AN UNEXPECTED AFFAIR
SKYE VON TRIESSEN

Copyright © 2024 Skye Von Triessen
ISBN: 979-8-333232-57-1

All rights reserved.

The characters and events portrayed in this book are fictitious. Names characters, places, and incidents are products of the author's imagination. Any similarity to actual events, persons, living or dead, is entirely coincidental. No part of this book may be reproduced, stored in a retrieval system, or transmitted in any form or by any means — electronic, mechanical, photocopy, recording, or any other without prior written permission from the author.

This book contains content that may be considered sensitive to certain readers, including adult themes and mature situations.

Dedication

For those of us who are often misunderstood because we are selective about who we share the best parts of ourselves with.

Table of Contents

Chapter 1
Chapter 2
Chapter 3
Chapter 4
Chapter 5
Chapter 6
Chapter 7
Chapter 8
Chapter 9
Chapter 10
Chapter 11
Chapter 12
Chapter 13
Chapter 14
Chapter 15
Chapter 16
Chapter 17
Chapter 18
Chapter 19
Chapter 20
Chapter 21
Chapter 22
Chapter 23
Chapter 24
Chapter 25
Chapter 26
Chapter 27
Chapter 28
Chapter 29
Chapter 30
Chapter 31

Chapter 32
ACKNOWLEDGMENTS
AFTERWORD

Chapter 1

Lane Remington hurried into Josephine's, the pub's dimly lit sign blazing against Seattle's somber skyline. The city's notorious mist was transitioning into a relentless downpour, compelling her to seek refuge. While her hotel was just around the corner, the prospect of solitary confinement held little allure. Plus, who would want to sleep alone on a rainy night, when the possibility of finding a gorgeous woman to take back to her hotel awaited within these walls? Giving a woman an orgasm or two was a far better way to spend her night, than alone with her errant thoughts.

Why can't I shake this restless energy that has consumed me since doing the interview? Yes, I want the job for both professional and personal reasons, but I don't need it. She shook her head as if to clear the nagging thoughts agitating her mind. *Regardless of my history with Alexandra, my professional track record speaks for itself and I just have to trust that she'll look past the fact that I wanted to fuck her wife. They weren't even married then.* Lane mentally rolled her eyes at herself, recalling that interaction with the infamous surgeon. *Guess that's what I get for propositioning a beautiful woman to my bed.*

Stepping over the threshold, she surveyed the bar, taking in the fusion of modern and nostalgic charm. Deep mahogany tables added a cozy feel, while walls adorned with global landmarks offered sophistication. Soft ambient lighting and soulful melodies created a romantic atmosphere. Scattered patrons enjoyed privacy in their secluded spots, adding a sense of discretion to the intimate setting. Josephine's seemed to live up to the raving reviews on Google claiming it was one of the city's premier lesbian establishments. *Nice. Maybe this can be my hunting ground if I get the job.* With a keen eye, honed by experience, Lane selected a table strategically positioned for optimal observation. History had taught her the social cues—casual singles gravitated to the bar, while those seeking intimacy or seclusion sought refuge in the tables and booths. Tonight, she was on the prowl, ready to navigate the intricate game of attraction with practiced finesse—a game that she barely ever lost.

She slipped off her coat, draping it casually over the chair before settling into another. The impromptu outing wasn't part of her evening agenda, but the confines of her hotel room—a temporary haven since her interview concluded at Parkwood Memorial—had grown stifling. She was hoping a walk would have helped to settle her mind, but after an hour of aimless strolling, it was obvious that her efforts were futile. Hooking up with someone also hadn't been on her itinerary for the night, but given her current unexplainable mood, she needed a distraction. And what better distraction than the primal act of physical intimacy? For Lane, focusing all her restless energy on bringing a woman to the highest peak of pleasure had always served as a reliable antidote to the tumult in her mind—a moment where all her troubles faded into blissful silence.

A gentle buzz interrupted her reverie, drawing Lane's attention to her pocket where her phone lay. Retrieving it, she couldn't suppress the grin that spread across her lips as she read the incoming message.

Nia: I hope you're staying out of trouble. But knowing you, I can bet some beautiful woman will fall prey to your charms and end up in your bed. I'm still bummed that I'm out of town while you're visiting, but I know you'll land the job, even though you wanted to fuck the owner's wife. Call me in the morning after your latest conquest untangles from your body.

Lane: Haha. Funny. You make my sex life sound so adventurous. I'm bummed you're not here as well to keep me out of trouble. Hopefully, the good doctor will look past my transgressions and hire me. I got a good vibe from her. She seems honorable. She said she wouldn't let that moment influence her decisions. But, I'm not worried, life always works out as it should. I have multiple offers lined up.

Nia: I'm hoping you land this job because having you home will be great. It will give us time to make up for all the years you spent conquering the world.

Lane: I know. Have a safe flight home. Talk to you tomorrow.

Lane lowered her phone to the table, exhaling a heavy sigh that seemed to carry the weight of her internal deliberations. The conversation with her best friend had stirred up a whirlwind of thoughts she had hoped the solitary walk would have quieted. She quickly pushed them to the back of her mind as she scanned her surroundings, wondering if she would find what she was looking for at Josephine's. Her gaze swept over the room, but none of the women grabbed her attention. The few who appeared to be alone seemed more interested in drowning their sorrows than in engaging in the kind of interaction Lane had in mind. She made brief eye contact with a couple staring at her with obvious interest, but she quickly looked away—she had no intention of ever playing on that field.

"Hi, what can I get for you tonight?"

Engrossed in her thoughts, Lane was caught off guard by the soft voice that broke through her musing. Startled, she looked up to find herself meeting the gaze of a young woman in her early twenties, with raven-black hair framing features flushed with a delicate blush. Lane offered a warm smile as she glanced at the name tag adorning the woman's black shirt.

"Hi, Kirsten," she greeted gently. "I'll have a Boulevardier on the rocks, please. Thank you."

Kirsten's cheeks flushed even deeper as she fidgeted nervously under Lane's gaze, her eyes lingering on Lane's face with a mixture of admiration and shyness. "Um... Would you like anything from the food menu?" she stammered.

Lane held Kirsten's stare, noting the nervousness that danced behind her eyes, more endearing than off-putting. "No, just the drink for now." As Kirsten nodded and turned to leave, Lane couldn't help but notice the way she nervously bit her bottom lip.

Lane chuckled softly once Kirsten was out of earshot. She was well aware of the impact her physical presence had on those around her, but she had never been the type to exploit it for personal gain. She prided herself on her inner depth, never succumbing to the allure of superficiality or using her appearance as a weapon. She was many things, but being shallow wasn't one of them. Confident, yes. Bordering on arrogant to some, but never veering into shallowness. Despite Kirsten's evident attraction, Lane's preferences lay elsewhere—women closer to her age or older, who shared her stance on commitment and understood the fleeting nature of their arrangements. Glancing around the bar once more, Lane's discerning eyes swept over the diverse array of women, still none of them captivated her interest. *Perhaps Josephine's won't deliver what I'm looking for tonight.*

"Here you go," Kirsten's voice once again broke through Lane's cogitations as she delicately placed the glass on the table, her movements graceful as she straightened—a faint brush of her hand down her thigh drawing Lane's attention. "Please let me know if you need anything else. Anything at all." The intensity in Kirsten's gaze—fixated on Lane's lips—didn't go unnoticed, nor did the suggestive undertones in her words.

"Thank you. I will," Lane responded, her tone deliberately neutral, a conscious effort to avoid giving Kirsten false hope. She had no intention of leading her on.

As Kirsten retreated, Lane couldn't help but notice the slight slump in her shoulders, a silent acknowledgment of unreciprocated interest. Though undoubtedly beautiful, Kirsten didn't trigger the spark that ignited Lane's desires. Chemistry was paramount, even in her non-committal liaisons. She didn't do relationships, but there had to be an undeniable connection between her and her partners—an unspoken understanding that transcended mere physical attraction.

Lane's fingers tightened around her glass as she lifted it to her lips preparing to take a sip, but her gaze snagged on a figure across the room, freezing her in place. The woman's caramel-toned skin seemed to radiate warmth, blending beautifully with naturally dark curly hair framing a strikingly beautiful oval-shaped face. Every curve of her body exuded an effortless sensuality that commanded attention and could bring any man or woman to their knees. Spellbound, Lane lowered her drink back to the table, mesmerized by the woman's graceful strides as she made her way to the bar. Amidst her air of elegance and sophistication, there lingered a faint shadow of sadness that tempered her beauty, adding a layer of complexity to her glamor. Lane's eyes strained to capture every movement as the woman settled onto a stool in the far corner of the bar.

Then, as if illuminated by a spotlight, the woman's smile lit up the room as she engaged the bartender in conversation. The transformation was quite dazzling and Lane's breath caught in her throat at the sight, her heart quickening as she beheld the woman's radiant beauty in all its glory. There was an undeniable magnetism emanating from her, and that spark that always helped her choose which women she brought to her bed, glowed brighter than the sun on its hottest day, drawing Lane in with an irresistible pull that sent a tingle racing down her spine.

As Lane's mouth grew dry with anticipation, she

finally took a sip of her drink, her eyes never leaving the captivating stranger. Despite the fleeting moment of brightness, Lane couldn't ignore the subtle return of sadness that clouded the woman's features once the bartender moved on to attend to other patrons. The huntress within Lane stirred to life, a primal instinct urging her forward. Determination flickered in her eyes as she resolved that this woman, with her enigmatic draw and hidden sorrow, would be the one to accompany her back to the hotel. In Lane's mind, there was no doubt—she would make it her mission to banish the woman's melancholy, if only for a night.

The woman turned toward Lane, her gaze briefly sweeping over Lane before retreating back to the depths of her drink, a veil of introspection descending upon her features. Yet, in that fleeting moment of connection, Lane felt a spark of recognition ignite within her, sending her heart into a rapid rhythm. A smile played at the corners of her lips as she contemplated the woman across the room, her mind whirling with possibilities. Deciding to bide her time, Lane allowed herself a few more moments to observe before she made her move.

Chapter 2

Miranda Hayes dashed into Josephine's, barely escaping the rain as large droplets echoed on the sidewalk and the doors swung shut behind her. It was the end of spring, and it seemed Seattle was hellbent on living up to its reputation for constant rain. In any other circumstance she might have preferred the comfort of home, curled up with a book and a glass of wine. But after the day she had, she needed something stronger and to be in an environment that would provide some distraction from her problems. Well, one problem in particular—her relationship with Trevor and her lingering uncertainty about moving in with him. That was why she opted for Josephine's, instead of going to Palmettos. Josephine's was one of Blake's favorite lesbian bars in Seattle and in the past, before Blake met Alexandra, they'd come here together whenever Blake felt the need to find a woman to take home with her.

Miranda made a beeline for the bar, a sigh of relief escaping her lips when she spied her favorite spot in the corner unoccupied. She craved solitude, and that secluded nook provided the perfect refuge from the bustling crowds elsewhere in the room. Although she could have taken a seat at a table, Miranda chose not to, being mindful of not monopolizing space that could be better utilized by couples or groups of friends.

Despite her despondency, Miranda found herself unable to suppress the wide smile that crept across her face as Josephine approached. The bar lights accentuated Josephine's ochre skin, casting her in an ethereal radiance as her dark brown eyes roamed seductively over Miranda.

"Miranda, sweetheart, are you here to finally rescue me from my misery and spend the rest of your life making me the happiest woman alive by becoming my wife?" Josephine's playful tone danced through the air as she leaned over the bar, enveloping Miranda in a warm hug and planting kisses on both cheeks.

Miranda laughed freely, the tension of the day melting away with each genuine chuckle. "You know, if I played on your team, I would have accepted your proposal the first time you asked, ten years ago."

"Well, sometimes we discover our true team later in life," Josephine quipped, a mischievous twinkle in her eyes. "So, I haven't given up hope that one day you'll realize a woman is the one who'll sweep you off your feet. Maybe you just haven't met her yet, or perhaps you already have," she added with a playful wiggle of her eyebrows, flexing her biceps for effect, which sent Miranda into fits of laughter.

"I think I would have figured it out by now," Miranda replied between giggles. "But if, by some miraculous twist of fate, I end up on your team, you'd definitely be my top pick."

"You better believe it. Ten years, Miranda. Ten years of pining after you," Josephine teased, reaching for a glass under the bar. "Your usual. Shall I make it a double? You looked like you needed a strong drink when you walked in."

Miranda nodded gratefully. "It's been a day."

"There's nothing a good Negroni or two can't fix," Josephine remarked as she expertly prepared the cocktail.

"And you make the best ones."

Josephine flashed a seductive smile that could make even the sturdiest knees weak as she placed the glass before Miranda, garnishing it with a slice of orange. "Yes, I do," she affirmed with a playful wink before glancing toward the other end of the bar where patrons awaited service. "I wish I could spend the whole night basking in your beauty, but duty calls. Give me a shout when you need a refill."

"Will do."

Miranda swallowed half of her drink in a single gulp, relishing the fiery trail as it blazed down her throat. It was far too early in the week for her to find comfort in a bar on a work night, but after the harrowing day she'd endured, who could blame her? The day had begun with the near loss of a patient and spiraled further when she found herself navigating two emergency surgeries back-to-back. But it wasn't just the chaos of the hospital that weighed on her, it was the heated argument with Trevor during her all-too-brief lunch break that cast a shadow over her evening.

At the mere thought of Trevor, the guilt she'd been grappling with for the past month reared its head, knotting her stomach with a discomfort that had nothing to do with drinking on an empty stomach. The argument they'd been rehashing for months loomed large—her reluctance to take the plunge and move in with him. Trevor was a genuinely good guy, a rarity in the murky waters of the current dating scene.

Logically, she knew she should seize the opportunity for something more with him, but she just wasn't ready. A nagging sensation, an elusive feeling of something missing, lingered at the back of her mind, casting doubt on her readiness for such a commitment. And it wasn't just with Trevor. It seemed to permeate her interactions with most men she dated, leaving her feeling as though she was holding back or that they simply failed to ignite whatever it was she yearned for in a relationship.

But, it was the hurt reflected in Trevor's eyes that made each argument about her reluctance to move in with him mentally exhausting. She knew he loved her deeply, and she cared deeply for him, but... Her thoughts were abruptly interrupted as another Negroni materialized before her, prompting her to raise a questioning eyebrow at Josephine, who sported a mischievous grin.

"It seems I'm not the only one who finds you irresistibly captivating and hopes to take you home tonight," Josephine supplied, nodding toward a secluded corner of the bar. "Courtesy of the brunette in the white top, whose eyes have been feasting on you since you walked through the door."

Miranda's gaze followed Josephine's indication, locking eyes with the woman she had briefly noticed upon her arrival. The striking brunette commanded attention like a magnetic force compelling Miranda to hold her gaze. Waves of rich, chestnut hair cascaded down her left shoulder, each strand catching the light and shimmering with a lustrous sheen. High cheekbones sculpted her face into a symphony of angles and curves, casting captivating shadows that only served to accentuate her natural beauty. Beneath delicately arched eyebrows, her eyes sparkled with an enigmatic depth—mysterious and beguiling. Full lips, painted a bold crimson, curved into a knowing smile, alluding to secrets untold and adventures yet to unfold. But it was the woman's eyes—veiled in shadow by the dim lighting—that held Miranda captive. Despite their indistinct color, their intensity seared through her, leaving her feeling oddly warm and vulnerable in their wake.

Absolutely, breathtaking.

Miranda felt like prey caught in the direct path of a beautiful predator, unable to evade the gravitational pull drawing her into the woman's seductive gaze. As the woman's lips curled into a teasing smile, she raised her glass in a silent toast, and Miranda found herself transfixed, unable to tear her eyes away. The woman exuded an air of undeniable sophistication and effortless confidence, evident in the relaxed ease with which she shifted in her seat, crossing one long, jean-clad leg over the other. However, it was the woman's unwavering confidence—bordering on arrogance—that gave Miranda pause, prompting her to narrow her eyes in scrutiny. She had encountered women with such self-assurance before, those who believed they could seduce anyone with a flash of their smile. Usually, Miranda found amusement in their attempts, but tonight, she wasn't in the mood for flattery.

As beautiful as the woman undoubtedly was, Miranda sensed a prowling danger beneath the surface. She knew the game all too well, recognizing the familiar dance of seduction unfolding before her. If she accepted the drink, it would only be a matter of time before the woman approached, seeking to engage her in conversation. Miranda had been her best friend Blake's wingwoman enough times to spot the signs—a shrewd invitation, followed by coy flirtation, all leading to the inevitable proposition. And tonight, Miranda wasn't willing to play along.

She turned back to Josephine, who raised an eyebrow at her curiously. "Return the drink to her. Tell her thanks, but no thanks."

Josephine's eyes widened momentarily before her lips morphed into another roguish grin as she retrieved the glass. "This should be interesting. I'll happily help get rid of any potential competition."

Miranda chuckled at Josephine's eagerness. "Of course you would."

As Josephine walked away, Miranda resisted the urge to glance in the brunette's direction. She knew it would be impolite, but she couldn't shake the feeling that this woman's ego wouldn't be easily bruised. Against her best efforts to maintain her composure, curiosity got the better of her, and she couldn't resist stealing a quick glance to observe the woman's reaction upon receiving Miranda's message. Expecting to see a flash of anger or annoyance, Miranda was taken aback when she was met with an even more devastating smile— one she suspected would make many women gladly accept a drink from her admirer. The woman cocked her head to the side, studying Miranda with an intensity that sent a shiver down her spine. Uncomfortable under the scrutiny, Miranda quickly averted her gaze and downed the remaining contents of her drink in an attempt to distract herself. She immediately longed for another drink, but Josephine was preoccupied with other customers, and no other bartender was in sight.

Maybe I should have taken the offered drink.

Before she could summon another thought, another Negroni materialized beside her empty glass. Without needing to turn her head, Miranda knew the owner of the long, slender fingers, painted with blood-red nail polish, that had placed the drink before her. The woman's intoxicating perfume—notes of white jasmine, lily of the valley, the velvety sweetness of vanilla, and a hint of sandalwood—invaded Miranda's senses, enveloping her in a sensation of pure intrigue, and lulled her into finally shifting in her seat to meet the woman's gaze. Hazel eyes, tinted more greenish than gold compared to her own, bore into her with unbridled lust. The intense desire shimmering in the woman's captivating gaze forced Miranda to swallow hard, her throat suddenly dry. She was tempted to reach for the unwanted drink, down half of it to alleviate the sudden scratchiness to get her mouth to work, and send this woman back to her seat.

"Seems like you could use another drink," her admirer pointed out, nodding toward Miranda's empty glass. Her voice smooth like honey, glided effortlessly through the air, leaving a trail of mystery and that untamed confidence in its wake. It possessed a gentle timbre, reminiscent of a soft caress, as each word she uttered carried a delicate invitation. An invitation that Miranda had no interest in.

Some people don't know how to take a hint.

Maybe it was her bad mood that was clouding her judgment, leading her to be uncharacteristically unfriendly, but the woman's cocky smirk irritated her, and she wanted to wipe it off her face.

Feigning indifference, Miranda gave the glass a

cursory glance before locking eyes with her unwanted guest once more. With as much disinterest as she could muster in her voice, she stated, "I can buy my own drink."

Miranda braced herself for a potential backlash, but instead of anger, the brunette merely regarded her with a long, assessing gaze. A deep sigh escaped her lips, and she shook her head in what seemed to be disappointment. However, she maintained an air of calm composure, as if allowing herself to be provoked was beneath her and she wouldn't give Miranda the satisfaction of seeing her ruffled.

Finally, a once alluring voice, now turned cold and calculated like a viper poised to strike, cut through the tension. "Don't tell me you're one of those women who find being offered a drink as offensive," the woman remarked, her sarcasm dripping like venom. "Of course, I know you can afford your own drink." With a delicate hand gesturing up and down Miranda's body, she continued, "You're wearing a limited edition Audemars Piguet watch and a 14-karat white gold infinity bracelet." Her eyes, now sparkling with gold flecks, roamed the length of Miranda's body. "You'd be highly financially irresponsible to be wearing tens of thousands in jewelry and can't afford a twenty-dollar cocktail."

The woman's mocking comment sparked the ire already brewing within Miranda, but what grated on her nerves most was the cool, calm delivery. "And yet the fact remains that I can afford my own drink," Miranda retorted, her tone laced with distaste. "So, I fail to see the relevance of your lecture on my financial status and management capabilities."

Her pursuer's response was swift and cutting. "The point is, I'm old school," she stated with a hint of disdain. "Regardless of how unfortunate certain societal norms may have been in the past, I prefer when women weren't so determined to overcompensate to prove their independence—to the point where being offered a drink seems to be misconstrued as offensive or a sign of weakness."

Miranda gritted her teeth, determined to appear unfazed by the woman's scolding comment. "So, you're one of those women who have a problem with feminism," she remarked sharply.

The brunette sighed dramatically, regarding Miranda with a mix of impatience and exasperation, as if she were dealing with a petulant teenager. Her full lips formed a thin line, and her eyebrows drew together slightly. The sudden change in demeanor seemed out of character compared to the composed facade the woman had maintained thus far, and Miranda couldn't help but find it somewhat endearing.

"Don't be so dramatic," her uninvited guest replied, condescendingly. "How could I possibly have a problem with feminism when its core principles aim to grant women countless rights and free us from the constraints of the patriarchy? It's these very rights that have empowered me to excel in my chosen career." Leaning in closer to Miranda, she lowered her voice to a seductive whisper. "They're the same rights that afford me the luxury of buying beautiful women as many drinks as I please, without expecting anything in return." She paused, a speck of mischief dancing in her eyes. "Unless, of course, they're so enchanted by my charm that they can't resist taking me home with them."

Her voice now danced with a dash of playfulness and the return of that immutable confidence. It was as if each syllable was carefully chosen to bewitch and conquer whomever this woman set her sights on. Miranda could see how women could fall prey to the magnetic appeal, intelligence and arrogant charm. This was one of those moments when Miranda envied Blake's skill at masking her emotions behind a stoic expression. Unlike her best friend, Miranda tended to wear her heart on her sleeve, and she found it challenging to conceal just how much this woman's presence was grating on her nerves. Though, it wasn't solely the woman's arrogance that had her grinding her teeth together—there was something else, something indefinable, stirring within her, a discomfort she couldn't quite articulate. Nevertheless, Miranda had reached her limit with this uninvited distraction, however entertaining it might have been.

Though challenging, Miranda maintained the interloper's gaze, summoning Blake's infamous blank expression. "Unfortunately for you, I don't find your arrogance charming, and there's likely an ulterior motive behind the offered drink."

A slender neck tilted to the side, amusement flickering in mesmerizing eyes as the brunette focused intently on Miranda, as if dissecting her every thought. "And what might that motive be?"

"Probably to lure me into your bed," Miranda replied bluntly.

The woman's lips curved into a sly smile. "And would that be such a terrible outcome?"

"I'm not interested," Miranda asserted firmly.

The woman arched an eyebrow. "And why is that?"

"Does it matter?" Miranda retorted.

Shrugging nonchalantly, the woman replied, "Women hardly ever turn me down. So, I'm curious to know why you're rejecting me before giving me a chance, and getting to know me better."

Miranda sighed, suddenly feeling exhausted from the unwanted interrogation. Beckoning her resolve, she reached for the words that would guarantee this woman left her alone. "I'm not into women, so there is no chance I'd want to take you home with me." Miranda was sure that would get the woman to leave her alone, but she only smiled, her eyes gleaming as if relishing the challenge presented by Miranda's resistance.

"Darling, I can guarantee that one night with me would have you questioning your sexuality," she purred, her voice returning to that timbre of a soft caress reaching again and extending the invitation to her bed. The richness of her tone—a smoothness that captivated and enticed—was like a siren's song luring sailors to their watery lair.

Miranda had to give this woman credit for her wooing skills. Still, she wasn't going to shy away from the challenge and shut her down. With a roll of her eyes and an air of boredom, she addressed the intruder in a cool, detached tone of her own. "I can see you're insufferable enough to think you're God's gift to women." Pausing for effect, she cast a mocking glance up and down the woman's figure. "Even if I was interested in women, I wouldn't invite you to my bed. I don't particularly find your brand of arrogance sexy."

Another sly smile graced the brunette's lips as she mirrored Miranda's action of appraising her. "And I find your brand of rejection very sexy." A brief pause as heated eyes did another slow trek of Miranda's body. "Your rejection doesn't bruise my ego, it only makes me want you more. I've never been attracted to easy. And I know if given the chance, I can have you screaming my name all night long."

Miranda lifted her hand, waving it in front of her unwelcome suitor. "Does all of this really work on women? Because I honestly can't see why it would."

Crimson red lips quirked into yet another smug smile, a sight that Miranda wanted so badly to wipe from her arrogant face. "Ninety-nine percent of the time, even with women who claim to be as straight as an arrow."

Why am I even entertaining this woman... Miranda thought as her eyes remained too long on the woman's full lips as she softly nipped at the bottom one before releasing slowly. She reached for the last piece of arsenal that would guarantee she was a part of the one percent of women who didn't fall prey to this insufferable seductress. "Well, I'll be a part of the one-percenters because one, as I said, I don't find all of this flair appealing. And two, I have a boyfriend."

As if Miranda's mention of having a boyfriend was inconsequential, the brunette merely shrugged and said, "A man cannot compete with me, darling. He can never give you the pleasure I can give you," she declared, her voice dripping with self-assurance. With a graceful gesture, she waved her hand through the air, dismissing Miranda's statement as trivial. "They're basic creatures, unworthy of women. All they seek is to assert control over us—to bend us to their will."

Miranda huffed out a sarcastic laugh. "That's a

bit hypocritical on your part because you're here attempting to bend me to your will, even after I've declined your drink, not once, but twice." With a mocking tilt of her head, she added. "Seems a classic case of pot calling the kettle black."

A flicker of something akin to hurt flashed in the woman's eyes, though before Miranda could discern the emotion, it vanished, replaced once more by defiance. "The only time I want a woman to bend to my will," she began, her tone low and suggestive, "is when she's yielding in my bed, overwhelmed by the pleasure I rain down on her... begging and screaming my name." With another casual shrug, she continued, "Outside of that realm, any woman I'm involved with stands as an equal in every aspect of our lives." Her expression became contemplative for a moment before she added, "Although, even in those moments of ecstasy, it's that woman who still wields the true power."

Miranda racked her brain for a suitable retort but found herself at a loss. Why was she even bothering to engage with this woman, knowing she'd likely have a counterargument ready to turn the conversation in her favor? Why was she allowing a complete stranger to monopolize so much of her time? Before she could ponder further, her phone buzzed against the bar. Seizing the opportunity, she reached for it, viewing it as her chance to bid this seductive stranger goodnight. Trevor's name flashed on the screen.

> *Trevor: Hey. I just arrived at your house, but you're not home. Can you come home, please? I really want us to talk about today. You know I can't sleep when we fight."*

And just like that, the guilt was back and the burden of uncertainty bore down on her shoulders.

With a heavy weight settling back onto her conscience, Miranda slid off the stool and slipped into her coat, disregarding the woman who now regarded her with genuine concern etched on her features. If Miranda didn't know any better, she might have believed the woman actually cared about her.

Hooking her handbag onto her forearm, Miranda met her companion's greenish orbs. "You should go find someone else to play with," she advised coolly, giving the woman a fleeting once-over. "Can't say it was a pleasure conversing with you."

The woman laughed and the rich sound caused unidentifiable sensations to course through Miranda's body. "You and I both know you're lying. You enjoyed every second of our little dance. And it was my absolute pleasure to tango with you."

Rolling her eyes, Miranda scoffed. "Keep dreaming."

To Miranda's surprise, the woman remained silent, offering no retort as Miranda walked away without a backward glance. Just as she reached for the door handle, a presence approached from behind. Miranda didn't need to turn around to confirm who it was. With a resigned sigh, she pivoted on her heels.

"You didn't give me your name," the woman uttered so softly that Miranda questioned if it was the same arrogant individual she had just engaged with mere seconds ago.

"And I won't. Chances are we won't ever cross paths again," Miranda replied, dismissively. She could admit that she felt horrible for replying so hostilely, especially considering the earnestness behind the request for her name.

Her tenacious admirer smiled— this one so very soft —as she whispered, "I hope we do."

Miranda narrowed her eyes wondering what games this woman was playing, but she didn't have time for it. "And I hope we don't. Goodbye." With that, she pushed open the door and hurried out into the pouring rain. She sensed the woman's gaze following her as she briskly made her way toward her car, but she refused to glance back, determined not to grant her admirer the satisfaction of winning the final move.

Chapter 3

A month after her interview with Dr. Alexandra Edison, Lane stared out the window of her new office, the dreary sky mirroring her subdued state of mind. She had successfully secured the coveted position at Parkwood Memorial and had spent the past month wrapping up her affairs in L.A. to relocate to Seattle. Today marked the beginning of a fresh chapter in her life, one that should have filled her with excitement and anticipation. Yet, contrary to her usual demeanor, she found herself feeling oddly out of sync. Normally, she would be buzzing with the thrill of embarking on a new professional journey, eager to tackle the challenges ahead and make her mark. After all, she had a knack for turning around struggling hospitals, a skill that had saved countless institutions from financial ruin. Even though on this occasion, she wouldn't be saving this hospital—thanks to the impeccable groundwork laid by the former CEO—she just had to keep the ship sailing.

But for some unknown reason, that sense of excitement seemed oddly absent. Perhaps it was the nostalgia of returning to Parkwood—a place imbued with sentimental significance for her—or perhaps it was the ambivalence of being back in Seattle, a city she couldn't decide if she loved or loathed. She was still grappling with the notion of leaving behind the vibrant nature of Los Angeles for Seattle's gloom—a prospect she never imagined entertaining. The idea of returning to Seattle after fleeing immediately after high school graduation to pursue her dreams at Berkeley College felt surreal. Over the years, her visits had been driven primarily by her enduring connection with the one person in Seattle she loved and who had refused to move to L.A., or follow her wherever her career had taken her. But now, despite her history of departure, Lane found herself drawn back to the city, hoping perhaps that a change in scenery would be a balm for the restless stirrings that had been haunting her for months. The constant whirlwind of high-profile contacts and glamorous events in L.A. had lost its appeal, and she yearned for a simpler, quieter life that better suited her personality. Plus, with Nia's return from London a year prior, the prospect of settling back into Seattle's rhythm seemed less daunting, maybe even comforting.

Then there was the fact that she had always harbored a desire to work at Parkwood, but previously, the hospital had consolidated the roles of Chief of Surgery and CEO; effectively closing the door for Lane, who wasn't a surgeon. It wasn't until two months ago, when rumors circulated that Parkwood was seeking an executive for the CEO position, that Lane saw her chance. Even though she knew the outgoing CEO and owner was none other than the infamous Dr. Alexandra Edison—the now wife of a woman Lane had pursued a year ago—she didn't let that dissuade her. Their less-than-amicable encounter at Alexandra's family's gala—where Lane had recognized Alexandra—did little to deter her pursuit. Only someone in their field living under a rock wouldn't know who she was. Lane had built her career on fearlessness and seizing opportunities with determination. So, she applied, confident in her qualifications to secure at least an interview, and hoped that Alexandra was professional enough to separate personal grievances from professional considerations.

Healthcare was Lane's passion, a career she embraced as a way of making a difference in the world. Despite earning a reputation for her unorthodox methods, which former coworkers labeled as cold and heartless, Lane remained unwavering in her dedication to ensuring the highest standard of care for patients in every hospital she touched. The opinions of those who judged her could be damned—she cared little for their perceptions. Rising to the top in the cutthroat world of corporate America had demanded a tough exterior and relentless perseverance, especially as she had to outpace her male counterparts tenfold. Hell, her entire life had required she operate on survivor's instincts.

Now, she was back where it all began—a place that had once saved her and launched her on a twenty-five-year journey of rising from the ashes. Hopefully returning here would reignite some lost spark in her life, despite the perpetual gloom of Seattle's weather. As Lane reflected on these shifting tides in her life, she couldn't help but wonder if her recent fortieth birthday played a role in her newfound sense of nostalgia. Age had a way of casting a retrospective gaze on one's life, prompting introspection and a reassessment of priorities. Her contemplation was broken by a soft knock on her office door.

"Come in," she called, shifting her focus from the

window.

The door creaked open, and Dr. Alexandra Edison stepped into the room, her smile radiating warmth and welcome. "I hope the office is suitable for your standards. Which I have a feeling are very high ones."

Lane chuckled softly, relieved that there was no awkward tension between them. Regardless of their history, she could admit that she liked Alexandra. "Yes, they surpassed my expectations. But I didn't expect anything less from you, considering your immaculate sense of style." She gestured toward Alexandra's attire. "Love the dress."

Alexandra laughed. "Smooth. Very smooth. I guess all this charm is what you use to have people eating out of the palm of your hand."

A cheeky grin played on Lane's lips. "Not many would label me as charming, Alexandra. I reserve this particular skill for my personal life with a select few. I get people eating out of the palm of my hand by understanding their motives, anticipating their every move, and…" her eyes now twinkling as her cheeky grin grew ever so slightly wider. "A little bit of fear."

"Ahh. So, I suppose I should have said that's what you use to have women eating out of the palm of your hand."

"More or less."

Alexandra shook her head, a smile lingering on her lips. "Well, are you ready to at least charm your new colleagues? I'm sure they would prefer that over your somewhat stoic demeanor."

"For you, I'll try," Lane said, stepping around her desk and signaling for Alexandra to lead the way.

As they made their way to the boardroom for

the weekly department meeting, Alexandra filled Lane in on tasks that required her immediate attention. Engaging in work-related discussions improved Lane's mood, and put her in a better frame of mind to handle introductions with the people she would be leading —individuals who might end up hating her because they didn't appreciate her particular management style. However, Lane approached each new hospital as a blank slate, refraining from judgment based on past experiences. Moreover, Parkwood's stable condition meant she wouldn't need to make drastic budget cuts or personnel changes to ensure the hospital's long-term survival.

As Alexandra swung open the boardroom door, Lane donned her professional mask—a cold exterior that maintained a necessary distance between her and her colleagues. Unlike some, she held little interest in forming friendships with those she worked alongside. Her primary focus was on executing her duties efficiently, and keeping a professional boundary made it easier for her to make tough decisions—like terminations—when necessary. Moreover, hospitals tended to be breeding grounds for gossip, and Lane cherished her privacy too much to indulge in workplace chatter—most of which involved women lamenting about their useless husbands or gushing about their kids. Contrary to popular belief, she wasn't one to bark orders or berate her staff. Instead, she chose to maintain an air of mystery, leaving her team to speculate about her and keeping her interactions with them limited to what was necessary for work. Only her assistants caught glimpses into her personal life, as their roles demanded access to her for job-related matters. For

Lane, work remained work, and she adamantly avoided mixing business with pleasure.

She squared her shoulders and entered the boardroom after Alexandra, ensuring her expression betrayed nothing. Yet, the atmosphere immediately shifted as she turned to face her colleagues, locking eyes with the most captivating woman she had ever encountered. Thoughts of her had consumed Lane's mind for the past month, lingering long after their somewhat hostile interaction. Lane had questioned her sanity, wondering if she was a masochist for still desiring the enchanting woman who had turned down her advances in spectacular fashion. That encounter— despite their sparring— had left her so aroused that she had returned to her hotel room alone, disinterested in the company of any other woman that night. Even after returning to L.A., days passed before she could bring herself to accept Gabriella's call and find the release she desperately needed. And now, with the stunning woman casting piercing glares at her, Lane felt that same surge of excitement from a month ago coursing through her veins.

I'm royally screwed.

Chapter 4

"What the actual fuck is she doing here?" Miranda whispered low enough for only Blake to hear, her eyes shooting daggers at the woman she never expected to see again as she entered the boardroom alongside Alexandra.

Blake shot Miranda a questioning look, leaning closer to her for an explanation. "That's Lane. I told you Alexandra hired her."

"She's... she's Lane?" Miranda spluttered, her eyes still fixed on the brunette, who stared right back at her.

Blake nudged Miranda with her elbow and asked, "What's going on? Have you two met?"

Before Miranda could respond, Alexandra started talking, but Miranda didn't hear a word her boss said. Her focus was consumed by the roaring in her ears, the annoyance coursing through her veins as she held the gaze of the most insufferable, arrogant human she'd ever met. Lane's memory of her was evident in the piercing stare she returned, accompanied by that pestilential smirk aimed squarely at Miranda. This woman, who seemed to think she was God's gift to women, had disrupted Miranda's peace with her supercilious demeanor and overall domineering behavior. Lane had loitered in Miranda's thoughts long after their encounter at Josephine's, simply because she had never encountered anyone so utterly infuriating. But the way Lane had asked for her name contradicted everything Miranda had assumed about her based on their conversation. And for some reason, that brief vulnerability had permeated Miranda's thoughts for days.

As Miranda studied Lane, clad in a bespoke black pencil skirt suit that accentuated her curves, with a crisp white shirt peeking from underneath, she couldn't help but notice the stark contrast in her demeanor. Gone was the carefree charm exhibited at Josephine's, replaced instead by a rigid and aloof aura. It was a striking departure from Miranda's expectations, adding another layer of complexity to the enigmatic woman before her. Yet, there was also an unsettling sense of familiarity and something else beneath the surface that irked Miranda to no end. Her damn presence alone seemed to stir up a tempest of agitation within Miranda. That same confident tone of voice, steeped in self-assuredness and commanding attention—but void of the charm she experienced at Josephine's—cut through Miranda's internal turmoil, compelling her to focus on the woman who continued to stare at her.

"There are other aspects of this place that I find more appealing than L.A.'s weather. Rather beautiful things, in fact," Lane replied to whatever question was asked, her eyes still trained on Miranda and her tone carried a teasing lilt despite her stoic expression.

Miranda couldn't resist rolling her eyes at the thinly veiled remark, fully aware that it was directed at her. Observing Alexandra's sincere smile at Lane, Miranda couldn't quite believe that the same woman who had tried to seduce Blake a year ago was now employed by Alexandra. Blake had recounted the encounter to Miranda, and now that she had met Lane, she understood why Alexandra had wanted to slap her that night. Shaking her head, she attempted to refocus on the introduction Alexandra was delivering.

"As you all know, I've decided to step down from the CEO role for personal reasons, choosing to primarily focus on my passion for performing surgeries. Today, I'm happy to introduce Lane Remington as my successor. With years of invaluable experience, Lane is here to lead us forward, ensuring the sustained growth and development of Parkwood. While we've come a long way in the past year, there's still a lot ahead of us, and Lane is instrumental in helping us reach those milestones. Let's extend a warm Parkwood welcome to her."

"Invaluable experience in being insufferable. Lord, help us," Miranda muttered softly as she crossed and uncrossed her arms.

Lane turned to Alexandra, nodding in acknowledgment, before redirecting her attention back to their colleagues. "Thank you, Alexandra. I'm looking forward to collaborating with each of you. My main focus will be ensuring the financial stability of this hospital, always considering the well-being of our patients and staff. Every decision I make will be geared toward long-term success. While I value teamwork, my commitment lies in doing what's best for the hospital, even if it may not be the popular choice at the time. As Alexandra mentioned, I've been in this field for a significant period and have successfully steered hospitals away from bankruptcy. Fortunately, Alexandra has done an outstanding job, and I'm here to build upon her achievements."

Lane paused, her eyes shifting purposefully to Miranda, mischief sparkling in them. "As heads of your departments, I'd like to schedule individual meetings to discuss budgets, your needs, and to learn more about each of you personally. I won't keep you much longer, because I understand your priority is saving lives rather than listening to me talk numbers. Thank you."

"God, she's so freaking arrogant," Miranda grumbled discreetly under her breath.

"Okay. You need to tell me what went down between you two immediately after this meeting," Blake whispered.

"Thank you, Lane. If there are no other matters you'd like to address, I suppose we can adjourn early today," Alexandra informed the group, her eyes quickly scanning the room before coming to rest on Blake.

Miranda smiled internally at Alexandra's obvious affection for her best friend and leaned closer to Blake. "Even after a year, you two can't seem to keep your eyes off each other. It just proves my point that you're both obsessed," she teased.

"It's called being in love, darling," Blake replied without breaking eye contact with Alexandra.

Miranda shook her head in mock exasperation at her friend's lovesickness and rose from her seat. She headed straight for the door, determined to avoid glancing in Lane's direction, even though she could feel the woman's eyes following her every move.

"Hey, wait up," Blake demanded, trailing behind her as she rushed to the elevators. "What's happening between you and Lane? For two people who are practically strangers, the tension between you two could cut diamonds," she added once she caught up with Miranda.

Miranda didn't slow down until they reached the elevators. She furiously stabbed the call button. "Let's go to my office and talk. The last thing I need is for her to come out and join us here."

Just as the elevator arrived, Lane and Alexandra emerged from the boardroom. Miranda found herself unable to resist stealing a glance at Lane, who shot her one of those cheeky smiles that seemed to be aimed solely at her. With an eye roll, Miranda stepped onto the elevator. She breathed a sigh of relief when Blake began checking her messages, encouraging Miranda to do the same. In the momentary silence, she took the opportunity to gather her thoughts and prepare to relay her encounter with Lane to her best friend.

"God. I swear the sight of that woman makes me want to drink something very strong this early in the morning," Miranda ranted as soon as the door to her office closed behind them. Her hands flew to her face and she let out a frustrated groan, then crossing her arms vehemently and whirling to face Blake. "I still can't believe Alexandra hired her after she hit on you. Now I can see why Alexandra wanted to slap her smug face," Miranda continued to rant as she pinched the bridge of her nose in both disbelief and realization of Alexandra's actions and decisions. She began pacing in front of her desk, her fingers anxiously running through her curls until firm hands gripped her shoulders, bringing her to a halt. Blake guided her gently into a chair, settling into one beside her.

"Alright. Take a few deep breaths and tell me what's going on." Blake urged.

At Blake's behest to breathe deeply and then explain her vexation, she closed her eyes and inhaled slowly through her nose, and exhaled slowly through pursed lips. Then Miranda turned to face Blake, doing her best to reign in her agitation with Lane—a feeling she was still grappling to understand. "Do you remember about a month ago I told you about that woman who hit on me at Josephine's? The one who was arrogant enough to tell me that one night with her would have me questioning my sexuality?" Miranda squinted as she emphatically pointed at nothing in particular on the ceiling. "Well, yes, that was our new CEO, Lane." She huffed as both her hands, palms up, presented the obvious conclusion. "That woman doesn't have a humble bone in her body and seems to think she is God's gift to women. I can only imagine how insufferable she'll be to work with."

Blake looked at Miranda, puzzled. "Yes. But why are you so annoyed? Women hit on you all the time." Blake animatedly waved her hand up and down at Miranda's body. "Have you seen you?"

Miranda inhaled deeply, slumping a little in the chair. "I can't explain it. She just gets under my skin. And the way she looks at me is just unnerving. Like she wants to have me for dinner." Her hand went back over her face as she aggravatedly muffled, "God."

Blake laughed. "Maybe she does want to have you for dinner."

Shaking her head, Miranda's eyes did a full three-sixty. "She's just one of those women who sees rejection as a challenge." She quickly threw her hands up in surrender, protesting, "Her words, not mine. After I turned down her advances, she said, and I quote, 'Your rejection doesn't bruise my ego, it only makes me want you more. I've never been attracted to easy. And I know if given the chance, I can have you screaming my name all night long.'" *Why the hell do I even remember everything she said verbatim?*

Blake's eyes widened before she burst into laughter. In between breaths, she added, "Oh my god. She said what? I mean, I'm not surprised. During our short interactions, I pegged her as a very confident woman who is not afraid to go after what she wants." Blake paused, attempting to restrain her laughter before continuing, "According to Alexandra, she does have boundaries. You should have just told her that you have a boyfriend. Although it seems like it's marriage she respects, since she didn't care that I had a girlfriend when she invited me to her bed."

Miranda shook her head once more. "You would think that would stop her. She said and I quote again, 'A man cannot compete with me, darling. He can never give you the pleasure that I can give you.' So, yes, boundaries my ass. Again. What was Alexandra thinking?"

Blake shrugged. "She did what she thought was best for the hospital. Lane is brilliant at what she does." Blake paused, cocked her head to the side and smirked. "As for Lane's comment, she kind of does have a point."

Miranda glowered, and Blake laughed.

"I can't believe you're siding with her at my expense," Miranda argued.

"I'm not siding with her. However, based on the context in which the statement was made, she does have a point in her claim that women are superior in the bedroom. A very strong point. But I know you're strictly Vitamin D, so just forget about it. And speaking of your man. I guess moving in with Trevor is still a no-go."

Miranda slumped even further into her seat, her demeanor shifting from fired up to despondent. "I can't explain it, but I'm just not ready to take the next step. I don't know exactly why." She kneaded her temples in an attempt to dissuade the same ominous feelings that would surface on this subject for the past few months. "Trevor is great, and I enjoy being with him, but I'm just not there yet. I can see that my hesitation is hurting him, and he thinks I'm not as committed to the relationship as he is. However, I can't force myself to do something that, deep down, I know I'm not ready for."

Blake reached for Miranda's hand and gave it a soft squeeze. "I understand. If you don't feel it, then it doesn't make sense to force it." She gently squeezed Blake's fingers in return, the corners of her mouth ticking up ever-so-slightly. "When the time is right, you'll feel it. Trevor loves you. I'm sure he'll wait until you're ready."

"We'll see. Speaking of being ready..." She grasped Blake's hand a little tighter with her fingers in excitement. "I still can't believe you're going to get pregnant. How are you feeling? Are you ready for the procedure this afternoon?"

Blake smiled as a touch of nervousness sparked in her eyes. "As ready as can be. It's a bit scary because, for the next ten months, my body will go through so many changes and be the home of a little human. But I'm just happy to make Alexandra's dream a reality. I want to give her everything she has ever wanted. Hopefully, we're lucky enough to get pregnant on the first attempt."

"Fingers crossed. I'm so very happy for you and

excited to be an aunt." Miranda smiled ecstatically now. "At least now Mom and Dad can stop hinting at wanting grandbabies. God, they are going to spoil this baby, rotten."

Blake's smile widened. "She's going to have four grandmothers lavishing her with gifts. I can only imagine."

"And the best aunt in the world of course," Miranda bragged, and then raised an eyebrow at her best friend. "But you do realize you just said 'she'? Does that mean you're hoping for a girl?"

"A healthy baby first and foremost. But maybe I want a girl more than a boy. When I picture our family, I've never seen a boy. Always us with our baby girl."

Miranda chuckled. "You're going to be an amazing mom."

"I'll try my best." Blake got up from the chair. "I should get going. I want to complete my rounds because I'll be off after the procedure. And don't worry about Lane. I think now that she's working here, she'll respect your boundaries. You should come over for dinner this weekend."

Miranda stood and pulled Blake into a hug. "I'll check on you later. Call me if you need anything before I see you. I love you."

"Love you too."

Miranda watched Blake leave, feeling grateful that at least one of them was living the epic romance she had always wanted for herself. Many would have thought she would have been the first to walk down the aisle, but surprisingly, life had other plans in store for them. Out of nowhere, Alexandra had swept Blake off her feet, and now they were happily married and starting their family. Miranda couldn't help but feel a pang of sadness because she wasn't sure she wanted kids, and despite the advances in modern medicine, her biological clock was running out. When they had discussed having kids, Trevor wasn't sure he wanted them either. So, that was one thing that contributed to her entering into a relationship with him. They decided they could revisit the idea in the future if necessary. Now, that future seemed so murky and Miranda felt like she was drowning, unable to tread water in the brewing storm of their relationship.

They'd only been dating a year, so there was nothing wrong with her wanting to wait to move in with him. Still, she knew it was more than just wanting to wait. She just hoped that Trevor would be patient enough to give her time to make up her mind and possibly figure out what was causing her hesitation. But how much time was he supposed to give her when he could probably be with someone who wanted to dive right in and be his everything? She knew she didn't want to break up with him. That much, she was certain of.

Her phone vibrating in her pocket interrupted her musings. She quickly retrieved it, expecting a page to the emergency room, only to find a meeting invite requesting her presence for a one-on-one introductory meeting with her new CEO. Annoyance prickled through her as memories of that night at Josephine's flashed in her mind. She hoped that after this initial meeting, they wouldn't need to interact much considering that Alexandra would remain as chief of surgery and, technically, Miranda's direct supervisor.

Lane Remington was the most self-centered individual she had ever met, and she intended to stay clear of her. Still, Miranda couldn't shake her curiosity about the woman. Surely, Lane must have an impressive resume to land the CEO role at such a young age compared to most in her field. Based on her physical appearance, she seemed to be in her thirties, just like Miranda. She pulled up Google to see what she could find, claiming it was to help her prepare for their meeting. There was nothing wrong with being prepared for what she imagined would be a very interesting encounter.

Damn. She looks amazing at forty. No wonder she's so damn arrogant.

Chapter 5

Standing by the window in the assisted living facility, Lane waited for Anita to come out of the bathroom. She focused on the raindrops cascading down the glass, attempting to calm her racing mind. It had been raining all day, but she braved the weather to visit the woman who was one of the main reasons she had chosen to return to Seattle. The week had been long, and she was grateful to finally have the weekend to relax. The past month had been crazy busy and she still needed to catch up on much-needed sleep. She blamed the chaotic events of the past month as the main reason why she was caught off guard by the sight of Dr. Miranda Hayes—the head of the cardiology department—in the meeting on Monday. Normally, she would have familiarized herself with the department heads at any hospital she was hired at before starting, but things had been so hectic while she wrapped up her obligations in L.A. that she just didn't have the time. When she'd walked into the boardroom and saw Miranda, her heart had pounded so fast in her chest that it was a wonder she was able to keep her expression neutral—even though she couldn't help smirking at Miranda to let her know Lane remembered her. She had wanted to laugh at the scowl on Miranda's face, followed by the eye rolls, aimed at her. It was quite evident she had left a less than impressive impression on the woman.

She could admit she had gone above and beyond to push Miranda's buttons that night at Josephine's because it had been such a long time since a woman had challenged her by not being so easily charmed by her—and God, did it give her an instant rush. On the rare occasion that a woman rebuffed her, Lane usually accepted the rejection and moved on, but that night she just couldn't resist Miranda's fiery spirit. She'd always loved a good challenge that required her to work hard to achieve the desired results. And the thought of getting a woman with so much passion and defiance—like Dr. Miranda Hayes with her vivacious spirit—to bend to her will in bed and challenge her in other areas of her life, caused excitement to sprint through her veins at lightning speed.

Miranda's infectious, carefree laughter lingered in her memory, especially during her conversation with Josephine, who seemed to share Lane's desire for Miranda that night. Miranda's head thrown back, and her luscious curls bouncing as her upper body shook with delight was an enchanting sight, capable of brightening even the gloomiest of rooms and exuding an abundance of warmth. It had been a while since she'd faced rejection from a woman, regardless of their sexual orientation. Prior to her encounter with Miranda, the last rejection she experienced was from Blake—though she hesitated to classify it as such, considering Blake's evident infatuation with Alexandra. Usually, women eagerly gravitated toward her giving her ample choice of the right woman to pursue—and her instincts rarely led her astray in her selection.

Now, Lane found herself in an even greater

quandary regarding her recent choice. Not only did Miranda assert her straight orientation and claim to be in a relationship, but Lane also recognized she was now Miranda's superior at work. While Lane might have navigated the other complications in stride, she firmly adhered to the principle of not dating colleagues, especially those under her supervision. Although Parkwood didn't discourage staff relationships—considering Alexandra's marriage to Blake—Miranda's rejection made Lane hesitant to pursue anything further and risk creating discomfort in their professional environment. Lane had harbored hopes of bumping into Miranda again and testing her luck, but never did she expect their paths to cross in her new job.

Guess that's why they say be careful what you wish for.

She was grateful she hadn't seen Miranda since their last meeting, granting her valuable time to ponder how to traverse the complex situation and her burgeoning attraction. It would undoubtedly be challenging, but she resolved to banish any thoughts of having any form of association with Miranda outside of work from her mind. Fortunately, it seemed Miranda still shared no interest in further interaction, which should make distancing herself easier. Considering their upcoming meeting next week, Lane speculated they wouldn't have many one-on-one interactions in the foreseeable future, as any requirements from Miranda's department would likely be communicated through Alexandra, circumventing direct contact with her. With the hospital's size, she should be able to avoid Miranda relatively easily. Right? Lane let out a sigh, her fingers gently massaging her temples as she contemplated the prospect of working closely with a woman who had occupied her mind with rather salacious thoughts for the past month.

God help her.

"Should I be concerned that after just one week at Parkwood, you're sighing as if you're carrying the weight of fifty crumbling hospitals on your shoulders?" A familiar voice came from behind her. "As far as I know, they're holding up just fine," Anita remarked as she strolled from the bathroom, persuading Lane to turn from the window and face her.

"I can see this place hasn't dimmed your winning personality," Lane replied with a chuckle, closing the distance between them in two long strides. With arms outstretched, she enveloped Anita in a tight embrace drawing in the familiar, comforting scent of vanilla and cinnamon. It stirred memories of soft embraces, warmth, and safety—of home. Easing back, she gently cupped Anita's smiling face, its rich chestnut complexion still radiant after seventy-five years of weathering life's trials. Laugh lines crinkled at Anita's eyes, a testament to the passage of time and shared laughter. In those light brown eyes, filled with warmth and love, Lane saw a reflection of her own affection mirrored back at her.

"I've missed you," Lane whispered, her voice quivering slightly with emotions only Anita could evoke—feelings that transcended words, spoken only between kindred souls. Anita, her guardian angel, her rock through life's storms.

Anita's eyes roved over Lane's face with the scrutiny of a concerned parent. "Should I be worried about all this emotion?" she asked, that parental concern now bleeding into her words. "You saw me just a month ago, and we video call almost every day."

Lane chuckled, guiding them to the small sofa by the window, offering a serene view of the garden. "You know you're the only one who gets to witness this side of me," she reminded Anita. "Stop fussing. I'm fine. Can you blame me after nearly losing you?"

As they sat facing each other on the sofa, Lane couldn't help but laugh at Anita's eye roll. "Maybe if you let others see this side of you, you might find a nice woman to settle down with," Anita suggested, gesturing to the teapot on the table between them. "Tea?"

Lane grinned. "Would I dare visit without indulging in your famous ginger and lemon tea?" she asked, playfully.

Anita shook her head, arranging cups for them. "Is that your secret? Flattery and charm to entice women into your bed, while keeping them at an emotional distance?"

"A little flattery and charm do work wonders in getting what I want, I won't deny that," Lane admitted with a smile. "As for the emotional distance..." She paused, shrugging slightly. "I guess I just haven't met anyone who makes me want to close the distance."

"Maybe it's because you're not letting them see beyond your armor," Anita suggested gently. "The one you've constructed so strongly that I fear I may never witness you allowing yourself to be truly loved."

Lane traced the rim of her cup with her index finger, contemplating Anita's words. "Maybe love isn't meant for everyone," she mused. "I'm content with how my life is. Relationships can be stressful, and frankly, everyone

I know has had terrible luck with them. So why bother?" She shrugged again, taking a sip of her tea, finding solace in its familiar flavors that always managed to soothe her, no matter the turmoil in her days as a teenager.

"Delaney," The scolding reprimand echoed through the room. "Please don't let the experiences of others dictate your own," Anita implored, reaching for Lane's hands with her fingers—calloused from years of cleaning the halls at Parkwood Memorial—gently scraping against Lane's skin. "You can learn from them, but don't assume that just because their experiences were bad, yours will be too. As you said, I almost died, and I don't want you to be alone when my time comes. I want you to find someone who will be there for you." Lane opened her mouth to respond, but Anita raised an eyebrow, silencing her in that familiar way that always made Lane pause. "Please don't mention Nia," Anita added softly. "She has her own family and won't always be there for you the same way a partner would. And all these women falling into your bed just for the fun of it, won't be there either."

Lane pondered her response but decided to shift the conversation's direction. Debating her love life with Anita, who had become a dog with a bone in recent months, seemed futile. "I'll definitely keep your advice in mind," she said with a grin, noticing Anita's narrowed eyes aimed at her. "When do you think you'll be ready to come home with me?" Lane hurriedly interjected, knowing this topic would swiftly divert Anita's inquiries into her dating habits.

"I'm not moving in with you, Delaney," Anita responded firmly, her gaze unwavering.

"Why not?" Lane pressed, her concern evident. "You despised this place when I pleaded with you to move here after your release from the hospital. I practically had to twist your arm to get you here." Lane took a deep breath, trying to push aside memories of the day she received the call about Anita's near heart attack.

"Because I don't want to impose on you. I'm sure having an old lady living with you won't do so well with the ladies when they sleep over," Anita replied with a dismissive wave of her hand. "I don't want to get in the way of you living your life."

Lane shook her head in disbelief, her voice barely above a whisper. "After everything you've done for me, do you honestly think I'd see you as a burden? You saved my life and gave me a home, for heaven's sake," she ended more firmly.

"That doesn't mean you owe me anything," Anita insisted. "You've repaid me by forging your own success despite the challenges of your upbringing. And you've done more than enough," she added, gesturing around the room. "This place alone comes with a hefty price tag."

"You're *deserving* of every penny," Lane retorted fiercely. "More deserving than anyone I know."

Anita sighed and once again reached for Lane's hands, her touch imbued with that motherly warmth that always reminded Lane that there was good in the world—sometimes coming in the form of angels like Anita—despite how shitty it was.

"Delaney, I know you moved back to Seattle because of me, even though I've told you a million times that I'm fine. I'm grateful you're home, but I don't want to burden you to the point where you're at work worrying if I'm lying on the floor with my blood pressure through the roof and unable to call for help."

A playful grin spread across Anita's lips, her eyes sparkling with mischief. "Besides, I've come to appreciate living here. It's nice being surrounded by people in my age group who I can share daily activities," she admitted, glancing out the window before meeting Lane's gaze again. "It's less lonely being here." Her grin widened. "And I have a hot grandpa here who brings me flowers and chocolate every day."

Lane threw her head back, laughter bubbling up from deep within her, a sound only Anita could coax out of her. Here was a woman who had weathered life's storms, yet still retained her sense of humor and humanity. "So, you want to stay because you've got some man wrapped around your finger?" Lane teased, a playful twinkle in her eyes.

Anita waved a hand in front of herself and smoothed her almost fully white natural curls. "Just look at all this gorgeousness," she quipped. "Can you blame him?" Her expression turned serious for a moment. "But it's not just about that. The environment here is incredible, and I love being surrounded by nature and breathing in the fresh air every day. There's a sense of community here that I've grown to cherish." She inhaled deeply. "So, you see," Anita continued, thoughtfully, "It's a good thing I talked you out of breaking your contract and losing millions of dollars just to move back here and babysit me. Things have a way of working themselves out, and sometimes we just need to go with the flow of life and embrace change."

Lane sighed, raising her hands in a gesture of surrender. "If staying here makes you happy, then I have no choice but to accept it. All I want is for you to be happy and comfortable."

Anita patted Lane's thigh. "I know, and I want the same for you," she replied, taking a sip of tea before fixing Lane with a cautious gaze. "Since I'll be staying here for the foreseeable future, I think you should sell the house to pay for it. I thought I'd live out my days there, but given the circumstances, I want you to sell it, invest the money, and use it to cover my expenses here. Technically, you'll still be paying for my stay since you paid for the house, so there's no point in arguing that you don't have a problem paying. Get Nia to invest the money, and use the gains to cover the costs of this place."

Lane met Anita's gaze with unwavering resolve. "That's because I don't have a problem paying. I'd spend every penny I have to do anything for you," she affirmed. "But I won't sell the house, just in case one day you decide you're tired of this place and want to return to the comfort of your home. I'll rent it for the time being." Her expression morphed into curiosity as she continued to regard Anita. "Where did you get this idea about selling the house?"

"Herbie mentioned that his daughter sold his house, invested the money, and is using the returns to cover his expenses here. That way, when he passes away, she'll still have the capital from the house for herself." She waved nonchalantly as she continued. "I've willed the house to you since you insisted on putting it solely in my name when you bought it. So, if you sell it and invest, when I'm gone you'll still recoup your investment."

Lane raised a questioning brow. "Herbie?"

A swoony smile lit up Anita's face. "Short for Herbert—hot grandpa who brings me flowers."

Lane laughed softly, but her expression quickly turned somber. "Please, let me take care of you. The house was a gift. I have more money than I'll ever be able to spend in this lifetime. I could live comfortably off the interest alone from my investments." She gestured around the room. "All of this pales in comparison to what you gave me when I had no one else. I'll forever be indebted to you." Her eyes landed back on her guardian angel before delivering her punchline. "Still, this isn't about repaying you—it's about doing something wonderful for someone I love. And you know there aren't many people in this world who I love."

"And that's because you keep allowing people to believe you're the dark lord, thus preventing anyone from getting too close to you and giving yourself a chance to fall in love," Anita pointed out knowingly.

Lane chuckled. "The dark lord persona is strictly for the office. Outside of work, I'm just naturally allergic to people and their lack of basic common sense."

Anita rolled her eyes affectionately. "You and your comebacks. Have you ever met anyone who didn't annoy you just by existing? Other than me and Nia, of course."

Miranda's image immediately flashed into Lane's mind. Nothing about Miranda Hayes annoyed her, not even when she was putting Lane in her place.

"What's that look?" Anita narrowed her eyes, as if trying to peer into Lane's thoughts.

"What look?" Lane feigned innocence.

"The one you get when you're debating whether or

not to tell me something."

Lane shook her head, deflecting. "No, there's nothing I want to tell you other than that I love you."

"Hmm," Anita hummed knowingly, reaching up to cup Lane's cheek, her eyes softening. "I know you better than you think," she said tenderly. "And I love you too, my sweet girl. Thank you for taking care of me and making me so very proud of the remarkable woman you've become. I know you didn't have to do anything for me." Anita shrugged with an air of indifference that didn't quite shroud the cloud of sadness behind her eyes. "After all, the children I gave birth to and scrubbed all those floors to put through college won't even give me a phone call."

Lane swallowed hard, the lump of emotions in her throat nearly choking her as she leaned into the warmth of Anita's palm. She gazed at the woman who, if it weren't for her generosity, Lane might not have survived past her teenage years—or might have been dealt an even harsher hand. Anita had been a complete stranger when they first met twenty-five years ago, yet despite her own hardships, she had shown Lane unwavering kindness without expecting anything in return. It was Anita's guidance that had set Lane on the path to success.

"I owe everything to you," Lane murmured, her voice thick with gratitude. "And your kids are morons. They don't deserve someone as wonderful as you."

Anita patted Lane's cheek gently before dropping her hand. "You owe it all to yourself. You put in the work and fought for what you wanted," she insisted, glancing around the room as if searching for something. Lane recognized it as Anita's way of avoiding talking about her son and daughter. "Now, are you ready for me to take all your money by beating you in a game of Gin Rummy?" Anita quipped with a daring twinkle in her eyes.

"You could certainly try," Lane replied with a grin as she rose to fetch the cards from the table on the other side of the room. These simple moments were the ones she cherished most in life. Few people knew this side of her, and she was forever grateful for those who did. They understood her at her core, and that was all that mattered. She knew they would never judge her or perceive her as demanding just because she had high standards, or entertain the myriad of other not-so-nice things people had said about her over the years. Yes, she didn't allow many to get close to her, and when people lacked access to a person, they often resorted to assuming the worst or fabricating stories to cast that person in a negative light to feel better about themselves.

Chapter 6

"Also, don't forget about dinner with my parents on Sunday," Miranda reminded Trevor on the other end of the video call. Glancing at the clock on her laptop screen, she realized it was almost time for her meeting with Lane.

"Do you want me to bring anything?" Trevor asked.

"No need. You know Mom always makes too much food anyway. They're just excited to spend time with us since we haven't been over in weeks." Miranda paused as a reminder popped up on the screen, signaling the impending meeting. "I was thinking of heading over on Saturday and spending the weekend with them since they'll be leaving for their European tour next week. You can join us on Sunday."

Trevor's expression darkened. "I was hoping we could spend the whole weekend together, especially since I didn't get to see you much this week because of your schedule."

That sense of guilt, as if she wasn't giving enough to him, crept along Miranda's spine whenever he pointed out the lack of time they spent together because of her —sometimes—very busy schedule. "I'm sorry I couldn't make it over. This week has just been insane. I promise to make it up to you next week. My schedule will be lighter and I won't be on call. I'll come home with you after the dinner."

Trevor nodded, but his expression didn't ease as much as Miranda had hoped after her explanation. "You know, all of this would be solved if we moved in together," he suggested, preemptively raising his hand to stave off any protest from Miranda. "I don't want to fight about it. Just putting it out there."

Why say it then if you don't want to fight about it... Miranda mused internally as she suppressed the urge to voice her thoughts. She didn't want to put herself in a worse mood, given that in the next fifteen minutes, she would be meeting with a woman who would undoubtedly get on her nerves. "I don't want to fight either. I think we've been doing enough of that lately," she admitted, trying to keep her tone neutral. "I have to go. I'll stop by the restaurant to see you after work."

Trevor shook his head clearly displeased with her dismissal of the moving-in-together issue. "Okay. I'll see you later."

"Bye," Miranda murmured, feeling suffocated by the tension that seemed to hang in the air every time Trevor broached the subject of them living together. Things had been going well between them, or so she had thought, until Trevor started pushing for more than she was ready to give. She hated feeling like the bad guy, because Trevor was so kind and caring toward her. But the passive-aggressive bullshit was starting to grate on her nerves.

She sighed, taking deep breaths to center herself. Remaining calm and focused was crucial for this meeting, especially since the last time she felt this way, she had met her new CEO and their interaction had been less than friendly. She could admit that she had been more curt with Lane than she normally would have been if she hadn't been in a bad mood. However, even if she had been in a better state of mind, the outcome might have been the same given Lane's egotistical nature. The way Lane had looked at Miranda was unnerving, to say the least. It wasn't lewd in a way that would turn one off, but it simmered with desire and lust, even when her demeanor was casually calm and relaxed. Miranda could understand why women would be drawn to Lane—she was undeniably beautiful, charming, and possessed a domineering aura that many found appealing.

Miranda shook her head to dispel the errant thoughts swirling in her mind. *Time to get this show on the road...* she thought as she headed two floors up to Lane's office.

"Hey you," Blake greeted as Miranda emerged from her office. "Heading somewhere important? I was hoping to go over a consult with you."

"I'm off to meet with your new CEO. I'm sure in her mind, it's very important," Miranda replied, pulling Blake into a quick hug.

Blake chuckled. "I'd pay big money to be a fly on the wall for this one. But please..." Blake eyed her imploringly. "Behave. I don't want you causing my wife unnecessary stress by making her search for another CEO."

Miranda glowered. "I can't believe you think I'd be the one to cause trouble."

"No, not usually," Blake admitted. "But I've never seen anyone get under your skin quite like Lane did after one meeting. You're usually Miss Sunshine and Roses— warm and friendly with everyone."

Miranda huffed in frustration. "That's because you

weren't there to witness what I had to deal with."

Blake shook her head, a smirk playing on her lips. "I've had firsthand experience with Lane's charms when she's trying to woo a woman into her bed, so I know exactly what you dealt with. That's why it's strange to see her get under your skin like this when it usually takes a lot to rile you up."

Miranda couldn't deny the smidgen of truth in Blake's words. Why did Lane affect her so deeply? The woman had an inexplicable effect on her. "Well, I don't want to cause any stress for your beloved wife, so I'll be civil to your new boss, even if she tries to provoke me into wanting to throttle her."

Blake grinned appreciatively. "Thank you. I really appreciate your thoughtfulness," she said, dipping her head in a mock bow.

Miranda narrowed her eyes at Blake's teasing act and laughed. Leave it to her best friend to lift her spirits without even realizing she needed it. "I'll let you know when I'm done, and we can meet up for that consult."

"Okay. See ya later," Blake said with a wave before heading off back to her office.

Miranda opted for the stairs, giving herself an extra moment to center her thoughts and approach the meeting with an open mind. She reminded herself not to let one negative encounter color her perception of Lane. Yet, with each step she took, she couldn't shake the uneasy feeling that had settled in her stomach since meeting Lane. Inhaling deeply, she practiced the new breathing exercises her yoga teacher had introduced earlier in the week, hoping they would help her find the serenity she sought.

"Hi, Kelsey," Miranda greeted warmly as she

approached Lane's assistant's desk.

"Hi, Dr. Hayes," Kelsey replied, her smile radiant enough to light up the entire room.

"Is it okay for me to go in?" Miranda inquired, pausing beside the desk.

Kelsey glanced at Lane's door before returning her gaze to Miranda. "Yes, she's expecting you."

Noticing the charm bracelet adorning Kelsey's wrist, Miranda pointed out, "I have that exact opal charm."

Kelsey's expression softened with fondness. "This was a gift from my sister. I wasn't into these things before she bought me my first pair. And now I'm hooked."

"Ahh, they can be quite addictive. I have an entire jewelry box of them," Miranda admitted with a chuckle.

Before Kelsey could respond, the phone on her desk rang, and Miranda waved goodbye, allowing her to take the call. Pausing outside Lane's door, Miranda took a deep breath, focusing on finding inner peace, before knocking.

"Come in," Lane's voice called out from the other side, clear and composed.

Miranda turned the doorknob, pushing the door open slowly, her heart pounding in anticipation of encountering Lane's trademark smug smirk—the same one she had flaunted just a week ago in the boardroom, a silent reminder of their brief but memorable encounter. However, what she saw caused her to pause in surprise as she took in the woman seated behind the desk.

Gone was the teasing glint and mirth in Lane's eyes that Miranda had observed during their interaction at Josephine's. Instead, they appeared distant and unreadable, like greenish icebergs gazing out into an abyss. Lane's body language lacked the casual familiarity of their prior meeting—there was no hint of the woman who had confidently offered her a drink, even after being turned down. This was Lane the CEO, a ruler cloaked in an aura of confidence and self-assurance that permeated the room. As Miranda observed her, she couldn't help but feel a sense of awe at Lane's presence. The woman exuded power, her whole countenance radiating authority as she sat behind her desk, poised and in control. It was as if she were untouchable in this setting, a formidable force to be reckoned with.

Lane's eyes, with their sparkling gold flecks, bore into Miranda, causing her to fight the urge to look away. Despite herself, Miranda couldn't help but swallow hard as she finally allowed herself to admire Lane's profile. She was stunning, with waves of rich brown hair cascading over one shoulder, and lips painted in her signature crimson red lipstick. Her eyebrows were perfectly sculpted, and the light makeup only served to accentuate her natural beauty. But it was Lane's eyes that left Miranda bewildered. The desire and lust that she had expected to see were conspicuously absent, leaving Miranda unable to decipher Lane's thoughts as she waited for her to shut the door.

Lane lifted a hand and gestured toward the chair in front of her desk. "Dr. Hayes, please close the door and have a seat."

Even her tone was different now—no longer smooth and charismatic like it had been at the bar, but cool, inscrutable, and impenetrable.

Miranda obeyed, closing the door behind her and

moving further into the office to take the offered seat. Just as she reached the chair before the desk, Lane stood and extended a hand for a handshake.

"Dr. Hayes, thank you for taking the time out of your busy schedule to meet with me," Lane said, her eyes fixed on Miranda's.

"Not like you gave me a choice in the matter," Miranda retorted, immediately regretting her words. Regardless of their history, Lane was her boss, and that demanded a certain level of respect. Lane tilted her head to the side, scrutinizing Miranda, but her expression gave no indication of what she was thinking.

As Lane began to lower her hand, Miranda quickly grasped it and completed the handshake. "Thanks for having me," she added, attempting to smooth over her blunder.

Lane slowly released her hand, and Miranda couldn't help but notice how soft and warm it felt, even as Lane's gaze bore into her with a coldness that she neither understood nor expected.

Maybe she's upset that I turned her down and this was payback.

Lane eased herself into her chair, her impenetrable gaze fixed on Miranda's face. Miranda mirrored her movements, the tension in the room palpable as they locked eyes, the silence stretching between them.

"In the future, if I request a meeting with you and it doesn't fit into your schedule, please feel free to set a time that is more convenient for you," Lane stated, her tone professional and formal. "I'm very flexible when it comes to accommodating staff's schedules, especially surgeons who can be pulled into the operating room at a moment's notice."

Miranda found herself at odds with the enigma before her, but this was their workplace, and if Lane was opting for formality, Miranda would oblige. Although, the stiffness of the interaction grated on her nerves. "Thanks for being accommodating," she said, mustering one of her most charming smiles, hoping to ruffle the composed facade of the stone-faced woman sitting across from her.

Lane's facial expression remained stoic, her demeanor unchanged. "You're welcome. Now, I don't intend to occupy more of your time than necessary, since it sounds like this meeting is of some hardship for you," she said evenly. "It seems you have more pressing matters to attend to than discussing the needs of your department with me and exploring ways to enhance its operations amidst the current economic challenges."

Miranda felt the sting of the dig, and she clenched her teeth to restrain the sharp retort poised at the tip of her tongue. Once again, she had to remind herself that this was her workplace, not Josephine's, where she could engage in not-so-polite banter with this woman. Lane's unreadable expression continued to pierce her, urging Miranda to maintain her composure. Taking a deep breath, she resolved that the sooner this meeting concluded, the better it would be for her sanity.

"The primary issues, of course, revolve around cost," Miranda began, her voice steady as she delved into the heart of the matter. "With the hospital garnering more attention since Alexandra came on board, we've seen an increase in patient volume that my current staff struggles to manage. Before the leadership change, my plan was to propose hiring two more surgeons and two additional cardiac nurse practitioners to Alexandra."

Miranda paused, expecting Lane to interject, but Lane simply nodded, signaling for her to continue.

Over the next twenty minutes, Miranda outlined her department's challenges and detailed her strategic plans for the coming months. Lane listened intently, asking insightful questions that demonstrated her deep understanding of hospital operations. It didn't surprise Miranda— after all, Alexandra had hired Lane for her extensive experience in the field.

"I'll need to see a business case for the new hires," Lane stated, her tone firm and measured. "As you're aware, we're focused on cost-saving measures, so any additional staffing must be thoroughly justified. However, providing optimal patient care remains our top priority, and I'll work with HR to explore ways to accommodate your request."

"Thank you," Miranda responded, maintaining eye contact with Lane, who had yet to look away throughout the meeting—an unnerving experience.

"Have a good day, Dr. Hayes," Lane concluded, the professional and distant cadence of her voice never wavering.

Miranda knew she should rise from her chair and depart, but Lane's demeanor—acting as if they were two strangers meeting for the first time—irritated her. She narrowed her eyes at Lane, who continued to regard her with cool indifference. Lane arched a sculpted brow in response to whatever she discerned in Miranda's expression.

Unable to suppress her frustration, Miranda blurted out, "Are you simply going to pretend that just a month ago, you weren't trying to lure me into your bed?"

Lane reclined into her chair, crossing one toned leg

over the other, a smug smile tugging at her lips—
the very one that had infuriated Miranda that night at
Josephine's. The distant and icy demeanor had melted
away, replaced by the familiar smooth-talker Lane,
mischief gleaming in her eyes.

"Why, Dr. Hayes," Lane drawled, sarcasm dripping playfully off of each syllable of Miranda's professional title, "it seems, despite your alleged disinterest in my advances, you haven't quite managed to forget about me." Miranda caught the minute flexion of Lane's fingers, resembling a dragon's talons twitching awake from disturbed slumber—her perfectly manicured nails, now lightly pressing into the armrests of her chair. "I thought you weren't interested in what I was offering that night at Josephine's."

Miranda chastised herself internally for simply not rising and leaving the office the moment she opened up that Pandora's box, especially now with Lane's pupils alternating between dilation and constriction—like a predator honing in on an unsuspecting prey. It made her feel like Lane wanted to consume her whole. She needed to escape this room before she uttered something she might regret later, yet once again, she found herself unable to resist the urge to respond. "Well, Ms. Remington," she rebutted, her voice tinged with sarcasm of her own, "I must admit, I've never encountered someone with such unyielding arrogance. So, it's no surprise that someone with your level of self-confidence would leave a lasting impression."

Lane's grin only widened, as though she were relishing the exchange at Miranda's expense. "I'll take that as a compliment. After all, said self-confidence has propelled me quite far in life…" The tips of Lane's nails began raking slowly back and forth on the armrests, synonymous to a tiger's claws extending and retracting before pouncing. "Particularly with the ladies. Most of whom find my self-confidence absolutely riveting."

Miranda's counter was swift. "I guess some women are desperate."

Lane only smiled wider. "Yes, very desperate for what I have to offer." She paused and ran her eyes up and down Miranda's body. "An offer which still stands for you whenever you're ready to explore the dark side."

Miranda rolled her eyes and stood from her chair. "Thanks, but no thanks. I'll pass on whatever you're offering, just as I passed on your drink. Have a good day."

Lane's laughter echoed through the room, its timbre sending a shiver down Miranda's spine. She found herself momentarily captivated, unable to look away from the enigmatic woman before her.

Beautiful Devil.

Miranda couldn't help but feel perplexed by Lane's actions. Here was a woman who had maintained a stoic facade throughout their entire meeting, yet now she was laughing so carefreely at Miranda's remark. It was as if Lane found amusement in their verbal jousting, despite the tension that had simmered between them. Miranda couldn't shake the feeling that Lane was trouble, and she made a mental note to keep her distance. With the size of the hospital and the fact that she got under Miranda's skin, avoiding Lane shouldn't be too challenging.

"Entertaining as always, Dr. Hayes," Lane remarked, her laughter still permeating the air. "It will be a pleasure working with you." As she spoke, Lane studied

Miranda beneath long lashes that fanned over high cheekbones, her eyes sparkling with a mixture of intrigue and something more potent. "Have yourself a wonderful day," she concluded, her tone maintaining a delicate balance between professionalism and a seeping undercurrent of playful challenge.

Miranda's eyes did another three-sixty as she fought the urge to respond, reminding herself of the professionalism expected in her role. Hastening her steps, she hurried out of the office. She silently thanked her stars that Alexandra would remain as chief of surgery. The thought of working more closely than necessary with Lane filled her with a sense of unease. She feared she'd inevitably find herself entangled in some form of trouble, unable to resist the barbs Lane effortlessly threw her way.

Chapter 7

"Damn, woman. This is what being a high-profile executive gets you," Nia announced, spinning around on her heels, taking in the view of Lane's penthouse as she entered the living room.

"And a whole lot more," Lane replied, approaching Nia and placing a hand on her shoulder to halt her spinning before pulling her into a tight hug. As they eased back from the embrace, Lane held Nia at arm's length, scanning her from head to toe. "You've gained back your exquisite derrière. I guess divorce has really done wonders for you," she teased, lifting a hand to run it through Nia's short, tight, natural curls. "I still can't believe you cut off all your beautiful hair. Even though you're wearing this new style better Eva Marcille in her prime."

"And I still can't believe you're moving back to Seattle. But, yes, being divorced and now finally being free to explore my bisexuality has done wonders for me." Nia wiggled her eyebrows. "Now, I have a little more understanding of why you haven't settled down with just one woman when you can indulge in the many wonders of more than one woman's body. There's something to be said about sex with a woman. I thoroughly regret wasting fifteen years of my life with a man before ever sleeping with a woman. Maybe I wouldn't have settled for less all these years."

Lane chuckled softly as she led Nia further into the living room. She poured a glass of rich red wine, the deep aroma swirling in the air as she handed it to her friend and settled beside her on the plush sofa. Nia took a long sip, her throaty hum indicating her appreciation for the wine's flavor, her eyes closing in a moment of pure indulgence. Lane seized the opportunity to study her friend's face, noting the major changes since their last get-together. After enduring a tumultuous divorce, Nia had shed layers of stress, regained weight, and emerged from the shadows of her ordeal. Her dark brown skin glowed with newfound vitality, and a spark had returned to her eyes with a glimmer of the resilience that had defined her. They had forged their bond during their first year at Berkeley College, both navigating the challenges of being financially strapped students without the cushion of affluent parents. Despite receiving only partial scholarships, they persevered by working tirelessly to finance their education. They were kindred spirits, survivors who understood that education was their ticket out of poverty.

Before meeting Nia, Lane had seldom encountered someone who embraced her unconditionally, unburdened by judgment or preconceptions. Even when their paths diverged across continents, they remained steadfast pillars in each other's lives. Besides Anita, Nia was the closest thing Lane had to family, a constant source of support and understanding.

"Well, I'm glad you're enjoying this side of your sexuality. I guess there's always a rainbow after the storm," Lane remarked, offering a nod of solidarity.

Nia raised her glass in agreement. "Cheers to that."

Lane clinked her glass against Nia's. "So, I take it things are still going smoothly with Kenya. No regrets about moving back here for her?"

A blissful smile graced Nia's lips, painted in a soft neutral hue. "None whatsoever. She's worth it. After everything with Brandon, it's a breath of fresh air to be with someone who respects and cherishes me as an equal partner. She values me for who I am, not as a possession or arm candy for social events."

"I'm genuinely thrilled for you. You deserve to be happy and to experience the freedom of self even when you're in a relationship."

Nia chuckled, shaking her head gently. "With all the wisdom you impart, I'm still puzzled why you prefer casual relationships over committing to one of these women who always fall head over heels for you."

Lane laughed lightly. "They don't really fall in love with me, Nia. They think they do, but then they start expecting more than I'm ready to give way too early into dating. And most of them are in love with the idea of who they think I am, or who they want me to be." She took a small sip of wine and waved her hand dismissively. "Besides, you know how demanding my career has been. The long work hours weren't exactly attractive to someone who was looking for a partner to have dinner with every night." She shrugged casually. "So why bother, when it's just going to end in heartbreak because I couldn't meet their expectations? Plus, no offense, but I've yet to see a couple who inspires me to want to give up my freedom and commit. Most of the people I know are constantly complaining about their miserable marriages and wishing they were single again. So, yeah, not much incentive to trade my freedom to enjoy as many women as I wish."

Nia regarded Lane with a mix of understanding and frustration, her brow furrowing slightly. "You know, to be fair to these women, you've never really given them a chance to get close enough to know the real you. You keep everyone at arm's length and trust only a select few."

Lane nodded in agreement. "I guess I just haven't met anyone who compels me to lower my defenses. And besides, I'm quite content with my life as it is. I have a career that fulfills me, and I've got you and Anita to berate me about my trust issues. What more could a girl ask for?" She took another sip of her wine, her gaze drifting toward the city skyline visible through the penthouse windows.

"As long as you're happy, that's all that matters to me. But that doesn't mean I'll stop supporting Anita in trying to get you to settle down or at least allow someone to sweep you off your feet," Nia said with a warm smile.

At the mention of Anita's name, Lane's heart warmed. She cherished having at least one person who loved her unconditionally and stood by her through thick and thin. Her guardian angel. "Anita is just worried I'll be alone when she passes away. Despite everything she went through with her ex-husband, she still believes in love."

"I guess Anita and I are just bleeding hearts. Unfortunately, we both chose terrible men to fall in love with," Nia said with a wry chuckle.

Lane lifted her glass in acknowledgment. "That, I can certainly agree on."

The sadness in Nia's deep, brown eyes didn't escape Lane at the mention of her ex-husband. Nia had fallen hard and fast for Brandon during their second year at Berkeley. They were both finance majors, and after graduation, Nia followed him to New York, sacrificing her own opportunities in Silicon Valley for his career at a major investment bank. Lane had never liked Brandon —she always saw him as an egotistical bastard with outdated, misogynistic views. But her smart, intelligent friend was blinded by love and had spent fifteen years of her life in a marriage that, by the end, almost destroyed her self-confidence. Nia realized she was bisexual after she started dating Brandon, so she never had the chance to explore that side of her sexuality until she met the woman who gave her the strength to walk away from her toxic marriage.

After witnessing what Nia had endured, who could blame Lane for not leaping headfirst into love? She preferred her life to be simple and uncomplicated. People often proved to be disappointments and she just didn't have the patience for them. Besides, she cherished her solitude and the freedom it afforded her— relishing in the lack of accountability to anyone else.

Nia glanced around the living room, her eyes taking in the elegant décor. "How long are you allowed to stay here? This is a really nice apartment."

Lane leaned back against the armrest, a faint smile touching her lips. "I can stay for free for up to a year. If I decide to stay longer, I can lease it going forward. It was part of my compensation package. The hospital owner wanted me to relocate quickly, so she offered this as a perk to expedite the process and save me the hassle of finding a place to live." She pointed a finger at the ceiling. "Interestingly, she and her wife live just two floors above in penthouse one. I think the apartment above mine is reserved for when her parents visit from L.A."

Nia shook her head, a wistful smile playing on her lips. "If you'd told me twenty years ago that our broke asses would, one day, be able to afford homes like this, I probably wouldn't have believed it." She raised her glass to her lips, sipped, and slowly lowered it with her index finger wiggling at her friend. "But you've always been a dreamer, Lane. You believed we'd achieve everything we wanted if we just kept working hard, regardless of our disadvantages. And look at us now. Hell, I've got more money than I ever thought possible."

Just the thought of those days reminded Lane why she didn't regret the countless hours she'd poured into climbing the corporate ladder. She knew all too well what it was like to have less than a hundred dollars, and even worse, not knowing where her next meal would come from. Nia's question drew Lane's attention back to the present.

"How long do you think you'll stay in Seattle? I know you moved back mostly because Anita's health issues scared you and you want to be here for her. But now that she insists on staying at the facility, will it change your mind about staying here long term? I know you're not a fan of this place."

Too many bad memories. "I'll play it by ear and see how leading the team at Parkwood goes," Lane replied. "The hospital is doing fairly well, so it shouldn't be too stressful to manage. But as of right now, despite the improvements in Anita's health, I want to spend more time with her. You know how much she means to me, and her health scare made me realize that if the worst had happened, I would have regretted not spending more time with her because of my career journey and her refusal to follow me around the world." Reaching across the sofa, Lane patted Nia on her thigh. "So, don't worry, my friend. You're stuck with me again for the foreseeable future. It's such a pity now that you're finally indulging in the female kind, you're already head over heels in love, and I can't reinvent our college days when you were my wingwoman."

Nia chuckled. "Those were the days. Even then, you were still as charming as ever, and that charm got us many free drinks."

"Well, we were broke as hell and couldn't afford all those fancy cocktails," Lane replied with a grin. "I'd be rather foolish to turn down free drinks that cost more than our weekly grocery budget."

"Even then, you had women eating out of the palm of your hands. Speaking of, have you met anyone to warm your bed since you've been here?"

Yes, a very stunning cardiothoracic surgeon who won't give me the time of day and thinks I'm an insufferable asshole.

Lane shook her head more to clear her thoughts of Miranda than to answer her friend's question. At this point, she didn't see any reason to bring up her interest in Miranda since nothing would happen between them. "Not yet. You know I'm very particular with my dating habits."

Nia lifted an eyebrow. "You mean very picky with the women you choose to lure into your bed."

Lane's mind immediately went to her meeting with Miranda, where she'd accused Lane of pretending that they were strangers after she tried to lure her to her bed. She bit her cheek to suppress a chuckle and kept her face as neutral as possible, aware that Nia was watching her closely. "I know what I want, and I'm willing to wait until I find it. You know I'm not that desperate for sex to sleep with just anyone."

"Oh, I know. You've always had very high standards in every aspect of your life. I'll personally buy a crown for any woman who lives up to your standards and tames the wild beast that is Lane Remington," Nia proclaimed with a playful grin. She rose from the sofa. "How about you give me a tour of this place?"

"Gladly. Then you can tell me about this new venture you want me to invest in. Even though, you know I'm already in without knowing the details. So far, your sound financial advice has made me a very wealthy woman and I don't intend to stop following you down the rabbit hole of making more money."

Returning to Seattle marked a significant shift for Lane and having her best friend nearby as she navigated this new chapter brought her comfort. Still, returning to this city stirred a mix of emotions—occasionally more painful memories than pleasant ones. Seattle was where she first experienced life's cruelty, where even those who were supposed to protect her were more unkind than strangers. It was a place that forced her to build walls around herself just to survive the harsh realities of the world.

Chapter 8

Miranda clenched her jaw in frustration as she read Trevor's message detailing his parents' unexpected visit and their eagerness to join their dinner plans at her parents' house. She'd interacted with Trevor's parents on a handful of occasions since they began dating, and with each encounter, she understood more why he had chosen to distance himself from them by moving away from New York. While Trevor possessed a laid-back, free-spirited demeanor, his parents exuded an air of elitism and condescension, treating anyone outside their Fifty-Seventh Street bubble with disdain, as if they were mere insects to be squashed beneath their designer shoes. Still, Miranda recognized the importance of Trevor's relationship with his parents and begrudgingly accepted their presence in their lives. Lately, their interest in his romantic affairs veered into uncomfortable territory, often revolving around the prospect of him siring a grandchild to uphold their prestigious family legacy—a child preferably conceived within the confines of marriage. Miranda couldn't shake the feeling that their acceptance of her—a half-black woman—was influenced by her family's substantial wealth. Their initial encounter had felt like an interrogation into her family's background, while subsequent meetings had been tinged with a more tolerable attitude, likely due to the realization that her family's net worth surpassed theirs. Money was power after all, and that was the only language people like Trevor's parents spoke. *Argh.*

"Sweetheart, why are you gripping your phone as if you want to squeeze the life out of it," her mom pointed out as she joined her on the patio.

Miranda jumped slightly. "Mom, you startled me." Miranda chuckled, relaxing her grip on her phone. She shifted to face Carolyn, her own surprise giving way to amusement at the sight of her mother with a face covered in a thick layer of facial mask, leaving only patches of her natural umber skin tone visible around her eyes. "If I'd known you were inside indulging in a facial, I would have joined you."

"I spent too long in the sun today without sunscreen at the tennis club, and despite all this wonderful melanin I'm blessed with, I still have to protect my skin from sun damage." Caroline glanced at the phone in Miranda's hand. "So, what's wrong? Why do you look like you want to strangle someone?" she asked, her voice carrying a note of concern.

Miranda hadn't discussed the recent tension in her relationship with her mom because her parents adored Trevor and were genuinely happy that she finally gave him a chance. Trevor was one of the few men she'd dated whom her parents liked, and she knew they were hoping that he would be the one to put a ring on her finger. While her parents supported her in all aspects of her life, she understood that they harbored hopes of her finding the kind of enduring love they shared and perhaps even some grandkids in the near future.

Miranda sighed internally. "Trevor asked if his

parents could join us for dinner. They're in town for a business trip and insist on meeting my parents. I wish I could refuse, but it would be seen as terribly rude in their eyes."

Caroline watched her for a long moment, her eyes assessing in that familiar, discerning way she had whenever she sensed Miranda was withholding something. "Well, luckily your father has made enough food to feed an army."

"Luckily…" She sighed again, this time audible and heavy. "I guess we should go and get dressed in our finest evening wear since having dinner in casual clothes in the presence of the McKinsons is akin to committing a First Commandment sin," Miranda quipped sarcastically.

Caroline chuckled. "You're joking, right? They invited themselves to our home, so they have to respect what we choose to wear to dinner. I, for one, am not in the mood to get all dressed up to accommodate their snobbery."

"I can only imagine the look on Bridgette's face when Dad comes out in his shorts and T-shirt," Miranda said, mimicking Bridgette's pinched expression whenever she thought something was unbecoming of civilization.

Caroline laughed once more. "I think that's just her normal expression daily." Then, her features grew somber. "I know you're not a fan of his parents, but is there something else going on between you two? Recently, there has been a lingering sadness behind your eyes whenever you speak about your relationship."

Miranda drew in a deep breath as she pondered sharing her relationship problems with her mother. They'd always been very close, and she often sought her mother's advice whenever she needed guidance. But now that she was thirty-seven and unmarried, she'd been feeling like she would disappoint her parents if her relationship with Trevor ended. Her family wasn't traditional extremists, but they valued marriage and family bonds. However, this was her mom, and perhaps talking to her would help shed some light on why she was reluctant to take the next step with Trevor.

"He wants us to move in together, but I don't feel like I'm ready for such a change. It's only been a year, and for Trevor, that's more than enough time. He doesn't understand my reluctance. He thinks I'm not as committed to the relationship as he is. We've been arguing a lot about it recently," Miranda admitted, the weight of her words heavy on her chest. The ever-present guilt that had been suffocating her recently made itself known.

"The whole situation has me reflecting on why my previous relationships failed, and I'm scared this one will also fail, even though Trevor is a really great guy compared to most that I've dated," she continued, her voice tinged with uncertainty. "Before Trevor, I could easily say that those men didn't deserve me and they just weren't the ones because I had really valid reasons for dumping them. But with Trevor, I've been wondering if I'm the problem... And I've just been feeling so guilty when he's so good to me and I don't have a valid reason other than that I'm not ready."

She exhaled a breath she didn't realize she was holding, and kneaded the sides of her temples with the pads of her fingers. "I care for him deeply, but I just feel like something is missing that should make me want to dive head-first into moving in with him. The puzzle is, I don't even know what that thing is."

Miranda didn't realize how emotional expressing her feelings was until she felt tears on her cheeks. "But, even though I'm not ready to move forward, I still don't want to lose him."

Caroline closed the distance between them and enveloped Miranda in a comforting embrace. Miranda melted into her mother's arms, finding contentment in the warmth and familiarity of her presence, despite the face mask smudging into her hair. Caroline's hands moved soothingly up and down her back, a gesture that had always brought comfort since Miranda was a child. She allowed herself to release months of pent-up tears, feeling the weight of her uncertainty and fears lift slightly with each drop. Maybe, she thought, all her exes were right, and she was the one with commitment issues. Maybe she truly didn't know what she wanted in a relationship.

A few minutes passed before Caroline slowly eased back, her hand still resting gently on Miranda's elbow as she held her gaze. "My darling child, there is nothing wrong with you. It's perfectly natural to not settle for anything less than fulfillment in every aspect of your life, especially in matters of the heart." She placed a warm hand over the base of Miranda's heart. "While Trevor may be an amazing guy, if he doesn't ignite that undeniable passion within you, the kind that makes you want to dive headfirst into moving in with him without a second thought, then perhaps he isn't the one who will awaken that feeling in you. Just because someone is wonderful doesn't automatically mean they're your perfect match. And you should never feel guilty for prioritizing your happiness.

"Relationships are complex, but they should never require you to sacrifice your well-being to appease your partner. True compromise should come from a place of mutual understanding and a desire to see each other happy, not from a sense of obligation or guilt." Miranda placed her hand over Caroline's, still resting on her chest, giving herself a physical anchor amongst the riptide of emotions evoked by her mother's words. "You deserve to be with someone who makes your heart sing, someone who challenges you to become the best version of yourself simply by being with them.

"Remember, my dear, you've witnessed firsthand what it's like to find that person who makes you want to leap into the unknown without hesitation. Who challenges your very understanding of yourself, compelling you to undergo a metamorphosis simply through their presence in your life. The one who turns your world upside down and shows you a love so profound that you'd move mountains just to be with them. Hold out for that kind of love, sweetheart. It's worth the wait." Caroline's lips curved into a fond smile, her eyes reflecting a depth of understanding and love that only a mother could possess.

Miranda smiled softly. "Yes, you and Dad are perfect examples."

Caroline shook her head. "While your father and I have a wonderful relationship, I'm not talking about us. You didn't witness the early stages of our relationship. I'm talking about Blake and Alexandra." A look of mild disbelief crossed Caroline's face. "You saw how much Blake changed to be with Alexandra. I honestly thought she would never settle down because she was so against relationships. But, when she met her person

—Alexandra—everything she thought she knew about herself went out the door." Miranda beamed internally, remembering how genuinely happy she was for her best friend to have finally found unconditional love. "She became a totally different person to be with Alexandra or maybe she just embraced her true self because she finally found someone with whom she could lower her guard. You were front row and center from day one, and look at Blake now—happily married with a baby on the way." Caroline lifted a hand and gently cupped Miranda's cheek. "Don't be too hard on yourself because you're not ready to give Trevor what he wants. If you move in just to make him happy, it will likely only make both of you unhappy because you would be miserable. If he can't wait until you're ready…" She shrugged. "Then it's okay to walk away."

"Don't you see me as a failure because I'm thirty-seven and haven't been able to maintain a relationship that lasted longer than three years? Even then, when Malcolm asked me to marry him, I still hadn't moved in with him after we had been together for three years." She tensed her shoulders and dropped her gaze to the floor, unable to meet her mother's eyes. "I've been successful in every other aspect of my life, except relationships. I can't seem to get them right." Miranda couldn't stop the slight tremor in her voice because her parents had always been supportive of her, and she didn't want to seem like a failure in their eyes.

"Absolutely not, sweetheart. Regardless of all the nonsense that certain people spew, there's no timeline for love. Some people are just meant to find their person later in life, and there's nothing wrong with waiting until then to commit to anyone. Furthermore, there's nothing wrong with being single and living your best life," Caroline firmly reassured.

She pointed a finger at Miranda. "You've always cherished your personal space when it comes to your home. You're open and friendly, but you also value your alone time. Even as a teen, when you were home, there were moments you spent all day in your room without speaking to anyone. So, I think constantly having someone in your personal space is something that you need time to get accustomed to. I believe that when you meet your person, you won't need time to get used to it. You'll embrace it without hesitation." Both hands lifted to Miranda's cheeks. "And yes, your father and I would love to see you married someday, but if it doesn't happen, we'll never see you as a failure. Especially when you've made us very proud of the remarkable, kind soul that you are."

Miranda sniffled as she fought back more tears from spilling over her lashes. "Thanks, Mom. I guess everything will work out as it should in time." Her phone vibrated in her hand. Glancing at it, she quickly read the message. "They're on their way. We should go get primped and lay out the red carpet." Hand in hand, they started walking to the door.

"As much as I love Trevor, not having his parents as in-laws is one silver lining if things don't work out between you two," Caroline remarked with a wry smile. "I don't understand people like them who believe they're better than others just because they're wealthy. I was raised in a wealthy environment, so having money is not a valid excuse for acting like pretentious snobs."

"I know." Miranda nodded. "That's one of the many reasons why I admire Trevor. He's so humble, kind, and compassionate, despite growing up around parents like that."

Hopefully, he won't run out of patience with me.

Chapter 9

God, I hate Mondays, Miranda thought as she pushed open the door of The Junction—Parkwood's staff go-to spot for the best coffee within walking distance from the hospital. The aroma of freshly brewed coffee did little to lift her spirits as she joined the lengthy queue, already dreading the day ahead. With at least ten people ahead of her, she resigned herself to the wait, craving the caffeine boost to jumpstart her sluggish brain for another hectic day of patient care. As she stood in line, her phone buzzed in her pocket, momentarily distracting her from her caffeine craving. An internal groan escaped her lips as she prayed it wasn't an urgent call pulling her away before she could savor her first sip of coffee. Relief flooded her when she saw Trevor's name illuminated on the screen.

Trevor: I miss waking up with you. I'll come over to yours after work tonight. Have a great day. Love you

Miranda's shoulders sagged as she read Trevor's message, her eyes scanning the words repeatedly as she wrestled with conflicting emotions. They had scarcely spent a night apart in the past week, and as much as she cared for him, she couldn't shake the overwhelming desire for solitude. The weight of his expectations bore down on her, knowing that any attempt to express her desire for space would only lead to another argument. Guilt gnawed at her conscience as she considered sacrificing her well-being to appease Trevor's desire for constant companionship. She knew she should feel grateful for his affection and attention, but a sense of suffocation engulfed her, battling the craving of freedom to breathe on her own in the comfort of her home. With a resigned sigh, she crafted a response, once again prioritizing Trevor's happiness over her own need for seclusion.

Miranda: I'll make it up to you. I'll see you later. Have a wonderful day. ♥

"I guess the wait is worth it for the quality coffee."

Miranda looked up from her phone to find herself under the intense scrutiny of a man standing too close for comfort. His blonde hair was impeccably styled, and his sharp green eyes seemed to bore into hers with a confidence that bordered on intrusive. Dressed in a sleek three-piece suit, he projected an air of self-assuredness as he flashed her a charming smile.

Argh. I'm so not in the mood for small talk right now... Miranda thought, mustering a polite smile to conceal her annoyance. "Yeah, it is."

The man chuckled softly, shifting to fully face Miranda as if her response had given him license to engage further. "But you know, waiting in such a long line isn't half bad when you have someone to pass the time with," he pointed out, extending his hand toward her. "I'm Eric Sloan."

Miranda eyed the offered hand, inwardly groaning at the idea of shaking a stranger's hand. She knew declining might seem rude, but she wasn't willing to compromise her comfort for someone she might never encounter again. With another polite smile, she responded, "I'm still taking COVID-19 precautions, so I'll have to refuse the handshake. Plus, I don't mind waiting alone. It gives me a chance to catch up on emails."

His smile widened as they shuffled forward in the line. "Understandable," he agreed. "If I hadn't spotted a beautiful woman such as yourself, I'd probably be using the time to catch up on emails too." He leaned a bit closer, his tone suggestive. "So, aren't you going to share your name with me?"

As the line progressed, Miranda artfully shifted to increase the distance between herself and the unwelcome presence beside her. "I'm not in the habit of sharing my name with strangers," she replied evenly, her firmness steadfast with a lack of inflection.

Eric chuckled once more, still not taking a hint. "Fair enough. So, how about you let me buy you coffee and we can get to know each other."

Miranda shook her head. "I'm getting mine to go," she responded brusquely, leaving no room for further negotiations.

Undeterred, Eric leaned in closer, his persistence overwhelmingly intrusive as he once again invaded her personal space. "How about dinner then?" he pressed, his mannerisms overly familiar. "I work in the area, and I'm assuming you do as well. I can pick you up anywhere."

Miranda's patience was wearing thin with this overbearing, forward man. She shot him a pointed look. "I'm not interested," she reiterated firmly, hoping to finally convey her lack of desire for further interaction.

His smile faltered for a moment before it returned even wider. "Come on. Don't be like that. Have dinner with me. I promise it will be worth it by the end of the night."

Before Miranda could articulate a response to finally get rid of this unwanted attention, notes of white jasmine, lily of the valley, the velvety sweetness of vanilla, and a subtle hint of sandalwood surrounded her. The scent enveloped her like a warm blanket causing an imperceptible shiver to run the length of her spine as her pulse thrummed in anticipation.

"Hi, sweetheart. The call took longer than planned," Lane said, her voice wrapped in tenderness and affection, echoing the sentiments of someone deeply in love. "I figured the line was long, so I thought I'd come and keep you company while you wait." Lane's lips curled into a sultry smile, her gaze lingering on Miranda's mouth.

She could repair a ruptured aortic aneurysm in a patient with high blood pressure, alarms and medical equipment blaring all around her, but now Miranda found herself struggling to process Lane's presence—her aura seemingly overpowering everything else in the coffee shop. Her gaze traced the contours of Lane's gorgeous face, lingering on lips painted in a striking shade of red, a small but noticeable beauty mark just above the right side of her lip, and eyes brimming with challenge. With a shuddering breath, Miranda tore her gaze away, focusing on Lane's neck as her mind raced to decide if she should play along with Lane's game. Playing along felt tempting, yet she feared it might turn out to be a case of jumping out of the frying pan into the fire. Still, Lane's presence offered a welcome relief from the unwanted attention of the persistent man.

Miranda narrowed her eyes as she once again met Lane's stare, summoning a loving smile to her lips. "Hi baby, unfortunately, this line seems to be moving at a snail's pace." As if on autopilot, her right hand lifted of its own volition to gently tuck a strand of Lane's hair behind her ear. She didn't miss the sharp intake of breath as Lane's eyes darkened slightly, blatant desire flickering within them. Miranda quickly withdrew her hand, hoping the act wasn't too conspicuous. *What the hell am I doing touching her?*

Lane's gaze lingered on Miranda's face for a moment longer before she shifted her attention to Eric, her expression hard as an uncut diamond. "Hello," she greeted him coolly as if he were merely an afterthought. "I'm the wife."

Miranda rolled her eyes internally. *Of course, she went for the big guns... not just, girlfriend... nope... had to be, wife.* Miranda turned to gauge Eric's reaction. His smile had transformed into a scowl, and patches of red crept up his neck to his face. His eyes darted between Miranda and Lane, a mix of anger and embarrassment flashing in them. "Seems every beautiful woman is a dyke these days," he muttered under his breath, then spun on his heels and stormed out of the coffee shop.

"I guess he didn't take too kindly to my interference in his attempts to charm a woman who clearly wasn't interested in his pedestrian advances," Lane commented.

Miranda turned sharply to face Lane, her eyes narrowing into slits.

Lane shook her head in amusement. "Men... such predictable creatures. They could stand to learn a thing or two about the art of seduction. Hitting on a woman in a coffee shop line? How utterly cliché."

"This coming from a woman who hit on me in a bar. Isn't that rather cliché as well," Miranda shot back, arching an eyebrow as she awaited Lane's response.

Lane's lips curved into that confident smirk, her eyes sparkling with mirth. "Now, now, Miranda darling, you can't possibly be comparing that man's lackluster performance to my artistry." She momentarily splayed a hand over her chest in feigned disbelief. "He went from a coffee rejection to a dinner invitation in less than a minute. I would have been more strategic with my approach than that."

Miranda's eyebrow arched higher in question. "And how long were you eavesdropping before you decided to play wife?"

"Long enough to realize you needed rescuing from Mr. Muscle Ken Doll, especially since he wasn't getting the hint from your polite rejections."

Lane's demeanor was one of gaiety, and once again, Miranda found herself grappling with reconciling this version of her with the woman she'd interacted with in her office just a week ago. How could someone transition so seamlessly from aloof to charming and engaging?

Glowering at Lane, Miranda earned nothing more than a soft chuckle. "I guess you're expecting a reward for your unsolicited heroics?"

Lane shrugged casually. "Consider it an act of pure altruism." Her eyes flickered down to Miranda's lips, a mischievous glint dancing in their depths. "But if you're looking to express your gratitude, I'm open to whatever you feel is fair payment. Although…" Her voice dropped an octave, volume low and hypnotic. "I think you have a pretty good idea of what I'd prefer."

Miranda's scowl deepened. "I knew I should have taken my chances with Ken Doll. At least I could've counted on never seeing him again. Whereas, unfortunately, I can't escape your advances as easily."

Lane moved up in the line, never breaking eye contact with Miranda. "Ken Doll would have bored you to death and turned you off your coffee. Whereas, I'm a far more interesting companion."

Miranda fought the urge to laugh, determined not to give Lane the satisfaction of seeing her amused by her quick-witted comebacks. Before she could respond the barista's voice shattered the cocoon of their private conversation.

"Next in line!"

Miranda offered the barista an apologetic smile, acknowledging the delay. "Good morning. Could I please have an extra-large honey almond flat white? My name is Miranda."

The barista's attention shifted to Lane. "And for you?"

"I'll have an extra-large Americano with an extra shot of espresso."

Miranda accepted the receipt and moved to the waiting area. "You know, you didn't ask if I was okay paying for your coffee."

Lane grinned roguishly. "Consider it payment for my heroic rescue from Kenny boy. And unlike you, I'm not offended by a woman paying for my drink."

"I wasn't aware you dealt in cheap labor, but I shouldn't complain since what you truly desire is out of reach," Miranda quipped, internally berating herself for steering the conversation into that territory. *Why can't I resist falling into this woman's damn traps?*

"For you, Dr. Hayes, I would have done it for free," Lane declared, her gaze dropping to Miranda's lips once more. "As for what I truly desire from you, I can be very patient when necessary and I believe in playing the long game to attain anything worth having. If it's meant to be mine, nothing and no one can stand in my way." Stepping closer, Lane's voice lowered, commanding attention. "And if you're meant to be mine, Miranda, there's nothing you can do to stop it." A lethal smile formed on Lane's lips. It was one of the polished charms —probably honed from years of practice in seducing women to her bed. "I'll be here, patiently waiting for you when you come knocking on my door."

They stood so close that Lane's breath brushed Miranda's cheek, her perfume the only scent filling Miranda's nostrils. Miranda instinctively took a step back, feeling the urge to flee from the sudden intensity. She held Lane's penetrating gaze, and what she saw in them caused her breath to hitch as she struggled to look away. Fortunately, their order was called, and Miranda quickly turned to retrieve hers. She snatched the cup from the counter and hurried toward the exit, not waiting for Lane to retrieve hers.

Once outside, Miranda paused to take a long, much-needed sip of her coffee, relishing the first shot of caffeine in her system. She hummed in pleasure, feeling the warmth spread through her. Sensing a presence behind her, she glanced over her shoulder to find Lane watching her. Before Lane could make any untoward comment that would surely irk her, Miranda stepped off the sidewalk and crossed the road toward Parkwood. Lane caught up with her, but she remained silent until they crossed the street.

"How was your weekend?" Lane asked casually, as if their previous exchange hadn't happened, though Miranda still felt the weight of it lingering in the air.

Miranda felt drained, unable to beckon her usual sharp retort. Instead, she settled for a solemn, "Good."

"Not in a talkative mood today, or is it just me you seem to can't have a cordial conversation with?" Lane's question was delivered with a certain edge, devoid of any emotion that would indicate whether she was serious or just trying to push Miranda's buttons. "You're quite friendly with everyone else at work. So, tell me, Dr. Hayes, why do I get such harsh treatment from you when you're a ball of sunlight with everyone else?"

Miranda chanced a glance at her companion, only to be met with a neutral expression that offered no insights into Lane's internal thoughts. "I didn't peg you as the type for small talk," she muttered before taking another sip of her coffee.

Lane didn't miss a beat in providing a comeback. "Oh, I'm not, Miranda darling. You're just the exception to my rules, as always."

Miranda turned her head to look at Lane, being mindful not to trip over her own feet. "And why is that? Is small talk beneath you, your highness?"

Lane took a sip of her coffee, staring at Miranda over the rim of the cup. "I'm not interested in delving into people's personal lives beyond what's necessary in our interactions. Often, it's just idle chatter devoid of substance. Women lamenting about their mediocre husbands or wives, or gushing over their children. Men prattling on about sports or objectifying women. Frankly, I have more productive uses for my time than indulging in such trivialities."

Miranda let out a sarcastic laugh. "You have such high opinions of people."

"Just stating facts, Dr. Hayes. You know I speak the truth, considering how readily you sacrifice your own time to engage in trivial conversations that offer you no real benefit."

Before Miranda could respond, they arrived at Parkwood, and Jessica, an intern in Blake's department, joined them just as they reached the entrance. "Good morning, Lane," Jessica greeted Lane with a shy smile before turning to Miranda. "Good morning, Dr. Hayes."

"Good morning, Jessica," Miranda and Lane responded in unison. Miranda couldn't help but feel a bit surprised that Lane knew the intern's name, considering it wasn't typical for someone in her position to be familiar with every member of staff. *Maybe something is going on between them. It's obvious Jessica is attracted to her. Probably not, since according to Alexandra, Lane prefers women closer to her age. Christ, why am I even trying to dissect this?*

Miranda observed Lane's demeanor shift, as if the mere presence of Parkwood invoked the stoic CEO she'd dealt with in Lane's office. Meanwhile, Jessica's bashful glances and flushed cheeks insinuated her admiration for Lane. Miranda expected a flirtatious response to such attention, but to her surprise, Lane's expression remained impassive, betraying none of the interest she anticipated given Lane's coquettish nature with her. Lane paused at the door to allow them to go ahead of her, expressionless eyes solely fixed on Miranda.

"So very chivalrous of you," Miranda whispered as she stepped past Lane. Lane responded with a fleeting wicked smile that vanished as swiftly as it had appeared.

Miranda made her way toward the elevator, engaging in conversation with Jessica about her weekend. However, beneath the surface chatter, she couldn't shake off her curiosity about Lane's thoughts on the conversation as Lane trailed behind them with an air of detachment, nodding briefly at any greetings thrown her way. As they waited for the elevator, more interns and nurses joined them, but Miranda noticed none of them approached Lane for conversation. Instead, they stole curious glances at her from the corners of their eyes, intrigued by her aloof demeanor. Rumors around the hospital painted Lane as enigmatic, with many staff members finding her icy temperament alluring, hoping to be the one to thaw her. When the elevator finally arrived, Miranda held back as others entered, noticing with a sliver of dissatisfaction that Lane remained behind as well due to the elevator space becoming increasingly crowded.

"Aren't you coming?" Jessica asked, glancing between Miranda and Lane just as the doors began to close.

"We'll get the next one," Lane replied quickly, forestalling any chance for Miranda to interject or command her legs to move to prevent her from sharing the next elevator alone with Lane.

"Okay. Have a great day," Jessica responded, her gaze lingering on Lane as she withdrew her hand, allowing the doors to close.

Fortunately for Miranda, another elevator arrived immediately. Unfortunately, no one else joined them, leaving her to be alone with Lane in a confined space. Miranda stepped inside and moved to stand at the back, expecting Lane to sidle up beside her and invade her personal space. However, to her surprise, Lane maintained a respectful distance, opting for a spot a few feet away. Yet, despite the physical space between them, Miranda felt as though Lane's presence still suffocated the air in the elevator. She took a deep breath, trying to shake off the feeling, only to inhale a lungful of Lane's perfume, a scent she would forever associate with this infuriating woman.

Lane's gaze shifted to Miranda as if she had detected her audible inhalation, a teasing smile playing on her lips. "Did you find Jessica's weekend kayaking adventure riveting?' she quipped. "That entire conversation perfectly proved my point about people's tendency to divulge mundane details of their lives that hold little interest for me—it's precisely why I tend to avoid such interactions."

Miranda couldn't help but notice the shift in Lane's attitude as soon as they were alone. It was as if the icy facade she wore at Parkwood melted away in the confines of the elevator. Regardless of her reservations about Lane, Miranda was intrigued by the bewildering woman. There was an irresistible allure to the mystery shrouding Lane's true self, a desire to unravel the complexities hidden behind her polished exterior. Was it a carefully crafted facade, or was this softer side merely a glimpse of the real person beneath the surface? Was this the authentic Delaney Remington, or merely another facet of her carefully constructed persona? And why did she prefer the shortened version of her name? These questions lingered in Miranda's mind, fueling her curiosity even as she remained resolute in not succumbing to Lane's charms. She refused to grant Lane the satisfaction of knowing she held any interest, wary of being drawn into the intricate game they seemed to be playing—a game in which Lane mistakenly believed she could win Miranda over with seduction.

Miranda leveled a withering glare at Lane. "I guess you get some kick out of annoying me. Why not indulge the numerous nurses and interns who appear to drool and gaze starry-eyed in your presence? They seem far more inclined to entertain your advances than I, who have no interest in becoming another conquest in your bed."

Both of Lane's eyebrows arched upward, her eyes widening slightly. "Drooling? I wasn't aware my staff was so enraptured by me."

Miranda's eyes rolled dramatically. "Oh, please. You can't deny you don't enjoy all the sidelong glances of admiration you receive."

"On the contrary, Dr. Hayes, I don't indulge in workplace romances. I pay little attention to lingering looks as I have no desire to pursue anyone I work with..."

"So, you've been toying with me just for the sake of it, knowing full well you have no genuine interest in me?" Miranda's voice rose with incredulity, each word laced with mounting frustration.

Lane took a deliberate sip of her coffee, her eyes locked on Miranda's face, seemingly relishing the tension she was causing. It was as if the act of drinking her coffee was her way of prolonging the moment, keeping Miranda on edge.

"If you hadn't so rudely interrupted me and allowed me to finish my statement, you'd have learned that you're the exception, Miranda darling," Lane said, her tone scolding. "Women tend to fall for me, and when it ends, things can get messy. I don't want that drama at my place of work. In all my years working at hospitals, I've never dated anyone I worked with. But for one night with you, I'm willing to make an exception to my rule." She paused, a slow smile spreading across her lips. "After all, you're worth the risk."

"Why?" Miranda questioned, her voice betraying the curiosity she hadn't intended to reveal. Her voice sounded breathy to her own ears and less assertive than she intended. *Fuck why did I even ask that?*

Lane's expression became contemplative as her eyes gleamed with the same intensity Miranda had noticed at Josephine's—the one that had lingered in her memory long after. "Because," she began, her voice a soft, almost a tender whisper, "you're absolutely breathtaking. And from the moment I laid eyes on you at Josephine's, I haven't been able to stop thinking about you." Her words seemed to hover in the air like a delicate embrace, reaching Miranda with a gentle touch that stirred something deep within her.

Miranda's mouth opened, but no words came out. Lane's tone mirrored the moment they parted ways at Josephine's, leaving Miranda disarmed once more by this unexpected vulnerability. Her head spun as she chastised herself once again for even entertaining the question of why she was an exception. Because why did it matter when she had no romantic interest in Lane? Still, she couldn't ignore the impact of Lane's words as an unknown sensation ran through her body, making her feel a little too warm and Lane's proximity a bit overwhelming.

Thankfully, the elevator stopped at her floor, and Miranda swiftly stepped out, avoiding any further interaction with Lane. She dared not speak, fearing her voice might not be strong enough to articulate a formidable response.

Before the doors slid shut, Miranda glanced back at Lane, their eyes locking in a silent exchange. At that moment, she was spellbound by the intensity in Lane's gaze, a depth of desire that left her breathless. No one had ever looked at her with such primal want and lust. It was as if given that chance she'd been asking for, Lane would do things to Miranda that no one else would have dared to try. The intensity of it all unsettled Miranda causing her to shudder involuntarily. Lane's knowing smile only added to the disconcerting moment, as if she could see through Miranda's thoughts, leaving her feeling exposed and vulnerable as the doors sealed shut.

Miranda massaged her temple as she veered toward her office. *It's way too early for my day to be this eventful already. Why do I keep allowing this woman to monopolize so much of my time? Why does she affect me this much when I find her so damn infuriating? Ugh.*

Chapter 10

Standing in a secluded spot at Parkwood's annual charity gala, Miranda studied Lane as she gracefully strode across the lawn toward Alexandra, who seemed entirely captivated by Blake who was engrossed in conversation with her mother and stepfather. Internally, Miranda couldn't help but smile at the evident love shining in Alexandra's eyes as she gazed at her wife. However, a soft sigh escaped her as she pondered whether she would ever experience such unbridled passion for someone. Though she cared deeply for Trevor, he failed to ignite the same level of intensity within her. Maybe it would develop over time. Maybe this unfulfilled longing was what held her back from taking the next step with him, as she yearned for a more profound connection. Her thoughts were interrupted by Lane handing Alexandra a glass of champagne, drawing her attention back to the present moment.

She couldn't tear her eyes away from the woman whom she hadn't engaged in another personal conversation with since their last encounter in the elevator. A conversation she had attempted to push out of her mind. Just as she had endeavored to suppress thoughts about who Lane truly was behind the various personas she presented. Or why Lane essentially ignored her whenever they crossed paths at the hospital unless it was absolutely necessary for them to interact. And when they did have to collaborate, Lane maintained a strictly professional demeanor—no flirting, no suggestive glances, nothing to indicate any attraction to Miranda. She chalked it up to nothing more than curiosity about a woman who seemed to derive pleasure from provoking her. That was all it was. After all, it wasn't unusual for her to be curious, especially when most people at the hospital shared her sentiments. Who was the real Delaney Remington?

As she observed Alexandra and Lane conversing, Miranda couldn't help but admire Lane. She was breathtakingly beautiful, with an aura of mystery that only added to her allure. Clad in a white dress that accentuated her well-toned physique, Lane's form suggested a dedication to fitness. Miranda couldn't help but notice the recurring motif of Lane's signature red lipstick. *Does she not wear any other shade?* Lane's hair, elegantly swept up into a bun at the nape of her neck, added to her sophisticated appearance. Soft tendrils escaped the neat bun, framing her face delicately and enhancing her appeal. Lane carried herself with a grace that suggested an aristocratic upbringing. Before Miranda could discreetly continue her scrutiny, Lane's hazel eyes met hers, arresting her attention. Their eyes locked, and Lane's appraisal of Miranda's body burned with the desire that had been absent when they crossed paths at the hospital. It left Miranda feeling as though her body was being reshaped by an unknown force. She supposed it was just unnerving to have someone staring at her as if she were being regarded as a sumptuous feast after a prolonged famine.

Miranda jumped slightly at the sensation of strong hands encircling her waist from behind, but as she recognized Trevor's touch, she relaxed into his embrace. Tilting her head to the side, she welcomed the tender kiss he placed on her lips.

"Did you miss me?" Trevor murmured, his breath warm against her skin as he drew her closer. "This dress is driving me crazy," he added, pressing his body against hers.

"Maybe," Miranda replied, turning around to face him and looping her arms around his neck. "Even though we've only been apart for a few minutes."

Trevor's grin widened, and his light blue eyes gleamed with the depth of his affection for her. "Even a mere second away from you feels like a lifetime, my love," he whispered softly.

Miranda gulped and threaded her fingers through Trevor's shoulder-length raven hair as she tried to push away the guilt that always crept in when he declared his feelings for her, knowing she might not be making him as happy as he deserved. "You're such a smooth talker." Drawing closer, she pressed a chaste kiss on his lips, attempting to dismiss her inner tumult.

Trevor smiled down at her. "No. It's just the truth. I can't help wanting to be with you all the time."

*Please don't bring up moving in together...*Miranda mused before she said, "Luckily, you have me all to yourself for the entire weekend."

Trevor brought his mouth to Miranda's ear and whispered, "And I'm going to spend every second doing very filthy things to you."

Inhaling deeply, Miranda eased back to meet Trevor's gaze, only to find his expression suddenly brightening as his attention shifted past her. "There's Alexandra. We should go say hi. I haven't seen her in a long time."

Miranda tensed slightly, hoping Lane wasn't still talking with Alexandra. The last thing she needed was for Lane to make an inappropriate comment in Trevor's presence, leading to potential awkwardness and explanations she wasn't prepared to provide. She didn't view her encounters with Lane as significant enough to warrant sharing with Trevor, but depending on Lane's behavior, she might have no choice but to explain. While Trevor generally had an easygoing nature, he had shown signs of jealousy in the past, particularly regarding Miranda's admirers. Glancing over her shoulder, Miranda confirmed Lane's location, and her eyes locked with Lane, who wore an inscrutable expression. Before Miranda could redirect her focus to Trevor and concoct a plausible excuse to delay greeting Alexandra, Trevor interlocked their fingers and guided her to her bosses. Lane's eyes remained fixed on them, and Miranda couldn't help but return the stare, caught in a moment of unspoken tension.

"Alexandra, it's so good to see you. It's been a while since our paths have crossed," Trevor greeted with a smile on his face coming to a stop before Alexandra and Lane. He turned his attention to Lane. "Hello."

Miranda held her breath as she noticed Lane's attention fixating on Trevor's hand wrapped around her waist. She may not be an orthopedic surgeon, but she could swear she saw a microfracture in Lane's otherwise stoic expression, evident in the faint twitch of a muscle in her jaw and the storm brewing in her usually ambiguous eyes. Despite Lane's adeptness at concealing her emotions, Miranda could discern the underlying current not visible to their companions. After what seemed like an eternity, Lane's gaze shifted to Trevor, and she offered a curt nod in greeting. Miranda resisted the urge to roll her eyes at Lane's dismissive attitude toward Trevor, opting instead to maintain a neutral stance to avoid drawing attention to their complex dynamic. She shifted her focus from Lane and tuned into the conversation between Alexandra and Trevor.

"It's been a crazy couple of months. Hopefully, we can all get together for dinner soon." Alexandra paused as if remembering something. She gestured to Lane. "My apologies for not doing a formal introduction. Trevor, this is Lane Remington. She's Parkwood's new CEO. Lane, this is Trevor McKinson, Miranda's boyfriend."

Trevor smiled over at Lane. "Nice to meet you, Lane."

"Likewise." Lane's tone lacked any form of affability and carried a chill that could cool Seattle on its warmest days.

Miranda sensed the chill in every syllable as if they were coated in ice. *What the hell is her problem? She couldn't quite possibly be jealous?* She resisted the urge to call Lane out for her rude and dismissive behavior toward Trevor, knowing it could escalate into a confrontation she wasn't prepared to handle. Miranda didn't know Lane well enough to predict her reaction, but past combats had taught her that Lane always had a sharp retort ready for any challenge Miranda presented.

Miranda cleared her throat and pulled Trevor closer to her, smiling at him. "Babe, I think it's our turn to have Blake and Alexandra over for dinner. You owe Alexandra one of your homemade poutines."

Trevor returned Miranda's smile, his eyes shining

with love as he stared down at her. "Yes, you're right." He redirected his focus to Alexandra. "Let us know when you're both available. We can show off our cooking skills while our paramours, who are not as good in the kitchen, gush over how amazing we are."

Miranda playfully swatted Trevor on his chest. "Hey! I'm very good at other things."

Trevor ran a finger down Miranda's cheek. "Indeed, you are."

Trevor's eyes sparkled with an abundance of love for her, and at that moment, Miranda felt a wave of gratitude for having someone who regarded her as their most precious treasure. Many women wouldn't hesitate to take the next step with someone like Trevor, yet here she was, hesitating due to an intangible feeling of something missing in their relationship. Perhaps she was the issue, undeserving of him. Maybe if she moved in with him, she could develop deeper feelings over time, fostering the connection she believed was absent. The one that would alleviate any doubts about moving in together. Their tender moment was abruptly interrupted by the chiming of Trevor's phone. Reluctantly, he withdrew his hand from Miranda's face to check the notification.

Trevor's features transformed, giving way to a visible expression of concern. "There's an emergency at the restaurant that I must attend to," he informed Miranda.

"Do you need me to come with you," Miranda inquired, her voice mirroring her boyfriend's worries.

"No. Stay and enjoy the party. Will you come over later?"

Miranda nodded. "Yes. I'll let you know when I'm leaving here."

Trevor turned to Lane and Alexandra. "Ladies, enjoy the rest of your evening. Alexandra, see you soon."

"Bye Trevor. Good luck with the emergency," Alexandra replied.

Trevor tenderly brushed his lips against Miranda's in a brief, affectionate kiss before taking his leave. As he walked away, Miranda stared at his departing figure and momentary sadness crept into her at the thought of losing him. She resolved at that moment to show him just how much he meant to her later that night.

"So, that's who I have to compete with?"

Miranda abruptly whipped her head toward Lane, her expression darkening into a scowl. "What are you talking about?"

Lane smirked and ran her eyes the length of Miranda's body. "For a night in your bed."

Miranda fixed her goldish-hazel spheres intently on Alexandra. "I thought you said she had boundaries when it came to women in relationships."

Lane interjected before Alexandra could respond, a mischievous smile curling upon her lips. "Yes, but those boundaries don't extend to boyfriends who are easily replaceable once a woman is touched, just once, by the *right* woman. And I know, I'm always the *right* woman."

A loud laugh erupted from Miranda's throat. "Could you be any more full of yourself?"

Lane merely shrugged, gleaming pupils fixed intently on Miranda. At that time, it seemed as if Alexandra's presence became an afterthought, their preoccupation was exclusively reserved for each other.

"I'm just stating facts and I have faith in my capabilities in the bedroom," Lane finally replied.

Miranda sobered and rolled her eyes. "Well, some

women want more than just a roll in the hay or meaningless sex."

Lane's eyes narrowed, and the subtle downturn of her lips betrayed that Miranda had struck a nerve, despite her attempt to conceal her reaction. "Oh, yeah? Then why aren't you moving in with Boy Wonder?"

Miranda's eyes widened, momentarily bouncing to Alexandra and then back to Lane. "How do you know about that?"

Lane tsked and shook her head as if Miranda should have known the obvious. "Walls have ears, Miranda, and you work in a hospital which is a cesspool for gossip." Before Miranda could respond Lane turned to Alexandra and said, "I'll see you at work on Monday. Enjoy the rest of your weekend." She refocused on Miranda, her lips ticking up into a devious smile, "Dr. Hayes as always, it was a pleasure talking to you. Remember when you're ready to explore the dark side, I'll be a willing teacher." Lane walked away without a backward glance and headed toward the exit.

Miranda turned to Alexandra and said, "Tell me again, why did you hire that woman? I swear she is a deviant."

Alexandra opened her mouth to respond but no words came out. She was no doubt probably wondering what the hell she had just witnessed between Miranda and Lane.

Miranda sighed and looped her hand through Alexandra's. "Don't bother responding. Let's join your wife and try to have some fun. I particularly need a very strong drink."

Chapter 11

Lane tossed back the remnants of her second drink since arriving at Josephine's thirty minutes ago. She wasn't accustomed to such heavy drinking, but after that encounter with Miranda at the charity brunch, she desperately needed something to take the edge off. What was she thinking, asking Miranda such an inappropriate question in front of Alexandra? *Damn it.* Regardless of her usual impulse to flirt with Miranda, at Parkwood she had maintained professionalism, doing her utmost to ignore her whenever they crossed paths or in the presence of their colleagues. The last thing she wanted was to be labeled unprofessional at work due to flirting with a subordinate who showed no romantic interest in her. And today, all her efforts to avoid such a situation blew up in her face when she saw another person touching Miranda—it had her seeing red. She prided herself on her ironclad self-control, but she couldn't stop the words from spilling out once *the boyfriend* left. *Why the hell do I always lose control of myself around this woman?*

Lane didn't understand the catalyst for her reaction when she knew Miranda was in a relationship. Granted hearing about it and witnessing it were two entirely different experiences. But, how the hell could she feel jealous? Because yes, it was intense jealousy that blasted through her the moment Trevor sneaked up behind Miranda and enveloped her in his arms. It felt as though he was laying claim to what should have been hers. But, how could she justify her jealousy when nothing had occurred between them? Lane had never experienced this level of jealousy with anyone she had dated before—a jealousy that set her blood roaring in her veins.

Maybe I need to get laid... she mused, scanning her surroundings to see if any of the women caught her interest. It had been weeks since she last had sex, and maybe she just needed to fuck someone else to get Miranda out of her system. *You did try to fuck her out of your system with Gabriella before returning here.* Still, Lane was a keen reader of people, and witnessing Miranda and Trevor interact, she sensed something was amiss on Miranda's end. Miranda didn't seem like the glowing girlfriend who was head over heels in love with her boyfriend. She also didn't miss the melancholy that had shrouded Miranda's features as she watched Trevor walk away.

Lane couldn't help but be curious about the foundation of their relationship, especially since Miranda confirmed the rumors Lane had been hearing around the hospital about her hesitation to move in with him. This was one of the many reasons Lane chose to keep her colleagues at a distance—she didn't want any of them prying into her life. She couldn't stop them from making up stories about her, but she could prevent them from asking her anything related to her life outside of Parkwood. Yes, it had given her a less-than-flattering reputation over the years, but she didn't want her staff discussing her personal life in the hallways the way those two nurses had been comfortable talking about Miranda's relationship. One of them had a crush on Trevor and thought he was wasting his time with Miranda, whom he admired for years before she finally gave him a chance this past year.

So, a fairly new relationship, and he already wants to move in, and she doesn't. Interesting.

Lane shook her head as if trying to dispel the thoughts of Miranda from her mind. However, the image of Miranda's melancholy—similar to the one she witnessed from their first encounter at Josephine's—lingered in her memory. It suggested that the source of Miranda's sadness that evening might have been issues with her boyfriend, leading her to drown her sorrows in alcohol.

Her thoughts drifted back to their encounter at the coffee shop, where she had pretended to be Miranda's wife to fend off that conceited man. Even then, Lane couldn't resist intervening, though Miranda had the situation well in hand. It was rather amusing to witness Miranda's firm rejection of the man's advances. However, what lingered most in Lane's mind was the moment when Miranda reached out to touch her, her hand trembling ever so slightly as if she felt the depth of Lane's attraction in that fleeting contact. She was unable to shake off the memory of how Miranda's touch had affected her when she brushed Lane's hair behind her ear. It marked their first physical contact out of a professional setting and it had ignited a firestorm of arousal within Lane as if someone had lit a match within her soul. Such a gentle gesture, yet it wielded an immense power over her. At that moment, Lane had yearned to bridge the small distance between them, to taste Miranda's full lips that were like temptation dangling before her. And when Miranda had questioned why she was the exception to Lane's rules, Lane found herself revealing a side of her she rarely showed—vulnerability. For reasons she couldn't quite understand, Lane felt secure revealing that side of herself to Miranda.

Why can't I stop thinking about this damn woman? She's in a relationship. She's straight. She can't stand my ass. Even though that's questionable since she never backs down from our little sparring matches. After all, there's a thin line between love and hate.

Deep down Lane knew why she was drawn to Miranda, but delving into those reasons would mean confronting parts of her past she had long buried. And that was something she refused to waste time doing.

"I know you love your own company, but should I be worried you're sitting alone in a dark corner of a bar, looking like you're contemplating murdering someone?" Nia's voice cut through Lane's reverie, snapping her back to the present.

Lane shifted her gaze from her glass to meet the amused eyes of Nia and Kenya, who had approached without her notice. "You know you're the first and only person I'd confide in if I ever had such thoughts." Lane flashed them a wry smile. "One, you'd talk me out of it, and two, you'd bail me out of jail." She rose from her seat to envelope Nia in a quick hug. "But fear not, I value my freedom too much to entertain such notions. Although, I think I'm smart enough to get away with it." With a gentle squeeze, Lane released Nia and extended a warm hug to Kenya. "Hey, Kenya."

"Hey, Lane. It feels like forever since I've seen you," Kenya greeted with a warm smile. Nia and Kenya settled into the seats across from Lane.

"What are you doing here? I thought you were going to Portland for the weekend to catch that Broadway show," Lane asked.

"My love has a work trip there next week, so we decided to turn it into a little getaway," Nia explained with a fond look at Kenya as they shared a smile.

Lane couldn't help but smile herself, witnessing the affection in Kenya's amber eyes as she locked eyes with Nia. The affectionate smile that graced Kenya's lips seemed to make her dark brown skin glow. After all that Nia had been through, she deserved this happiness.

"I meant to call you earlier to let you know about the change of plans, but the day just flew by before I had the chance," Nia explained, focusing back on Lane.

"How's the new company treating you?" Lane asked Kenya, who still had her eyes fixed on Nia.

Kenya planted a quick kiss on the side of Nia's mouth before turning her attention to Lane. "Amazingly well. After being in Europe for so long, I was a bit hesitant about returning to the harsher corporate life here. But I managed to negotiate everything I valued in Europe into my contract, which allows for a better work-life balance. Plus, the owners are wonderful people who share the same values as I do." Kenya's brows furrowed in thought. "I think their daughter works at your hospital... Dr. Miranda Hayes."

Sighs. Just the person I'm avoiding thinking about... Lane thought as Kenya looked expectantly at her, awaiting confirmation. Lane suppressed the urge to inquire further about Miranda's parents to glean some insight into her life beyond Parkwood. It wasn't her style and she didn't want to draw attention to her interest in Miranda. Nia knew her well enough to recognize it would be unusual for her to be asking personal questions about her staff. And since Kenya was a construction engineer, she could assume that Miranda's parents were into property development. "Yes, Dr. Hayes works at Parkwood. She's the head of the cardiology department," she finally replied casually as if Miranda was just any member of staff and not the woman she wanted to do rather unprofessional things to.

Kenya nodded. "That's right, they did mention she's a heart surgeon. We met briefly when she stopped by the office to see her parents. She's absolutely breathtaking with those Terrence Howard type eyes."

Lane arched a questioning eyebrow at the vivid description of Miranda's eyes.

Kenya chuckled. "Come on, Lane. Just because I'm head over heels in love with Nia doesn't mean I can't notice another beautiful woman, especially someone as gorgeous as Miranda. I'm sure you've noticed her. It's hard not to, considering she's also your type."

"Lane doesn't date people she works with, baby," Nia interjected.

Lane relaxed back into her seat, her lips ticking up slightly at the corners. "And what, pray tell, is my type? I'd like to think I'm very open-minded with my dating habits."

Kenya laughed. "Oh, come on. Since we've known each other, you've always been drawn to women with that standout, natural beauty. The ones who walk into a room and command attention." Kenya paused, briefly studying Lane before continuing. "I think it's the challenge you enjoy. The challenge of winning over a woman who captivates everyone's attention with just her mere presence."

Lane shifted her focus to Nia, raising another questioning eyebrow. "What exactly have you been telling your girlfriend? She seems to be under the impression that I'm some version of a female Lothario?"

Nia chuckled and snuggled closer to Kenya. "I haven't been telling her anything other than showing her a few pictures of women you've dated over the years." She shrugged nonchalantly. "I mean, she does have a point. You do tend to go for women who stand out in a crowd."

"I beg to differ on that point. I just like what I like, and if I have to work for it, I will." Lane countered. "I'm just a hard worker in every aspect of my life."

"And why hasn't your hard work paid off since you're still single," Kenya jested.

"That's by design. Being single is a choice… one I quite enjoy," Lane replied.

"I can't wait for the day when that choice is snatched from you and you have no choice but to submit to a relationship," Nia added, enjoying seeing Lane being put on the spot.

Lane rolled her eyes. "How did we get from talking about Kenya's job to my dating habits? I'm sure you didn't come over here to give me life lessons about falling in love."

"Maybe we did. Since you were over here brooding into your glass like a woman who couldn't have what she wanted," Nia retorted knowingly.

Lane narrowed her eyes at her friend, wondering where she got that assumption. She hadn't confided in Nia about her attraction to Miranda. Even though given their years-long friendship, Nia could simply be astute enough to pick up on subtle cues, or perhaps it was just a lucky guess. "Well, Nia dearest, you more than anyone should know that once I set my mind on achieving something, I work tirelessly until I accomplish it. So, worry not, my friend. I always get what I want in the end."

Both women across from Lane laughed. "I have no doubt you will, with that perseverance of yours."

Lane's spirits dimmed a bit as she mulled over her own thoughts. *For once, it may not be able to get me what I want, since the object of my desire sees me as a nuisance.*

"Enough about me. I don't know how we went from talking about your Broadway trip to my personal life," Lane waved a hand across the table. "Aren't you going to get something to drink?"

"Because your life is way more entertaining. But yes, we need something to drink," Nia replied, scanning the bar for a server.

"Speaking of Broadway, why don't you come with us?" Kenya asked.

"God, no. Definitely not my scene," Lane replied.

Kenya chuckled. "You know, you're very stuck in your ways."

"Again, I just like what I like and know myself well enough to know that I couldn't endure three to four hours of such artistry." Lane rose from her chair. "I don't see a server. I need a refill, so I'll just go get it. Do you want the usual?"

"Nice escape from explaining your Broadway aversion," Nia remarked with a laugh. "Yes, the usual, please. Make mine a double shot."

"How about you, Kenya? Single or double?"

"Single. I need to be sober for what I have planned

later when we get home," Kenya replied, turning her attention to Nia and giving her a suggestive once-over that would no doubt make her friend wet.

Lane pivoted on her heels and made her way to the bar, scanning the area for anyone who might catch her interest. Witnessing the affection between Kenya and Nia, she felt a pang of longing for companionship, preferring not to go home alone and dwell on a woman she may never have. As she reached the bar, her phone vibrated in her pocket. Retrieving it, she read the message and smiled. It seemed like the gods had heard her pleas and decided to reward her.

Gabriella: Sweetheart, I'm in Seattle for the weekend. Can I see you tonight and every night while I'm here?

Anticipation course through Lane's body while she drafted a response. If anyone could take her mind off Miranda, it would definitely be Gabriella.

Lane: I'm all yours for the entire weekend for whatever you need.

Chapter 12

"Can't you take the day off and spend it giving me a repeat of our weekend activities," Gabriella purred, her voice filled with desire, as she pushed the sheets down her body, revealing her breasts— a tantalizing invitation for Lane to shed her clothes and crawl back into bed with her. Lane watched, transfixed, as Gabriella exposed herself further, baring her glistening sex—a sight that reminded her of the rather filthy things she did to it over the weekend. With purposeful strides, Lane closed the gap between them, placing a knee on the bed and capturing Gabriella's lips in a bruising kiss. Gabriella gasped, submitting to Lane's will and she reveled in the impact she had on this woman who was one of Hollywood's most sought-after actresses. Tracing her hand over Gabriella's curves, Lane ventured between her thighs, hissing in pleasure as her fingers met an abundance of moisture.

Lane severed the kiss, holding Gabriella's heated gaze. "As tempting as the offer is, I don't want to be late for work," she said as if she was reading tedious paperwork instead of slowly circling Gabriella's clit with two fingers.

"You're the boss. There's no one to reprimand you," Gabriella panted, her breath catching with each movement of Lane's fingers. She lifted her hands to her dark pink nipples, teasing them with firm touches, her emerald green eyes darkening into a deep forest green.

"Even then, I need to set a good example for my staff." Emphasizing her unwavering standards, she increased the applied pressure of her fingers. "Plus, I abhor tardiness from anyone including myself," Lane replied, her fingers now exploring the slickness below as she slowly pushed two fingers inside Gabriella's dripping core.

Gabriella inhaled deeply, opening her legs wider to accommodate Lane's long deep thrusts. "Yes, I'm well aware of the high standards you set for yourself and others." With a sharp intake of breath, Gabriella pinched her nipple hard, a mixture of pleasure and pain eliciting a deep, primal moan from her throat. "I... have... no... complaints," she continued, her words punctuated by the rhythm of their passion. "Your standards always ensure that whenever you fuck me, I'm guaranteed multiple orgasms." Each muscle from Lane's shoulder to her hand flexed, procuring a growl from Gabriella's throat. "And I can feel you between my legs for days after."

Lane flicked her wrist to check the time on her Breitling, her thrusts becoming more urgent. "Be that as it may," she began, her voice husky with desire, "I'm cutting it close here. And since, as you say, I have very high standards, I need to ensure that you orgasm before I leave." She leaned in closer, her gaze intense. "So, how about you lower your right hand to your clit and let me watch as we work together to push you over the edge?"

Gabriella pouted. "But then I'll come too quickly and you'll leave and I don't want you to go," she husked out, her hips rising off the bed to match Lane's strokes.

A devious smile formed on Lane's lips as she curved her fingers, pumping harder while using her thumb to circle Gabriella's clit. The effect was immediate and Gabriella's walls clenched around her fingers, her screams reverberating through the room as her orgasm crashed over her.

Lane lowered her mouth to Gabriella's ear and whispered, "Or I can just make you come all by myself." She dragged her lips from Gabriella's ear to her lips and kissed her softly. "I have to go," she whispered as she pulled away from the woman beneath her panting hard. Slowly, Lane removed her hand from between Gabriella's thighs. She waved her fingers, glistening with arousal, at Gabriella. "I'll wash my hands and see myself out. You should try and get some more sleep. You have a long flight later."

"You don't play fair, Delaney," Gabriella, purred as she stretched like a feline cat waking up from a long slumber.

Lane paused at the use of her full name. Gabriella was one of the few people who called her by it. "I never claimed to," she said as she continued into the bathroom to wash her hands.

She needed to make a quick stop by her apartment to change and grab her laptop. She hadn't intended to spend the entire night with Gabriella, but after the events of the night, numerous orgasms had left her too exhausted to leave once Gabriella fell asleep. She had known Gabriella Mancini for the past ten years, and their arrangement had been beneficial to both of them whenever they were in the same city. Of all the women she had dated over the years, Gabriella was one of the few with whom she would have considered taking the next step if either of them had been inclined. Not many people understood the person she was, but Gabriella did, and she didn't expect more than Lane had to offer or wanted more. So, it worked out perfectly for both of them—wonderful company and plenty of mind-blowing sex.

When she returned to the bedroom, she found Gabriella pushing her hands through her silk robe. "Why are you up?"

"I want to walk you to the door," she replied, tightening the belt around her waist.

"If I didn't know better, I'd think you're becoming attached, Miss Mancini." Lane quipped, retrieving her bag from the chair in the far corner of the room. She scanned the area to ensure she wasn't missing anything. Gabriella had chosen to rent a house for the weekend instead of staying at a hotel, which Lane found strange, but she didn't see it necessary to question, as it was inconsequential.

Gabriella laughed. "I've been attached since the day we met, Delaney. Isn't it obvious whenever we're together or the fact that after ten years, I still can't get enough of you? You haven't been able to erase the lust I feel for you."

Lane stared at the woman before her, running her eyes over her beautiful face, her sex-mussed, mahogany hair, wondering how to reply to words she wasn't sure were being communicated in their usual casual rapport. There was an underlying longing in Gabriella's voice which was foreign to Lane. She decided not to read too much into it and opted for the dynamic she knew. "That's because you love sex and no one fucks you as good as I do."

Gabriella shook her head and flashed her that world-famous sultry smile. "That confidence of yours is one of the many things I find so very sexy about you."

A glint of self-assurance glimmered in Lane's eyes as she moved to the door. "I know."

Gabriella followed behind her as they descended the stairs. "I'll be in Europe for a few weeks, then back in L.A. for an extended period. Hopefully, I'll see you once I get back. You moving to Seattle really sucks. I don't how you could have given up L.A. for all this rain."

Lane paused at the main door, her hand resting on the handle. "I have my reasons. Have a safe flight home. Let me know once you've landed." Leaning forward, she planted a tender kiss on Gabriella's forehead before opening the door to leave.

Before she could step over the threshold, Gabriella grabbed her hand and pulled her into a deep kiss. Lane was momentarily stunned, her mind racing with the awareness that the door was open and anyone could see them, even though the streets were empty and the sun wasn't fully up.

She slowly pulled away from Gabriella, raising a questioning brow. "Aren't you concerned about someone snapping photos of us?"

"The streets are empty and I needed a proper kiss goodbye." Gabriella ran her fingers down Lane's cheek. "Thanks for an amazing weekend. You never disappoint. Have a wonderful day at work.

"You too," Lane replied, trying not to read too much into Gabriella risking someone seeing them together for a goodbye kiss.

She squeezed Gabriella's hand one last time and briskly walked to her car, mentally calculating how fast she would have to drive to her penthouse to make it on time for work.

One hour later, Lane was in the back of a town car, on a video call with Anita as her driver navigated through morning traffic. Accustomed to having a driver in L.A., during work hours, she decided to enlist the same services in Seattle. With time being a precious commodity, she saw commuting as an opportunity to catch up on emails and get a head start on her day. Fortunately, traffic was still light, so she would make it to Parkwood on time.

"What do you want me to bring for you when I visit later? And please don't say nothing," Lane asked as she watched Anita watering her plants through the phone.

"I don't need anything, so naturally, my answer will be nothing, Delaney," Anita replied, punctuating her response with a playful eye roll.

Lane grinned, her heart swelling with admiration for one of the most resilient women she had ever met. "Well, I'll think of something because showing up empty-handed isn't an option for me. You may be stubborn, but when it comes to ensuring your comfort, I can match that stubbornness with determination."

Anita picked up her phone and settled on the sofa, finally giving Lane her undivided attention. "Oh, I know too well from experience how stubborn you can be when you set your mind to something. I won't even bother debating with you. Bring whatever you want."

Lane nodded, her smile widening. "I'll take that as a compliment."

"You should. How was your weekend?" Anita tilted her head to the side, her eyebrows lifting in question. "Did you get into any trouble with the ladies? I assume that's why you chose to visit today instead of yesterday."

Lane couldn't help but laugh as she watched Anita's raised eyebrows, a clear attempt to mimic her. "If you weren't so utterly cute when you try to imitate me, I might take offense." Lane shook her head in mock exasperation. "But yes, I changed plans because Gabriella was visiting for the weekend. I also wouldn't exactly classify what we did as getting into trouble."

Anita sighed heavily. "A decade of being that woman's secret. I understand your arrangement suits you both, especially since you refuse to have a relationship with anyone. But I can't help but wonder if you're holding out hope for something more from her. Sure, there's no commitment on either side, so you're both free to date other people whenever you're in different parts of the world, but I can't help wondering if, along with all your other reasons for not trying to give yourself a chance of experiencing love, it's because you're waiting on her. You have so much to offer to anyone lucky enough to break down those walls you've built around yourself and see your heart. Yet you waste so much time on these meaningless affairs."

It was Lane's turn to sigh heavily. If it had been anyone else expressing those sentiments, irritation might have been her initial response. But this was Anita and she recognized the genuine concern stemming from love. Before Anita came into her life, Lane didn't have anyone who cared enough to fuss over her purely out of love and concern for her well-being.

"The cruelty of this world built these walls, Anita. You, more than anyone, know that. They are there to protect the heart you want me to share with said world." Lane flicked an invisible speck from her dress, attempting to divert her thoughts from the harsh realities that shaped her. "However, that's not the only reason why I haven't had the epic romance you so badly want me to have. I simply haven't met someone who I believe is worthy of my heart. Someone who inspires me to seek more than just a fleeting connection. Yes, maybe I've grown used to my lifestyle and struggle to see myself settling down, given it's all I've known and I do cherish the freedom it affords me. But the underlying truth is, I haven't met that special someone who ignites a desire for something deeper within me."

Anita attempted to interject, but Lane raised her index finger to stop her. "And let's be clear, I'm not Gabriella's clandestine affair. You know I value my privacy and have no desire for my personal life to become fodder for the media, regardless of Gabriella's circumstances. Our relationship is founded on mutual enjoyment of each other's company without expectations, which is why we've remained a part of each other's lives for so long. It's not because I'm some hidden secret." Lane softened her gaze as she held Anita's. "Please, stop worrying that I'll be alone if something happens to you. I'll be fine, I promise you."

"I know you'll be fine because you overcame so much to reach this point in your life. But in spite of the world's cruelty, having the right person to navigate it with is infinitely better than going it alone. You deserve to experience all the wonders this world has to offer, Delaney, including being deeply in love with someone who will love you just as much. I want that for you before I leave you."

Lane bit her cheek, suppressing the emotions churning within her. She comprehended Anita's perspective but staunchly refused to yearn for love or affection. Her life felt satisfactory as it stood. Besides, relationships were intricate and frequently concluded in heartache and disillusionment. So, what was the point? As the car decelerated to a halt, signaling her arrival at work, she silently thanked the stars for providing a convenient excuse to conclude this conversation.

"I know," Lane said softly. "I've arrived at work. I should be there around five, later. Have yourself a wonderful day. I love you."

Anita smiled wistfully, causing Lane's heart to tighten in her chest. "Love you more, my child. I'll see you later. Since you insist on bringing me something, how about a box of coconut-crusted donuts from The Junction."

"You know you're not supposed to eat so much sweets," she teasingly scolded with a mock frown of disapproval. "Doctor's orders."

Anita rolled her eyes. "These doctors know nothing about what is or isn't good for my health when it comes to food. I have been feeding myself for over sixty years without any dietary restrictions, and until recently, I've been fine. A donut or two won't send me keeling over."

Lane chuckled. "Okay, you're the boss. See you later." Anita waved bye and ended the call. Lane sighed and collected her belongings, then stepped out of the car making a concerted effort to push the conversation to the back of her mind.

"Thanks, Constantine. I'll be ready to leave a little earlier than usual today. Around four fifteen," she informed her driver.

"I'll be here. Have a great day, Miss Remington."

"You too. And just Lane will do," she replied and then hurried toward the hospital entrance.

Craving a cup of coffee, Lane debated that she didn't have time to fetch one herself. She strode briskly to the elevators, grateful that no one attempted to stop her for frivolous conversation. However, as she turned the corner, she stopped abruptly, spotting Miranda waiting by the bank of elevators. *Christ. Of all the people to run into. Universe why do you keep throwing temptation in my path?*

Miranda lifted her gaze from her phone, her eyes widening slightly before her expression shifted to impassive. She gave Lane a quick once-over, then returned her attention to her phone.

Lane smiled inwardly at the casual dismissal, maintaining her composure as she approached the elevators at a slower pace. "Good morning, Dr. Hayes," she greeted, coming to a stop a few feet away from Miranda.

Miranda once again raised her eyes from her phone and looked at Lane, her expression neither hostile, nor friendly. "Good morning, Lane," she replied coolly.

I guess she's pissed off because of what I said at the charity event. Then again, she's always pissed off with me since the day we met.

The elevator arrived and Miranda stepped on without another word, moving to stand at the back. Lane followed suit, choosing to stand at the front to ensure there was enough space between them. Unfortunately for her, the elevator doors closed with just the two of them, leaving Lane to endure the tension brewing between them. She didn't dare turn around to face Miranda, but she could feel her eyes boring into her.

It seemed as if she was unable to control herself around this woman, so to prevent herself from saying something inappropriate again, she chose to remain silent. The elevator felt as if it were moving slower than usual and the urge to strike up a conversation with Miranda pushed down on her shoulders. Lane reached for her phone, seeking something to focus on instead of the woman behind her, who was probably shooting daggers at her.

Just as Lane opened her messages to respond to a text from Nia, Miranda's chilly tone cut through the tense silence. "Does this hot and cold tactic work on the women who fall for whatever you offer them?"

Lane wanted to laugh but swiftly suppressed it as she slowly turned to face the woman behind her. Tilting her head to the side, her expression became quizzical. "Excuse me?"

Miranda rolled her eyes and shot her an exasperated look. "Don't pretend you don't know what I'm talking about," she retorted in edged frustration.

God, this woman is entertaining. Intelligence and sass. Such an appealing combination. Who can blame me for wanting her? Lane summoned her most innocuous expression. "I'm afraid I don't follow Dr. Hayes. Could you please explain?" she asked with feigned innocence.

Miranda let out a frustrated huff. "One minute, you're trying to lure me into your bed, prying into my personal life—like it's any of your business. And the next, you're ignoring me, as if less than forty-eight hours ago, you weren't bragging about your prowess in the bedroom, insinuating you could easily replace my boyfriend with said prowess."

This time, Lane couldn't contain her laughter,

marveling at Miranda's ability to evoke amusement even while scolding her. Lane drew in a shuddering breath, attempting to reel in her laughter. "I thought you weren't interested in me bedding you? So, why would you want me to constantly be hot with you?" Lane cocked her head to the side, trying hard not to laugh at the glower on Miranda's face. "For someone who claims to have no interest in what I have to offer, you sure pay a lot of attention to my behavior around you. I thought you'd be glad when I'm not inviting you to my bed, Dr. Hayes."

Miranda narrowed her eyes and leveled her with a withering glare. "God, you're so insufferable. I don't even know why I bothered opening my mouth to ask you anything."

"Could it be that despite your insistence that you're not attracted to me, you actually are? And instead of succumbing to temptation, you find other ways to interact with me?" Lane's tone carried a hint of challenge. "Your behavior toward me is rather ambiguous, Dr. Hayes. You claim one thing, yet your actions say otherwise." To underscore her point home, Lane slowly traced Miranda's body with a heated stare, her eyes lingering on her very kissable lips, before returning her gaze to meet Miranda's. She couldn't help but notice the audible swallow and the pounding pulse point she wanted to bite.

Miranda held Lane's gaze, and for a moment, they simply sized each other up. Miranda's eyes dropped to her lips, and Lane couldn't resist biting her bottom lip, unconcerned about ruining her lipstick. The temperature in the elevator seemed to soar, and Lane fought the urge to close the distance between them and kiss the pout off Miranda's lips. But, it was the intensity in Miranda's eyes, brimming with unspoken questions, that kept Lane frozen in place. They were utterly mesmerizing, even as they seemed to shoot daggers straight into Lane's defenses, piercing through her armor. *Kenya was right, her eyes did resemble Terrence Howard's.*

The opening of the elevator doors shattered the charged moment and Miranda stepped around her to exit. However, before stepping over the threshold, she paused at Lane's side and uttered "Keep dreaming."

"Oh, I will, Miranda darling," Lane replied, low and sultry. "After all, what better way to prepare for our eventual reality than to have you occupy my subconscious, especially when you're such an enticing thought."

Miranda merely rolled her eyes and hurried out of the elevator before the doors closed. Lane sighed heavily and massaged her temples. *So much for being nothing but professional with this woman.* Where was her self-control when it came to Miranda Hayes? The aggravating reality was that Miranda wasn't helping the situation—often initiating these provocative conversations between them. Despite Miranda's insistence to the contrary, Lane couldn't shake the feeling that there must be at least some curiosity there.

Guess only time will tell.

Chapter 13

"Has anyone else noticed how little we know about Lane?" Allison Boyd questioned, casting a curious glance around the room at her colleagues. "I mean, I was curious enough to Google her, but found nothing beyond tidbits about her professional achievements. It's like she doesn't even exist on social media."

"I've noticed that too." Bradley chimed in. "She's so mysterious. Very intriguing. During our first meeting, I expected her to ask something about my life outside of Parkwood, but she kept it strictly business. I tried to venture into personal territory and she shut it down."

"I just find her mysterious personality hot," Dr. Bhavani, the head of the neonatal team added. "I can appreciate a woman who knows how to keep her personal life out of the cesspool of gossip here at Parkwood. Not to mention, many of the nurses and interns seem to have a crush on her. Seems many of us find her just as intriguing as you, Allison."

"Plus, she's breathtakingly gorgeous. I can see why many are so enthralled by her." Allison replied. "Maybe we should invite her to one of our weekly get-togethers at Palmettos."

"That would be a great idea. Who's brave enough to ask her, knowing there's like a ninety percent chance she'll say no?" Bradley asked. "I find her a bit intimidating, so I'll pass."

"I'll pass as well. What all of you find intriguing, I find rather disrespectful to us as her staff," James, the head of the plastic surgery team, sneered.

"I wouldn't classify her as being rude. She's just not very sociable," Allison answered, her brows creasing together as if she were trying to see Lane the way James did.

"Well, she acts like she has a stick up her ass. She's been here almost three months now, and we know nothing about her outside of Parkwood. I've tried to strike up conversations with her, but it's like talking to a brick wall. All she does is look down her nose at me, like I'm scum beneath her shoes," James argued, scoffing.

*Maybe that's because you were probably trying to flirt with her and she wasn't interested in your lackluster come-ons...*Miranda thought as she listened to her colleagues discuss Lane while they waited for her to arrive for their weekly department meeting. For some reason, hearing them talk about Lane behind her back made her uncomfortable, and she felt the urge to come to Lane's defense.

"Did your conversations involve inviting her out for a drink with you? Not everyone finds your personality charming," Bradley deadpanned, a microdose of sarcasm coating his riposte.

"Oh, please. I wouldn't date a woman like that who is so frigid. I can't recall ever seeing her smile since she's been here. She wears that ever-present blank expression, looking at you as if you're not worthy to be breathing the same air as her. Good luck to any man who is looking to tolerate someone like her," James retorted, his words dripping with disdain and highlighting the bruised ego of a fragile man.

She's not interested in men, you moron. Miranda clenched her teeth, her irritation simmering beneath the surface as she shot James a venomous glare. She had never been fond of him—he epitomized the type of man who viewed women as second-class citizens, believing they should be confined to being barefoot and pregnant in the kitchen. James was hired to be the Head of Plastic Surgery by their former CEO, Bheatti, and became Bheatti's personal lapdog, flaunting his power without accountability. Miranda had hoped Alexandra would have found cause to fire him after assuming leadership, but James had managed to fly under the radar since Bheatti's departure, and now seemed to be resurfacing with his toxic behavior. Perhaps he had underestimated Lane by assuming he could speak down to her, and now, faced with his miscalculation, he resorted to badmouthing her.

"Maybe you're taking it a little too personally, James. She's not the talkative type with anyone, not just you. The consensus around the hospital is that she is reserved and distant, but no one has accused her of being rude or mistreating them. If anything, most are simply curious about her because we know so little," Allison replied, her features now mirroring Miranda's distaste for their colleague.

"She's just a dictator who thinks she's better than us. Maybe she has some dirty little secret that she doesn't want people to know," James shot back.

"Okay, that's enough!" Miranda's voice thundered through the room, her eyes ablaze with fury as she fixed James with an unyielding stare. "Lane's personal life is none of your business or anyone's in this hospital.

It bears no relevance to her role as our leader. A sentiment which you seem to have forgotten while you sit here talking about her in such a *disrespectful* manner. Your disrespect is unacceptable. As you said, you know nothing about her, so all your arguments are simply based on your fragile male ego. Which I'm assuming is bruised because she doesn't give you a second glance. So how about you show her the respect she deserves as your boss? Because she is your boss, even if you don't like the fact that you have to bow to a woman."

By the end of her statement, Miranda was so angry that her hands trembled. Regardless of her history with Lane, hearing this moron spewing such venom about her didn't sit well with her. She summed it up to her defending another woman from the misogynistic tyranny of men. Nothing else. All eyes were now trained on her, but Miranda didn't care. She held James' stare, conveying her contempt without hesitation. As he prepared to retaliate with probably another senseless remark, the door swung open, and Lane entered the room. Clad in impeccable black attire, her expression inscrutable, she commanded attention effortlessly. An eerie silence descended upon the room in her wake.

Glancing around at her staff, she strode confidently to the head of the table and took her seat. "Good morning, everyone," she began, her voice projecting calm authority. "Dr. Edison and Dr. Westmore won't be joining us today." With a tap on her tablet screen, she brought it to life. "Let's commence with the budget forecast." She paused, allowing her words to sink in before continuing. "Overall, the hospital concluded Q3 on a strong note, but some departments are still operating in the red. My goal for Q4 is to transition all departments into profitability as we approach the new year."

Leaning forward, Lane's gaze swept across the room, her expression thoughtful yet resolute. "To achieve this, I'll be scheduling meetings in the coming weeks with those of you whose departments are experiencing losses. I want us to collaboratively explore strategies to improve your financial standing." She emphasized each word, her tone unwavering. "In preparation for these sessions, I need each of you to prepare a detailed report outlining the primary factors contributing to your department's financial challenges, as well as your proposed solutions." Pausing again, Lane met the eyes of each individual seated around the table. "While I have my own insights, I value your feedback in understanding the intricacies of your respective departments."

*No pleasantries and straight to business...*Miranda mused, smiling internally knowing it probably pissed off James.

"I doubt many of us will find the time to do these reports with surgeries filling our schedules. Why not just tell us the problem and *your* plan for fixing it?" James objected, drawing the focus of the room.

"I'd like to think your colleagues are perfectly capable of expressing themselves, Dr. Michael. Moreover, I'm quite certain when you signed your contract to lead your department, you understood that paperwork is part and parcel of the role," Lane retorted in a chillingly composed tone, her expression betraying no hint of emotion.

"Yes, but we studied medicine, not business. So, it's not our job to know how to balance a budget. I believe that responsibility shouldn't fall on us, allowing us to focus on what's truly important... saving lives," James countered, seeking validation from his peers with a glance around the room. However, none of their colleagues dared to blink in agreement.

Miranda's eyes remained on Lane, scrutinizing every minuscule movement on her captivating face. Sensing Lane's irritation, Miranda couldn't help but admire her adeptness at concealing her emotions. Watching Lane calmly facing down James, Miranda understood why her colleagues found her so intriguing. There was an esoteric quality about Lane that compelled one to unravel the mysteries behind her facade. The Lane Miranda knew seemed worlds apart from the woman seated before her now, or the persona her colleagues were familiar with. It left Miranda contemplating whether she should feel special in having glimpsed beneath the surface or not, considering the side she knew was often insufferable.

"I didn't ask you to balance a budget. I simply asked for insight into why you're exceeding your allocated funds and how we can address it. Managing your budget falls within your responsibilities, as you're the one approving invoices under a certain threshold. It doesn't necessitate a business degree to grasp basic arithmetic," Lane replied phlegmatically, conjuring a deathly calm resembling the stillness before a storm.

"Well, you must understand that before Alexandra's arrival, we weren't required to handle these matters. It's only since the change in leadership that we've been burdened with additional administrative tasks," James shot back, once again seeking support from those around the room.

Speak for yourself. The rest of us always had to manage our budgets but since you were Bheatti's pet, you got off with doing nothing.

Lane peered down her nose at James. "And that's precisely why, unlike the previous leadership that you seem to miss, Alexandra was able to save the hospital. She possesses the competence to balance a budget, unlike Bheatti."

"I didn't say that Alexandra hasn't done a good job. I'm just saying that these additional admin tasks prevent us from focusing on surgeries."

This man is really a moron. He really doesn't know when to shut up.

Lane rocked back in her seat and crossed one leg over the other. "If administrative tasks interfere with your ability to focus on surgeries, I can assign someone else to lead your department. I'm certain there are many on your team eager for the opportunity, and who wouldn't mind handling paperwork." James began to speak, but Lane raised a hand to silence him. "I consider this conversation a waste of my time, as well as that of your colleagues. You have a choice—fulfill your duties, or I can find someone else to do it for you." She turned to the rest of the group. "If any of you share similar sentiments as your colleague's, please let me know. I'll be more than willing to assist with transitioning you out of your role. After all, at Parkwood, employees' well-being is a priority. I wouldn't want any of you to be unhappy while fulfilling your well-compensated responsibilities."

Miranda glanced at her colleagues, noting the array of expressions on their faces. Apart from James, none of them appeared visibly angry. Some seemed taken aback, while others seemed to be suppressing smiles behind their hands. Aware of the general negative opinions about James among her peers, Miranda assumed they were pleased to witness someone challenging him.

After a tense moment of silence, Lane's voice sliced through the air, relieving the collective tension as if everyone had been holding their breath, waiting for James's response. "Now, since that's settled," she continued, "I'd like to address the expectation gap between the roles of doctors and nurses. Based on the results of the anonymous survey I conducted two weeks ago, it's apparent many nurses feel doctors expect them to shoulder the bulk of their responsibilities. Some doctors seem to undervalue the vital contribution of nurses to patient care. Since your staff reports directly to you, and not me, it's imperative that you eradicate this attitude. Make it clear to your team that this is not a place for egos, especially among doctors and nurses who must work together. If doctors can't treat their coworkers with respect..." Lane's gaze shifted pointedly to James, "...then perhaps they need to seek employment elsewhere."

Lane paused, her gaze sweeping over each person in the room, though she lingered slightly longer on Miranda, a detail surreptitious enough not to be readily apparent. "Okay. I want to dedicate the remainder of this meeting to reviewing the results together and to receive your feedback. Is there anything else you want to bring to my attention?"

Everyone unanimously agreed that they had nothing to highlight. They then devoted the next twenty minutes to dissecting the survey results. Miranda couldn't resist stealing glances at Lane throughout the discussion. For someone who pretty much just threatened to fire them if they had a problem doing paperwork, Lane was genuinely concerned about the morale of the nurses. Miranda voiced her concurrence with the need for a shift in some doctors' attitudes toward their subordinates. She also couldn't help but notice James maintaining a conspicuous silence throughout the discussion, presumably because he was among those doctors who offloaded a significant portion of his responsibilities onto the nurses.

As her colleagues shared their perspectives, Miranda mulled over Allison's observation that Lane wasn't necessarily disrespectful to her staff—a point Miranda was inclined to agree with. While Lane didn't appear to give a damn what anyone thought about her, Miranda couldn't deny that Lane's personality wasn't inherently rude. But people often misinterpret individuals with Lane's reserved personality as aloof or rude simply because she didn't allow them to get close enough to know her. And when people lack access to you, they tend to assume the worst. Throughout the meeting, their eyes met on several occasions, but in the presence of others, there was no indication of Lane's attraction to her—as usual. Nevertheless, Miranda couldn't ignore the intense magnetism in Lane's gaze—a pull that simultaneously drew her in and made her want to flee.

"Thanks for your input. I'll take everything into consideration when determining our next steps. In the meantime, if you have further ideas, please don't hesitate to share them. That's it for today." Lane turned her attention to Miranda. "Dr. Hayes, could you please stay back for a moment."

Miranda paused halfway up from her seat. "Sure," she

replied, settling back into her chair.

Bradley and Allison exchanged teasing glances with her, as if Miranda was a student being asked to stay back for reprimand. Miranda also caught the venomous glare James directed at Lane as he exited the room. Once they were alone in the boardroom, Miranda shifted her attention to Lane, only to be met with an unnerving expression. They locked eyes, and for a moment, the silence enveloped them as they simply stared at each other. Suddenly, Miranda's lips felt dry, prompting her to instinctively moisten them with the tip of her tongue. Lane's eyes followed the movement and Miranda felt the heat of her gaze increase tenfold.

Lane took in a long, slow breath, and Miranda braced herself for a comment unrelated to their work. However, Lane simply said, "I've reviewed your business case for additional hires in your department. Although my objective is to reduce costs, you presented a compelling argument for why you require more staff. Therefore, I'm willing to meet you halfway. For now, I'm giving you the go-ahead to hire an additional surgeon and two cardiac nurse practitioners. We'll reassess the potential for hiring another surgeon at the end of Q1 next year."

I can't keep up with this woman's moods. "Thank you. I can work with this arrangement for the time being. I'll do my part to explore other areas where we can cut costs in my department to contribute to funding the hiring of an additional surgeon next year."

"Perfect. I have faith in your ability to do so. Your department is among the few that have consistently operated within budget since you took over, which is commendable. If you require any assistance, my door is always open. That's all for now."

Miranda nodded and rose from her seat, feeling Lane's stare lingering on her as she made her way to the door. Catching Lane's mischievous smile, Miranda arched an eyebrow in question. Lane's smile only widened, teasingly. With an exasperated eye roll and a shake of her head, Miranda reached for the door handle.

"Oh, and Dr. Hayes, thanks for so fiercely defending my honor." Lane's words prompted Miranda to turn around and face her. Before she could respond, Lane continued. "I was genuinely touched by your impassioned speech, putting your colleague in his place. I was surprised that you, of all people, chose to defend my less-than-lovable personality. Then again, you're the only one special enough to have any insight into who I am outside of Parkwood. I'm just shocked that, given our history, you took that stand against people who you've known far longer than me. So, tell me, Dr. Hayes..." Lane leaned back in her chair, uncrossing and recrossing her long, toned legs. Her perfectly symmetrical face pensive, as if trying to interpret a rare art piece. "Should I assume I'm growing on you?"

Miranda stared at Lane, her mind racing as she tried to figure out the woman watching her with an underlying curiosity, as if she too were attempting to decipher who Miranda was. Still, regardless of the facts, Miranda wasn't going to give Lane the satisfaction of an answer to her question. "I was defending the honor of women in general," she said firmly. "So, please don't let it get to your head."

That ridiculously devastating smile—that people like James weren't privy to—formed on Lane's lips.

"Whatever you say, Dr. Hayes. If that helps you sleep better at night."

Miranda chose to disregard Lane's reply and posed her own question. "How do you remain so composed after hearing everything that was said about you? You showed no signs of being affected by the less-than-flattering remarks. Many would have stormed into the room, frothing at the mouth upon overhearing such cavalier comments from a colleague. But you entered with one of your, now-famous, blank expressions."

Lane shrugged. "I've encountered men like James throughout my career. Their opinions about who I am mean nothing to me, so I won't waste my time reacting to them. Besides, people have said far worse things about me," she added with another shrug. "And honestly, I couldn't care less. These individuals hold no significance to me beyond my responsibilities as their boss, so whether they like or dislike me is inconsequential. I'm here to fulfill a job, not to make friends. Therefore, I won't squander my time trying to prove anything to anyone. People are entitled to their opinions about me. It doesn't impact how well I sleep at night. And James is just mad because he tried to flirt with me during our first meeting and I shut him down."

Miranda recognized that some people used a facade of indifference to shield themselves from hurt, but she sensed that Lane genuinely didn't care about her staff's opinions about her. It made Miranda ponder what experiences had shaped Lane into the woman she was. To navigate the world without investing energy in those she deemed unworthy of her time was intriguing, albeit somewhat intimidating. However, Miranda refrained from probing further out of fear of provoking a line of conversation she'd rather avoid. "Next time, since you don't care what your staff thinks about you, I'll know better than to rush to your defense."

Lane rested her elbow on the table and propped her chin in her palm, amusement marring her gorgeous features. "I thought you weren't defending me, but women in general, Miranda darling."

Miranda noted the shift in Lane's tone and couldn't ignore the effect of Lane calling her *Miranda darling* in that sultry way of hers. "An act that I'm starting to regret. Have a good day, Lane. Please, at least try to occasionally smile with your staff, instead of walking around here like the muscles in your face don't work."

Lane burst out laughing and the sound of it kept Miranda frozen to the spot, watching the woman who confounded her in so many ways. Her laughter revealed a side of Lane that left Miranda perplexed yet fascinated —a side that should grace the world more often, for it was a beautiful laugh, one that made Lane appear younger and carefree.

"As always, you never fail to amuse me, Dr. Hayes," Lane said, making an effort to rein in her laughter. "I'll take your advice under consideration, although I'd rather share my smiles with only you."

"Goodbye, Lane," Miranda replied, turning on her heels and finally opening the door. Lane's laughter trailed after her as she went through the door and Miranda couldn't stifle the smile that formed on her lips now that Lane wasn't seeing her face. She could admit that behind her cold exterior, the woman did have a sense of humor.

Charming devil.

Chapter 14

"And please don't sleep with this instructor." Nia lectured, pausing with her hand on the door handle as she turned to face Lane. "You know how hard it is to find a class that meets your very specific, high standards. We had to wait a month to secure our spots here and this studio is one of the best within a fifteen-minute drive for both of us."

Lane resisted the urge to roll her eyes at her friend's oversimplification of the events that had led them, or rather her, needing to find a new yoga class. "When we were involved, she wasn't a yoga instructor. And when we initially joined that class, she wasn't our instructor then. It's not my fault she's still hung up on our casual relationship, which ended over two years ago."

Nia released the door and rested her hand on her hip, fixing Lane with a scolding look reminiscent of the one Anita often gave her when she wasn't pleased. "Regardless of the circumstances, I still feel the need to warn you. Women can't seem to help but fall in love with you, and when you don't return their feelings, some of them tend to go bat shit crazy."

"Again, nothing you say is my fault." Lane smirked. "Not my fault if women find me charming. They know what they signed up for when they agree to date me. Not my fault if they breach the terms of our agreement and then expect me to follow along with it."

Nia burst out laughing. "Breach? You talk about dating as if it's some business transaction. Delaney Remington, love isn't like one of your ironclad contracts that is all clear-cut rules and guidelines." Nia shook her head in amusement at her best friend's pragmatic approach to relationships. "People can agree to casual, but then feelings develop. It's not as simple as you make it sound to follow your staunch rules of 'don't fall in love with me because I'm not looking for a commitment.' God, I can't wait for the day when Cupid shoots you in your ass."

"I think Cupid knows better than to waste her arrows on someone like me who isn't looking for love," Lane responded drily. She pointed to the door. "Now, if you're done with your lecture, I'd prefer not to be late for our first class. I wouldn't want us to make a bad impression on the instructor—who I shall not charm into my bed."

"I swear the older you've gotten the more lethal your sarcasm has become," Nia remarked, reaching for the door once more. "But, I'm serious, stay far away from the instructor."

This time Lane did roll her eyes. "Maybe you should warn the instructor to stay far away from me. I'm not always the instigator in these entanglements."

"Just do as I ask," Nia demanded, finally opening the door and stepping into the building.

Lane chose not to respond and silently followed Nia. She could admit that she did feel bad about the situation that led them here. The fact that a past affair was the reason they needed to seek out a new yoga class weighed on her conscience. Their previous instructor turned out to be Valentina, a woman Lane had dated for a year. She had met Valentina during one of her visits to Seattle to see Anita, and they had shared a passionate weekend. A month later, Lane returned to Seattle for Anita's birthday and a mini vacation for herself. During that trip, she reached out to Valentina—who was then a software engineer—and they spent the week together. After that, for over a year, whenever Lane visited Seattle, they would meet up. Eventually, Valentina expressed her desire for an exclusive relationship. Lane, on the other hand, had just signed a one-year contract to relocate to Denmark to oversee the opening of a new hospital for the corporation she was working with. Valentina wanted to continue dating long-distance until Lane returned, but Lane wasn't interested in a committed relationship at the time and declined Valentina's proposal. And let's just say Valentina was less than thrilled about Lane ending things.

Fast forward to the present, and between the end of their arrangement and Lane's relocation to Seattle, it appeared that Valentina had left her tech career behind and transitioned into a full-time yoga instructor. They exchanged brief words at the end of their first class together, and by the time Lane arrived home, she found a message from Valentina, asking her out for a drink to catch up. Lane politely declined, expressing that she didn't think it would be a good idea. Unfortunately, Valentina didn't take the rejection well and proceeded to send Lane a series of messages detailing how much she had been hurt two years prior. To avoid an uncomfortable situation, Lane immediately called Nia and informed her that they needed to find a new yoga class.

"We just made it on time," Nia whispered as

they crossed the threshold into the studio. It felt like stepping into a serene park, with lush green grass and the soothing trickle of water fountains. Soft instrumental music played in the background, enhancing the tranquility of the space as participants settled onto their mats. The studio's ambiance was reminiscent of an oasis, providing respite from Seattle's rainy weather. It was the perfect atmosphere for days when classes couldn't be held outside, offering participants the chance to immerse themselves in nature.

They left their shoes at the designated area at the back and stepped onto the faux grass, which remarkably felt like the real thing. Most patrons were already on their mats, engaged in various stretches, and the space was nearly full. Silently, they made their way to the other side of the room where there was just enough space for two more people. Just as Lane was about to roll out her mat, her eyes zoomed in on the woman in front of her, who was seated with her head between her legs, stretching her back muscles. Waves of curly brown hair cascaded over the mat, unmistakably belonging to someone Lane could spot from a mile away. And as always, her pulse quickened, and a rush of warmth flooded her veins. Lane groaned inwardly, trying desperately not to dwell on the flawless, light brown skin that had occupied her thoughts for the past couple of months, the slender waist that flowed into wide hips, and the spandex-clad ample backside that she had thought about doing rather filthy things to.

I swear the universe is hell-bent on torturing me. Because why... WHY? Of all the yoga studios, why did I have to end up at the one Miranda... freaking... Hayes attends? Just...

why?

"Are you okay? Why are you just standing there staring at her ass?" Lane silently cursed herself for being obvious enough for Nia to notice her fixation. "I mean it's a beautiful ass, but still...?" Nia whispered in her ears.

Lane shook her head and released the breath she hadn't realized she had been holding. "Yes, I'm fine," she whispered, her voice steadier than she felt.

So much for calming my mind and releasing pent-up energy when the source of some of that pent-up energy will be stretching and bending her body into various positions right in front of me.

Lane glanced around the room in search of another spot, but nowhere else seemed suitable and the instructor announced that the class was starting. Resigned to her fate, Lane continued to roll out her mat and did her utmost best to ignore the woman in front of her. Even though she smiled internally at the thought of Miranda's reaction when she finally spotted her. Lane did a few breathing exercises to calm her racing heart and to find the self-control she needed to avoid getting distracted by the temptation in front of her.

The class began and Lane did her best to focus on the instructor's guidance, but much to her utter dissatisfaction, she couldn't prevent herself from admiring how Miranda moved with fluid grace. Miranda seamlessly transitioned from one pose to the next, her agile body effortlessly navigating through each asana. As the class progressed, Lane couldn't tear her eyes away as Miranda gracefully flowed into a deep backbend, her spine arching elegantly as she lifted her chest heavenwards. The sight of Miranda's body, strong and flexible, stirred the hunger she had been working hard to bury for the past months. God help her. She wanted this woman. Lane held her breath bracing for Miranda to finally see her, but Miranda kept her eyes closed for the entire pose, her face a picture of relaxation. From one pose to the next, Lane's eyes eagerly tracked every movement of Miranda's supple body, observing the way her muscles rippled beneath her skin with each controlled breath.

As they transitioned into the Cow Pose, much to her absolute dismay, Lane felt her arousal stir. Try as she might, she couldn't remove her eyes from Miranda's ample backside as she arched into the pose, her chest lifting and expanding with each breath. The intensity of the pose caused a surge of lust to course through Lane's body, her breath hitching as she watched Miranda's shapely ass lift higher and release tension, her body surrendering to the stretch. Lane felt a rush of heat spreading through her body, her heart rate quickening—not from her own exertions, but the woman in front of her. There was just something undeniably sensual about the way Miranda moved, a raw beauty that left Lane powerless to look away and everything disappeared around the two of them. *What the hell is happening to me? Why can't I control my body's reaction to this woman?*

Lost in the moment, Lane found herself imagining Miranda in a similar pose, but not in the yoga studio —rather, in Lane's bed. She envisioned herself sinking deep into Miranda from behind, feeling the surrender and release that she witnessed now. The fantasy consumed her—Miranda begging for more, her voice echoing in the room, her body trembling with pleasure as Lane took her harder and faster. The thought sent a flush of warmth between Lane's thighs, and she cursed the universe for its cruel games. *Because why? Just... why?* As the class moved from one pose to the next, Lane wished fervently for it to end faster so that she could escape this torturous situation.

As they transitioned into the Lord of the Dance Pose, requiring the class to face the left side of the room, their eyes met and it was as if time stood still. Lane found herself lost in the hazel orbs that seemed to drown her in waves of lust. Miranda's eyes widened in surprise, then quickly shifted into her signature scowl, seemingly reserved just for Lane, who couldn't help but smirk at the reaction. Before she could even take another breath, Miranda lost her balance and began to tumble to the ground. Acting on instinct, Lane immediately righted herself and reached out a hand to prevent Miranda from falling. She caught her just in time, their bodies inches apart. Lane could feel the heat emanating from Miranda's touch as her fingers wrapped around Lane's forearm, sending a jolt of electricity through her. Standing in such close proximity, their breaths mingling, Miranda's soothing scent of vanilla and shea butter wrapped around her like a comforting blanket. Miranda's eyes wandered over Lane's face, and at that moment, Lane wished she could read minds, to decipher what was going on behind those mesmerizing eyes. Miranda's eye color shifted from goldish green to deep forest causing Lane's heart to race with anticipation, wondering what thoughts lay hidden beneath that intense stare. With both of them not wearing heels, Lane realized that Miranda was actually an inch shorter than Lane's 5'8". This only made Lane want her even more, as she had always preferred being the taller one in her arrangements.

"Ladies, are you okay?" The instructor asked from the head of the room.

Miranda immediately released Lane's forearms and took a step back, but Lane kept her hands wrapped around Miranda's. "Be careful, Dr. Hayes. I wouldn't want you to damage these hands of yours, which are needed to save lives."

Miranda only glared at her and leaned in a bit closer to Lane, lowering her voice, "Maybe if you weren't ogling me, then I wouldn't have lost my balance. Please keep your eyes to yourself."

Before Lane could respond, Miranda pulled her hands from hers and resumed the pose. Lane fought the urge to laugh as she moved back to her mat. She didn't miss the questioning look that Nia shot her, but she chose to ignore it. Because it was neither the time nor the place to discuss her attraction to Miranda Hayes—which it seemed she had no control over, since even in a room full of people, the sight of the woman made her aroused. *Maybe it was just the poses that triggered my reaction.*

Lane sucked in a shuddering breath and tried to focus as they moved on to the next pose. But now that Miranda was aware of her presence, it was like some invisible force was pulling them together, because for the rest of the class their eyes kept finding each other, and she couldn't stop the rush of excitement that shot through her each time Miranda shot daggers at her. As the class came to an end, Lane realized that it wasn't just the yoga poses themselves that stirred her arousal—it was the woman who embodied them. A woman whose strength, grace, and sensuality had ignited something deep within her.

Rolling up her mat, Lane felt tempted to talk to Miranda but remained rooted to her spot, hesitant to approach her with Nia within earshot. She didn't want to give Nia ammunition to grill her about Miranda. However, Miranda took the initiative when she whirled around and faced Lane. She opened her mouth to speak but stopped suddenly when Nia wrapped her arm around Lane's waist. Lane noticed something fleeting in Miranda's eyes, but it vanished before she could decipher it.

"I'm going to the bathroom. Please stay out of trouble while I'm gone." She teasingly patted Lane's cheek with her free hand. "Please wipe the drool from your mouth before you speak to the woman you spent the entire class ogling," Nia whispered.

Before Lane could respond, Nia released her and headed to the bathroom. Lane watched her walk away, her mind racing with thoughts about whether her admiration for Miranda had been as conspicuous as Nia seemed to imply.

"Should I be concerned that of all the many yoga studios in Seattle, you ended up at the one I've been attending for the past five years? Life couldn't be this cruel to me for it to be a mere coincidence," Miranda said, prompting Lane to shift her attention to her.

Lane shot Miranda an affronted look. "Dr. Hayes, as devastatingly alluring as you are, I would never stoop to stalking just to be in your presence." Her lips then curved at the corners in a daring smirk. "I think fate is trying to tell us something since we keep ending up in the same places. Maybe you should just let nature take its course."

Miranda folded her arms across her chest. "And what course is that, exactly?"

"You know *exactly* what I'm talking about." Lane stepped closer to Miranda. "But if you insist on me spelling it out for you..." She leaned in a little closer, her voice barely above a whisper, "You. Naked. In my bed. Screaming my name. Over... and... over." And as the words left her mouth, Lane cursed herself internally for once again not exercising self-control around this woman, who seemed to always know how to push her buttons. *Damn it! Damn it! Damn it!* Miranda drew in a deep breath and Lane took a step back, scrutinizing every nuance etched in Miranda's expression.

Miranda swallowed hard and stared at her for a long moment. Then, she narrowed her eyes and glanced around the area, as if checking to ensure that no one was within listening distance. "Don't you already have someone here with you, who unlike me, wants to be in your bed screaming your name? I'm sure she wouldn't be happy about you hitting on another woman when she is only a few feet away. I know you don't have any qualms about cheating, but I do, and I would never get involved with someone who is a cheater."

Lane's eyebrow arched in question as she wondered who the hell Miranda was referring to before it dawned on her that she must be talking about Nia. Lane chose to ignore that part of Miranda's statement, because if Miranda was probing for information about her relationship with Nia, then she would prolong putting her out of her misery. "I've never cheated on anyone before."

With her arms still folded across her chest, Miranda shifted her weight to her right hip. "In my book, if you knowingly get involved with someone in a relationship, then you're a cheater just like them."

God. Is that what she thinks of me? That I'm just some womanizing cheater? Lane was tempted to say something scandalous to push Miranda's buttons, but instead, she ended up saying, "I absolutely agree with you. However, I'm temptation. It's up to the person in a relationship to avoid temptation. They are the ones who promised to be faithful to their partner, not me. Some people are in open relationships and it's up to them to let me know if they're not. If their relationship isn't open, then I don't get involved with them. But I rarely ever go that route because commitments are sacred to me. And marriage is an absolute, no. I don't care if it's open. I would never knowingly sleep with someone who is married."

She crossed her arms in a mirrored pose to Miranda's. "And for your information, Miranda, I'd never cheat if I'm in a relationship. I'd also never get into a relationship with someone who cheats, because if they cheat with me, then they would cheat on me." *Christ. Why do I always feel compelled to explain myself to this woman and try to erase whatever abhorrent assumptions she makes about me, when I don't normally explain myself to anyone?*

Miranda's eyes became ice cold as the frown on her face deepened into anger. "So, all this time you've been flirting with me, it's just because you want to fuck me, knowing you wouldn't want a relationship with me because I would have cheated on Trevor with you."

"For someone who has no interest in fucking me, why do you care so much, Miranda?" Lane asked, intently studying the woman before her who was just as beautiful in anger as she was in laughter. *God, she's breathtaking.*

"I *don't* care," Miranda gritted out.

"If you say so. But to answer your question—you would have been the exception to my moral compass, Miranda darling. Because one, you are involved with a man, two, you've never been with a woman, and three, I know you wouldn't have cheated on me if we were to have a relationship."

"How do you know I wouldn't cheat on you?" Miranda asked, sounding both confused and curious at the same time.

Lane lifted a shoulder in indifference. "Because it's extenuating circumstances that would have led to you cheating, not because you're a natural cheater."

"What!? What do you mean extenuating circumstances?"

"You realizing for the first time in your life that you're attracted to women or perhaps specifically to me. Under those circumstances, I wouldn't miss out on a chance to have a relationship with you if you slip and stumble into my bed before you get rid of the boyfriend. I don't condone cheating, but life isn't as black and white as people make it seem at times. I wouldn't have been successful in my career if I wasn't able to analyze situations from various angles before drawing a conclusion. But I have full faith that you would dump the boyfriend before you take a bite of the forbidden fruit and embrace the dark side."

Miranda burst out laughing. "Oh my god... oh my god... You always have an answer for everything even when they are so far-fetched." Miranda shook her head. "God, you're aggravating."

"I don't hear you denying that you're attracted to me."

"That's because I'm not, and it's a waste of my time to even give your wild assumptions a second thought." Miranda bent down and picked up her mat and gym bag. "Goodbye, Lane," she said, heading to the door without another glance in Lane's direction.

Lane watched her leave, her mind reeling with the fact that she was even more turned on from the damn conversation. Every interaction they had left her yearning for more. Being in Miranda's presence made her feel things that she didn't understand—this burning lust she feared that could only be quelched by fucking the damn woman. When did she become a masochist? Because why couldn't she just get thoughts of this woman out of her system? And why did her damn self-control evaporate in her presence? *Arrgh!*

"Are you ready to go?" Nia asked, interrupting Lane's train of thought.

"Yes, I am." She reached for her gear, doing her best to avoid Nia's questioning gaze.

She thanked the stars when Nia's phone rang, which provided a temporary relief from Nia's inquisition as they exited the studio. Just as they reached outside, she spotted Miranda standing a few feet away, typing on her phone. And it was like a magnet to steel, because Miranda immediately lifted her head and met Lane's gaze. They stared at each other until a silver Mercedes-AMG GT Coupe pulled up at Miranda's feet, forcing her to look away. Lane watched as the boyfriend slipped out of the driver's seat, wearing a huge smile on his face, walked around the car, and enveloped Miranda into a tight hug—his hands dropping to rest on her ass. Miranda wrapped her arms around his neck and they shared a brief sweet kiss that made Lane grind her teeth as jealousy shot through her. Trevor released Miranda, took her gym bag, opened the car door for her, waited for Miranda to settle into her seat, and then closed the door. Then he walked back around and slipped into the driver's seat.

At least he has the attributes of a real gentleman. A commodity that is so very rare among the current species of men roaming the earth.

"Are you ready to tell me why you're looking at that man like you want to murder him for kissing the woman you spent the entire class drooling after," Nia said from behind Lane.

Lane pivoted on her heels to face Nia. "There's nothing to tell, nor is there anything wrong with admiring a beautiful woman."

"I know you well enough to sense there's more to it than you're letting on. But, I'll let it slide for now. I don't have enough evidence to prove my assumptions and I know you won't share with me until you're ready." Nia looped her arm through Lane's and started walking to the parking lot. "Still, the way you look at that woman says more than you realize. I've never seen you look at anyone the way you do her."

"Hmmm," Lane murmured, finding no other words to offer. Denying what must have been obvious to Nia seemed pointless.

She resolved to exert better control over her attraction to Miranda, perhaps even extinguishing it altogether. Especially now that for the foreseeable future, they might run into each other at the yoga studio. The last thing she needed was to endure another session of agonizing arousal while watching Miranda

contort her body into various poses that sent her mind tumbling into the gutter.
This woman is going to be the death of me.

Chapter 15

Miranda once again found herself seated at another dinner with Trevor's parents, struggling to subdue her irritation. She silently wished his father's business matters in Seattle would conclude sooner rather than later. Three dinners in the past month had stretched her patience thin. Tonight's gathering had sparked yet another argument with Trevor when she expressed her reluctance to rearrange her plans to accommodate their last-minute invitation. She believed her time was just as valuable as theirs and saw no reason to bend over backward for people who expected the world to cater to their every whim. Trevor, however, viewed it as an opportunity for her to bond with his parents, emphasizing that she would soon be a part of their family once they were married. While Miranda understood his efforts to be more tolerant of his parents after his mother's health scare, she found it difficult to overlook their condescending behavior. Nonetheless, she acquiesced to Trevor's request, mainly to end the argument and alleviate her weariness.

Now, she was trapped in a conversation about their affluent social circle and the increasing wealth they had amassed since the year began. The more time she spent with them, the more she admired Trevor's resilience in carving out his own path in life, distinct from theirs. Still, despite her disdain for their elitist attitude, Miranda saw their genuine love for Trevor, particularly his mother, who interrupted her thoughts with a sharp call of Miranda's name.

Miranda shifted her focus to Bridgette. "Sorry, could you please repeat your question?"

Bridgette's expression tightened with displeasure, indicating her annoyance at Miranda's apparent lack of attention to the conversation. "I asked, what are your plans for my son, since you've been reluctant to move in with him."

Taken aback by the question, Miranda shot a quick glance at Trevor, expecting him to intercede and address his mother's intrusive inquiry. However, to her dismay, Trevor remained silent, leaving her to face the interrogation alone. While she wasn't surprised that he had discussed their relationship with his parents, she was shocked by Bridgette's audacity in demanding an explanation from her. And as nice as she was, Miranda didn't take kindly to people who had no say in her relationship, demanding that she justify her choices to them. Since Trevor showed no inclination to defend her, she realized she would have to handle the situation herself.

She refocused her attention on Bridgette. "Your son already knows my plans and he's aware of my stance on moving in together. Plans he must have relayed to you during your discussion about *our relationship*."

The frown on Bridgette's face deepened, her disapproval of Miranda becoming increasingly evident. "Yes, he mentioned you don't want to move in because you claim you're not ready. I'd like to understand why you're not ready, especially after dating for over a year. That's ample time to determine if you want a committed relationship with someone."

Miranda bit the inside of her cheek to contain her rising anger. "As I said, your son knows why and I don't wish to explain myself to you. There's no defined timeline to relationships and that's all I'll say on the subject."

Bridgette wasn't to be deterred, and like a dog with a bone, she continued. "Well, he doesn't understand what's holding you back if you intend to be his wife and give us some grandkids. Neither of you is getting younger, and as you know, your biological clock is running out. So, you need to make up your mind about what you want, and don't waste my son's time."

"Mother, that's enough," Trevor said, though his tone lacked the anger Miranda would have expected from the man she'd spent the last year getting to know. Something inside of her shifted as she wondered what picture of their relationship he had painted to his parents. She had never been more disappointed in him than in that moment.

Bridgette scoffed and fixed her gaze on Trevor. "No son, don't tell me 'enough'. You've been more than patient and she insists on giving you the runaround. So, I'd just like to know why." Bridgette shook her head, disgust creeping into her features. "This dating culture is what's wrong with today's society, where women feel they can date one man to the next without a thought for commitment. No woman should be her age and not married with children. It's unbecoming of a civilized society. If we still existed in a world where this behavior was frowned upon, instead of being celebrated, then she wouldn't be dragging her feet with you."

Trevor opened his mouth to speak, but Miranda had enough and refused to sit silently while this woman degraded her, even if she was the mother of the man she was involved with. "What should be frowned upon," Miranda stated, her voice steady but charged with anger, "is your audacity to judge me for aspiring to more in life than popping out babies for a man and keeping his house. After all, those are the traditional values that you're alluding to. Where women were expected to marry a man as soon as she started bleeding because a woman's purpose is only to serve men. Well, newsflash Bridgette, this isn't the archaic ages where I need to marry your son to feel a sense of self. Nor do I feel any shame about being thirty-seven and not married with kids. And I definitely won't allow your backward views on the role of a woman in society to guilt me into doing something I'm not ready to do."

Brigette's eyes widened in surprise as if she were shocked that Miranda responded to her in that manner. She began to speak, but Robert intervened, placing a firm hand on hers to silence her. "Let it go, Bridgette," he ordered with staunch finality, brokering no room for argument.

Bridgette huffed and like a good little wife, she kept her mouth shut. A tense silence settled around the table and Miranda expected Trevor to suggest they leave. However, he only looked at her as if he was disappointed in her. Miranda held his gaze, refusing to back down because if he was pissed at her for putting his mother in her place, then she was equally pissed at him for not standing up for her. He lowered his eyes first, reached for his glass, and knocked back his whiskey.

"I'm going to the bathroom," Miranda announced,

feeling the urgent need to distance herself from Trevor and his parents. Trevor moved to pull out her chair, but she stopped him with a raised hand. "No need," she insisted, pushing her chair back and rising to her feet.

Before she could take her first step her eyes connected with the last person she expected to see, who was watching her with that intense gaze that unnerved her. *Fuck... my... life.* Unfortunately for her, she couldn't detour from passing Lane's table to go to the bathroom. Miranda inhaled deeply and continued her journey. Lane kept her eyes on her, and Miranda watched as a slow smile spread across her face, as if she knew Miranda wished she didn't have to walk by her table. *Damn deviant.* Drawing closer to Lane, she noticed she was dining alone, halfway through her main course and a bottle of red wine. *Why is she having dinner by herself?*

Miranda stopped beside Lane's table, glancing down at her half-eaten meal and then back at the woman, looking at her with amusement sparkling in her eyes. "Did your insufferable charms not work on your date and you got stood up?"

Lane held her stare, her eyes now glinting with that familiar challenge—the one that always seemed to emerge each time they interacted. "On the contrary, Dr. Hayes, I'm on a date with myself. I heard this place serves one of the juiciest filet mignons and I decided to treat myself to a night out on the town."

Miranda studied the woman before her, who after months of working with her and their occasional banter outside of the hospital, she still couldn't get a clear read on who Delaney Remington was. Here was a woman with a tough exterior and a no-nonsense leadership style, yet in another breath, she displayed a surprising level of care for the people she was entrusted to lead, especially those in lower-level positions. Miranda had also observed Lane interacting with janitors and cafeteria staff, noting how gently she spoke to them with such sympathy and compassion, and the respect she accorded them—a stark contrast to some of their colleagues who barely acknowledged the ancillary staff's existence. As much as Miranda tried to resist, she found herself unable to quell her curiosity about this woman who often managed to get under her skin. Lane's throat-clearing brought Miranda back to the present.

"You don't find it weird to be dining by yourself?" Miranda finally asked.

"No, I don't. I love my own company," Lane replied matter-of-factly. "And there are only a select few other than myself that I can tolerate sharing a meal with." An inquisitive eyebrow lifted on Lane's face "Why? Do you find it odd?" Lane held Miranda's gaze, her curiosity evident in her expression, as if Miranda's perspective on the matter was genuinely important to her.

Miranda's eyes traveled skywards and back. "With that ego of yours, it comes as no surprise you love your own company," she remarked dryly. "And no, I don't find it weird you're comfortable dining by yourself." Miranda's curiosity stemmed not from Lane's solo dining choice, but from people often telling her she was weird to go to the movies and dinner by herself.

"And is there something wrong with loving myself? I believe self-love is the most important love of all. Because if you don't love yourself, then you won't know how to love others or how to truly be happy?"

Lane's earnestness was evident, devoid of any

sarcasm or jest, leaving Miranda momentarily taken aback by the genuine sentiment behind Lane's words. "Finally, something we agree on. Even though loving yourself doesn't give you the right to be insufferable."

Lane flashed one of her signature cheeky grins. "What you consider insufferable, others find charming, Miranda darling. Even though, given that you can't resist having a conversation with me, I'm of the opinion that you *do* find me charming." Lane's long, flawlessly manicured index finger began tracing slow circles around the rim of her wine glass. "Because surely you wouldn't give someone who is insufferable so much of your time, even when you're out having dinner with your boyfriend and what seems to be his parents. Were you that bored that you jumped at the opportunity to come over and talk to me?"

Miranda sighed dramatically. "You know, maybe you should have been a lawyer because you always have an argument for everything and often twist situations to fit your narrative." Miranda curled each finger, making a fist, and then relaxing them down by her sides. "I had no choice but to pass your table to use the bathroom and I didn't want to be rude by not saying hello."

"You could have just said, 'hello' and been on your way. Yet, here you are indulging in scintillating dialogue with me." Lane effortlessly changed the direction of the circles she drew on the rim of her glass as her lips ticked up into that infuriating smirk. "So, Miranda darling, don't you think it's time you admit that you like me and enjoy my company?"

Miranda channeled her most bored expression. "You have such a wild imagination. Keep weaving your tales. I guess it's more comforting than reality."

Lane relaxed back in her chair, casually reaching for her wine glass. "Whatever you say, Miranda. As much as I'd enjoy continuing this little chat, your boyfriend is on his way over and he doesn't seem too happy."

Miranda glanced over her shoulder to find Trevor walking toward them.

"If you want to end the night on a better note, how about you ditch the boyfriend, and his stick-up-the-ass parents, and come home with me? You seem to enjoy my company much more than theirs," Lane proposed, the notes of temptation melodically wafting through the air, leaving no room for doubt about her intentions.

Miranda whipped her head back around to Lane, but before she could respond, Trevor materialized by her side.

"We're ready to leave," Trevor addressed Miranda, then turned his attention to Lane, offering a smile that didn't reach his eyes. "Hello, Lane. Good to see you again."

Lane gave a curt nod, her expression blank. "Hello."

Under normal circumstances, Miranda might have been annoyed by Lane's obvious dismissal of Trevor, but she was still irritated and felt little concern if Trevor perceived it as a slight from Lane. Following their first encounter at the charity brunch, Trevor had told her later that evening that he didn't think Lane liked him.

"Enjoy the rest of your dinner, Lane." Miranda said.

"Good night, Miranda."

Miranda trailed behind Trevor to their table, her steps measured and her mind swirling with unspoken frustrations. She quietly thanked the stars his parents had excused themselves, sparing her the discomfort of their presence. She gathered her belongings and they walked outside in uncomfortable silence. As they stepped outside into the cool night air, the tension between them thickened, overshadowing any sense of ease. Ire swirled in the air around them, evident in the rigid set of their shoulders and the silence that stretched between them like a yawning chasm. She contemplated calling a rideshare to take her home, seeking refuge from the uncomfortable atmosphere. But deep down, she knew they needed to address the unresolved conflict that had marred their dinner.

Once the valet pulled up with their car, Trevor opened the door for her, the gesture tainted by the forcefulness with which he closed it. Miranda noted the subtle display of his fury, though she couldn't fathom what had stoked it to such intensity. She had stood her ground against his mother's belittlement, refusing to tolerate disrespect. She had the utmost respect for her parents and as such would have respected his, if they had earned it. Because for her, respect was earned and not something people with money thought they were entitled to, even when their personalities were of the lowest caliber of humans.

"Please take me to my house," Miranda directed as soon as they pulled off the curb, her voice carrying a hint of weariness.

Trevor shot her a sideways glance, his expression tight with tension. "I thought you were spending the weekend at my apartment."

Miranda met his gaze evenly. "Well, given the events of the evening and the anger radiating off you in waves, I think it's best if I go home." She kept her tone measured, unwilling to escalate the situation further, because she simply felt drained and didn't want to fight with him.

"Great, because we already don't spend enough time apart. Can you blame me for being upset?" Trevor shot back, his tone cutting like glass, though his voice remained eerily calm. That was the thing with Trevor—his anger simmered beneath the surface, never erupting into shouts, but always present in the sharp edge of his words.

Miranda turned sideways, resting her back against the door. "And what exactly are you upset about, Trevor?" Her tone was steady but tinged with frustration. "You expected me to just sit there and let your mother speak to me like I'm some kid she has authority to tell how to live their life?"

Trevor sighed heavily. "It's not like some of what she said wasn't true regarding our relationship." He shifted uncomfortably in his seat, his hands gripping the steering wheel tightly. "It's been over a year, and you've been dragging your feet, Miranda." His voice softened slightly, but the edge remained. "Just like my mother, I don't understand your hesitation. I do everything to make you happy, yet you insist that you're not ready. And you can't give a valid reason as to why."

Trevor's words hung heavy in the tense atmosphere of the car. Miranda's hands folded into fists in her lap, her eyes trained on Trevor's profile. "Oh, because I don't do everything, other than wanting to jump into moving in together to make you happy?" Disappointment reverberated in her throat, and her brows furrowed in exasperation. "You're talking like we've been together for years instead of just one. When we got together, we discussed taking things slow, and now all of a sudden, there's this rush to move in together."

She took a deep breath, her chest rising and falling with emotion. "And based on whatever discussions you've been having with your mother, there seems to be an expectation that I should be walking down the aisle and popping out two point five babies in the near future. So, please don't make it seem like you're the victim here and I've done nothing to make you happy." She paused and took a calming breath. "I care deeply for you and your desires, but I won't jump into moving in together just to make you happy when I'm not ready."

Trevor shifted his attention to her, his eyes flashing with a mix of hurt and defiance. "Well, as my mother said, neither of us is getting any younger, Miranda, and if I'm going to have children, I'd prefer to start soon and not five years from now." His hands gripped the steering wheel even tighter. "Look at Blake and Alexandra, they got married within a year of dating and now they're starting a family."

Miranda took a moment to let Trevor's words sink in as she studied him. She couldn't help but feel a pang of confusion and mounting vexation at the sudden shift in his attitude toward their future. Over the last few months, things had shifted between them, and she couldn't pinpoint the exact moment when Trevor's expectations had begun to diverge from their previous discussions. They had the necessary conversations about marriage and children. He knew she wanted to get married someday, and children were a maybe. "Trevor, where is all of this coming from?" she asked, her tone calm but infused with concern. She needed to understand what had sparked this change in him, why he suddenly seemed so eager to rush their relationship forward.

"It's coming from the fact that I'm deeply in love with you, Miranda," Trevor confessed, his voice earnest and filled with emotion. "You're everything I want in a lifelong partner. You're kind, compassionate, intelligent, and a genuinely good person. I want the whole nine yards with you—kids and all. But it's obvious you don't, because if you did, then you wouldn't be thinking twice about us moving in together. I want us to take the next step and start building our life together. Our schedules have been so hectic that we barely saw each other the last two weeks. Living together would solve that problem and allow us to spend more time together, building toward our future."

Miranda's shoulders tensed, the weight of Trevor's words pressing down on her like a lead blanket. Guilt gnawed at her insides, a familiar ache she battled every time their discussions turned to their future together. She fought to keep her emotions in check, refusing to let her tears spill over. While she didn't want to lose him, she simply couldn't do what he wanted to appease him when she knew deep down, she wasn't ready. It wasn't as if she hadn't invested as much as he had in their relationship. She did her part, ensuring to make time for him no matter how busy her schedule was. True, there were times when hospital duties consumed her, and they only saw each other once a week. But she always tried her best to prioritize him. And yet, it seemed like it just wasn't enough for Trevor. She couldn't help but feel he was being unfair to her.

"I'm sorry my best isn't good enough for you at the moment," Miranda uttered, her voice stifled with exhaustion. She felt drained, the strain of their unresolved conflict bearing down on her like a heavy burden. She knew some might see her reluctance as selfishness, but to her, moving in together was a significant commitment—one that demanded careful consideration and mutual readiness.

Trevor sighed heavily, but remained silent. Miranda turned to face the window, the soft hum of the car's engine providing a backdrop to their silent exchange for the remainder of the drive. Getting closer to her house, Miranda felt a wave of conflicting emotions wash over her. Initially, she had craved solitude, but now she couldn't shake the urge to address the rift that had formed between them. Trevor was right—they had barely spent any time together this past week, and she couldn't deny the pang of guilt that tugged at her heart. Before she could gather her thoughts to bridge the gap between them, Trevor stepped out of the car and walked around to open her door. The simple gesture made Miranda's heart squeeze painfully in her chest. Despite their current conflict, Trevor possessed qualities that were so rare and precious in the current pool of men—a fact Miranda couldn't ignore. As she emerged from the car, a feeling of vulnerability engulfed her. Maybe she was foolish for wanting to take things slow, knowing if they broke up, her chance of finding someone with his inherent good qualities was slim.

Facing Trevor, she couldn't help but notice the myriad of emotions swirling within his cerulean spheres, but the most striking was acute sadness—one that she couldn't bear to see and wanted to erase. Miranda closed the distance between them, her heart pounding in her chest. Without a word, she enveloped Trevor in a tight embrace, nestling her face against his chest, inhaling deeply and drawing comfort from the familiar scent of his cologne. For a moment, Trevor remained stiff in her arms, his body taut with tension. But gradually, he began to relax, his arms encircling her, pulling her closer as if he never wanted to let her go.

"I'm sorry," Miranda whispered, her voice muffled against his shirt, the fabric soaking up her remorse.

"Me too," Trevor murmured, his tone lacking its usual warmth.

Drawing back slightly, Miranda met his gaze, searching for a glimpse of the affection she cherished. "Do you want to come inside?" she offered tentatively.

Trevor shook his head, a pained expression crossing his features. "Maybe we need the night apart to cool down."

"I don't want us to fight either," Miranda admitted, vulnerability coloring her voice. "But I don't want us to part ways like this, with unresolved tension hanging between us."

Trevor searched her face for a long moment. After a beat, he nodded slowly. "Okay," he finally agreed, his voice subdued.

Trevor locked the car and slipped his hand into Miranda's. Each step toward her front door felt like trudging through thick mud, the strain of their situation tightening around her like a constricting python. She grappled with the dilemma of how to pilot their relationship without sacrificing their individual happiness. While she hoped the natural inclination to move in together would have developed with time, it remained elusive. Their one-year dating anniversary hardly seemed enough time to justify such a significant step, considering the layers still to uncover about each other. Miranda held onto the belief that taking it slow wasn't a sign of hesitation but rather a desire to ensure the authenticity and strength of their connection. Because yes, that thing that she couldn't define still hadn't made itself known, and she was hoping that with time she would feel it with him. Maybe there was nothing more to feel, and she was just being idealistic.

Chapter 16

"I'm going to miss you so much," Miranda whispered against Trevor's lips, lingering for one more kiss before he departed. Since their heated argument two weeks ago, an undercurrent of tension still existed between them, despite her efforts to reaffirm her commitment to their relationship and show him how much he meant to her. Trevor was en route to New York to fulfill his long-held dream of opening a restaurant in Manhattan, a venture he'd been tirelessly working to achieve. While Miranda supported his ambition, she couldn't shake the conflicting emotions about the timing of his departure amidst their unresolved issues. On the other hand, maybe distance would afford them both the necessary space and perspective to address their concerns and return to each other with renewed clarity and resolve to continue working on their relationship.

Trevor gently pulled away from the kiss but kept his hands around Miranda's waist. "Hopefully you'll be able to fly out for a weekend. I know you're not a fan of my parents, especially after the way things ended at the last dinner, but it would be great for you to meet some other members of my family. My sister has been eager to meet you, so this trip could be a perfect opportunity."

Miranda nodded, her mind already calculating potential dates, given that it was the holiday season and she already had plans to spend Christmas with her mother's parents. "I'll do my best to make it work."

Trevor leaned in for a final, chaste kiss on her lips before releasing her. "I'll call you as soon as I land."

Miranda held the door open as Trevor picked up his luggage. As he stepped over the threshold, he paused, studying her face as if he were committing every feature to memory. There was an inkling of uncertainty in his eyes, a flicker of emotion she couldn't quite place. Before she could voice her concerns, he leaned in and kissed her softly, his lips lingering for a moment before he pulled away and continued toward his rideshare. Watching Trevor walk away, Miranda felt a pang of unease settle in her stomach. She hoped that his trip would bring a resolution to their problems, and perhaps pave the way for a smoother path forward. Hopefully, by then she would be ready to move in with him. Closing the door behind him, she went to the kitchen in search of her phone. She had placed it on silent the previous night because she wanted to devote all her attention to Trevor without any disturbance. Her heartbeat stuttered when she saw the messages from Blake and Alexandra—a sense of foreboding washed over her as she read them, her mind racing with apprehension.

Blake: Something might be wrong with the baby. On our way to the hospital.

Two hours later.

Alexandra: Blake needs you. Can you come to the hospital as soon as possible?

Miranda didn't bother to check the other messages.

She rushed back to the living room, snatched her bag, and bolted through the door. On her drive to the hospital, she tried to call Blake and Alexandra, her heart pounding with each unanswered ring. She tried to not let her mind wander to worst-case scenarios, but the images kept flooding in, each more terrifying than the last. This was her best friend—her sister—and the thought of anything happening to Blake or the baby was unbearable. The drive passed in a blur of anxious thoughts and gripping fear. Twenty minutes later, she was threading her way through the maze of hospital corridors, her steps quick and purposeful. At the nurses' station, she hastily inquired about Blake's whereabouts. Armed with the information she needed, Miranda rushed to the elevators. The ride up felt as if it was the longest two minutes of her life. The elevator doors opened, and in her haste, Miranda ran straight into someone, almost toppling them both to the floor. But strong arms wrapping around her prevented what could have been a terrible fall. The familiar perfume she had grown accustomed to over the last few months filled her nostrils as she inhaled deeply to calm her racing heart.

Miranda shifted her head to meet Lane's intense gaze. They stood mere inches apart, their breaths mingling with each rise and fall of their chests. For a moment, Miranda remained frozen in Lane's arms, unable to pull herself away. Being this close to Lane, staring into her hazel orbs, Miranda felt as if she was being pulled into the deep lust lurking in them. Lane's eyes dropped to her lips, tracing their contours with a hunger that sent ripples down Miranda's spine. Slowly, Lane lifted her gaze back to Miranda's eyes. It had been months since

Lane had looked at her for the first time as if she wanted to devour her alive, yet even now, as Lane looked at her the same way as she did then, Miranda couldn't deny that the impact remained the same. The intensity of Lane's stare unnerved her, making her feel like she needed to escape a predator who would absolutely ravage her if she got too close.

"Dr. Hayes, I know you're worried about Blake, but please be careful not to cause any accidents. I wouldn't want anything bad happening to you, resulting in broken bones," Lane said, her hands still gently wrapped around Miranda.

Finally realizing their proximity, Miranda stepped back, granting herself some much-needed space. Though her words were casual, she detected a hint of concern in Lane's eyes. Since their last banter at the restaurant, they had only crossed paths twice over the past two weeks. Lane had been out of town at a medical convention, and Miranda had taken a few days off to spend time with Trevor before his trip. During that period, Miranda couldn't deny feeling Lane's absence keenly. It was as though she had grown so accustomed to Lane's antics that she had come to expect them, a realization that struck her as peculiar.

Miranda cleared her throat. "Sorry...," she started to apologize, then frowned. "Were you visiting Blake?" She knew Lane and Alexandra got along well—a fact she was still wrapping her head around given the way they had met—but she was surprised that Lane would make a personal visit to Blake's room, given how much she typically kept her personal life separate from her professional one.

"You sound surprised, Dr, Hayes." Lane cocked her

head to the side, scrutinizing Miranda's face. "Do you find it so hard to believe that I would take time out of my busy day to visit a colleague who has been hospitalized?"

Miranda sighed because she honestly didn't have the energy to banter with Lane. She needed to get to Blake and find out if something was wrong with the baby. And the truth was, more often than not, she still didn't know what to think of Lane. The woman was a paradox —one who didn't allow anyone at their workplace to get close to her, resulting in a slew of contradictory rumors about her. While some admired her no-nonsense approach and efficiency, others resented her strict standards and unwillingness to tolerate slacking off. The conflicting rumors about Lane only added to the mystery surrounding her.

"I know you love occupying my time to bring some excitement into your life, but I really don't have time to be your entertainment right now. Bye, Lane."

Miranda expected a sharp retort, but Lane's voice softened as she said, "She's strong and will get through this," her tone soothing, reminiscent of the gentleness she had shown when asking for her name at Josephine's.

This was precisely what puzzled Miranda about this woman. One moment, she could be as cold as ice, and the next, she exuded warmth and compassion. Miranda nodded in acknowledgment, sidestepped Lane, and continued to Blake's room. Pausing outside the door, she took a deep breath, willing her racing heart to calm down and summoning the strength she needed to support Blake. With resolve, she pushed the door open and entered to find Alexandra cradling Blake, her comforting words filling the room. As Blake lifted her head from Alexandra's shoulder, Miranda saw the depth of her worry, and her heart sank. Closing the door behind her, she approached the bed and rested a hand on Alexandra's shoulder, giving it a gentle squeeze.

Alexandra released Blake and rose from the bed, sadness leaking from every pore on her face. "Hey, Miranda. Thanks for being here. I'm going to update our parents while you two talk."

"Of course. I would have been here sooner, but my phone was on silent." She gave Alexandra a quick hug as she made her way to the door.

Blake watched Alexandra walk to the door, and Miranda could see the concern etched not just for their child, but also for Alexandra. Taking a seat on the bed, she gently clasped Blake's hands in hers. "What's happening with the baby?" she asked, her voice projecting more strength than she felt inside.

Blake drew in a deep breath, her eyes fluttering shut momentarily. "The baby is currently fine, but I have placenta previa," she murmured, her voice barely above a whisper as if she feared the weight of the words themselves.

Miranda's heart clenched at the intimate familiarity of the condition, understanding the risks it posed to both her friend and unborn child. She fought to suppress the rising tide of emotion, swallowing hard against the lump in her throat as she battled back tears. She knew she had to remain composed, steeling herself to be the pillar of strength that Blake needed in this moment of uncertainty.

"I'll be staying here until it's safe to deliver the baby or my condition changes and forces delivery," Blake continued, her voice faltering as tears welled up in her eyes.

"You have one of the best doctors in the world who I know will do everything to save your lives. I have faith you'll get through this and have a successful delivery. You're the strongest person I know, and you'll beat this thing, just as you have overcome every obstacle life has thrown at you." Miranda reassured with conviction. She reached out, gently wiping away the tear that had escaped the corner of Blake's eye. "Besides, lord knows I can't exist in this world without you. Who else would be the bestest friend a girl could ask for?"

Blake smiled weakly, but her expression quickly turned somber. "You're the one who is bestest friend anyone could have asked for. That's why if the worst should happen and I don't make it, I need you to promise to always be there for Alexandra."

Miranda understood the gravity of the situation and couldn't begin to fathom how much courage it had taken for Blake to speak those words. "You'll be fine. But I promise to always be there for Alexandra. I'll also be here with you every step of the way until it's safe to deliver the baby, or for whatever you need."

"Thank you," Blake responded, her voice strained with emotion. Despite her efforts to stay composed, tears spilled over her lashes and ran down her cheeks.

Miranda pulled her best friend into a tight hug, allowing her to silently cry on her shoulder. Their bond stretched nearly two decades, and she knew Blake's strength better than anyone. Miranda drew comfort from Blake's resilience, knowing her friend's love for Alexandra and their unborn child would fuel her fight. As Blake wept, Miranda couldn't help but reflect on the powerful love shared between Blake and Alexandra—a love that had stood the test of time and adversity. It was the same kind of love she aspired to have for herself, the kind she hoped to build with Trevor. While Blake and Alexandra's love had been a certainty from the start, Miranda believed that great love could manifest over different timelines for different people. She trusted that with time, she and Trevor would reach a point where she wouldn't hesitate to take the next step with him.

Chapter 17

Lane emerged from the car at Parkwood's entrance, the scene exploding into a chaos of flashing lights and relentless voices. Paparazzi swarmed around her, their cameras thrusting forward as they bombarded her with questions. With no escape from the frenzy, Lane steeled herself to confront the onslaught head-on. Even the alternative entrances to the hospital were besieged by paparazzi, leaving her with no choice but to brave the storm. A security guard rushed to her side, offering a welcome barrier against the persistent vultures she deemed among the worst humanity had to offer. Lane adjusted her sunglasses and tightened her coat around her, seeking some semblance of protection from the overwhelming clamor surrounding her.

"Miss Remington, are you having an affair with Gabriella? How long has it been going on?" one reporter shouted above the raucous, his voice amplified by the crowd's excitement.

Lane gritted her teeth and quickened her pace, ignoring the question as she walked briskly to the hospital entrance.

"Miss Remington, can you confirm Gabriella's sexual orientation? Is she a lesbian, bi, pan... Where does she fall on the spectrum?" another journalist yelled, thrusting a phone in Lane's face.

"Are you the reason Gabriella broke up with Thierry Gagne last year?"

The questions continued to relentlessly pierce the air, each one more intrusive than the last. Lane felt her irritation mounting, reminding her of the many reasons she hated the society they lived in. It was a world where revolting individuals like these creatures felt entitled to pry into someone's personal life simply because of their chosen career. Lane's jaw clenched tighter, her resolve hardening against the onslaught of invasive inquiries. For a brief moment, her steps faltered, but she quickly regained her composure, striding forward with renewed determination.

Arriving at the entrance, the automatic sliding doors parted to welcome her to the curious glances of her staff. Their hushed murmurs ceased abruptly as she strode past them to the elevators. Lane met the stares of those who dared to look at her, her eyes emitting an unyielding steel that bore into them, compelling them to swiftly lower their gazes. Did they believe she would cower from appearing at work? Or worse, walk with her head bowed as if she had committed some transgression or had reason to be ashamed? *I can bet they've been frothing at the mouth with eagerness to gossip about me.*

Reaching the elevators, Lane breathed a sigh of relief upon finding them empty. The last thing she needed was to endure an uncomfortable ride with employees who might offer well-intentioned but unwanted sympathy or, worse yet, pry into the chaotic state of her life with officious questions. Once the doors had closed, Lane took out her phone and tried to call Gabriella again, only to be greeted by the familiar sound of voicemail. With a frustrated sigh, she sent off another text message instead.

Lane: Call me, please. I just need to know how you're handling the situation.

Stepping out of the elevator, Lane found Miranda waiting there. She opened her mouth to offer a greeting, but the words caught in her throat as she registered the expression on Miranda's face. In the months they had known each other, Miranda had often regarded Lane with a mix of exasperation, annoyance, and curiosity, but there was something different in her eyes now—an icy detachment that Lane had never seen before. Even during their initial encounter, Miranda had retained a hint of warmth in her eyes when rejecting Lane's advances. *Ah. She must have seen the photos. But why does she seem so upset about them?*

Before Lane could address the tension between them, Miranda's words cut through the silence like a blade. "If it isn't the mystery woman who's had the media blowing up Parkwood's phones to learn more about her," Miranda accused in blatant sarcasm. "Couldn't you have waited until you were inside the house before shoving your tongue down Gabriella's throat? Or was it all part of a publicity stunt for her upcoming movie? After all, Hollywood is known for these things. People are willing to do anything for fame." The disdain in Miranda's words left Lane speechless, unsure how to respond to her unusual hostility.

On any other day, Lane might have relished the chance to engage in their usual banter, but today wasn't one of those days. "I've thought many things about you, Miranda, but being vindictive wasn't one of them," Lane responded, her voice calm but firm. "I know you enjoy our little dance, but I'm not in the mood to tango with you right now. This is someone's life the media is tearing apart for sport. While your comment about Hollywood is true, not everyone craves attention to the extent that they'd out themselves for publicity. You don't know anything about Gabriella—or me, for that matter—to make such assumptions."

"Well, given your track record, who can blame me for making such assumptions." Miranda's retort was sharp, like a sword parrying for another strike.

Lane's eyebrows furrowed, a flicker of frustration crossing her features. She took a moment to compose herself before responding, her voice measured but tinged with irritation. "And what track record is that, Dr. Hayes?"

"The one where all these months, you've been flirting with me relentlessly while you've been in a relationship all along, or whatever arrangement you have with Gabriella—considering the world thought she was straight," Miranda chastised, condemnation rumbling from deep within her—far from anything Lane had ever heard.

Lane's expression hardened at Miranda's accusation. The weight of her words floated around them, stirring a mix of emotions within her. She observed Miranda's tense demeanor, searching for clues in her expression. She couldn't understand why Miranda appeared so disturbed by the notion of Lane being in a relationship. She couldn't have been naïve enough to think Lane was celibate because she flirted with her. Lane paused, a realization slowly dawning on her as she considered

Miranda's reaction. *Is she... jealous? No way. She couldn't be jealous...could she?*

Regardless of her current state of mind, Lane couldn't resist the temptation to put her theory to the test. She knew she probably shouldn't be participating in this conversation, not with everything else resting on her mind, but there was an undeniable pull toward Miranda Hayes that she couldn't ignore.

With a boldness born of both desire and indignation, Lane closed the distance between them, her voice low and intimate as she spoke. "I love to fuck, Miranda. And until you decide to share my bed with me, I'll seek pleasure elsewhere," Lane murmured, her words coated with a teasing edge. Leaning in closer, she whispered, "But don't let jealousy consume you, Miranda darling." Lane edged forward, leaving just a paper-width space between them. "Just say the word, and I'll be at your mercy. You'll get to explore every fantasy you've ever harbored about me." Lane watched Miranda's reaction closely, noticing a flicker of confusion in her eyes as if she were genuinely surprised by the notion that she might be jealous. It was a curious reaction—one that only fueled Lane's desire to have Miranda Hayes in her bed.

Miranda suddenly stepped back as if she were repelled by the very idea of intimacy with Lane. With a derisive scoff, she said, "God, you're so full of it. What makes you think I would waste a single thought on you outside of this hospital, let alone fantasize about fucking you?" She squared off to Lane, raising herself to her full height. "If I wanted to fuck a woman, you'd be the last person on my mind. In fact, I wouldn't entertain the idea of fucking someone like you, who views women merely as vessels to fulfill your sexual desires." Miranda paused, her gaze unwavering as she continued. "You're everything I dislike about men, so I'd definitely not want to get into bed with you—to be just another conquest, another notch on your bedpost, only to be discarded like a rag doll come morning."

Miranda's harsh words struck Lane deeply, though she fought to conceal the hurt beneath her usual facade of indifference. But Lane was not one to suffer a blow without a retaliatory strike. "I happen to be the fantasy of many women, Dr. Hayes," she retorted sharply, her tone dripping with sarcasm. "After all, I do have one of the most renowned women in the world warming my bed whenever I desire." She cast a mocking glance over Miranda. "And judging by the fact that you're here, acting like a jealous girlfriend who was betrayed, it seems I might be your fantasy as well. You can deny it all you want, or perhaps you just haven't come to terms with it yet, but deep down... you... want... me." With a deliberate step, Lane closed the distance between them, lowering her voice to a dangerous whisper. "But let me make something clear. I only chase for so long, and when I stop, I don't ever turn back. So, don't wait too long to take advantage of what I've been offering, because it won't be on the table forever."

Miranda's glare hardened, distaste swirling in her hazel orbs. "Yes, sure. I should be so very grateful for the wonderful opportunity to have sex with you. Bye, Lane," the unmistakable mock rippling like a shockwave around them.

Lane remained silent, opting not to engage further. She had already expended enough energy on this pointless exchange. But for the life of her, she just couldn't avoid this damn woman who always seemed to know how to push her buttons. And right now, she was one sentence away from saying something she might regret. And she was still Miranda's boss even if both of them seemed to have forgotten that little tidbit of information while they stood in an open area where anyone could come along and hear them. Without another word, she stepped around Miranda and continued to her office.

Lane paused at her personal assistant's desk, bracing herself for the same reaction as other staff members, who had gawked at her as if she were some novelty. Surprisingly, Kelsey's demeanor didn't falter as she met Lane's gaze with staunch professionalism. "Good morning, Kelsey. Please hold all my calls until after the department meeting. Thank you."

"Good morning, Lane," Kelsey replied with a tentative smile. "Will do."

"How's your mother doing? I hope she's feeling better. If you need to leave early today, please don't hesitate to do so."

Kelsey's features softened with gratitude. "Thanks, Lane. She's doing much better. I think you need me more today. I'll do my best to ensure unwanted calls don't get through. I'm sorry about everything that's happening."

"Thank you. But if you need to go, don't hesitate. I'll manage just fine. Your mother's well-being takes precedence over shielding me from vultures."

"Okay." Kelsey nodded. "I'll see how the day unfolds and then decide."

Lane continued to her office, closing the door with a decisive click. She dropped her bag onto her desk with a resounding thud before sinking into her chair with a heavy sigh. Umbrage billowed within her, triggered by Nia's call earlier, disrupting her morning routine with news of leaked photos of her and Gabriella splashed across the internet. As she brooded over the situation, the sting of Miranda's words lingered, cutting deeper than any damn media scrutiny ever could. Lane prided herself on her indifference to public opinion, but Miranda's judgment held a different significance. It was a twisted irony that despite the futility of any potential relationship, she still harbored a ridiculous intense desire for the woman. It was as though some unseen force kept intertwining their paths, fueling Lane's desire even in the face of rejection.

The banter between them had been electric from day one—a constant dance of facetiousness and intellect that left Lane yearning for more. Miranda's sharp tongue and quick wit were like a drug to Lane, infusing her with a sense of exhilaration she rarely found elsewhere. In a world of mundane interactions—where people often bored her to death—Miranda's presence was a breath of fresh air, an intoxicating reminder of what it meant to truly connect with someone who wasn't offended by her personality. Not many people appreciated her blunt nature. People often wanted sugar-coated words and spun tales to soften the hard truth—Lane didn't have time for that.

Yet, in the wake of Miranda's acerbic remarks, Lane couldn't shake the unsettling notion that perhaps what she mistook for hidden attraction was simply Miranda's way of firmly stating she had no interest in someone like Lane. The very idea ignited a surge of fury within her, compounded by the fact that Miranda's judgment was unfounded. After all, Miranda didn't truly know Lane— her comparison to manipulative men felt unjust. Lane was many things, but she had never used a woman for sex. Women had always gravitated toward her and she had always been forthright about her intentions—never needing to manipulate or coerce like men often did. With a weary sigh, Lane reached for her phone, determined to focus on more pressing matters than dissecting her interactions with Miranda Hayes.

Lane opened Google, bracing herself for the latest onslaught of headlines regarding her association with Gabriella. Each gossip rag seemed to have concocted its own version of falsehoods about their relationship, each more sensationalized than the last. What grated on Lane's nerve even more was the betrayal from a few women she had dated, eager to gloat about sleeping with Hollywood's darling's "girlfriend". While deeply bothered by having her private affairs splashed across the media, Lane's primary concern lay with Gabriella. She couldn't shake worrying over how Gabriella was coping with being outed in that manner, especially considering her deep-seated fear of jeopardizing her career by coming out.

Despite the progress in societal attitudes, Lane knew all too well that Hollywood's prejudice against LGBTQ + actresses still persisted, often hidden beneath a veneer of progressivism. Many nights after intimacy, wrapped in each other's arms, Gabriella had confided her fears to Lane. She empathized and had been fine with accommodating Gabriella's wish to keep their affair discreet. Other than Anita, no one else knew the truth—not even Nia. To witness Gabriella's worst fears materializing was a gut-wrenching blow for Lane, igniting a fierce determination to shield her from further harm. Though their relationship was casual, Lane saw Gabriella not only as a lover but as a trusted friend, someone with whom she had shared private details of her life that she had never disclosed to any other woman she had dated. As Lane's thoughts spiraled in introspection, Gabriella's name flashing on her screen interrupted her train of thought.

Lane's thumb instinctively tapped the green icon. "Hey, are you okay?" she asked, concern etched in her tone as Gabriella's face filled her screen.

"Hi, sweetheart. I'm sorry it took me so long to reach out. It's been a whirlwind morning. I've been knee-deep in damage control with my team," Gabriella's voice carried traces of weariness and remorse, her eyes betraying signs of exhaustion. "I hate that you're being dragged into all of this. I know how much your privacy means to you."

"Don't worry about me," Lane reassured her. "What's the next step for you?" she inquired, wanting to know how she could support Gabriella through this ordeal. "How did they even get those photos of us? You said not many people knew where you were staying when you visited."

"Becca had assured me that the location was private. But when it comes to the media, we all know the levels they'd stoop to." Gabriella let out a frustrated sigh. "Rob is arranging a series of interviews and then we'll go from there. What's it been like on your end? I'm so very sorry for bringing the paparazzi to your doors." Lane could see the remorse in Gabriella's eyes as she continued, "Becca told me that many of the articles have been trying to dig up as much information about you as possible." Gabriella's eyes dropped, and she swallowed hard before whispering, "I'm sorry." When she looked back up, Lane saw guilt written all over her face.

Lane wasn't surprised by Gabriella's obvious guilt for dragging her into the spotlight because she knew how much Gabriella cared for her. "I'll be fine," Lane assured her, offering a comforting smile. "And apart from doing interviews, I'm here for whatever you need." Lane's voice softened with empathy. "I know this is incredibly difficult for you, but try to look at the bright side. Now you won't have to live in fear of someone discovering your true self. You can live your life openly and authentically."

Lane paused, her expression supportive yet pragmatic. "And if anything, you can be certain the LGBTQ community will stand by you. Hollywood will have to think twice about turning its back on you. You just have to ensure your team handles the situation in a way that shows it wasn't shame that kept your sexual orientation a secret, but a genuine fear for your career that you've worked so hard to build." Lane's voice carried a hint of resilience. "We all do what we must to survive in a world that hasn't always been kind to people like us."

Gabriella's smile brightened faintly through the weariness. "I wish you were here," she admitted softly. "Would you mind if I came to spend a weekend with you? It would be a relief to escape from all the chaos happening here."

"Absolutely, whatever I can do to support you through this," Lane responded without hesitation. "Just let me know as soon as possible so I can clear my schedule for you." A soft knock on Lane's door interrupted their conversation, prompting her to glance away from her phone. "I have to go now," Lane said reluctantly, meeting Gabriella's eyes on the screen. "I'll call you later. Everything will be fine."

"Okay. Bye." Gabriella said softly, blowing Lane a kiss before disconnecting the call.

Lane straightened in her chair, adopting her professional mask. "Come in," she called out, her voice steady and composed.

The door opened and Alexandra entered her office. "Hi Lane, do you have a minute?" she asked, closing the door behind her.

"Hi Alexandra, yes, I do," Lane replied, maintaining her composure as she watched Alexandra approach. She couldn't help but wonder if Alexandra's visit was prompted by dissatisfaction over Lane's media attention, potentially tarnishing the hospital's reputation. Since Blake had been hospitalized, Lane had taken great care to ensure Alexandra's workload outside of surgery remained light. Lane genuinely respected Alexandra, seeing her as one of the few people she truly liked. Having worked closely with her over the past few months, Lane understood why Blake had fallen in love with her. Since their interview, Lane had always found it easy to converse with Alexandra. It was rare to encounter someone who could handle brutal honesty and reciprocate it.

Alexandra settled into the chair opposite Lane. "How are you holding up?" The unexpected question caught Lane off guard. Her confusion must have been evident in her expression because Alexandra quickly added, "As someone whose personal life was also splashed across the front pages of almost every gossip magazine in the world, I understand it's not a pleasant experience or an easy pill to swallow."

Lane felt a sense of relief wash over her. The last thing she wanted was to explain her personal life to the woman who was technically her boss, since she owned the hospital. "I've weathered worse storms," Lane replied, her voice steady with resolve. "I'll manage. Hollywood has a short attention span—they'll move on to the next story soon enough."

Alexandra observed Lane for a moment, her gaze assessing. "You know, it's alright to not always be strong or feel the need to put on a brave front," she counseled gently. "It's okay to be vulnerable, Lane. And if you ever need to talk, I'm here to listen." Leaning forward slightly, Alexandra offered a small smile. "Until then, based on my experience with the media, the best advice I can give is to pull a Beyoncé."

Lane frowned in confusion. "A Beyoncé?"

Alexandra chuckled softly. "You know, just take a page from Beyoncé's playbook," she suggested. "Ignore the media, no matter what they say about you. She never dignifies their rumors with a response. Instead, she drops an album and eloquently puts all the naysayers in their place. Beyoncé lets her work speak for itself, rather than partaking in social media wars or feeling the need to explain herself to anyone."

"Ah. I see. Well, a strategy like that I can get behind," Lane responded with a nod. "I don't believe in explaining myself to people who are of no consequence to me either."

Alexandra rose from her chair. "Good. It's a waste of time to give people who contribute nothing positive to our lives an ounce of our time," she affirmed. "I have to get back to Blake, but I just wanted to check in on you. You've been doing an excellent job, so your well-being is very important to me. I truly appreciate you stepping in to ensure that my schedule was lighter so that I can be with Blake."

Lane's lips curved into a teasing smirk. "Who would have thought that one day you would be concerned about the well-being of the woman you wanted to throttle, because she dared to make a pass at your beloved wife?"

Alexandra laughed. "What can I say, Delaney Remington, you're an acquired taste. A woman with a heart of gold behind that armor of yours. One day, you'll meet someone who will shatter that armor of yours without you even realizing when it happened."

Lane chuckled. "I'll take that as a compliment. How's Blake doing?"

Worry creased Alexandra's features as her smile faded. "She's holding up as well as can be expected given the situation. Her blood pressure has remained steady over the last few days."

Lane nodded, her concern mirrored in her expression. "Well, I'm here for both of you if you need anything at all."

"Thank you. I'll see you later," Alexandra responded, offering a small nod as she turned to leave.

As Lane watched Alexandra walk to the door, a wave of contemplation swept over her. Would she ever find someone with whom she could share the same depth of love that Blake and Alexandra had for each other —who made her willing to sacrifice her freedom? Did she even desire such a connection? While she wasn't opposed to falling in love, it just hadn't happened with any of the women she'd dated. Fortunately for Lane, she didn't harbor a burning longing for an epic romance. From a broader perspective whether or not she had her own great love story seemed inconsequential. After all, she wasn't dissatisfied with her life—quite the opposite. Lane recognized that love wasn't a universal necessity for everyone and that happiness manifested in various forms for different individuals.

Chapter 18

"Did any of you know that she is a lesbian? So many women have come forward about their time together. I had absolutely no idea," James commented, his voice vibrating with excitement as he continued to scroll through articles on his phone. "I mean she hardly speaks to any of us outside of work-related matters, so I guess I'm not the only one who is surprised."

"Speak for yourself, James. Why should it be a surprise to any of us?" Allison interjected, her voice sharp with disapproval. "We shouldn't be concerned about who Lane chooses to sleep with. It's of no consequence in the grand scheme of things. If Gabriella was a man, I'm sure you wouldn't be asking if we knew she was straight, much less be surprised by it," she added, her voice now charged with annoyance.

James glanced up at Allison, his eyes widening with shock. "I didn't mean it like that, Allison. I'm just making an observation," he replied, defensively.

"Well, what you're saying isn't relevant or important," Allison retorted, her frustration with their colleague more evident. "I don't understand why society always makes it such a big deal about someone coming out as anything other than straight. You don't see the media picking apart someone's life for being heterosexual. It's time society realizes that being homosexual is just as normal as being heterosexual."

James rolled his eyes. "No need for all that. It's not about her being a lesbian," he countered. "It's just that we finally have some insight into her personal life, since we don't know much about her outside of these walls."

"You seem to forget that she doesn't owe any of us her private life," Allison defended vehemently. "She's doing an excellent job of running the hospital and that's all that matters, even if not everyone loves her no-nonsense approach."

"I must agree with Allison," Bradley chimed in. "While Lane may not be the friendliest of people with us outside of the necessary work-related conversations, she's leading us in the right direction to continuous growth."

"Well, tell that to the intern she fired last week for being late. The poor kid was sobbing on his way out the door," James reminded them with faux sympathy for the dismissed intern.

"He deserved to be fired for being late ten times in one month. That's not the type of behavior we want to encourage," Allison stated firmly.

Miranda listened to the conversation happening around her as they waited for Lane to appear for the weekly meeting, silently grateful that Allison was defending Lane against James' dimwitted comments. Irrespective of her current irritation with the woman in question, she agreed with Allison that Lane's sexual orientation shouldn't be a topic of discussion for her staff or the media. To Miranda, homosexuality should be seen as the natural order of things, just as heterosexuality.

Her mind drifted from the conversation to her

earlier confrontation with Lane. Miranda found her own behavior confusing. She couldn't understand why she had reacted the way she did. Perhaps Lane was right, and Miranda had acted like a jealous girlfriend who had been betrayed. She chalked it up to being annoyed by Lane's months-long flirtation, especially given the media's portrayal of Lane and Gabriella's long-term relationship. Miranda acknowledged that people engaged in open relationships, but Lane had never given any indication of being in a committed arrangement with anyone.

Miranda knew she shouldn't believe everything she read in the media, but the pictures were irrefutable evidence of the affair—images of Gabriella and Lane displaying clear affection for each other. They had stirred an unsettling feeling in the pit of Miranda's stomach. Almost every photo depicted them with their tongues down each other's throats, their passion evident. Gabriella licking ice cream off Lane's stomach by a poolside. Lane embracing Gabriella from behind on a balcony while kissing her neck. And as she had scrolled through the photos, each one seemed to stoke her anger further. But beneath her anger lay a bigger question. Why did she feel this way? Lane didn't owe her anything. Still, Lane had insisted she wasn't a cheater. So, why had she never mentioned being involved with someone if she was as honorable as she claimed? Miranda strongly disliked people who misled others about their relationship status. Still, despite her principles, why did she care so much?

What puzzled Miranda even further was the fleeting hurt that flashed in Lane's eyes when she had compared her to a lying, cheating man. Lane had recovered quickly, masking the emotion behind a veil of indifference, but Miranda had seen through it. In the heat of the moment, Miranda had felt justified in her anger, especially after Lane threw her relationship with Gabriella in her face, while in the same breath dared to tell Miranda that she still wanted to fuck her. However, upon reflection back in her office, Miranda's sense of justification waned. She realized her words had cut Lane deeply, and given the circumstances, maybe she had overreacted. Perhaps, worrying about Blake and the uncertainty surrounding her relationship with Trevor might have fueled her short-tempered response to Lane. She was many things, but Lane was right—Miranda wasn't a vindictive person. Lost in her musings, the opening of the boardroom door snapped Miranda back to the present. She looked up to see Lane enter, her expression impassive. Not a single emotion on her beautiful face betrayed how she felt about her life becoming the most talked-about topic in the media.

Lane strolled to her chair and gracefully settled into it. Glancing around the table, she made eye contact with everyone except Miranda. Miranda, however, recognized the act for what it was and couldn't help but admire Lane for not faltering under the scrutiny of her colleagues. Lane was well aware that they all must have seen the photos, and she intended to meet each of their gazes to convey her apathy to their opinions.

"Good morning," Lane greeted, her voice emanating nothing but cool professionalism. "I want to use the first thirty minutes to discuss my plans for revamping the internship program. Parkwood has always been a teaching hospital, and while Alexandra has made strides in restoring it to its former glory, there's only so much she could have accomplished in two years. We're training future doctors, so it's imperative that, whether or not they remain at Parkwood, we send out the best physicians into the world," she continued as she connected the projector cord to her laptop.

"I understand that we now live in a society where everyone seeks coddling, and the brutal truth is often considered unkind. However, our interns need to understand that once they step through these doors, people's lives are in their hands. If they can't handle the mental and physical demands of being a doctor while prioritizing patient care, then they need to consider another profession." Lane's gaze lifted to meet her staff, once again bypassing Miranda as her eyes scanned the room. "People's lives are no laughing matter, and those who can't take this profession seriously will be kicked from the program. I refuse to squander resources on interns who view this profession as merely a pathway to prestige…"

As Lane continued to speak, Miranda attempted to decipher her expression, but Lane remained an oracular figure as she seamlessly transitioned from one slide to the next, outlining a rigorous training plan that would have impressed Miranda when she had started as an intern at Parkwood twelve years ago. That was the thing though, Lane herself was an impressive CEO —she was so knowledgeable and proficient. While she maintained a professional distance from her staff, she was very hands-on with each area of the hospital's operations. It was no wonder that, at just forty, she was one of the most sought-after CEOs in the medical industry. Miranda couldn't help but acknowledge Lane's appeal—beautiful, charming, funny, and intelligent.

Lane possessed qualities that many would appreciate in a partner. It was easy to see why Gabriella would have been drawn to her.

And why am I even sitting here analyzing her? Oh yes, my stupid guilty conscience. I'll just apologize once this meeting is over.

"Is there anything else any of you would like to bring to our attention?" Lane's question snapped Miranda out of her reverie.

After a brief silence, James spoke up. "What do you intend to do about the paparazzi outside? They've been there all morning and it's not good for patients coming in and out of the hospital."

Miranda narrowed her eyes at James, knowing his question was asked from a place of provocation, intended to draw attention to Lane's personal life. She wished she could reach across the table and slap his smug face.

Lane's eyes slowly drifted to him, her expression bored. "What do you expect me to do about it? I'm not a member of the government who has the power to implement laws to prohibit vultures from terrorizing citizens. If you have a problem with their so-called right to freedom of the press, then I recommend you reach out to the offices of Gerrard Boucher. I believe he's the US representative for this district."

"But it's your drama that brought them here. So, maybe if you go outside and give them a statement, they would leave. I'm just concerned about the safety of staff and patients," James pushed, clearly toeing the line between being an asshole and a concerned staff member.

Lane relaxed back into her chair, her expression still

bored as she stared at James. "As far as I'm concerned, I don't owe the media or *anyone* an explanation about anything concerning my private life. And I'm not in the habit of feeding gossip mongrels. Now, it's obvious you don't have anything of consequence to update us on, so this meeting is adjourned. I don't believe in wasting time debating frivolous matters when I have a hospital to run."

Lane rose from her seat, signaling an end to any further discussion. Before Miranda could second-guess herself and lose her nerve, her mouth moved of its own accord. "Lane, may I have a minute before you leave?" she heard herself ask.

Lane paused after the first step, turning to face Miranda, finally holding her eyes since she entered the room. With a fluid movement, Lane lowered herself back into her chair, and they sat silently while waiting for the rest of their colleagues to exit the room. Once they were alone, Miranda found herself at a loss for words. She didn't know how to begin apologizing, especially when she didn't fully understand why she had reacted the way she did. Plus, knowing Lane, she would likely gloat if Miranda said anything that might imply she was remotely attracted to her, even when she wasn't.

"Dr. Hayes, I have better things to do with my time than to sit here waiting on your mouth to work. So, if you don't mind, could you please utilize the minute you asked for?" Lane's impatience sliced through the air like sharp ice.

Miranda gritted her teeth, suppressing the biting retort on the tip of her tongue as she contemplated abandoning her plan to apologize to this damn insufferable woman. However, she reminded herself that she was an adult capable of admitting when she was wrong and apologizing for it. "I just wanted to apologize for earlier," Miranda began cautiously. "My remarks were uncalled for, and I'm sorry."

Not one muscle moved on Lane's face as her eyes bored into Miranda with a coldness she had never seen before. "I don't need your apology, Miranda. You spoke what was on your mind. I have the power to decide whether or not I let your words affect me, so in hindsight, it doesn't matter."

Miranda opened her mouth to speak but before she could find words, Lane continued, her voice cool and detached. "But I'll say this to you for future reference, whenever you feel the need to judge the way I choose to live *my life*, without actually knowing who I am outside of these walls, or what you saw in the media… Even though I don't do relationships, I've never once misled a woman. I've always been upfront about my intentions. If I'm dating someone who lives in the same city as me, I only ever date that person until the arrangement no longer works for either of us. So, I don't appreciate you putting me in the same category as men who treat women like they're things that should be used and discarded as they see fit—I've never done that. Every woman who I've dated has always wanted a relationship with me. Not one left because I mistreated them or used them. They only left because I wasn't able to fall in love with them the way they did with me."

Lane got up from her seat and looked down at Miranda. "And since you dislike me so much, I'll do my best to stay out of your way unless we must correspond, because I'm your boss." Lane flicked her wrist and glanced at her watch. "Your minute is up. Have a good day, Dr. Hayes."

Without waiting for a reply, Lane opened the door and exited the room, leaving Miranda to grapple with the sting of her words. Miranda's mind raced as she struggled to understand why she felt as if someone had punched her in the gut. In fairness, Lane's harsh words were justified—they were a response to Miranda's actions. Still, Miranda had hoped for the Lane whom she had interacted with over the last couple of months, the one who would respond with something scandalous and charming, not this cold and harsh version she had just encountered—a version she had never been on the receiving end of before. She didn't understand why, but it deeply bothered her. Perhaps it was for the best that they stuck to strictly professional conversations.

Miranda sighed, finally finding the strength to rise from the chair. She worked her neck from side to side, trying to alleviate some of the stress lodged there—stress that had been accumulating since Blake was hospitalized and Trevor remained in New York longer than planned. Hopefully, with Trevor coming home this weekend, some of the tension would dissipate from her body.

Maybe Lane won't be so upset with me by then either.

Chapter 19

Miranda scanned the table one last time, confirming that every detail was impeccable. The soft glow of the candles cast a warm, inviting ambiance, and the delicate scent of fresh flowers filled the air. With a satisfied nod, she stepped back inside from the terrace, her heart fluttering with anticipation. The sun was beginning its descent, painting the sky in hues of orange and pink, setting the ideal backdrop for a romantic dinner. Trevor was on his way over, and she was determined to make the evening perfect. It had been a month since they last saw each other, and Miranda longed to reconnect with him in every way possible. They had much to discuss about their future, but tonight was about rediscovering their connection and savoring each other's company. Returning to the kitchen, Miranda checked on the simmering pot of chicken tagine, a dish she had meticulously prepared for Trevor. She didn't like cooking, but she had poured her heart into making something special just for him. Trevor always appreciated her efforts, and she wanted tonight to be no exception. With a contented smile, she turned off the stove and headed to her bedroom. She needed to grab a quick shower and change into the dress that would make it difficult for Trevor to focus on anything but her.

As Miranda reached the bottom of the staircase, the sound of the door opening caught her attention. She turned, her heart leaping with joy as Trevor stepped inside, closing the door behind him. A radiant smile lit up her face as she rushed to him, her eagerness palpable. In her haste, Miranda nearly collided with Trevor, throwing her arms around him in a tight embrace. He reciprocated, but his embrace lacked the usual warmth she was accustomed to. His body felt rigid against hers, his arms wrapping around her with a subtle hesitance. Undeterred, Miranda pressed closer, her lips seeking his in a tender kiss, hoping to ignite the familiar spark between them. Trevor responded, but the kiss felt restrained, lacking the fervor and passion they usually shared. Easing back, Miranda studied Trevor's expression, noting the shadow of sadness clouding his features. She held his gaze, searching for answers in his eyes, but the melancholy she found only deepened her concern. He was not a man who was happy to see his girlfriend after not seeing her for a month.

Miranda cupped Trevor's cheek, using her thumb to smooth out the muscle ticking in his jaw. "What's wrong?" she asked softly with genuine care and affection.

Trevor's expression remained somber as he stepped away from the doorway, gesturing for Miranda to follow him to the sofa. "Let's sit down, so we can talk."

"I made your favorite for dinner," Miranda offered, her voice laden with worry. She paused by the sofa, studying Trevor as he sat down, his demeanor still distant. "Do you mind if we talk while we eat? I just need to grab a quick shower."

Trevor shook his head. "I think it's best if we talk

first."

Disquiet settled in Miranda's stomach as she lowered herself beside Trevor, her eyes fixed on his face, attempting to gauge his mood. She knew him well enough to sense that something must be terribly wrong. He could hardly maintain eye contact and his body emitted so much tension it could have caused an earthquake.

Miranda folded her hands in her lap, pressing them against her stomach to calm the queasiness that had settled there. "Okay. Whatever you need."

"Where do you stand on us moving in together?" Trevor asked calmly.

Miranda frowned, her brows knitting together in confusion. "That's the first thing you want to discuss after not seeing each other for a month?"

"Yes, Miranda," Trevor replied resolutely. "Because it will determine how we move forward. I need to know if you're ready for the next step in our relationship so that I can plan my future accordingly."

Miranda's pulse quickened as shock and anger coursed through her veins. After weeks of separation, this wasn't the conversation she expected for their first night together. She understood the importance of discussing their future, but she had hoped for a more romantic start to their evening. Suppressing her rising emotions, she chose to remain calm. "Your future... I thought it was our future, since we're in this relationship together. And what exactly do you mean by 'determine how we move forward'?"

Trevor ran his hands through his hair, a sign of his frustration. He blew out a slow breath before speaking. "You know how much I love you, Miranda, but I can't keep waiting in limbo, uncertain about our future together. The time we spent apart gave me a lot to think about regarding my future and our relationship. And the truth is, our current situation isn't working for me anymore. You didn't even come out to New York once to visit me. With the new restaurant there, I need to know where we stand, so I can figure out how much time I should spend in New York."

"My best friend, who is like a sister to me, is in the hospital fighting for her life and the life of her baby. I needed to be here for her," Miranda explained, her voice marked with an undercurrent of anger. "I thought you understood when we spoke about it. I told you I'd take some time off from work during the week if you came home since you were mostly needed in New York on the weekends. I tried to meet you halfway."

"Yes, I understand, but you didn't even try to come, Miranda. Yes, Blake is your friend but I'm your boyfriend. I wasn't asking you to come there for more than a few days. If Blake's condition had changed while you were there, I would have used my family's private jet to bring you back immediately," Trevor countered. "But that's the past and it's our future that we need to discuss."

Miranda's heart thudded rapidly against her ribs, her stomach churning with dread as she forced herself to whisper, "Are you breaking up with me?"

"I've been doing a lot of thinking," Trevor said, his voice strained. "I think it's best to end things now, or at the very least until you're sure if you want a future with me."

The words hit Miranda like a blow to the chest and she struggled to process them. "What do you mean?

Just because I haven't moved in with you, doesn't mean I don't want a future with you. Our relationship is still new, Trevor."

Trevor shook his head, his expression pained. "I know, but I can't ignore how I feel anymore. Being apart put things into perspective for me and I just can't deal with the uncertainty anymore. Since you're not ready to move forward, I think it's best we part ways now to save us further heartache."

Tears welled up in Miranda's eyes as she struggled to contain the flood of emotions threatening to overwhelm her. "So, what you're saying is either I move in with you or our relationship ends?"

Trevor dropped his eyes to the space between them on the sofa. When he returned his gaze to Miranda, the emotions in them answered her question before he spoke. "If I ask you to move in with me right now, what will your answer be?"

The question hung in the air, suffocating Miranda with its implications. An ultimatum—in so many words, he was giving her an ultimatum. She felt like her world was crumbling around her, and what she needed to do to save it, she couldn't do. Yes, she could agree to move in with him, but at what cost? Moving in with him before she was ready would probably make her resent him, because she would only be doing it for him, and it would probably lead to them ending up right back at this point. He would probably see it as her not loving him enough to choose to save their relationship, but what he was doing was unfair. While it hurt that this was where they ended up, she knew deep down she had to do what was best for herself. Still, she didn't want to just give up on what they had.

"Can you just give us some more time? I just need more time. I don't want to lose you," she pleaded, her voice trembling.

Trevor reached across the space, gently taking her hand in his. His palm felt warm against hers, contrasting with the cold numbness overtaking her body. "You're doing what's best for you, Miranda, and I have to do what's best for myself. It's just sad that our best self-interests aren't aligned. I'm truly sorry, but I just can't give you any more time. But if you do ever reach the point where you want to fully be with me, if I'm available, I'll gladly try again with you. You're an exceptional woman and I wish things could be different, but I need to be with someone who is certain of their feelings for me."

Miranda shook her head, fighting hard to keep her tears from flowing. "My feelings for you have nothing to do with why I don't want to move in with you. I'm certain of my feelings for you and that I want to be with you."

Trevor smiled sadly. "They're not mutually exclusive, Miranda. If you were certain, then you wouldn't still be hesitating, even in the face of losing me."

With a heavy heart, Miranda whispered, "So, that's it then. Either I choose to move in with you or it's over?"

Trevor squeezed her hand and then released it. "I guess so. I'm truly sorry. I was hoping that you would choose us."

Miranda fought back the surge of anger rising within her, realizing the futility of directing it at him when she couldn't give him what he wanted. "I'm sorry too. I was hoping that I was worth waiting for."

Trevor's sigh carried the weight of disappointment

as he spoke. "And I wasn't worth taking a leap for." Leaning across the sofa, he enveloped Miranda in a tight embrace, holding her close for a moment. "I'm sorry," he whispered, pressing a gentle kiss to the side of her head. Releasing her, he stood, his gaze lingering on her with a mix of sadness and resignation. "Goodbye, Miranda. Take care of yourself."

Miranda stared at his handsome face, her heart breaking with every passing moment. She desperately wanted to tell him that she would move in with him, to salvage what was left of their relationship, but the words seemed to stick in her throat. In the end, all she managed was a barely audible whisper, "Goodbye, Trevor."

Trevor nodded silently, staring at Miranda for a brief moment before he turned toward the door. Miranda didn't dare to look back as she heard the soft click of the door closing behind him. The sound was like a key to the floodgates she had been desperately trying to hold shut, and with his departure, her tears finally spilled over her cheeks. Curling up into a ball on her side, Miranda surrendered to the waves of emotion crashing over her. She cried, the sobs wracking her body as she grappled with the turmoil of her shattered relationship. While she wasn't ready to move in with him, she cared deeply for him and really wanted things to work out for them. But she was old enough to know that if she had agreed to move in together just to appease him would have been a mistake.

As the tears continued to stream down her face, Miranda couldn't help but question herself. At thirty-seven, shouldn't she have figured out what she wanted by now? Why was it so hard for her to find the epic romance she had always dreamed of? She believed in love, in the kind of love that sweeps you off your feet and makes you want to throw caution to the wind. But somehow, it always seemed to elude her grasp. What was wrong with her? Why couldn't she get it right? Why couldn't she find someone who made her heart race and her pulse quicken with just a glance? With each passing moment, the weight of her loneliness felt heavier, suffocating her with its crushing grip. Miranda cried until exhaustion finally overtook her, pulling her into a deep and dreamless sleep. In the darkness of her slumber, she prayed that when she woke, it would all have been nothing more than a nightmare.

An hour later, Miranda jolted awake to the persistent ringing of her cell phone. With a heavy sigh, she fumbled for it on the table across from her, wincing as the dull ache in her head intensified. "Hi, Mom," she greeted, her voice betraying the strain of her emotions despite her efforts to sound composed.

"Sweetheart, Blake's placenta ruptured, and they have to deliver the baby now. Alexandra tried calling, but you weren't answering. Your father and I are on our way to the hospital," Caroline's voice trembled with concern as she relayed the distressing news.

Miranda sprang from the sofa, her heart racing with worry. "I'm on my way," she urgently assured her mother.

"Please drive safely, sweetheart," Caroline advised with a hint of apprehension in her tone.

"I will. I'll see you there," Miranda affirmed before ending the call and rushing into the kitchen to grab her keys.

Regardless of the turmoil in her own life, Miranda's

priority was now her best friend and niece, both of whom were in danger—she needed to be there for them. She could deal with her emotions later, once Blake and the baby were safe. As for Trevor, perhaps there was still hope to salvage their relationship. Sometimes, after a break-up, people realized they couldn't bear to be apart and found their way back to each other. Alternatively, maybe her path forward didn't include Trevor. Perhaps her true happily ever after awaited her with someone else, someone with whom she would find what she was searching for. Maybe love would find her when she least expected it, opening a new chapter in her life. But right now, Blake was her sole priority and it was the fear of losing her best friend that consumed her as she burst through her front door, hoping and praying that Blake would survive.

Chapter 20

"God, you're incredible," Gabriella purred, her fingers tracing lazy patterns on Lane's stomach.

Lane glanced at her with a teasing smile. "What made you come to that conclusion, Miss Mancini?"

Gabriella trailed her fingertips from Lane's stomach to her mouth, using her thumb to outline Lane's bottom lip. "The things you do to me with this mouth of yours, for instance," she murmured. "I've been with my fair share of women, and none please me quite like you do, Delaney. Plus, you're not clingy and don't need my attention 24/7. Even though our relationship has been casual, with either of us free to date other people, you've always been here for me whenever I needed you, without expecting anything in return." Gabriella smiled, her eyes brimming with affection. "And did I mention that you're an amazing lover?"

I'm glad someone thinks I'm amazing since Miranda Hayes thinks I'm despicable. The gall of that woman. Ugh. I really need to stop dwelling on how she views me. She doesn't know me, so it shouldn't matter, especially when there's no chance of me kissing that judgemental look off her beautiful face. What is it about this damn woman that seems to erase all my self-control? I can't seem to refrain from interacting with her, even when I know I shouldn't. But after those hurtful words. I really need to. No more flirting. No more banter.

"Sweetheart where did you go?" Gabriella asked, tapping Lane on her ribs.

Lane shook her head. "Nowhere."

"I know you don't share much about yourself with me, but you know you can tell me anything. I want to be more for you," Gabriella said, her voice carrying a trace of longing.

Lane turned to face her, catching the wistful expression in Gabriella's eyes. It gave her pause, inducing her to study Gabriella's face more intently. Their relationship had always been physical—pure carnal desires—devoid of deep emotional connections. Friendship, yes, but nothing deeper. Yet, there was something different in Gabriella's eyes now, something that made Lane cautious. She hesitated, unsure of how to respond. While she had noticed subtle hints of this before, it now felt more pronounced.

Deciding to tread carefully, Lane chose not to address the underlying emotions directly. "You give me everything I need from you and then some," she replied, attempting to maintain the status quo of their relationship.

"But don't you want more?" Gabriella's question swirled in the air, laden with unspoken meaning.

Lane considered her response carefully. "That's a very open-ended question. Explain more," she encouraged, preferring clarity over assumptions.

Gabriella took a deep breath before exhaling slowly. "Like a relationship. You know. Someone to love and for them to love you. Not meaningless flings with a deadline stamped on them from the start."

Lane pondered the statement for a moment. A year

ago, her immediate answer probably would have been no—she didn't want more than casual relationships. But since being in Seattle, and even before that, she had been feeling off. It was as if the way she lived her life wasn't enough anymore—like something was missing. At first, she dismissed it as boredom, but now she wasn't so sure. Overall, she liked her life the way it was. She relished the freedom to do as she wished without worrying about anyone else's feelings. She could just get up and go anywhere in the world for work without worrying about the impact on her partner. Moreover, she genuinely enjoyed meeting a new woman and the excitement that came with the novelty of dating. Lane loved women and wasn't sure if she could commit to only one for the long haul. She firmly believed in offering only what she could give.

She chose to defer answering. "Does our arrangement not work for you anymore, Gabriella? You know I'll understand if you want to end things between us."

Gabriella sighed, eased up on her elbow and looked down at Lane. "That's not what I asked you, Delaney. But, no, I don't want to end things between us." She paused, uncertainty crossing her features. "I was hoping you'd consider trying for more with me. Give us a chance to date exclusively and see where it goes. I know that with me being in the closet in Hollywood, there was no chance to pursue a relationship with you, because you told me from day one you could never be in a committed relationship with someone who was in the closet. So, now that everything is out in the open, I want to know if you're willing to try with me."

Lane attempted to answer, but Gabriella placed a finger on her lips. "Don't answer now. Think about it.

I know it's a lot to consider. But there's no one else I'd rather have my first openly lesbian relationship with. It will be a huge adjustment for either of us, but we can take it slow. Keep the lines of communication open as we always have." Gabriella sat up, dropped a chaste kiss on Lane's lips and hopped off the bed. "I really need to use the bathroom."

Lane's eyes tracked Gabriella's curves as she sashayed into the bathroom, her mind slowly processing Gabriella's request. Gabriella's words surprised Lane because, since the day they had met and started sleeping together, Gabriella had never once alluded to wanting more than what they shared. They were both career-driven, and their arrangement—seeking physical comfort from each other—worked perfectly over the years with their schedules. But the sincerity in Gabriella's words proved she was serious. The least Lane could do was consider what she asked. After all, she was forty, and maybe it was time she tried committing to one woman. Still, it seemed Gabriella's feelings had grown into something more, and Lane didn't want to get her hopes up, only to hurt her later by realizing she couldn't commit.

Plus, Gabriella lived in L.A., and Lane didn't see herself moving back there anytime soon. At this point, she wasn't even sure if she would remain in Seattle. Lane had moved back to take care of Anita, but since she insisted on staying in the assisted living facility, Lane wasn't needed as much as she thought she would be. Though it was nice to spend time with Anita every week, and Nia, too. They were the only family she had, so being close to them over the last few months was nice. Other than them, she had no reason to remain in Seattle, especially since her role at Parkwood wasn't as challenging as she thought it would be. The hospital didn't need saving—one of her main reasons for applying for the job—she only had to lead it into increased and consistent profitability. But she missed the challenge that came with taking over a hospital that needed to be saved—doing what others before her failed to do.

Maybe that was her problem. She viewed dating the same way she viewed her career—she enjoyed the challenge of meeting someone new and the excitement that came with fucking a woman for the first time. Just like her job, she often grew bored when dating a woman for longer than a few months. However, Gabriella was the exception. Spending time intermittently over the years had prevented boredom, and in many ways, Gabriella had become a friend as well as a lover. Perhaps it wouldn't be such a bad idea to try with her. If it didn't work out, at least they both understood the terms of their arrangement. It was worth considering, especially since Gabriella had been honest about her feelings. And who knows, maybe this could be the start of something meaningful for both of them.

Lane sighed. It was too early for such deep introspection before her first cup of coffee. She reached for her phone on the bedside table, only to realize she had grabbed Gabriella's phone instead of her own. As she moved to put it back, a message notification from Gabriella's manager popped up on the screen. Lane frowned as she read the part of the message that briefly appeared. She would never intrude on anyone's privacy by reading their messages, but the context in which her name was mentioned sent off alarm bells in her mind. She thought about asking Gabriella to explain the message, but hesitated—she didn't want to make something of it if it was nothing. Still, she needed to appease her mind. She decided she would just read that message and, if it was nothing, let it go. She knew Gabriella's phone code because Gabriella had given it to her when Lane's phone fell into the toilet and she needed to use Gabriella's. However, Lane prided herself on being honest and above board, and she didn't feel right about invading Gabriella's privacy.

Just as she attempted to return the phone to the bedside table, another message popped up on the screen. This time, she could no longer deny herself—her moral code be damned. Lane's fingers flew over the screen, and as she read the messages, she felt anger surge through every fiber of her being.

Rob: Everything is going according to plan. Did you get Delaney to agree to date you openly? You know how people love a good love story. Your fans already love the idea of the two of you together. They find her mysterious aura seriously hot. Getting her to agree to accompany you to the premiere would be a bonus.

Rob: Are you sure you don't want to have some pictures of this weekend together leaked? I know you're not fully comfortable with this path, but this is Hollywood, and you have to do what you have to do to stay ahead of the game. Call me to discuss logistics.

The bathroom door opened and Lane looked up to find Gabriella's smile fading as soon as she saw Lane's expression. "Is everything okay?" she asked with both concern and nervousness. "What are you doing with my phone?" she continued as she drew closer to Lane.

Lane handed her the phone with the opened messages. "Do you mind explaining your manager's messages?" she requested calmly.

Gabriella took the phone, her face draining of color as her eyes scanned the screen. She looked up at Lane, guilt and remorse visible in her expression. "Delaney... I can explain. I know it looks bad... but please, let me explain."

Disappointment and anger thrummed within her, but Lane had honed the skill of concealing her emotions over the years, revealing vulnerability only when she chose to. She suppressed those feelings and assumed her impassive mask. With a wave of her hand, she signaled for Gabriella to explain. "And please do me the honor of at least being honest. The last thing you want to do right now is insult my intelligence."

Gabriella nodded, perched on the edge of the bed and clasped her hands tightly in her lap. "First, you must know that I never intended to hurt you. I care for you too much to ever do that."

"Please spare me the platitudes," Lane interjected, her tone dismissive. Gabriella swallowed hard, tears welling up in her eyes. Lane couldn't help but wonder if the emotional turmoil she was witnessing was all just a performance. After all, Gabriella was a brilliant actress.

"As you know, Rob and Andrea are aware of my sexual orientation, and they've done everything to keep it under wraps because, in their eyes, a lesbian often doesn't land leading roles in Hollywood, especially if they're required to play a straight character. I'm thirty-five and I'm just tired of hiding," Gabriella explained. "So, I told them as much. They asked why now, and I told them I'm in love with you and I needed to give us a chance to be together before I lose you."

Lane almost flinched at the use of the word love, but managed to keep her expression neutral.

"They agreed that coming out now wouldn't be the right time, especially since I'm at the peak of my career," Gabriella continued. "But I told them I no longer wanted to choose my career over happiness. So, they came up with a plan to ensure my coming out coincided with my movie premiere. I told them I couldn't use you like that, but traction for the movie was lower than expected, so in the end, I decided to go along with their plans. After all, if I was going to come out, why not try to benefit from the publicity? There was nothing I could do to prevent the media from digging up my personal life anyway."

Gabriella dropped her eyes, shaking her head. "I know it sounds bad, and it was wrong of me not to ask you if you would be okay with being in the spotlight like that, especially given how much you value your privacy. After the first set of photos leaked, I felt sick to my stomach each time I thought about you. But it was done, and I felt a huge weight lifted off my shoulders at not having to hide anymore. Rob wanted to take more pictures this weekend, but I told him absolutely not." Gabriella's voice trembled. "I'm so very sorry. Please know that despite everything, I did it for us because I truly want a future with you."

"For us? First of all, there would have to be an 'us' for you to claim you did anything for 'us'," Lane replied, her voice remaining deadly calm despite the emotions beneath the surface. She flung the sheet off her body and rose from the bed. "Second of all, if there was an 'us', then you wouldn't have betrayed me like this. If you truly love me as you claim, then you wouldn't have used me this way." Lane scanned the room for her clothes and began getting dressed.

"Please don't leave like this. Can we just talk about it some more?" Gabriella pleaded desperately.

Lane continued putting on her clothes, struggling to keep her anger in check. She wasn't going to be all sad and weepy about what happened—she didn't have high expectations of humans. From a very young age, she had seen the ugliness that came with humanity. Throughout her life, she had witnessed how cruel people could be, and at her age, nothing surprised her anymore. She expected them to be disappointing. Still, there were few people she allowed to get close to her because she trusted them to always be honest with her, and Gabriella was one of them.

Closing the button on her pants, Lane met Gabriella's gaze, now filled with tears. "In your plotting and scheming, did you ever once consider asking if I'd be willing to help you with your plan to come out?"

Gabriella sniffled and shook her head. "No, because I know you wouldn't have agreed to it. You're a very discreet person and wouldn't appreciate the attention."

Lane smiled ruefully. "And there you have it. So how can you sit there and tell me that you never intended to hurt me, yet you proceeded to do something that you knew I wouldn't have agreed to if you had asked me."

Gabriella's tears flowed down her cheeks now, pain and regret palpable in her eyes. But as Lane stared at the woman she had expected better from—someone she deemed a friend in many ways—she couldn't discern whether Gabriella's tears were genuine, born from a fear of losing Lane, or if it was all an act.

Gabriella rose from the bed and closed the distance between them, reaching out to take Lane's hand. "I'm truly sorry for hurting you," she whispered.

Lane withdrew her hand sharply. "Please, don't touch me," she replied with lethal calm.

She moved around the bed to retrieve her phone, scanning the room to ensure she hadn't left anything behind. Satisfied that she had everything, she headed to the door. Pausing with her hand on the doorknob, Lane glanced back at Gabriella. "I'm not hurt. I'm just disappointed," she said quietly. "Take care of yourself, Gabriella. I wish you all the best with your coming-out story. You can confirm with Rob that I won't be joining you on the red carpet. And let your team know they don't have to worry about me going to the media. Please don't contact me again."

Gabriella let out a soft cry and stepped toward Lane. "Delaney, please…"

Lane steeled herself against the hurt in Gabriella's voice and closed the bedroom door, cutting off any further pleas. She grabbed her bag from the sofa where she had left it the night before and made her way to the front door. Stepping outside, the cool morning air offered a welcome relief, and she took in a lung full, hoping it would help soothe her broken spirit. They had chosen to meet at a cottage on the edge of a lake, away from prying eyes, and now as Lane walked to her car, the scenery around her offered little comfort. She knew that, like every other disappointment in life, this too would pass. All she had to do was keep moving forward. People were who they were, and she couldn't change that. The only thing she could control was her reaction to being let down by them. And as always, she chose to cut them off and move on—it was as simple as that. But regardless of her resolve, the loss of someone she had cared about for ten years still stung. Lane couldn't help but feel the weight of that loss, reminding herself that no matter how strong she was, she couldn't deny being human and the ache that came with it.

Chapter 21

Miranda studied Lane while she waited for her to finish a call. They hadn't seen much of each other over the past two weeks since their argument about Lane's relationship with Gabriella. The few times their paths crossed, Lane had treated Miranda like any other employee—professional and distant. Gone were the playful banter and suggestive glances that used to characterize their exchanges, replaced by a demeanor void of any personal connection. It was as if Lane no longer found Miranda intriguing or worthy of her attention. The change in Lane's behavior toward her was palpable, her once warm gaze replaced by a chilly detachment that struck Miranda like a sharp jolt, leaving her puzzled and unsettled. She had expected to feel relieved at the absence of Lane's admiration, but instead, she found herself strangely missing their usual interactions. She couldn't quite explain it, but Lane's flirtatious nature had become a familiar part of their routine, and its sudden absence left a void. She assumed it was natural to miss something that you had gotten accustomed to.

What perplexed her, even more, was how much she was bothered by Lane's attitude. Didn't she know how to forgive and move past mistakes? Didn't she know how to accept an apology? For someone who had professed attraction to Miranda, Lane's interest sure seemed to have evaporated overnight. But whatever, it shouldn't matter—she had her own issues to deal with. For one, she hadn't spoken to Trevor since he walked out her door. He hadn't reached out, and since she couldn't give him what he wanted, she thought it best not to give him false hope by calling him to talk. His patience had run out with her, and there was nothing she could do about it, apart from agreeing to move in with him. But more than anything, her heart was hurting because her best friend was currently in a coma from complications during her C-section. Miranda felt adrift with worry for Blake, Alexandra, and their daughter. She just couldn't fathom the thought of Blake not waking up. She was one breath away from breaking down due to the stress she felt, barely hanging on by a thread.

However, she had promised Blake she would be there for Alexandra if anything should happen to her. Therefore, when Alexandra asked her to step into the chief of surgery role, there was no way she could have said no, knowing that Alexandra needed to take time off to care for Amara and deal with the additional stress of Blake being in a coma. That was how she ended up sitting across from Lane in her office, waiting on her. Now that Miranda was chief of surgery, it required them to work more closely than before. While it chafed that Lane was giving her the cold shoulder, she had to remain professional in her role. Still, the damn woman frustrated her with her ever-present blank stares that lacked the warmth usually reserved just for Miranda.

Not warmth, but lust. She only ever looked at me with unbridled lust. But why do I care though? I should be glad to not be on her radar.

Lane removing the phone from her ear broke Miranda's introspection. She fixed her steely hazel eyes on Miranda, her expression inscrutable. "Dr. Hayes, sorry for keeping you waiting. Given the circumstances of your promotion, if you need some time off before stepping into the role, I can manage your duties until you're in a much better frame of mind to return to work. I know how much Dr. Westmore means to you, so I understand if you need the time off."

Is this her way of asking how I'm dealing with Blake's condition? Showing me that she cares despite still being royally pissed off at me? Whatever it was, Miranda needed an icebreaker from the unfriendly tension that surrounded them.

"Am I correct to assume that since you're offering to double your workload on my behalf, you've finally accepted my apology?" Miranda asked neutrally, pushing for genuine clarity because she honestly didn't know what Lane's motives were.

Lane's gaze remained fixed on Miranda's, leaving her yearning to decipher the thoughts hidden behind those eyes. "It's about ensuring the well-being of an employee through a trying ordeal," Lane said, her monotonous syllables as emotionless as the professional poker face she had in place. "Surely, you're familiar with the robust mental health initiatives spearheaded by Alexandra. I'm simply extending the same support I would offer to any employee in similar circumstances. While I would suggest delegating to another colleague, Allison has stepped in for Blake, and considering the impending number of surgeries, I prioritize having our surgeons in the operating room rather than bogged down by paperwork. Besides yourself and Allison, there's currently no one else I'd recommend for the role, given the hospital's current needs."

Miranda felt the sting of Lane's detached response like a sudden slap across her face. Before she could contain her rising irritation, her words spilled out impulsively. "Are you planning to be upset with me forever? Treat me as if I'm merely someone you begrudgingly tolerate because of our professional proximity. I've admitted my mistake and apologized. Don't you understand the concept of forgiveness and moving forward?" Miranda struggled to keep the vitriol out of her voice. Because seriously, what was Lane's problem?

Lane's head tilted slightly to the side, her expression remaining impassive. "Dr. Hayes, I'm simply adhering to the standards of professionalism I uphold with all employees," she stated evenly. "I assumed that was your preference. And just because you've offered an apology doesn't automatically necessitate my acceptance of it. My acceptance isn't something you're entitled to."

"You've never treated me like any other employee. You've always..." Miranda's voice trailed off as she struggled to articulate her thoughts. Because why did it matter? She should be content with a strictly professional relationship. Why did she care if this damn insufferable woman ignored her, or no longer glanced at her with a teasing smirk.

"I've always, what, Dr. Hayes?" Lane's question landed with the precision of a programmed response, akin to dealing with a robot designed to push Miranda to the brink of madness.

Miranda inhaled deeply, steadying her frayed nerves.

She was here to do a job and whether or not this woman was friendly toward her shouldn't matter as long as they maintained professionalism to get the job done. "It doesn't matter. Let's just get on with the reason for our meeting."

"Why are you so upset, Dr. Hayes?" Lane's voice carried a hint of curiosity, almost clinical in its detachment. "I was under the impression that a strictly professional relationship was all you wanted from me. Considering your apparent distaste for my character, shouldn't you be grateful for the current state of our interactions?"

This damn woman is impossible. Miranda gritted her teeth, her frustration simmering beneath the surface. "Maybe you're right. If this is how you choose to behave, then so be it," she retorted, sitting up straighter in her chair, her resignation set in the tension of her shoulders. With a firm touch on her laptop screen, she brought it to life. "Let's proceed with our *strictly professional* meeting, shall we?"

With a dismissive gesture, Lane shifted her focus to her own laptop screen. "We have a lot to cover," she began, her voice brisk and businesslike. "I need you to review the proposal for implementing automated dispensation robots and assess its potential impact on our staff. Alexandra was supposed to offer her insights on this venture, but since she hasn't, I'll need you to familiarize yourself with the proposal and provide your feedback as soon as possible."

Irritation skirted along Miranda's veins like a current. "Understood. I'll make it a priority," she replied tersely, matching Lane's robotic professionalism with her equally clipped formality.

Lane's sharp, greenish-gold eyes bore into her, their intensity palpable. "I'll provide you with a high-level overview, outlining the rationale behind my decision and the objectives I aim to accomplish through this approach."

Miranda nodded, mentally fortifying herself to focus on Lane's words, determined not to let the sting of Lane's attitude distract her. After all, her feelings shouldn't be bruised because they weren't even friends. Their dynamic mostly consisted of Lane's flirtations, especially outside of the hospital, where chance encounters seemed far too frequent. It was as if Seattle had somehow shrunk since Lane's arrival, leading them to cross paths more often than expected. Maybe it was just the stress of her failed relationship and worry for Blake causing her to be emotional. Still, why did she feel this emptiness settle over from Lane's harsh treatment? Thirty minutes later after being briefed on what was required of her, Miranda rose from her chair, feeling even more disheartened than when she entered Lane's office.

She stared at Lane who was watching her with that familiar blank stare. "Have a good day, Lane," she uttered softly before turning to leave.

Lane remained silent until Miranda's hand rested on the doorknob. "Dr. Hayes," she called out, prompting Miranda to glance back at her. "My offer still stands. If you require time off to cope with Blake's coma, I'm here to assist with your workload." Lane's tone retained its business-like quality, yet there was a glimmer of softness, an undercurrent of genuine concern woven into her words.

Miranda simply nodded, suddenly feeling too

drained to put any more meaning behind Lane's mercurial behavior. She decided to take Lane's words at face value, accepting that she was being offered the same support any other employee would receive—not because Miranda held any special significance to her. "Thank you," she murmured as she opened the door and stepped out of the office.

Rounding the corner toward Alexandra's office—which had now become hers—Miranda caught the murmur of voices coming from the nearby supplies closet. The voices belonged to Melanie and Kelsey, her and Lane's personal assistants. Recognizing Lane's name, she paused, curiosity piqued, and silently eased closer to listen in on the conversation.

"Why were you so pissed off with Derek today at lunch? You literally bit his head off when he mentioned Lane," Melanie asked.

"Because he was talking shit about her, which simply isn't true. Just because she doesn't stroll around the hospital flashing smiles at everyone and gossiping, doesn't mean she's a horrible boss," Kelsey replied with indignation. "Not everyone, including myself, likes small talk. Most of those who have negative things to say about her are simply disgruntled because she doesn't tolerate their nonsense and holds them accountable for doing the job they're paid to do."

"I haven't had many interactions with her, but whenever she stops by Alexandra's office, she's always pleasant with me," Melanie chimed in. "I mean, we don't have lengthy conversations, but she always says hello."

"Yes, she's pretty reserved, but she's one of the best bosses I've ever had. I didn't tell you this before, but when my mom was sick, she gave me time off to take care of her without me even having to ask her. When I returned, I expected my work to be backed up, but she pretty much handled everything herself. I know what her day is like, so I know it must not have been easy for her to manage without an assistant. She also treats the ancillary staff with a lot of respect. I've been around many execs who treated their PAs and the cleaning staff like shit. Lane is a good person behind the hard exterior that everyone else is focused on, instead of seeing all the good she is doing," Kelsey said.

"We know how people in this place like to gossip, especially when they don't know anything about you outside of work. They're all probably even more pissed because they can't just waltz up to her and pry into her personal life. Guess that's why they were all so happy to see those pictures of her and Gabriella," Melanie added.

"People are just assholes." A drawer slammed shut. "We should get back. I think her meeting with Dr. Hayes should be ending any moment now," Kelsey stated.

Miranda hurried away from the door, not wanting to risk being caught eavesdropping. She decided to take a walk to The Junction for a coffee, hoping the fresh air would help clear her head. Briefly, she entertained the idea of asking Lane if she wanted an Americano, but quickly dismissed it. It was obvious that Lane was still upset with her, and it was best to respect her boundaries. Strolling to the elevators, Miranda mulled over the conversation she'd overheard between their assistants. She was a bit surprised that Lane's assistant held her in such high regard since Lane kept her staff at a distance. Though to be fair, Lane was always professional when interacting with staff and keeping people at arm's length didn't equate to being a horrible boss. She had also witnessed firsthand how Lane interacted with the cleaners and cafeteria workers, always polite and respectful. Kelsey was right—there was undoubtedly so much more to Lane than what met the eye.

Unfortunately, at this point, it seemed that Miranda wouldn't have the chance to delve deeper into the woman behind the professional veneer. It was clear that Lane no longer desired any interaction with her beyond their strictly professional relationship.

Chapter 22

Lane stared at her reflection in the window, the overcast sky mirroring her mood. For some reason, she couldn't shake the funk she had been in since the whole Gabriella debacle. Gabriella had called her multiple times and sent messages begging Lane to forgive her, but each call went to voicemail, and Lane deleted the messages without opening them. She didn't trust many people, but she had trusted Gabriella. And to be used in such a way made Lane lose every ounce of respect she had for her. As far as she was concerned, Gabriella no longer existed to her. She wasn't perfect by any means, but she despised dishonest people and those who used others as a means to an end without considering how their actions affected them. Yes, she would have said no to the staged photos if Gabriella had been forthright, but she would have supported her if she had chosen to share her coming-out story authentically. That's what friends did. Instances like these were one of the main reasons she didn't have many friends. It was so hard to find genuine people who truly understood the meaning of friendship. She had learned a long time ago that not many people understood loyalty and that friendship was a commitment just as strong as an intimate relationship.

Usually, Lane found it effortless to move on when

people disappointed her, but since leaving the cottage, she had been in an unshakeable foul mood. Even her usual outlets—a beautiful woman in her bed — for relaxation held no appeal. Instead, she found herself stuck in a monotonous routine of work, home, and occasional outings with Nia or visiting Anita. But if Lane were to be truly honest with herself—and she always endeavored to be—she knew that the primary source of her peculiar mood was the tension between herself and one, Dr. Miranda Hayes. Their close working relationship in recent weeks hadn't been easy, especially with Lane's persistent urge to flirt with the damn woman every time they had a private meeting. However, Lane had made a conscious decision to maintain strict professionalism with Miranda, given the woman's earlier comparison of Lane to a disliked and unscrupulous individual—an audacious accusation, in Lane's opinion. Though Miranda had offered an apology, the damage had been done, and Lane believed it was best to keep her distance.

A distance that was increasingly challenging to maintain as Lane saw the evident sadness etched into Miranda's demeanor since Blake's coma. She had witnessed the close bond Blake and Miranda shared and knew it must not be easy for her to deal with the uncertainty of not knowing whether or not she would share another moment with someone she loved. To Lane's surprise, she wanted to provide support and comfort to Miranda during this trying time. The melancholy in those eyes tugged at something inside of Lane, motivating her to offer to alleviate certain aspects of Miranda's chief of surgery responsibilities, aiming to ease the burden of her days. Ever since that day, they had existed in a tension-filled professional dynamic. Miranda hadn't attempted to apologize again and Lane had stuck to her plan not to flirt with her. Still, it was difficult to ignore the sidelong glances that Miranda cast her way, or the fact that she often caught Miranda watching her whenever she thought Lane wasn't paying attention to her. Those hazel eyes studied Lane with a curiosity that unnerved her. It was as if Miranda was trying to unravel some mystery whenever she looked at Lane these days.

She thought Miranda would be happy to keep their relationship strictly professional, however, she noticed genuine dejection in Miranda's eyes when Lane didn't accept her apology. This lingering despondency persisted whenever they were in the same room—a sorrow Lane yearned to dispel, to witness once again the radiant smile capable of brightening the darkest spaces. To be honest, Lane found herself puzzled by both her own actions and Miranda's. Despite everything that had transpired over the past few weeks, she still harbored a deep attraction to Miranda. What confounded her even more was that, while she had swiftly cut Gabriella out of her life after feeling disappointed, she couldn't seem to do the same with Miranda—whose words had wounded her more deeply than Gabriella's actions. Miranda didn't really know her, and Lane shouldn't have cared about her opinion, yet she did. Even more unsettling was the realization that she missed the banter with Miranda. *Sighs. I really need to stop thinking about this damn woman.*

"Do you plan on brooding and staring daggers at the windows every time you come here these days?" Anita's voice broke through Lane's reverie, announcing her arrival as she made her way to the sofa. She patted the space beside her. "Come, sit with me."

Lane relinquished her vigil by the window and settled onto the sofa beside Anita, reclining and resting her head on Anita's lap— a familiar gesture reminiscent of the motherly comfort she sought as a teenager. Without a word, Anita began to stroke Lane's hair, offering the expected affection that Lane had come to rely on. "I wasn't brooding," Lane murmured.

"Oh, yes you were." Anita countered gently. "You keep forgetting I've had many years to deal with your moods. I can tell when something is bothering you." She peered over to see Lane's face. "So, tell me, what's on your mind? You've been here every day after work this week, and each time, you've just been... *brooding.*"

Lane remained silent, grappling with the challenge of articulating her temperament when she couldn't even make sense of it herself.

"I know Gabriella's actions hurt you and your response was to cut her out of your life because whenever people hurt you, that has always been your way of dealing with the pain," Anita pointed out gently.

"I'm not hurt. Just disappointed," Lane replied with a mixture of resignation and sadness.

"You're hurt, Delaney. It's okay to admit it," Anita insisted, her voice laced with understanding. "Admitting you've been hurt doesn't make you weak. In fact, it takes courage to acknowledge your vulnerabilities. It's also okay to forgive those who have wronged you. I'm not making excuses for Gabriella, but you need to learn to forgive, Delaney." Her gentle fingers continued combing through Lane's voluminous strands to ease the uneasiness radiating from her body.

"Humans are flawed and prone to making mistakes. All we can do is learn from them. I know you don't think much of people in general because of your past experiences, but not everyone is a shithole who deserves to be burnt at the stake."

Lane chuckled softly, rolling onto her back to stare up at Anita. "Humans can be quite ugly, but I'm fortunate enough to know a few who strive to make the world a better place," she mused. "I'm looking at one of them right now. If more people had your heart, the world would be a better place." She paused, reflecting on her own experiences. "Regardless of everything, I always give people a fair chance to show me who they are. I'm just not surprised when they turn out to be disappointing. But that's life—I just have to keep moving forward."

Anita's light brown eyes, wise with wisdom, softened with motherly affection. "But sometimes, my dear, it's not easy to move forward, especially when we care deeply for someone. This was ten years of whatever you two were doing. So, it's natural to feel the loss."

Lane smiled softly. "I promise, I'm fine. Yes, in some ways I'll miss Gabriella, but I've accepted that what we shared had an expiration date. Even if I had entertained the idea of a relationship with her, I doubt it would have lasted. She's not the reason I'm *brooding,* according to you."

Concern slowly stained Anita's features. "Then what's been bothering you?" she asked, her eyes searching Lane's for answers.

"Nothing really," Lane deflected with a faint shrug. "I guess, I've just been feeling a bit off lately. Restless. Work isn't as challenging as I'd hoped it would be and with you deciding to stay here, I guess I've just been feeling adrift."

Anita's expression shifted to one of sadness. "Are you thinking of leaving? I mean, even though we're not living together, I've enjoyed having you home. It's been nice seeing you every week. But you know I'll always support whatever you decide. I don't want you to stay here out of some misguided obligation to take care of me."

"No, I'm not going to leave. It's been nice spending time with you too. I just have to find other avenues outside of work to challenge me." Lane shot Anita a scolding glare. "And will you stop thinking that me wanting to be here for you is out of some misguided obligation? I'm here because I want to be here for you, the same you have been for me since the day we met. While I owe you a lot, you're not a burden, you're my family." Lane paused, her voice catching. "The only real mother I've ever known."

Tears shimmered in Anita's eyes. "You're my family too, and you know I love you as if I had given birth to you," she murmured, her voice thick with emotion. She placed her hand on Lanes. "That's why I want you to take my advice. Mothers know best," Anita continued, her voice filled with maternal wisdom. "You need to find a woman you can tolerate for more than just a few months. Give yourself a chance to experience love. You want a challenge? Love is the ultimate challenge. Find someone who will challenge you, who won't hesitate to call you out on your bullshit. Someone who is kind and compassionate, yet strong-willed. Someone who will see beyond the surface and push you to be vulnerable. You need someone who will challenge you, Delaney.

With your personality, anything less will likely bore you or annoy you to death."

I think maybe I have found someone like that. A certain surgeon who pushes my buttons and gets under my skin like no one else ever has before. Unfortunately, I'm the last person she would ever want to have a relationship with. And I keep forgetting she's straight. Although, being straight is irrelevant because many women discover other aspects of their sexuality later in life. Ugh. I need to stop thinking about this damn woman...

"Delaney, where did you go just now?" Anita asked, bringing Lane back to the present.

Lane inhaled deeply. "Nowhere. Just thinking about your theory. What you see as a challenge, I see as trouble that will likely end in heartbreak." She huffed out a defeated sigh. "I'll find something else to occupy my time."

Anita playfully patted Lane on the cheek. "Well, I'm not giving up hope that one day you'll find love. Yes, relationships can result in heartbreak, but overall being in love is something wonderful that I wish for you to experience. Everything in life comes with good and bad, Delaney. Just because we're afraid of getting hurt doesn't mean we shouldn't open our hearts to love. It's all a part of living. And I want you to experience everything that life has to offer."

"I know you do. But I also believe that whatever is meant to happen will happen. So, if I'm supposed to find love, I will. If not, then I'm okay with that too." Lane sat up. "Now, no more of this nostalgic talk. I brought your favorite dessert, let's eat and watch one of your soap operas."

Anita chuckled. "Okay fine. I'll take the bribe and

drop the subject."

Lane went to the small kitchenette to unpack the bags she brought, mulling over Anita's words. While she wasn't opposed to the idea of love, she also believed that love unfolded naturally, not something that could be forced. People either loved you or they didn't—there was no middle ground. Even those who were supposed to love you might not and there was nothing you could do about it. It was as simple as that. So, if love were to find her, it would happen in its own time. Until then, she would continue to savor life's pleasures—often found in the company of beautiful women.

Chapter 23

Miranda pushed open the glass doors of the yoga studio, rushing to secure a spot before the class commenced—barely making it on time after sleeping through her alarm. Though she briefly contemplated skipping the session, she hadn't attended in weeks and craved the mental rejuvenation it offered. Her life and work had been tumultuous over the past month, leaving her feeling mentally and physically drained. Arriving home later than planned from work due to an emergency surgery, she had resisted the temptation to stay in bed. Such was the rhythm of her life since assuming the role of chief of surgery—work being busy and providing the necessary distraction from the ending of another failed relationship.

She had come to terms with Trevor's decision to prioritize his needs, acknowledging the necessity of letting him go. Though initially hurt, she had been coping adequately and had found peace in accepting his choice. Learning from her colleagues at the hospital that Trevor had temporarily relocated to New York to manage the new restaurant had stung, especially considering his lack of a goodbye. She expected better from him in many ways, seeing that their relationship hadn't been terrible. Then again, he had blindsided her with the breakup, so maybe she was stupid for feeling hurt that he hadn't informed her of his move. Then there was the constant worry for Blake, who had been in a coma, leaving Miranda in a state of numbness for weeks. Thankfully, Blake was now awake and on the path to recovery. When Alexandra had called with the news, Miranda had collapsed in her chair, overcome with relief, shedding tears for nearly thirty minutes. Since then, she had slowly drifted into a better mental space, able to focus on healing and rebuilding her mental fortitude.

Lowering herself to her mat, Miranda looked across the room to find Lane watching her. Their eyes locked, and that now familiar emotion swept through Miranda like a wave coming to shore. She couldn't resist holding Lane's gaze, consumed by a feeling that had perhaps been there for a long time but had become more prominent since Lane began treating her as if she didn't exist outside of necessary work interactions. It was a classic case of never realizing the significance of something until it was gone. From the day they had met, Lane had always puzzled Miranda. However, especially in recent weeks, Miranda found herself unable to shake thoughts of her, longing for their usual banter. Getting accustomed to the brick wall between them was difficult, leaving her unsure of how to breach it. She had tried a few times, but Lane hadn't been receptive and Miranda decided to let it go.

However, what confused Miranda was Lane's contradictory behavior. Despite the cold shoulder, Lane had been lightening Miranda's workload and showing concern for her well-being in her own way. The more they worked together, the more Miranda's feelings toward Lane grew increasingly muddled. She was slowly coming to a realization that shocked her in more ways than one, leaving her bewildered and unsure of what to make of it. The woman Miranda now learned was Lane's friend—Nia—said something to Lane forcing her to shift her attention from Miranda.

The instructor signaled the start of the class and Miranda made a conscious effort to divert her attention away from the woman whose presence seemed to hold her spellbound. Through each sequence of movements, Miranda twisted and stretched, gradually feeling the weight of mental exhaustion dissipate. She urged her thoughts to retreat to a place of tranquility, pushing aside the chaotic whirlwind within her mind. However, it appeared her mind had its own agenda, fixating instead on Lane's serene transitions between poses. There was an effortless grace to Lane's movements, a fluidity that belied the physical demands of each posture. Miranda's thoughts then wandered to the contours of Lane's physique—toned yet yielding a softness that intrigued Miranda. The defined curve of Lane's ass, accentuated by the snug fit of her yoga attire, captured Miranda's attention. Her eyes drifted to Lane's full lips and she wondered what it would be like to kiss her. *Wait, what? Why am I even thinking about kissing her? Ugh.* She rationalized it as simply appreciating another woman's gorgeous assets—after all, it was natural to appreciate beauty in others. And Lane was undeniably beautiful. But was it also normal to contemplate what it might be like to kiss her? She reasoned that perhaps it was, especially considering Lane's apparent confidence in her prowess in bed. Nothing was wrong with her wondering if Lane could live up to what she had implied.

It couldn't be that unnatural for Miranda to be curious about Lane, considering the woman had been flirting with her for months. Still, the pressing question remained—why had Miranda never been put off or offended by Lane's advances? Did she enjoy the attention? Was that why she found herself missing it, now that Lane had ceased her flirtatious behavior? But what puzzled Miranda even more was her lack of similar reactions to other women's advances. Josephine, for instance, had been flirting with Miranda for years, yet she had never entertained thoughts of her in the same way she did with Lane. While Josephine was undoubtedly beautiful and Miranda would have gladly dated her if she were queer, she had never felt any sexual attraction toward her or dwelled on her physical attributes. Nor had she given much thought to the underlying attraction or the frequency of Josephine's flirtations.

Women had always flirted with Miranda, but she had never felt this level of curiosity about any of them as she did with Lane. Maybe it was merely the emotional upheaval of the past few months that had her questioning everything. After all, if her newfound realization were genuine, wouldn't she have recognized it years ago? Or was this realization tied solely to one Delaney Remington? A woman who got under Miranda's skin like no one else ever had. A woman who looked at her as though she perpetually harbored a desire to push Miranda against a wall and fuck her right then and there. Even now, amidst Lane's frustration with her, Miranda couldn't ignore the unmistakable lust in Lane's eyes whenever she thought Miranda wasn't watching her.

"Miranda? Are you okay?" A soft voice asked, stopping the runaway train that was her thoughts.

Miranda looked over her shoulder to find Natalia, the instructor, staring at her with concern. Miranda transitioned from the bridge pose to a sitting position. "Yes, I'm fine. Why do you ask?" she inquired in a hushed tone, mindful not to let her voice carry across the room.

"You were stuck in the bridge pose for the past three transitions," Natalia whispered, her worry becoming more apparent.

Miranda's eyes widened slightly. "Really? I guess I was just lost in my thoughts."

A faint smile curled on the edges of Natalia's lips. "Yes, you were. Must have been something important to have you distracted to the point where even my techniques couldn't calm your mind."

Miranda shook her head, releasing a heavy sigh. "Trust me, it's not you. Thanks for checking on me. I'll do my best to stay focused for the rest of the class."

"If you need to talk after class, I'm a good listener," Natalia offered with a soft smile, her lingering gaze suggesting an openness to more than just conversation.

"Thanks. I'm sure I'll be fine by the time we're done," Miranda replied, noting that Natalia's admiration didn't have the same impact as Lane's.

Natalia nodded, announced the next pose, and strolled back to the front of the class. Just as Miranda attempted to follow Natalia's instructions, her eyes drifted to Lane, who was watching her with curiosity. Miranda lifted a questioning eyebrow, but Lane simply smirked and went back to her pose. That single act caused a tinge of excitement or relief to shoot through

Miranda's body, as it was the first sign of playfulness from Lane in weeks. *God. This is ridiculous. When did I go from being annoyed with her knowing smirks to being thrilled by them? Was I really ever annoyed though?*

Miranda shook her head, attempting to clear her thoughts of the conflicting feelings swirling around Lane. Unsure of what to make of them, she wondered if her guilt over hurting Lane's feelings was adding to her emotional unrest. Determined to push these thoughts aside, she resolved to ignore them, believing they would eventually fade with time. After all, she reasoned, she was simply dealing with a lot at the moment and might be fixating on something that wasn't even there. With much relief, she managed to maintain focus through the final minutes of the class. While the other participants began to pack up their belongings, Miranda decided to use the child's pose to stretch her lower back muscles. A minute into the routine, she was startled when she sensed a shadow looming over her. Lifting her head, she expected to see Natalia but instead locked eyes with Lane, whose intense hazel gaze bore into her with curiosity. Miranda sat back on her haunches, meeting Lane's gaze with uncertainty.

"Did you enjoy the show?" Lane asked, a mischievous glint in her eyes.

Miranda frowned, eyebrows knitting together, betraying her bafflement. "What are you talking about?"

"You know, the one where you spent the entire class ogling me. Did you get your fill of my very fine ass, Dr. Hayes?" Lane's tone was neutral, but there was an undercurrent of challenge in her words.

Miranda laughed. Though she couldn't deny she had

stolen many glances at Lane during the class, she would never give her the satisfaction of admitting to it. She decided to take the conversation in another direction. "Since you're having a conversation with me that doesn't involve discussing financial and strategic planning, am I to assume that you're no longer pissed at me for committing the unforgivable sin of offending you?"

"Am I to assume that your answer is 'yes', since you're avoiding my question?" Lane shot back.

"Why do you care since our conversations are supposed to be strictly professional?" Miranda retorted defensively.

Lane waved a hand between them. "So, we're playing twenty-one questions now?"

Miranda rose from her mat and faced Lane squarely. "No, we're not playing anything. I'm simply respecting your wishes to keep our relationship strictly professional."

"You're just finding excuses to avoid telling me the truth. But I saw you, Miranda, your eyes were glued to me for most of the class. So much so, that you zoned out, and Natalia had to come and ask if you were okay. My question is, why were you ogling me since you have no interest in sleeping with someone like me? Someone you dislike. And before you consider lying, remember your eyes say a lot more than you think. You aren't as good at hiding your emotions as you think." Lane's words were direct, cutting through any pretense with a sharpness that demanded a response.

"And my question is, 'why do you care?'" Miranda countered coolly, but remaining firm. "And if you weren't ogling me as well, how could you have seen everything that you claimed just now?" Miranda folded her arms against her chest. "I've already apologized for my overreaction to your personal life and you insist on holding it against me. If you can't forgive and move on, then that's your problem. I won't keep apologizing for it."

"Have you considered why you overreacted to seeing me in the arms of another woman? Have you come to the same conclusion as me—that you were, in fact, *jealous*?" Lane's eyes blazed with an intensity that made Miranda's breath catch in her throat.

Miranda bit her lip, stalling to formulate a response that didn't involve outright lying. Months ago, she could have easily denied any jealousy, but now she wasn't so sure, given the absence of any other logical explanation for her reaction. Reflecting on it now and over the time Lane spent being mad at her, she couldn't deny the possibility that jealousy had played a part. Gathering her resolve, Miranda bent down to pick up her mat and began rolling it up. "What do you want, Lane? You want me to agree to your theory so you can gloat?" Her tone was guarded, a shield against Lane's penetrating gaze.

Lane shot Miranda an exasperated look. "I'm not a teenager, Miranda, to gloat about a woman being jealous over me." Stepping closer to Miranda, Lane lowered her voice. "You already know what I want. But do you know what *you* want?" Her words were a gentle challenge, probing Miranda's intentions.

Before Miranda could gather her thoughts, she heard someone calling Lane's name behind them. Miranda glanced over her shoulder to see Nia, signaling to Lane that she was ready to go.

"See you around, Miranda. I hope you enjoyed the

show," Lane said casually, taking a step to leave, then paused and added, "I do love a woman who loves to watch," her words dripping with seduction, as she slowly ran her eyes up and down Miranda's body.

Miranda swallowed hard as sensations she would need to analyze outside of Lane's presence surged through her body. Her eyes remained on Lane until she exited the studio leaving Miranda in a cloud of confusion. Why did this woman have such an impact on her? And why her, out of all the women in the world? If she was to have some late awakening, why did it have to be with the most arrogant woman she had ever met? And why did she enjoy their sparring matches so much? So many questions, all pointing to one inevitable conclusion.

Chapter 24

Stepping onto the patio at Blake and Alexandra's house, Lane felt drawn to soak up the beautiful view of the lake. She had visited the couple a few times since Blake was discharged from the hospital and had grown to love the scenic vista from their backyard. Reflecting on her history with the two women, Lane could admit that she was surprised to regard Alexandra as a friend in many ways. Alexandra had looked beyond their history and treated Lane as more than just an employee during their months of working together. Alexandra possessed a warm and inviting personality that naturally drew people to her, and despite Lane's aversion to people, she appreciated their budding friendship. Still, she couldn't shake off her astonishment when Alexandra extended an invitation to the post-birth baby shower being held for Blake after her coma. The guest list comprised mostly family and close friends, making Lane even more perplexed by the invitation upon her arrival.

Spotting Blake standing by herself, gazing out at the lake, Lane approached her. She watched as Blake's attention shifted to the balcony as if drawn by some unseen force. Following Blake's trajectory, Lane spotted Alexandra standing there, her eyes fixed on her wife. Despite the challenges they had overcome, their connection only seemed to strengthen with each hurdle they faced, exemplifying the type of love Blake and Alexandra shared. Lane had never encountered another couple as devoted, or frankly as obsessed with each other, as these two women. Witnessing the silent exchange between them, Lane couldn't help but ponder what it would be like to love someone so deeply—enough to be willing to sacrifice everything for them—and let her guard down and be that vulnerable with someone herself. Though, at this point, she questioned whether she was even capable of it. Lust and passion she understood, but love remained a daunting enigma that had eluded her for years. Maybe, she simply wasn't cut out for it.

Drawing closer to Blake, Lane noticed that she was so captivated by Alexandra that she hadn't even sensed Lane's approach. "Had I witnessed the intensity with which you gaze upon her before I endeavored to capture your attention, Blake Westmore, I wouldn't have dared to entertain the thought of coaxing you into my bed," Lane said, mischievously breaking the spell Blake was under. With a subtle flourish, Lane inclined her head toward the balcony and waved at Alexandra.

Blake shifted her attention to Lane. "Lane, thanks for coming. It's great to see you." Blake's features grew contemplative for a moment, then she added with a wry smile. "And regarding your observation, I guess I'm pleased to know that my love for my wife is unmistakably evident."

Witnessing the genuine happiness in Blake's eyes as she professed her love for Alexandra persuaded Lane to ask a question she had been contemplating, considering Blake's dating history before meeting Alexandra. "Why did you choose a life of commitment after years of casual rendezvous? You had a trail of admirers, women vying for your attention. What made you trade the appeal of freedom for the choice to settle down with just one woman?"

A soft ripple of laughter spilled from Blake's lips. "Rendezvous? I wouldn't label my past dating habits as such. Nevertheless, I'm intrigued. How did you come to the conclusion that I had a legion of admirers and engaged solely in casual dating?"

Lane tsked. "Come on, Blake, we work in a hospital and unfortunately people in that setting don't seem to know how to mind their business. And your transition into married life seems to be a fascinating occurrence that many on staff didn't think would have happened."

"What's the motivation behind your question? Has someone managed to capture your attention to the point where you're contemplating a journey down a path similar to mine?" Blake asked, curiosity evident in her eyes.

A flicker of longing briefly shot through Lane, only to be swiftly shrouded by the cloak of indifference that she so adeptly wore. "I'm just curious," she remarked, nonchalantly, "to understand how someone who had never ventured into a committed relationship seamlessly transitioned into married life within a relatively short span. And, from what I've witnessed, you're genuinely content."

Blake studied her for a moment, likely attempting to discern Lane's motives behind asking such probing questions. "Love," she stated, "I fell deeply in love with an incredible woman who outshone every other woman. It's as simple as that, Lane. When you meet the person destined for you, surrendering everything to be with them becomes second nature. And Alexandra is my destiny."

Lane began to formulate a response, but the words caught in her throat when she spotted Miranda walking toward them—a surge of excitement rippled through her body. Dressed in form-fitting, tailored white slacks and a baby blue, high-neck, sleeveless top, with her natural curls cascading around her shoulders, Miranda was the epitome of beauty—her caramel skin glowing under the sunlight. Lane had been wondering why she hadn't seen Miranda since arriving but had assumed she would eventually make an appearance. Ever since their conversation at the yoga studio, there had been an undercurrent of tension between them, more intense compared to before their disagreement about Lane and Gabriella. Lane had been with many women, so she knew it wasn't uncommon for women to realize their attraction to another woman later in life. While she hadn't been certain before about Miranda's feelings toward her, seeing the way Miranda had admired her during yoga class had confirmed what Lane had so desperately wanted to be true since that night at Josephine's.

At the end of the class, her initial intention had been to leave and maintain the professional barrier she had erected between them, but Lane couldn't resist the temptation of calling Miranda out for watching her throughout the entire session. Miranda's eyes had conveyed everything that she was unwilling to admit to Lane. And as usual, their banter had caused excitement to burn through Lane's veins like a blazing fire coming to life after months without oxygen. However, regardless of what she saw in her eyes, if Miranda didn't admit it to herself, then there was nothing Lane could do about it. While she had resolved to forget about anything ever happening between them, her attraction to Miranda hadn't diminished over the weeks, despite keeping her at a distance. Lane still desired Miranda more intensely than she had ever desired another woman. She attributed it to the time they had spent working together and the fact that Miranda was an intelligent and stunning woman who could rival any Greek goddess. So, who could blame her for being captivated by Miranda, even if her own attraction puzzled her? Normally, if a woman rejected her—a rare occurrence—Lane would simply move on to the next, but it seemed the same principles didn't apply to one Miranda Hayes.

Miranda's expression remained stoic as she locked eyes with Lane, but a bright smile unfurled across her lips when she directed her focus to Blake. *Wonder if she will ever smile at me like that?*

Without sparing another glance at Lane, Miranda closed the distance and pulled Blake into a tight hug. "I've missed you so very much," Miranda whispered as she stepped back and planted kisses on both of Blake's cheeks. "Sorry to be late, but I got called into an emergency surgery just as I was on my way out."

"I've missed you too. There's no need to apologize. I'm just happy that you're here," Blake replied.

As Miranda shifted to face Lane, the atmosphere changed. Her features, once warm and friendly, now betrayed an undercurrent that Lane didn't want to make any assumptions about. "Lane," she greeted with an elusiveness, as if saying Lane's name were some hardship.

Lane smirked as she lifted a quizzical brow. "Ah, Dr. Hayes, no hugs and kisses for me? Surely, you must be aware that your chilly reception wounds me deeply."

Miranda, unimpressed, rolled her eyes. "Wounding requires having feelings, Lane, and I'm not convinced there's anything resembling a heart inside your chest."

In response, Lane feigned injury, placing a hand dramatically over her chest. "Ouch. Your words cut deep, Dr. Hayes. But since you're the esteemed cardiothoracic surgeon, I'm open to letting you examine what's beneath my clothes anytime you want to check for a heart."

Miranda narrowed her eyes at Lane, while Blake struggled to suppress a laugh. Before Miranda could retort, Lane smoothly turned her attention back to Blake, appearing calm and collected as if she hadn't just invited Miranda to her bed. "Blake, it was good to see you. I look forward to having you back at the hospital," Lane said as she stepped away, pausing beside Miranda. "Dr. Hayes, I'll see you at work on Monday. Have yourself a wonderful weekend."

Miranda clenched her jaw, maintaining a stony silence. Lane smiled and continued to the house. That was what she was attracted to—not many women understood Lane's sarcastic nature and could match it. But Miranda never missed a beat, and Lane felt like an addict craving a hit whenever their paths crossed. She had no idea what their future held, but sometimes the unexpected happened when you least expect it. Until then, she would leave everything up to the law of attraction.

Chapter 25

"I can't believe you didn't bring Amara with you," Miranda remarked as she settled into her seat across from Blake on her patio.

A soft smile graced Blake's lips as all the love she felt for her daughter shone brightly in her eyes. "I was so very tempted to," she admitted, "but I wanted to give you my undivided attention. We haven't had any alone time since I woke up, and we need to catch up properly."

"You're right," Miranda agreed, nodding. "Work has been incredibly busy. Being the chief of surgery is no easy feat. You and Alexandra made it seem effortless, but the paperwork alone is tedious. Now, I fully understand why Alexandra wanted to step back from the CEO role. I honestly don't know how she managed both positions and performed the number of surgeries she has since she took over." She shook her head in disbelief. "It can be very exhausting, especially for people like us who thrive in the operating room. But it has been an amazing learning experience."

Blake reached out for Miranda's hand, their fingers intertwining as a symbol of their bond of friendship. "Thank you so much for stepping in when Alexandra needed you," Blake expressed, gratitude evident in her voice. "It gave her peace of mind to focus on me and Amara without worrying about the hospital. She didn't doubt Lane's capabilities to cover both roles, but Alexandra wanted one of her surgeons to gain the experience."

Miranda did her best not to react to the mention of Lane's name—a task growing increasingly challenging as Lane seemed to constantly stare at her as if she could see Miranda's thoughts about her. "You know I would do anything for you—you're my family. You asked me to look out for her, so it was the least I could do," she replied, striving to divert her mind from the ache she had felt not knowing if she would have another moment like this with Blake.

Blake squeezed her hand, her eyes conveying understanding of Miranda's inner turmoil. They had been friends for years and they knew each other very well. "You're my family too, and that's why I know something is going on with you," Blake observed astutely. "So, spill. Start with what's going on with Trevor. Then, I need to know about all that tension between you and Lane at the party. It's obvious she's still attracted to you, and your reaction to her wasn't what I would have expected, considering you've described her as the most insufferable person you've ever met."

Miranda briefly panicked at the thought that her feelings for Lane might be that obvious. She had been making a concerted effort to keep them hidden, especially from Lane herself. However, she quickly reminded herself that this was Blake—someone who knew her better than anyone else. Blake was the only person who could likely help her figure out her conflicting emotions. Miranda had been yearning to confide in Blake, but she wanted to be certain of her feelings before broaching the topic. Furthermore, they hadn't had a chance to discuss her relationship status with Trevor either. In fact, aside from her parents, she hadn't confided in anyone about it. She hadn't been in the mood to explain another failed relationship. This was why she was immensely grateful to have her best friend back. If Blake had been awake when her relationship ended, Miranda wouldn't have had to confront her emotions alone. Blake would have been there to support her through it all.

Miranda massaged her temples, trying to ease the tension building in her head. "Where to start..." She took a sip of her mocktail before continuing. "Trevor dumped me on the day of your C-section. He grew tired of waiting for me to decide if I wanted a future with him. Apparently, moving in together was supposed to symbolize my commitment, but to him, it seemed like I wasn't taking things seriously enough. He practically gave me an ultimatum."

"I'm so sorry to hear that," Blake responded, her voice filled with compassion. "I was really hoping things would eventually smooth out between the two of you."

Miranda swallowed hard, fighting back the tears threatening to spill. She didn't have to hide her emotions from Blake, but she simply didn't want to cry anymore over the end of her relationship. "I wasn't ready, so he ended it," she explained, her voice wavering slightly. "In some ways, I wasn't surprised, but I still felt blindsided. There was tension between us while he was in New York, but he gave me the impression that he still wanted us to continue working on our relationship once he got home. At the same time, I'm not mad at him for doing what he needed to do to make himself happy. I couldn't give him what he wanted at the moment, so it's only fair that he tries to find it elsewhere."

"I'm not surprised you're looking at it that way," Blake commented, nodding in understanding. "You've always tried to see things from other people's perspectives. How have you been dealing with it? I know you cared deeply for him. I imagine you're hurt."

Miranda sighed, her gaze turning introspective. "That's the thing that made me accept his decision without much animosity," she admitted. "While I'm hurt, I'm not devastated. Trevor was deeply in love with me, and if our feelings were on the same deep level, I would have chosen to move in with him to make him happy. We were just at different emotional places. We can't force love to happen on our terms—it will happen how it's supposed to. Trevor is great, and I wish him well." She shrugged. "He's probably the only guy I've dated who I would give another chance to if he asked me. Sadly, the timing just wasn't right for us, I guess." Miranda took another sip of her drink, pausing to collect her thoughts. "I've just been working a lot since the breakup and focusing on healing."

"I'm glad you're doing okay. Sorry, I haven't been here to help you deal with everything." Blake's eyes softened, concern emanating like a warm blanket of compassion. "Why did you take so long to tell me?"

Miranda glanced out at her garden, collecting her thoughts before responding. "You've been through a lot over the last couple of months, and I just wanted you to focus on healing and bonding with Amara. My relationship woes felt insignificant in the grand scheme of things."

"Well, I'm here now, anytime you need me," Blake offered reassuringly as her hand grasped Miranda's, her thumb slowly massaging out the fatigue embedded in her knuckles.

Miranda once again found herself staring out at her garden, admiring her blooming peonies, contemplating how to broach the next topic Blake had asked about. She didn't even know how she had ended up where she did when it came to Lane, and she still had so many questions for herself. She decided to pose a question that, before, she thought was an easy one to answer. After all, she believed that people were simply attracted to who they were attracted to, regardless of sex, and that they would just feel it. But when you're thirty-seven and have never felt any sexual attraction to another woman before, was it really that simple?

She brought her gaze back to Blake and held her eyes, watching as worry etched itself into Blake's features at whatever she saw on Miranda's face. "What made you certain of your sexuality? What made you a hundred percent sure you would never want to sleep with a man?" At the mention of sleeping with a man, Blake made a face, causing Miranda to laugh. "I guess your reaction should answer my question."

Blake chuckled softly. "I guess so." Her expression then turned serious. "I guess you're asking because of Lane?" Miranda nodded, not at all surprised by Blake's intuitiveness. "I just knew because I had never been drawn to a man sexually. I've never felt the urge to kiss them or found jocks appealing when I was in high school. Cheerleaders and female teachers, on the other hand, I used to have very vivid fantasies about." Blake winked in amusement, before returning to an indifferent expression. "I've just never felt any attraction for a man. I don't find anything about them sexually appealing. It's that simple for me, but I also recognize that it may not be that easy for some people, especially given the society we're raised in, which often implies that something is wrong with us." She shrugged nonchalantly. "And then some people realize later in life that they're attracted to the same sex. I think there's no one way of realizing that you're queer, or a timeline for that matter."

Miranda groaned in indignation. "I think I might be attracted to Lane," she rushed out. "So much has happened over the last few months causing my emotions to be all over the place and I'm not even sure of what I feel for her or understand it. Because why her? I've always been open-minded and accepting of people's sexuality, but I've never thought of another woman the way I do Lane. I mean, no other woman has pursued me the way she has or been so upfront about wanting me." Miranda threw her hands up in the air. "Of all the women. Ugh." She shook her head in disbelief. "You're probably the most lesbian-lesbian, I know. You're hot, brilliant and so sexy, but I've never felt any intimate attraction for you. Hell, I've seen plenty of women naked and never felt any desire for them."

Blake chuckled. "Well, you have thought about sleeping with Halle Berry."

Miranda laughed. "It's... Halle... freaking... Berry. Every black woman has probably thought about sleeping with her. So, that doesn't count." Miranda snapped her fingers and pointed at Blake. "Plus, I also allowed Brittany to kiss me the night of my high school graduation because she had a massive crush on me. She told me if she had one wish for her graduation, it would be to kiss me. So, I allowed her to do it. I didn't think anything of it, or was even remotely turned on by it."

She covered her face in her hands, before running them through her long luscious curls in an attempt to quell her agitation. "I'm just so confused by these new feelings, and I've been looking at other women to see if I feel anything, but I don't. Natalia, my yoga instructor, has the hots for me, and while she's absolutely stunning, I don't feel any desire for her. It's just Lane—the most insufferable, arrogant woman I've ever met." Just saying Lane's name caused Miranda's pulse to beat harder.

Blake's features grew contemplative. "Look at it this way. It's not every guy that you see you're attracted to, right? Or find attractive?" Miranda nodded. "Same as it's not every woman that I meet I'm attracted to sexually." Blake waved a hand between them. "What if you've just never met a woman who you were attracted to sexually until Lane? Love or attraction is a strange thing and sometimes we just end up liking or loving the last person we expected, even if they're the same sex. We just love who we love. And you don't need to label it or yourself. Or put yourself in a box. Just love who you want to love and live your life for you. It's that simple." Blake smirked and wiggled her eyebrows. "If you feel an attraction to Lane, if you want to explore it, then do it. I'm sure she is more than willing to allow you to explore all you want. That woman looks at you like you're her dinner."

The intensity with which Lane always stared at her flashed into Miranda's mind. The heated, lingering looks that always made Miranda feel naked under her gaze. The want and hunger in those eyes. *What would it be like to have sex with someone who looks at me with so much desire? Is that why I'm so drawn to her? Sigh.*

"I wish it was that easy. Since realizing my feelings for Lane, I've been doing a lot of soul-searching about why my past relationships failed. You know my dating history. Before Trevor, I could have confidently said that my exes just weren't the right fit for me. But Trevor was different, he was great, and I genuinely wanted things to work out with him. However, just like all the others, there was always something missing. They were all able to fall in love with me within months, but I either wasn't ready or didn't feel the same level of love for them at the same time. So now, I'm starting to think that maybe I was the problem all along. And how does my newfound attraction to women, specifically Lane, factor into all of this?"

Blake nodded with understanding. "What you're feeling for Lane will probably make you question your entire life. But don't put too much pressure on yourself trying to figure it out now or in days. Give yourself time and just take it one day at a time." She paused, taking a sip of her drink before continuing. "What made you realize you're attracted to her? I mean, there was always this tension between you, but I always thought it was because Lane was always flirting with you and you found her arrogant."

Miranda let out a long, slow breath. "From the night we met at Josephine's, something about her left me feeling unsettled. It was unnerving. At first, I thought it was annoyance with her unabashed desire for me and her cockiness. And I enjoyed bantering with her. Some days, I even looked forward to it when we ran into each other at work. But I didn't realize it then, because I was in a relationship, and you know I would never cheat.

"Do you remember when the pictures of her and Gabriella were leaked?" Blake nodded. "Well, for some unknown reason, I felt betrayed by her, since she had been flirting with me for months. I said some not-nice things to her about it, and she reacted by putting up a wall between us. Once she did, I realized that I missed our interactions. It was so weird. The more she pulled away from me, the more drawn I was to her.

"Then, we started working closely together, and I started noticing things about her. The woman she is behind the stone-cold persona she dons at the office. It was like I became attuned to everything about her. Her beauty. Her intelligence. Just everything. I can't stop thinking about her."

"I can see why you're attracted to Lane. She's exactly your type, but this time only with C-cup boobs and a vagina," Blake said with a chuckle.

Miranda's brows furrowed in confusion. "What do you mean?"

"You've always been attracted to high-pedigree men who know how to write a complete sentence and speak proper English. From the day I've known you, you've always gone for the suit and tie types. Trevor was the only guy you dated who was more laid back. But he is from upper-class New York and has many of the attributes you're attracted to behind his bad boy appearance—he is a true gentleman."

Miranda looked at Blake puzzled, still not seeing the connection to Lane. "Lane always looks like she stepped right off the runway," Blake continued. "I don't think I've ever seen her wearing jeans and a T-shirt since she's been here. She is always so well put together and carries herself with a certain level of confidence and self-respect. Plus, she's charming as hell and very intelligent. Regardless of her background, her mannerisms are that of a refined, sophisticated woman. These are things that you've always been attracted to."

Miranda tsked. "Refined until she's inviting me to her bed in not-so-sophisticated ways. That woman is a devil."

Blake laughed. "Maybe she's a lady in the streets and a freak in the sheets." Her grin widened. "A charming devil who has you twisted up in knots."

Miranda grabbed some mixed nuts from a bowl on the table and playfully tossed them at Blake. "Stop teasing me. It's not funny. I don't want to even imagine how much she would gloat if she ever found out that I'm attracted to her. Ugh. She already insists that I am, but unless I confirm it, it will only be an assumption."

Blake's eyebrows shot up in surprise. "You're not going to tell her and take up her offer to introduce you to—according to her—the dark side?"

Miranda shook her head adamantly. "God, no. At least not now. Maybe my attraction to her will go away. I can't deal with her arrogance. It will be like losing a damn battle if I admit my feelings to her. If I want to explore my sexuality, I'd be better off dating another woman. Definitely not Lane. She's just…. Ugh."

"Everything you'd want in a partner. Except this one comes in red bottom stilettos and curve-hugging dresses," Blake said with a grin, then she sobered as Miranda glared at her. "Seriously though, don't write off Lane. You know she's more than what meets the eye. I think you should explore your feelings for her with her. You might be surprised by what you find."

"I'm perfectly fine being single for now. I'm still

healing from my breakup and the trauma of you almost dying. Some time alone is what I need for a reset."

Blake got up from her chair and rounded the table, stopping in front of Miranda. She pulled Miranda from her chair and enveloped her in a warm hug. "Do whatever you need to do. I'll be right here to support you. I know what you're feeling can be overwhelming and confusing, but life is what you make of it and you're free to live it as you see fit to achieve happiness. Even if it comes in the form of a gorgeous brunette who drives you crazy."

Miranda chuckled, snuggling deeper into Blake's arms. She wholeheartedly agreed with Blake about living her life to be happy, but she definitely wasn't sure if happiness came in the form of Delaney Remington. Plus, Lane didn't do relationships. And if it was a woman she was supposed to find happiness with, wouldn't it be better to date someone who was at least open to a relationship? Open to love? Lane had made her intentions clear—she only wanted to fuck Miranda, nothing more. Then again, since she was so confused about her feelings, wouldn't it be better to pursue casual relationships to explore this side of her sexuality before any form of commitment? Time... she would just give herself time to figure everything out. She would have to do her best to hide her attraction from Lane. No need to give her anything more to be insufferable about.

Chapter 26

Lane leisurely strolled down The Ave, veering toward a quieter section after an hour of brisk walking. Restless nights had become her unwelcome companion lately, and she hoped an afternoon stroll would help clear her mind before visiting Anita. Long walks had always been her go-to when her thoughts spiraled out of control. The restlessness that had haunted her before starting her role at Parkwood had returned with a vengeance in recent weeks. Initially, she believed she had conquered whatever had been troubling her, as the feeling had dissipated for months after joining Parkwood. However, since the incident with Gabriella, a sense of despondency and foreboding had taken root within her. She needed an outlet for her agitated energy, but nothing seemed to provide lasting relief. Maybe it was the slower pace of Seattle compared to the bustling atmosphere of L.A.—the quieter environment was still an adjustment for her. She was also traveling less for work and had more time on her hands. Even though she had always lived a somewhat subdued life while in L.A., dating had been more frequent back then as well. But maybe that was precisely the issue. Perhaps she needed to revert to her old dating habits. Women had always been a welcome remedy whenever she needed to silence her racing thoughts.

However, even that theory was flawed because upon further reflection, Lane came to the conclusion that she was bored. And much to her utter dismay, lonely. It was a rather ghastly thought considering she could have numerous women in her bed if she wanted. But strangely enough, these days when she woke up with a woman's limbs wrapped around her, she still felt lonely. Bored. Other than work, the only other thing—or well, person—that kept her mind interested was, Dr. Miranda Hayes. Miranda was a dichotomy to Lane at times—sweet and gentle, yet strong-willed and a hurricane at the same time. Miranda had been doing her best to avoid Lane like the plague for the past two weeks. She avoided every situation where they would be alone unless it was absolutely necessary. Miranda also avoided making eye contact with Lane whenever they talked, again, unless it was absolutely necessary. It was as if Miranda was afraid of what Lane would discover if she stared too long at her.

Lane sighed. Maybe pursuing a woman who had explicitly stated that she would never sleep with her —even if Lane were the last person on earth—was the challenge she needed. That would explain why, after months of dancing around this woman, she still desired her. Perhaps at this point she needed to get her head examined for still carrying a torch for Miranda.

Turning the corner to a quieter stretch of the street, Lane's attention was immediately drawn to a striking mural adorning a large panel of glass. Depicting teenage girls in vibrant colors, it exuded a sense of empowerment and community. Intrigued, Lane took a few steps closer, peering through the windows into the space beyond. Inside, she observed a dynamic environment bustling with activity. Teenage girls of diverse backgrounds engaged in lively conversation, while others focused intently on their tasks at hand, tapping away on computers and tablets. The open-concept layout fostered collaboration and camaraderie, creating a welcoming atmosphere. Spotting a door further down the street that appeared to lead to an office, Lane felt compelled to learn more about the center. With a determined stride, she made her way to the entrance, eager to uncover the purpose behind this inspiring hub of activity.

Opening the door, Lane was met by a white woman with a friendly face and auburn hair, casually dressed in jeans and a T-shirt bearing the slogan *"Found Family: You're Never Really Alone"*.

"Hello," Lane greeted her, stepping inside. "Could I speak with someone about the programs you offer here?" She paused, adding almost as an afterthought. "I'm Lane, by the way."

"Hello, Lane, I'm Ava," the woman greeted with a warm smile. "I'm one of the program coordinators here, I can offer you a detailed overview of our operations. If you need more information beyond what I can provide, our website is quite comprehensive and should address all your questions."

Lane returned Ava's smile appreciatively. "I'd love a tour while I'm here. It would be great to see the setup of the space, if that's allowed. I realize this area is separate from where the teenagers are on the other side."

Ava nodded in agreement. "Yes, only authorized personnel are permitted in the area you saw through the windows. It's a safe space for them, and outsiders aren't allowed in there."

"I see. This is a safe space for only girls?" Lane inquired, her curiosity growing.

Ava paused, her fingers hovering over the keyboard of her laptop. "Before I provide more information, may I ask why you're interested in knowing the details? May I also have your last name, and the purpose of your visit?"

"Last name is Remington. If you're making a log for security purposes, you can log me as Delaney Remington. I was just walking by and the mural caught my attention, and then I noticed the teenagers socializing." Lane's lips curled into one of her trademark smiles that she used to charm people when she felt the need to. "Call it an information-gathering visit from a curious mind."

Ava nodded, accepting Lane's explanation. "We're always thrilled to share our work with those interested in supporting our cause and raising awareness about the programs we offer for teenage girls in need of a safe space." Rising from her desk, she gestured for Lane to follow her. Together, they passed through a glass door, obscuring the view of what lay beyond. Stepping into a spacious area divided by glass walls on either side, Lane saw young women and girls engrossed in various activities.

"Found Family is a haven for teenagers from troubled homes, those being bullied at school, or anyone who feels alone, depressed, or like they don't fit in anywhere," Ava explained as they strolled slowly along the corridor. "Our offices are open from 8 a.m. to 8 p.m. every day, and there's a 24-hour helpline. Our operations are somewhat like a membership club you apply for, ensuring that resources go to teenagers who genuinely need help. As you can see, the facilities are very upscale, so over the years, we've had people who just wanted to take advantage of what we offer because they thought it was cool.

"If someone needs help, they simply walk through the door and share their stories with a counselor. We know that sometimes it's difficult, but we need to ensure that we're offering help to those who truly need it. If they're from a troubled home, we work with child services to rectify the problem. We have temporary housing upstairs where if someone runs away from home, they can call the helpline, and we'll give them a place to stay for the night until we can get them help in the morning. Then we have kids who just want to be somewhere they feel safe to be themselves and socialize with people they are comfortable being around. We offer counseling, tutoring, and various programs designed to empower and uplift these girls from a very young age."

As Ava elaborated on the center's services, Lane's gaze wandered, absorbing the bustling activities on both sides of the partition. She couldn't help but be impressed by the supportive atmosphere and diverse offerings. Reflecting on her own teenage years, Lane wished she had a sanctuary like this one—a refuge where she could have escaped to, during challenging times.

At the end of the corridor, Ava pointed to the left. "Over there, we have two therapists who are always available to the girls whenever they need someone to talk to. We also offer free therapy sessions to parents who want to mend their relationship with their daughters but need guidance in bridging the gap between them." Ava turned to Lane, her eyes brimming with pride. "In summary, we do incredibly meaningful work here. The girls feel like they're part of an exclusive membership club where they can freely express themselves and receive the support they need to grow into their best selves."

Lane's mind swirled with questions, eager to learn more about the impactful work being done for young women in this space. "I must agree. The setup is quite impressive. May I ask about funding? Is it privately funded or by the government?"

Ava's response was immediate. "The government? God, no. If we had to depend on government funding, we would probably be a rundown shack." She didn't mince words, making her distaste for Seattle's elected officials clear. "We're one hundred percent privately funded."

"If I were to make a donation, would it be possible to receive more detailed information on how funds are allocated? Like an expense report or the last fiscal financial statements?" Lane inquired, hoping her request wouldn't come across as odd, which would be a red flag for her and she would leave without donating.

"I don't handle that aspect of our operations, but our director will be in on Monday and she can provide all the details you need. You can leave your contact information, and she'll reach out to you then." Before Lane could respond, Ava's expression shifted as if she had just recalled something important. "Actually, the owner is here today. She usually stops by once a week to check in. She's very nice and I'm sure she wouldn't mind answering your questions. Let's head back to the front, the executive offices are on the other side."

Lane nodded in agreement and followed Ava back along the path they had taken. As they walked, her eyes continued to absorb the scene around her, growing increasingly intrigued by the incredible facility dedicated to supporting young women. She understood firsthand the challenges of navigating a world that could be unforgiving to young women. With nowhere to go or kind strangers to offer a home, so many teenagers lose their way and never recover from the trauma, and some lose their lives.

Reaching a small office space on the other side of the reception area, Ava gestured to the sofas. "Please have a seat while I check if she's available to speak with you now."

The area was warm and inviting, decorated with three small cream leather sofas, a small table adorned with flowers, and art that appeared to have been painted by students who were members of the center. For some reason being there triggered memories of her own troubled childhood and she couldn't prevent her mind from revisiting places that she had long buried.

Chapter 27

Miranda opened the door to her office, stopping dead in her tracks upon spotting Lane talking to Ava. *What the hell is she doing here? I swear Seattle has gotten smaller since this infuriating woman moved here,* Miranda thought as she fought the urge to retreat back into her office to hide. Because, yes, she had been avoiding Lane in an attempt to quell her attraction and resist temptation. However, since they worked together, it was a rather difficult task, and it seemed some invisible force kept conspiring to put them in each other's path from the very first night they had met. Before she could decide on fleeing, Lane glanced over Ava's shoulders, and their eyes connected. Surprise briefly flashed in Lane's eyes, but it disappeared just as quickly as it had appeared. Caught in Lane's piercing gaze, Miranda felt a magnetic pull drawing her forward, compelling her to step out of her office and confront the inevitable encounter.

Ava spun around, her expression brightening as she noticed Miranda. "Hi, Miranda. I was just on my way to see you..." Her voice trailed off as she registered Miranda's bags. "Oh, you're leaving?"

Miranda nodded, trying her best to avoid meeting Lane's gaze—who seemed to be watching her with curiosity. "Yes. Do you need help with anything before I leave?"

Ava stepped aside and gestured to Lane. "This is Delaney Remington. She's interested in making a donation, but she'd like more details on how her donation would be spent. Since you're leaving, I can arrange for Daria to call on Monday." She then turned to Lane. "Would you mind if the director contacted you on Monday?"

Lane's eyes gleamed with mischief, and Miranda braced herself for whatever was about to come out of her mouth, knowing it likely wouldn't be to her liking. "Yes, I do mind," Lane said firmly, causing Ava to frown. "I'd much rather Miranda contact me. Better yet, since she's on her way out, I can walk with her. I wouldn't want to unnecessarily keep her behind." Lane flashed one of those charming smiles that would get any woman to do her bidding. "Miranda, are my suggestions agreeable to you?" she finished, her voice carrying a hint of challenge.

Miranda fought the urge to glare at Lane in Ava's presence. Instead, she forced a professional smile and said, "Ava, it's fine. I'll accommodate our potential donor's request. Have a wonderful weekend, and I'll see you next week."

"Okay. Have a great weekend as well," Ava said, turning her attention to Lane. "Lane, it was nice meeting you. Take care."

"You too, Ava. Thanks for the tour." Lane glanced at Miranda and added, "I think I might be visiting more often in the future. Though, that depends on whether or not Miranda will be able to convince me to open my checkbook."

Ava chuckled. "I'm sure she will."

"Thanks for your confidence in me, Ava. Take care," Miranda stepped off toward the exit, gesturing for Lane to follow her. They walked in silence until they exited the building, with Miranda trying hard not to focus on how aware she was of Lane's presence. The scent of her perfume which was different from the one she often wore, the lack of makeup, and casual clothing that still made her appear as if she stepped right out of a magazine, and pink lips that were only covered in lip gloss. This was the most dressed down she had ever seen Lane, and the woman was even more devastatingly alluring like this.

Stopping on the sidewalk, Miranda turned to Lane and asked, "Why are you here? Should I be concerned about you stalking me, or are you genuinely interested in donating?"

Lane grinned, and the site of it made Miranda's pulse flutter. "Miranda darling, as tempting as it would be to stalk you, I have no desire to resort to such machinations. I love my freedom too much and if I'm behind bars, then I'll never get what I desire the most. So, fear not, I haven't planted a tracking device on you or have hidden cameras in your office."

Miranda scowled. "You sure know a lot about stalking. I won't even ask what you desire the most..."

"That's because you already know," Lane interjected, cutting off Miranda before she could finish the sentence.

Ugh. This woman. "Whatever. I'm starving and need to eat. If you're serious about donating, you can walk with me to get lunch. If not, have a great weekend, Lane."

"I'd love to join you for lunch." Lane made a sweeping

motion with her right hand. "Lead the way."

Miranda rolled her eyes and started walking to the small park at the end of the block. She really wasn't in the mood to deal with Lane's presence, but she would never do anything to jeopardize a potential donation. "We have various programs that you can donate to, or you can make a general donation that the team decides on how to use. We also have a scholarship fund that goes toward awarding ten college grants each year. The amount varies depending on how many donations we receive or funds raised through our yearly events. I don't believe in wasting resources, so we only send a copy of our financial statements to donors who request it. I can have Daria send you last year's statements if you need more granular details on how your money will be spent."

Miranda glanced sideways at Lane to see her reaction, which caused her to lose her footing as she stepped off the sidewalk to cross the street. Miranda stumbled, but before she could fall flat on her ass, strong arms wrapped around her waist and steadied her. Righting herself, she came face to face with Lane, a mere breath's distance apart—their chests rising and falling in tandem. Lane's eyes bounced between Miranda's and her lips, her pulse point hammering in her neck. Miranda's body suddenly felt too hot as her heartbeat skyrocketed. Every sensation that she had been trying to suppress while in Lane's presence came alive and she felt like she couldn't breathe. They were standing so close that if Miranda just leaned forward an inch, she would taste lips that—much to her horror—she had dreamt about kissing two nights ago. She dared to meet Lane's eyes and the desire in them made Miranda want to squeeze her legs together as her core began to throb. *Why, why, why? Please, not now.*

Lane pulled Miranda closer and logic told her to step out of the embrace, but her body remained rooted to the spot, losing the battle against her mind. Miranda felt as if she was under some spell that kept draining her resistance when it came to Lane. Staying away from her hadn't diminished the damn attraction and she felt exhausted fighting her feelings. She just needed to give herself time to figure out her confusing feelings for this damn insufferable woman.

"Hey, you two, get a room!" a young man on a bicycle shouted as he zipped past them.

It was the bucket of cold water Miranda needed to snap out of the trance she had fallen under. "Thanks," she muttered, breaking away from Lane's embrace. Without waiting for a reply, Miranda crossed the street, putting some distance between them.

Lane caught up with her and they walked in silence to the taco truck a few feet away. Miranda was surprised by the lack of commentary from Lane about her reaction to being in her arms. Lane was perceptive enough to have noticed Miranda's heart pounding away in her chest.

"Hey, Miranda. How are you?" Mateo greeted as they approached the truck.

"Hey, Mateo. I'm starving and could probably eat everything on the menu. But, I'll settle for spicy fish and my usual side today," Miranda said with a grin. "How are Lucia and the baby doing?"

"Muy buena," he replied excitedly. "The little princesa has me wrapped around her fingers. Thanks again for ensuring that everything went smoothly for us at the hospital."

"It was the least I could do for all the years you've been keeping me fed with the best Mexican food in Seattle."

"Always such a charmer," Mateo said with a chuckle.

Miranda shifted her attention to Lane, who was silently watching the exchange. "What would you like? They have almost every type of taco you can think of."

"I'll have what you're having," Lane said, giving her a look that Miranda couldn't quite read.

Miranda turned back to Mateo. "Make my order two of everything. I also need a regular chicken, and orange soda to go. Please make the chicken around thirty minutes from now. I'm going to sit over there to eat, and I'll grab it when I'm leaving."

"Make that two of the same to go as well. Thanks," Lane added casually. Miranda shot her a questioning glance, but Lane simply shrugged.

"You got it," Mateo said as he wrung up the order and handed Miranda the POS machine.

Miranda tapped her card, leaving a generous tip, then stepped to the side to wait, hoping Lane wouldn't initiate conversation. She needed a break from the suffocating tension between them, a chance to rebuild her defenses against temptation. Miranda inwardly sighed with relief when Lane took out her phone to check her messages. Following suit, Miranda scrolled through her own notifications, grateful for the distraction. However, Lane's proximity, her body heat palpable, made it challenging to ignore their closeness. After a few minutes, Mateo popped his head out of the truck, announcing their orders were ready.

"Thanks, Mateo. I'll be back in a few," Miranda said, taking the containers and handing one to Lane.

They walked in silence to a picnic table in a quieter area of the park, away from the hustle and bustle. Miranda settled onto the bench, positioning herself in the middle to discourage Lane from sitting beside her. She suspected Lane would sit next to her just to annoy her, so she was putting controls in place to prevent it. Opening her box, the delightful aroma made her mouth water and her stomach growl, and the first bite elicited a soft moan from Miranda. A gentle laugh from across the table made her look up to meet Lane's gaze. Lane was watching her with a soft smile—not the usual knowing, teasing smirk she often directed at Miranda, but something more tender, as if she were seeing Miranda for the first time. The effect of it caused strange stirrings in Miranda's stomach.

"Are you just going to sit there and watch me eat?" Miranda asked with less bite than she intended. She was too hungry to find energy for Delaney Remington's wit.

"Would you mind if I did? Those little moans are a bit of a distraction and I like watching you," Lane replied, her eyes drifting to Miranda's mouth.

Miranda sighed in resignation. "Yes, I would mind. And the food is better when it's hot."

"As you wish. I don't like cold food, so you make a valid point," Lane replied as she opened her container.

Surprisingly, Lane remained silent as they ate. Each time Miranda lifted her eyes from her food, they met Lane's and she felt like she was sitting under a microscope, being examined to discover everything that she wanted to keep hidden. Halfway through the meal, Miranda couldn't take the silence any longer. It wasn't in her nature to share lunch with someone without engaging in conversation. Knowing Lane, it would suit her perfectly well to sit there without saying a word. She was confusing as hell and half the time Miranda couldn't predict which version of her she would get—the one who flirted, or the one who could sit through a meeting without exchanging a word unless absolutely necessary.

"What other information do you want to know about Found Family, if you're really serious about donating?" she asked, breaking the silence which was neither comfortable nor uncomfortable, to be honest.

"Ava said that you're the owner." Miranda nodded. "How did you start it and why?"

Miranda stared at Lane for a moment, searching for any signs of an ulterior motive, but all she found was genuine interest reflected in Lane's eyes. The center was Miranda's pride and joy, a labor of love she poured her heart into. She felt a swell of pride whenever she talked about the services they offered to girls in need. Setting aside her apprehension about Lane, Miranda decided to speak candidly about her passion project that morphed into Found Family.

"The idea started back in my high school days," Miranda began, her voice tinged with nostalgia. "It was a class project where we had to come up with a concept to improve our communities if we were given a million dollars. I crafted the concept and penned a business plan for Found Family. My teacher, who had connections in local government, was so impressed that she proposed it to the city council. I was thrilled at the prospect, but unfortunately, they said it was too costly and dismissed the idea as a waste of resources. I was so heartbroken that I asked my parents for a million dollars to do it."

Miranda chuckled softly, remembering how brazen she was to ask her parents for so much money. "They didn't say no, but explained that the timing wasn't right as I needed to focus on graduating high school. They promised to revisit the idea when I was older and could invest more time into it. Reluctantly, I agreed. I went off to college, and the project faded into the background."

Pausing for a moment, Miranda took a sip of her mango drink, studying Lane's reaction. Surprisingly, Lane's genuine interest was still visible, convincing Miranda to continue. "After I finished my residency, I bought a new house and while packing up to move, I found the project. It reignited something within me, and I decided to turn it into a reality. My parents owned the building where the shops had closed down. I proposed the idea of using it for Found Family, and they gifted it to me. I used some of one of my trust funds as seed money and have been persuading my family's wealthy associates to open up their checkbooks to continuously fund operations."

Lane's eyes widened slightly, a playful glint dancing in them. "How many trust funds do you have?"

Miranda arched an eyebrow, unamused. "That's all you got from what I said?"

Lane shrugged, a smirk tugging at her lips. "What can I say? You just casually threw it out there, like having multiple trust funds is the norm."

Miranda sighed, her patience wearing thin. "That wasn't my intention. I'm simply sharing the information you asked for. And it's none of your business, anyway."

Lane raised a hand in surrender. "Please continue. You can tell me how rich you are the morning after we...."

Miranda scowled. "Must you...." She gestured vaguely between them, "flirt with me now? I thought you wanted information to help you decide if you should donate."

Lane laughed, her shoulders shaking and Miranda was enraptured by the infectious sound of it, soaking up the sight. "Can't I have both? Flirt with a beautiful woman while she tells me how brilliant she is. Plus, it was your mind that went to the gutter. You don't know what I was going to say." Miranda's glare intensified, warning Lane to reel in her laughter. "Okay fine. Please continue."

Miranda let out a frustrated sigh. "God, you're insufferable. I don't even know why I bother with you."

"Because you like me," Lane said.

"No, I do not," Miranda retorted, praying the ground wouldn't open up and swallow her for such a bare-faced lie. *Of all the women in the world, why did it have to be this infuriating woman? You only find her infuriating because you like her.*

"Yes, you do. I know when a woman likes me, Miranda. But you can deny it all you want. My offer still stands. Whenever you're ready to explore the dark side, you know where to find me," Lane said with confidence as if she could see inside Miranda's mind.

Lane's confidence only fueled Miranda's frustration. "Keep dreaming," she shot back, taking another sip of her drink to moisten her suddenly dry mouth.

"Oh, I will. I *love* dreaming about you," Lane said, her eyes a few shades darker now as they scanned up and down Miranda's body.

Miranda's body began to react to the smoldering gaze,

sending a wave of heat through her, causing her to jump up from her seat as the need to flee consumed her. "Since you're only interested in flirting with me, I'm going to go. Goodbye Lane."

Lane's expression softened, regret washing over her features. "Please don't go," she said earnestly, her voice tainted with that rare vulnerability she hardly showed. "I'm sorry. I'm really serious about donating and would love to hear your story. Please sit down."

Miranda shook her head and continued packing up the remainder of her lunch. "I must go. I can book an appointment with you next week in a more professional setting to provide you with whatever else you might need. Just know your money will be used to help many young girls in need."

Lane stood up, disappointment vivid in her eyes. "Why have you been hiding from me, Miranda? And now you're running away because I flirted with you?"

Miranda chose to sidestep Lane's question, already having told one white lie in an effort to conceal her feelings, and that was the limit of her moral flexibility for the day. She had always been accused of being honest to a fault, but desperate times called for desperate measures. "I'm tired, Lane." That was the truth. "It's been a long week, and I had intended to just grab something quick to eat and go home. I'll provide you with all the information you need next week."

Lane studied her for a moment, her expression suggesting she might want to pick apart Miranda's excuse for fleeing. However, she ultimately nodded and said, "Okay fine. I know you had a busy week at work and I can see how exhausted you are. I'll let you off the hook on one condition…"

Miranda paused, apprehensive about agreeing. With Lane, she never knew what to expect and the woman was smart enough to trap her into agreeing to something Miranda wouldn't like. However, her exhaustion was kicking in and she just wanted her bed. "Okay fine," she relented, albeit with caution. "Even though I could just walk away. As much as I would love for you to donate, I know plenty of rich people who are willing to donate to feel good about themselves and brag to their friends about helping the less fortunate. So, while I'll appreciate your money, I won't succumb to any and every request."

Lane glared at her. "God, then you accuse me of being exasperating. Jesus. I don't even want to know what you think I was going to request." Lane rolled her eyes dramatically and Miranda had to bite her lower lip to prevent herself from laughing. It was such an out-of-character act from the woman. "I was simply going to ask that you continue to tell me about your journey with Found Family and why you chose to focus on teenage girls. That's all. Not anything that you were thinking."

"Well, who can blame me for thinking you would have requested something untoward," Miranda muttered, pulling up her bag on her shoulder. "But, yes, I can finish telling you about my inspiration."

"Preferably over dinner or lunch," Lane piped up. It was Miranda's time to roll her eyes. "Come on. You're the one who is always buying me food. I owe you at least one meal."

"Okay, whatever. There's no point arguing with you," Miranda grumbled as she started walking back to the food truck.

Lane matched her pace, seamlessly falling into step with her. "Thanks for being so accommodating. I'm looking forward to it," Lane replied, sincerely.

As they strolled toward the parking lot, each carrying their to-go bags, they slipped into a comfortable silence. Miranda felt a spark of electricity in the air as their hands brushed against each other, sending a pleasant tingling sensation through her fingers. When they reached the corner before the entrance to the parking lot, they both paused and handed the bags to the homeless woman sitting there with a sign asking for food. She accepted the bags, nodding thanks profusely. Miranda turned to Lane, eyebrows raised in surprise at the unexpected act of kindness. While it was typical for her to buy a meal for the woman whenever she visited the center, she was intrigued by Lane's decision to do the same.

Once they continued walking before Miranda could express her curiosity, Lane said, "I see you're a good Samaritan through and through. It's admirable. The world could use more people like you who see the plight of the less fortunate and give of themselves to make the world a better place without expecting anything in return."

The wistfulness in Lane's voice compelled Miranda to stop and turn to face her. She studied the woman intently, attempting to decipher her emotions, but was met with Lane's trademark neutral expression. "I think I could say the same about you," Miranda replied, her tone measured. "It's just that I'm more open about showing the world that I care. Whereas you... you hide behind a veil of indifference to keep people at arm's length. To shield them from seeing that beneath those blank stares and 'don't give a fuck what anyone thinks of you' attitude," she pointed a finger at Lane's chest, "there's a heart in there."

"Didn't you tell me a few weeks ago that I didn't have a heart?" Lane reminded, teasingly.

Miranda's eyes did a full three-sixty. "Fine, I take back my words. Maybe I'm trying to see something that's not there." Lane chuckled. Before she could respond, Miranda decided to assuage her curiosity. "Why did you choose to buy her food, instead of just giving her money?"

"She probably would have used the money to buy drugs. If I buy her food, then she is guaranteed one meal for the day. How about you?"

Miranda smiled internally at Lane's intuition. These days it was like everything about the woman impressed her. "More or less the same as you. I offered to get her help at a treatment center and she refused. I know no matter how much money I give her, she'll only use it to buy drugs. Giving her a meal is better."

Lane didn't reply, instead, she just stood there staring at Miranda. Not with lust or that burning intensity that often sent a shiver down Miranda's spine, but something like veneration. The impact was still the same as if Lane was staring at her with lust-filled eyes. Miranda cleared her throat and said, "I'm parked right there. Have a great weekend. I'll see you at work on Monday."

Miranda expected some flirtatious comment, but Lane simply said, "You too, Miranda. Please get enough rest."

They remained rooted to the spot, locked in a silent exchange that seemed to stretch on endlessly. Miranda felt an unexpected tug, a desire to linger in Lane's company a little longer. She couldn't deny that she had enjoyed their time together, and seeing another side of Lane always left her wanting more. The more she fought her attraction, the more it seemed to intensify. She wanted Lane, and the realization both thrilled and terrified her. But to what extent she wasn't sure. Was it only a sexual desire or something deeper?

A distant car honk shattered the trance, jolting Miranda back to reality. She cleared her throat, breaking the silence. "I'll see you," she said abruptly, her voice betraying none of the turmoil inside her. With swift steps, she walked briskly to her car, refusing to look back. She felt Lane's eyes on her, but she dared not meet them, fearing Lane might see the longing in her own.

Chapter 28

Miranda's breath caught in her throat when her eyes landed on Lane approaching her table. She wasn't surprised to see Lane weaving her way between tables toward her because she knew they would be sitting together. What surprised Miranda were the somersaults happening in her stomach as her eyes roamed over Lane's body, taking in the white floor-length gown that hugged her curves like a glove made just for her. Under the golden lights of the ballroom, Lane was a vision in white. It felt as though everything and everyone around her disappeared, leaving only Delaney Remington gliding to her with that confidence that made the woman simultaneously alluring and intimidating. Her gown clung to her like a second skin, accentuating her curves and highlighting the perfection of a body that Miranda had witnessed bend and twist in various yoga poses. The dress was daring yet elegant, with a plunging neckline that drew the eyes and a slit up the left thigh that revealed just enough to capture one's imagination. Her mahogany tresses fell in waves down one side, leaving her striking features visible—high cheekbones, a gentle jawline, and eyes sparkling with mischief and charm, all fixed on Miranda. Her makeup was impeccable, with smoky eyes and her signature red lipstick.

Miranda was spellbound, the smoldering rapacity in Lane's eyes preventing her from looking away. She felt a surge of red-hot lust coursing through her body, mingling with a longing she had been unable to deny. She didn't know what she would do if Lane made a move tonight because how much longer could she deny herself what she truly wanted to explore?

"Wow. Who is that?" the doctor beside her—whose name Miranda's Lane-filled brain couldn't remember at the moment—asked, breaking the trance she had fallen under.

Before Miranda could muster a response, Lane was already beside her, effortlessly pulling her to her feet. Lane's signature fragrance enveloped Miranda, tempting her to lean in closer and breathe in the scent at Lane's neck. *God. So much for keeping my distance to lessen my attraction.* Lane greeted her with an air kiss on each cheek and a shiver that had nothing to do with the temperature in the room ran the length of Miranda's spine.

As Lane started to pull back, she leaned in closer, her lips brushing Miranda's ear with a whisper, "I'm happy to see my attire had the desired effect. It seems you already can't take your eyes off me, just as I won't be able to keep mine off you tonight." Miranda could feel the fervency in Lane's hooded eyes as they flicked to her lips. "You look absolutely breathtaking." Her low, tantalizing voice and the warmth of her breath against Miranda's ear left her heart racing and her thoughts scattered.

Miranda quickly stepped back from the embrace, torn between the urge to either glare at Lane or draw her even closer, acutely aware of their audience. She managed to force a polite smile as she reclaimed her seat.

Lane, ever composed, scanned the table, acknowledging their colleagues with a poised nod. "Hello, I'm Lane Remington," she introduced herself smoothly, taking the seat between Miranda and the doctor whose name still eluded Miranda.

Miranda quickly reached for her glass of champagne, draining the contents in one gulp to steady her racing nerves. It had been a few days since she saw Lane—their last encounter being the lunch Lane had insisted on to learn more about Found Family. To keep things professional and stave off any intended flirtation, Miranda had strategically suggested they meet in the hospital's cafeteria. She considered the hospital a neutral ground where they could discuss the cause as colleagues. Lane always maintained decorum in front of their colleagues—a behavior Miranda relied on to keep her at a safe distance until she could sort out her conflicting feelings. During that lunch, Lane had paid keen attention and posed insightful questions about Found Family, demonstrating genuine interest. However, her intense gaze had unnerved Miranda, piercing her as if she knew about Miranda's attraction and was simply biding her time, waiting for Miranda to capitulate. They had concluded their meeting with Lane suggesting they share a car to this gala they were both scheduled to attend on behalf of Parkwood. Miranda had swiftly refused—there was no way she would willingly trap herself in the backseat of a car with Lane for almost an hour.

Now, here they were, and Miranda found herself unable to look away from Lane, who was deeply engaged in conversation with their colleague whose name still escaped Miranda. The dark-haired woman seemed enraptured by Lane, hanging on her every word and inching closer with each minute that passed. Miranda watched, a knot forming in her stomach, as the woman leaned in to whisper something into Lane's ear, placing a hand over Lane's. Lane responded with a smile, leaning in to reciprocate the whisper, eliciting a laugh from her admirer. Roaring jealousy flared within Miranda, her jaw tightening as she observed their interaction. The urge to pull Lane away, to declare some sort of claim, surged powerfully within her. It was then that Lane turned her head, locking eyes with Miranda. Her gaze was penetrating, a knowing smirk curling on the corners of her red-painted lips, as if she could see the tumult of emotions Miranda was experiencing.

"So, Lane, no husband or kids for you?" the smarmy suit sitting across from Miranda inquired with a sly smile. "I read your bio because there have been talks at Mason Ridge about poaching you from Parkwood. You've built quite the reputation in the industry. It would have been challenging to balance that with a family."

Miranda couldn't help but wonder how stupid he was not to pick up on the dynamics between Lane and Dr. Tomlin—Miranda finally remembered the woman's name—who was clearly flirting with Lane. Lane's face remained neutral, betraying no emotion, but Miranda caught the subtle signs of irritation. The slight clench of her jaw and the blank stare that seemed to question his intelligence were tells Miranda had come to recognize in their time working together.

"No wife or kids for me. However, I'm positive that

if I had taken that route, I would have still been able to achieve everything I have in my professional career and maintain a happy marriage," Lane replied, her voice calm, but carrying an icy undertone that checked his presumptions.

"Oh, you like women," the man replied, his surprise lifting his eyebrows toward his hairline.

"No, I love women. I'm a lesbian," Lane stated confidently, holding the man's gaze as if daring him to make another stupid comment.

Dr. Tomlin's eyes sparkled with excitement as if Lane's confirmation of her sexual orientation was the highlight of her year. Meanwhile, Miranda's eye shifted back to Lane, her thoughts stuck on the earlier mention of Mason Ridge potentially recruiting Lane. That hospital was located all the way in New York. Was Lane thinking of moving? And why did the mere thought of Lane leaving stir a pang of sadness within her?

Before the man could respond, the MC took the stage, signaling the start of the dinner. As the evening unfolded with a lavish three-course meal and varied entertainment, Miranda increasingly felt drawn to Lane. Throughout the dinner, Lane effortlessly commanded attention among their peers, her charm and confidence shining as she discussed the medical industry with passion and insight. Miranda had always recognized Lane's brilliance, but hearing her articulate such a deep commitment to healthcare reaffirmed that her motivations extended far beyond personal gain —she genuinely cared about improving patient care. What fascinated Miranda even more was how Lane seemed to shed her usual reserved demeanor in this social setting, appearing more extroverted than she typically did at the hospital. It was as if Lane wore different masks in different environments, and Miranda yearned to uncover the authentic woman behind those carefully constructed facades.

Three hours into the event, Miranda found herself swirling across the dance floor with a fellow surgeon she had known since med school. They had kept in touch over the years, and she was grateful when he approached her table to invite her for a dance, especially after Dr. Tomlin had all but dragged Lane onto the dance floor when the MC encouraged everyone to let loose and have fun. The woman couldn't have been more obvious with her intentions for Lane, which involved ending the night with Lane in her bed. Lane, who had all but ignored Miranda since their brief greeting, and seemed totally fine with the woman fawning over her like a lovesick puppy. Miranda knew she had no right to be jealous since she was the one choosing to deny herself what Lane had offered since the day they met. But it seemed these days she had no control over her emotions when it came to Lane, who was watching her across the dance floor instead of paying attention to the woman in her arms.

"Are you seeing anyone at the moment?" Terrence asked, drawing Miranda's attention back from Lane.

"No, I'm not. But I'm not interested in dating at the moment," Miranda replied with a smile.

Terrence chuckled. "The timing never seems to be right for me since med school," he replied, his dark brown eyes scanning Miranda's face as a coy smile formed on his lips.

Miranda took in Terrence's strikingly handsome features—reminiscent of Morris Chestnut's— and wondered why she had never considered dating him despite always finding him attractive and genuinely nice. "I guess not," she replied thoughtfully.

Terrence nodded, his expression reflecting understanding rather than disappointment. "Please keep me in mind when you do decide to start dating again," he said softly. "I'd love to take you out to dinner."

Before Miranda could respond, slender fingers painted a deep red tapped on her shoulder, pausing their movements. Miranda glanced over her shoulder to find Lane standing behind her, eyes fixed intently on Terrence with possessive assertion, like a tigress declaring her territory.

"May I cut in?" she asked with a smile that didn't quite reach her eyes.

Terrence glanced between Lane and Miranda, sensing the tension. "As long as Miranda doesn't mind," he replied, holding Miranda's gaze.

Miranda knew she should say she minded and continue dancing with him, but the overwhelming urge of not wanting to hurt Lane's feelings consumed her. She smiled at Terrence and said, "Thanks for the dance. It was nice catching up with you."

He stepped back, taking Miranda's hand in his, raised it to his lips, and planted a kiss on her knuckles. "The pleasure was all mine. Enjoy the rest of your night."

As Terrence walked away, Lane immediately stepped in, her strong hands finding Miranda's waist from behind. She gently pulled Miranda into the rhythm of the music, leading them effortlessly into the dance. Miranda unconsciously relaxed into Lane's embrace, Lane's warm breath brushing against her ear. Every nerve in Miranda's body seemed to ignite, her senses heightened by the closeness of Lane's presence. As they moved together, Miranda struggled to focus on anything but the sensation of Lane's body pressed firmly against hers.

Struggling to regain some semblance of control over her body's reactions, Miranda managed to find her voice. "I thought by now you would have been on your way home with Lydia." She internally sighed in relief that her voice remained steady, despite the turmoil erupting inside of her from being so close to Lane.

Lane spun Miranda around in her arms, not missing a beat as they continued to dance. A playful smile was dancing on her lips, but it was the appetency in her eyes that almost made Miranda gasp. "Is that jealousy I'm hearing, Miranda darling?"

"Why would I be jealous, Delaney?" Before Lane could respond, Miranda pressed on, the question burning too brightly to hold back. "The bigger question is why did you interrupt my dance after practically ignoring me all night?"

Lane's eyes burned with desire as she smoothly twirled Miranda back into her arms. "I know jealousy when I see it, Miranda. But you have no reason to be jealous when the only woman I want to go home with tonight is you. As appealing as Lydia may be, she doesn't hold a candle to you." She paused, her gaze sweeping over Miranda appreciatively. "Did I mention how absolutely ravishing you look in this dress?" Not giving Miranda a chance to respond, Lane's tone softened as she posed her own question. "The *bigger* question is why have you been avoiding me, Miranda? You seem to be doing everything in your power to reduce our interactions. Why is that?" Her eyes searched Miranda's for an iota of the truth, her playfulness fading into genuine curiosity.

Miranda's heart raced, her instincts screaming to look away from Lane's intense gaze knowing she wasn't good at hiding her emotions, but she forced herself to hold it, even though every fiber of her being trembled under that scrutinizing look. "I thought that was what you wanted," she countered. "You were the one who put up barriers between us."

Lane tsked, a modicum of exasperation mingling with her persistence. "No, Miranda. That was then, and it's not why you're pulling away now." Her voice softened, almost pleading, "Please be honest with me. Don't you think I've seen the signs? Hmm?" Lane pulled Miranda closer, maintaining just enough distance to search her eyes deeply. "Do you think I haven't noticed the way you've been watching me? The way you stare at my lips during our meetings? The way you probably wanted to slap Lydia for fawning over me all night." Lane's voice dropped to a whisper, intimate and coaxing. "Why are you afraid to take what you want from me, Miranda darling? It's yours for the taking. So, why torture yourself with fantasies about me instead of indulging in the real thing?"

Lane's voice was smooth, and compelling, like a skilled predator circling its prey—the siren calling sailors to their doom. It was almost too much for Miranda, who felt an overwhelming inclination to surrender to the emotions battling within her—desire pulling her one way, reason tugging her another.

Taking a deep, shuddering breath to steady herself, Miranda ceased their dance, pulling back just enough to look Lane directly in the eyes. "What do you want from me, Lane?" The words barely escaped her lips, so quiet she wasn't even sure Lane had heard her. She posed the question partly to divert her own thoughts, to stall, because Lane had always been clear about her intentions. But Miranda needed something—anything—to help her resist the pull of her desires, if only for a moment longer.

Lane stared at Miranda for a long moment, her gaze softening as if she saw the turmoil in Miranda's own and wanted to comfort her. Gently, she drew Miranda closer, her lips brushing against the shell of Miranda's ear. "You *know* what I want, Miranda," her voice a seductive murmur that resonated with every word, stirring the tension between them as they swayed slowly to the music. "But if you need specifics, I can provide that as well." Her hand trailed lightly down Miranda's back, sending waves of arousal through her. "I want you to grant me the privilege of fucking you until you beg me to stop." Miranda couldn't prevent the audible gasp that escaped her at Lane's frankness, even though she shouldn't be surprised. "I want you to allow me to strap and stroke you from behind with long, deep, hard thrusts while my fingers play with your clit, driving you to the edge and back until you beg me to make you come." Miranda's nipples suddenly felt too hard against her dress. "Then I want you to come so hard that my sheets would be ruined with an abundance of your wetness." Her fingers continued their teasing ascent on Miranda's spine. "I want you to allow me to eat your pussy while you lay spread eagle on my desk, willing and eager for my tongue." A very vivid description of that scene flashed in Miranda's mind. "But more than anything I want you to allow me to kiss you. Because for some reason, I want to kiss you more than I want to fuck you," Lane finished, her voice a blend of desire and earnestness.

Miranda's heart thudded wildly against her ribcage, its beats louder in her ears than the pulsing music. A feverish desire coursed through her, igniting every nerve as her mind helplessly spun images of what Lane had just described. She became acutely aware of her tight grip on Lane's dress only when Lane gently pulled away, breaking the physical connection but not the emotional thunderstorm rumbling between them. As Lane stared at her, the raw honesty and desire in her eyes caused Miranda's resolve to crumble. She knew that if Lane were to kiss her right then and there, she wouldn't—couldn't—resist. A person could only withstand so much temptation, and Miranda was at her limit. Yes, she might be confused about her feelings for this infuriatingly irresistible woman, but her body harbored no such doubts—it craved everything that Lane was offering.

Lane lifted her hand, gently cradling Miranda's cheek, her thumb tracing Miranda's skin—branding her. Miranda held her breath, anticipation building as Lane leaned in, her eyes a deep, mesmerizing pool of desire. Miranda's eyes fluttered shut, expecting the tender press of lips against hers. However, instead of a kiss, Lane's breath caressed her ear, whispering the access codes to her penthouse in a sultry undertone. As quickly as she had closed the distance between them, Lane pulled back, planting a chaste kiss on Miranda's cheek. Miranda's eyes snapped open in surprise as Lane released her and stepped back, her demeanor as cool and collected as if she hadn't just seduced Miranda like a pro.

"Enjoy the rest of your evening, Dr. Hayes. Get home safe," Lane said with a polite nod, then turned and walked toward the exit, leaving Miranda in a state of bewilderment.

What!?

Miranda stood frozen, watching Lane's retreating figure, feeling as if she were slowly awakening from a spell cast by Delaney Remington herself. Miranda's mind spun as she replayed the last few minutes over and over wondering how the hell Lane could have walked away from her. Did she want Miranda to beg? Was that it? Because clearly, she must have seen the havoc her words were wreaking on Miranda's self-control. A mix of arousal and frustration pulsed through Miranda, an intense combination that made her want to scream. Again, why did she have to be attracted to the most arrogant, infuriating woman on the planet? She could almost see the smug satisfaction in Lane's strides as she walked away, leaving Miranda in such a state. *Fuck her*, Miranda thought as she grabbed a glass of champagne from a passing server. *Yes, that's exactly what you want to do to her.*

Chapter 29

Lane stared out the floor-to-ceiling windows at her penthouse fighting the impulse to check the time once more. It had been an hour since she had arrived home from the gala and she had gambled on Miranda arriving a few minutes later to give in to desires, but it seemed once again she had misjudged the woman. Lane had always been good at reading the signs of when a woman desired her. She might have doubted Miranda's attraction in the early days of their interactions, but over the past weeks something had changed—other than the fact that Miranda was now single—and Lane had seen the signs. No woman who didn't want to sleep with her would look at her the way Miranda did. The woman wasn't good at hiding her emotions and Lane saw the desire in her eyes—the curiosity. She had been waiting patiently for Miranda to make the first move, but the woman had been avoiding her instead of jumping her bones. The avoidance was another sign that she was right in assuming that Miranda felt some attraction to her. She was curious to find out what had changed, though she believed that there was always something between them from the start. Something that kept her desiring the woman even when she didn't want to and even when Miranda insisted that Lane was the last woman on the planet she would want to sleep with.

Lane wasn't big on fate, but since she had been in Seattle, life kept putting Miranda in her path. It was like they couldn't resist each other. And my dear god did she want to fuck the woman. She should applaud herself for the iron-clad self-control to walk away from Miranda earlier and to ignore her most of the night just to see if she would be jealous. A test that had proven her suspicions because all night Miranda shot daggers at Lydia as if she wanted to slap her for touching what was hers. And Lane had wanted so badly for Miranda to have claimed what was hers. But the infuriating woman had chosen to dance with some guy causing Lane to lose her patience. At that moment as she watched Miranda dance with that man, she was the one who had been jealous. A feeling that was foreign to her because she didn't do jealousy.

At this point when she went to work on Monday, she should get her head examined for still wanting the exasperating woman even after so many months when she could have a woman like Lydia in her bed right now. Lydia had sent all the signs that she was willing to follow Lane home, even when Lane had done her best to keep her at bay. While she found the woman attractive her mind had been too consumed with thoughts of how the golden dress hugged Miranda's curves, highlighting her bountiful behind that Lane had fantasized about doing rather indecent things to. Plus, Lydia didn't cause intense lust to burn through her veins the way Miranda did nor did she challenge her the way Miranda did. Maybe if Miranda hadn't been in such close proximity, she would have gone home with Lydia but she just couldn't when all her thoughts were centered on Miranda... fucking... Hayes. Jesus. When did she become this? If she had accepted Lydia's offer to go home with her, she would probably be knuckles deep inside of her, but no, here she was alone with a throbbing clit because her damn libido seemed to be attracted to one woman.

Lane sighed and downed the remainder of her whisky. She was so fucking horny and didn't know why she was punishing herself. She loved sex and was denying herself because of a woman who she couldn't stop lusting after. *Fuck this* she thought as she decided to take Lydia up on her offer. She turned from the windows to retrieve her phone but stopped suddenly when she heard the elevator doors open. She held her breath daring to hope as she waited for someone to appear. Seconds later Miranda appeared, fire and fury burning in her eyes when she spotted Lane. Lane didn't dare move as she watched Miranda approach her in slow cautious steps as if she was afraid of disturbing a sleeping beast. Lane noted the tremor in Miranda's hand as she drew nearer, stopping directly in front of her.

Lane swore her heart stopped momentarily when Miranda reached behind her and unzipped her dress, letting it fall to the ground, leaving her standing in her heels and black laced underwear. Lane dug her nails into the palm of the hand not holding the tumbler in an effort to quell the urge to reach for Miranda, push her up against the glass, and sink three fingers inside of her. Her body, God almighty, her body was everything that Lane had imagined it would be and then some—full breasts, flat stomach, and generous hips that one half of her race was known for. Lane had never felt anything like what she was feeling at that moment. As if she were finally being given her most prized obsession. Like she, a mere mortal, was being granted an audience with a goddess. But though she wanted to reach for Miranda, Lane remained rooted to the spot waiting for her to make the first move. She forced her eyes to meet Miranda's instead of focusing on her breasts.

"You win," Miranda said, a slight tremor in her voice as her eyes misted over. "So, if you want us to fuck, then let's do it because I'm tired of fighting what I feel for you." Miranda lifted her hands helplessly, tears now forming in her eyes. "I don't even fully understand what I feel for you or why I want you when you're the most maddening woman I've ever met." Miranda swallowed hard as if she was trying to prevent herself from crying. "Here I am... you won."

Lane stared at Miranda as her mind struggled to process the words she was hearing as her desire to fuck the woman clashed with the logical side of her mind. Did Miranda honestly think that it was all just a game to Lane to see if she could get Miranda in her bed? Did she really think so little of her? Regardless of what her mind was struggling to grasp, it was the tears, fear and vulnerability in Miranda's eyes that stirred something in Lane and doused her desires. Because no matter how much she wanted to fuck the woman she would never take advantage of her when her mental state was obviously fragile.

"No," Lane replied firmly.

Before she could say another word, Miranda shouted, "What?!" her trembling hands balling into fists. "Months you've been pursuing me and now that I'm here offering myself to you, you're turning me down!" Her voice cracked on the last words.

Lane sighed and reached out a hand for Miranda to take. "Let's sit down and talk, Miranda."

When Miranda didn't take her hand, Lane wrapped her hand around Miranda's, tugging until Miranda finally stepped off and followed her to the sofa. She went for the duvet folded on one of the smaller sofas. Returning to Miranda's side, she wrapped it around her shoulders noting how Miranda was watching her with a mixture of aggravation and curiosity. She then went to her wet bar to pour a glass of whiskey for both of them, trying hard not to question her sanity at turning down what she wanted more than anything. Returning to the sofa, she handed one of the glasses to Miranda and sat beside her. Miranda continued to stare at her as Lane took a sip of her drink, eyeing her over the rim of her glass.

Their eyes remained locked for what felt like minutes until Lane decided to break the silence. "I can see that this isn't as simple as sleeping with a woman for the fun of it or just curiosity. You're confused about your sexuality." Lane paused, allowing her words to sink as she watched Miranda's reaction. "I've slept with straight women who only wanted the experience of sleeping with another woman, so I know the difference between that and what you're feeling. As much as I would absolutely love to bend you over on this sofa and fuck you, I have never been intentionally calloused with a woman's feelings or taken advantage of their vulnerabilities. So, talk to me, Miranda. Why did you decide to sleep with me after all these months of me chasing you?"

Miranda studied her wearily for a long moment before taking a long sip of her drink. She licked her lips and once again Lane wondered why she insisted on torturing herself where this woman was concerned.

"I don't know why I'm attracted to you when I've never felt any sexual attraction for another woman. Women are beautiful creatures who I've always admired, but never felt the overwhelming desire to sleep with any of them... until you." Miranda took another sip of her drink as if she was buying time to find her words. "I'm not in the habit of hooking up with random people just for sex. And it would be insensitive of me to just start dating women to figure out if I'm in fact bisexual, only to have one of them fall in love with me, and I realize I'm not. I'm just so confused about my feelings for you." Miranda shook her head slightly, sniffling. "So, is it a case where your insistence on wanting to sleep with me has made me want to try, or am I naturally attracted to women and you're the first one to bring out this side of me? I just don't want to hurt anyone by putting myself out there just for experimenting to figure my shit out."

"I can guarantee it's me. You just couldn't resist my charm for much longer, even though you claim that I'm insufferable," Lane teased, earning a soft chuckle from Miranda that did funny things to her insides. *This woman has a very strange effect on me.*

"Maybe you're right and it's just you, since I don't seem to want anyone else," Miranda said with a shrug.

"So, use me then, to explore your attraction. You'll get to figure out your feelings without worrying about hurting anyone or feeling like you're using them. We'll take it slow and see how things go," Lane offered.

"What do you mean 'use you'?" Miranda asked cautiously.

"Date me. We'll go out as two people who are attracted to each other. If the attraction is still there after a couple of dates, or date, then we explore our desires for each other," Lane answered, questioning her sanity for those suggestions knowing that if Miranda decided after a few dates she didn't want to sleep with Lane she would probably lose her mind.

Miranda narrowed her eyes at her. "And what do you get out of helping me when you could have someone like Lydia who knows exactly what she wants from you?"

Lane laughed. "Still jealous, are we?" Miranda glared at her. "I get you, Miranda. I get to fulfill my very wicked fantasies about you. It's that simple for me." Lane's eyes bored into her. "Neither of us is looking for a relationship so there is no harm in me helping you to figure out your late awakening. I know it can be confusing when a woman realizes later in life that she is attracted to women, so I'm willingly offering my services. Doing my part to ensure you get the most wonderful experience from your first time with a woman." Lane grinned. "Satisfaction guaranteed."

Miranda rolled her eyes and shook her head. "You're so full of yourself."

"And you like it," Lane replied, feeling relieved to finally see the fear and sadness disappear from Miranda's eyes.

"Sadly," Miranda replied with a smile as her shoulders relaxed even more. "Okay. I'd love to go out with you," she added after a beat.

"Then it's settled. I'll pick you up at seven p.m. on Saturday. I'll let you know the dress code by Thursday since I need to plan our date," Lane said, trying hard not to laugh when Miranda looked at her suspiciously.

"I should have known you would be a bossy control freak," Miranda said.

A slow, unhurried smile made its way onto Lane's lips. "I'm a freak alright. But only in the bedroom and that's also the only place I like to give orders. In other areas of my life, I'm more accommodating. A team player."

Miranda's eyes darkened as if she was picturing Lane giving her orders in bed. She quickly took a sip of her drink and then rose to her feet, clutching the duvet to her chest. "I guess I better get going."

Lane rose from her seat thinking it was a good idea because she was really pushing the limits of her self-control by turning down sex with Miranda. But instead of agreeing to Miranda's statement, she heard herself say, "You can stay in the guestroom or my room if you need someone to cuddle you after an emotionally charged evening."

Miranda cocked her head to the side, studying her. "You're telling me you have that much self-control to hold me close all night without making a move."

"Why don't you find out for yourself?" Lane dared her.

"I'd rather not. I'll get my dress and go." Miranda then sobered and closed the distance between them, leaning in and kissing Lane on the cheek. "Thanks for being so understanding and not taking advantage of my earlier emotional breakdown."

"You're welcome," Lane replied, fighting the impulse to caress the spot on her cheek that still tingled from the touch of Miranda's lips.

Miranda nodded and went to retrieve her dress off

the floor by the window. Lane watched her get dressed, wondering why she was so willing to go to such lengths for her. Deep down she knew why. But it wasn't something she wanted to examine.

Chapter 30

Miranda stared at Lane sitting at the table across from her on the date Lane had meticulously planned—a date that so far left Miranda even more intrigued by the woman. As promised, by Thursday, Lane had provided the dress code for their evening and arrived five minutes before seven to pick her up. Now, here they were at Navia—a rooftop restaurant that provided a stunning view of Seattle's skyline and waterfront. The atmosphere was quiet and romantic, with enough privacy for them to talk. Miranda thought she would have been nervous but she felt relaxed in Lane's company. Though to be fair, she had always felt comfortable around her, even when she flirted relentlessly. Even more surprising was the difference between Lane the CEO and the version she was currently on a date with. The woman was so charming, well-mannered and had given Miranda her undivided attention since picking her up. She now understood why the women who had fallen in love with Lane did so, even when they knew she didn't want a relationship.

"Penny for your thoughts, Miranda? Why are you just sitting there, staring at me?" Lane asked, shattering Miranda's introspection.

Miranda's eyes flickered with curiosity as she responded, "Tell me about your career journey. How did you become one of the most sought-after CEOs in our field at such a young age? Plus, you're a woman and we all know it's not that easy for women to rise through the ranks in corporate America."

Lane paused, her gaze steady and contemplative, as if weighing the decision to share her story. New to the nuances of casual dating, Miranda felt a mix of eagerness and uncertainty about what was appropriate to ask. She couldn't help but be captivated by the mystifying woman before her, eager to understand the experiences that had shaped Lane into the formidable leader she had become.

Finally, Lane spoke, her voice measured and reflective. "A combination of long hours, unwavering determination, sacrifices, and a bit of luck. I've always been ambitious and achievement-driven. Failure was never an option for me. After college, I was recruited by the hospital where I completed my final-year internship. While the other new hires left after eight hours, I stayed late, focused on securing a promotion within a year." She paused, a feline smile playing on her lips. "During those extended hours, I developed a strategy to streamline the hospital's operations, aiming to improve efficiency and turn a profit for the first time in years. When I pitched the idea to my manager, she dismissed it as too ambitious and unworkable."

Lane's smile widened, a glint of defiance in her eyes. "But the confidence you sometimes find insufferable drove me to bypass her and present my plan directly to the CEO. Fortunately, she was new and shared my visionary outlook. She loved the idea, greenlit its implementation immediately, and promoted me to be her personal advisor and lead strategist for the project.

She said she saw the hunger and determination in me and wasn't about to let another hospital snatch me away, even if my manager was too stuck in her old ways to recognize my potential."

"Just like that, you went straight to the top of the food chain. Weren't you afraid of being fired for going over your manager's head?" Miranda asked, fascinated by Lane's brazenness.

"No, I wasn't afraid," Lane replied confidently. "I graduated at the top of my class with multiple job offers, and I knew my skill set was in high demand. I was willing to take the risk because I wanted to work with people who were serious about making a difference in healthcare. If their objectives didn't align with mine, I was ready to move on."

Lane took a sip of her wine before continuing. "My strategy was a success, and within two years, the hospital was turning a profit. A year later, the CEO received a job offer in New York and asked me to join her. With no ties in Berkeley, I followed her, and she promoted me to Director of Operational Efficiencies. She credited my strategy for her new role and rewarded me accordingly. Two years later, I was promoted to Vice President of Operations. During that time, I updated my original plan to incorporate technological advancements, making it even more effective.

"Just as I completed the modifications, I heard that my former hospital was looking for a new CEO. All the progress Eileen and I had made had been undone, and they were operating in the red again. I applied, confident that I could turn things around, and at thirty, I secured my first CEO position. Eileen didn't take credit for my strategy, and the owners knew it was my idea that had made them profitable, so they took a chance on me. Since then, hospitals have been courting me. Word of the Remington Technique spread throughout the industry, and for the past ten years, I've been conquering the medical field doing my best to ensure the best patient care at any hospital I touch."

Miranda was impressed by Lane's journey but not surprised. With Lane's confidence, she could easily see her daring to apply for a CEO position at just thirty. "Have you always been this confident and sure of yourself?" Lane slowly ran her tongue along her bottom lip and the sight of it caused Miranda's pulse to jackhammer as she wondered what it would be like to sink her teeth into those full kissable lips.

Lane smirked at her as if she knew exactly what Miranda was thinking. Miranda narrowed her eyes, and Lane chuckled. "Your beautiful face always tells your secrets, Miranda darling. But to answer your question, no, I wasn't always this confident. But to survive in this cruel world and corporate America, I had to learn to be. It was either let the world destroy me or grab it by the horns and take what I wanted from it." Lane's statement piqued Miranda's interest, but before she could ask her to elaborate, Lane said, "Now, it's your turn. Tell me about your vision for Found Family. Where do you see it ten years from now?"

Miranda smiled, touched by Lane's genuine interest in Found Family. God, everything about Lane impressed her and she couldn't deny how much she enjoyed being in her company. *You've always enjoyed her company, even when you claimed she annoyed you.* "I'm hoping to expand to other areas in the city and to add more programs. But my overall goal is sustainability and consistently raising funds to maintain the level of service we have always offered."

"I know you will," Lane said, her voice steady and sincere. "If you're interested, I'd be more than happy to help you strategize. I already have a few ideas that could be beneficial. You're doing important work, and if you don't mind, I'd like to donate more than just money," she offered. Miranda thought she detected a hint of nervousness in Lane's demeanor, but the moment passed quickly, leaving her uncertain.

"I'd love that. We appreciate all the help we can get." Miranda locked eyes with Lane seeing, beyond the many masks to the kind-hearted woman behind them. Lane's heated gaze sent a flutter of nervous anticipation through Miranda's stomach making her wonder what might come later. God, it still felt so surreal that a woman had such an impact on her, but she was absolutely certain she wanted to be there and nowhere else.

For the rest of their meal, the conversation continued to flow smoothly with both of them sharing more tales about their individual career journeys and places they had traveled over the years. Miranda had to admit she was even more impressed by Lane after hearing how she outsmarted men who thought they could belittle her and put her in her place simply because she was a woman. Lane had become who she was through sheer will and determination. After dinner, Lane took her to a floral exhibition, which surprised Miranda since she didn't recall sharing her love for plants with Lane. One of her favorite pastimes was tending to her garden during the months that the weather allowed and maintaining a small greenhouse for the less friendly seasons. Curious, she had asked Lane where she got her information, but the woman had said she couldn't divulge her sources. Overall, Miranda had enjoyed herself more than she expected and loved every minute of being in Lane's company.

An hour later sitting in the back seat of the car on their way to her house, Miranda eyed Lane out of the corner of her eye. Reflecting on the events that led to this moment, she still couldn't believe she had walked into Lane's penthouse, stripped naked, and declared they should have sex. But between Lane leaving her so very aroused and frustrated and her decision to finally leave the gala, her emotions had been all over the place. She had just wanted to stop fighting her attraction. In those moments leading up to her bold declaration, she had felt defeated. All she knew was that she was painfully horny and at her wit's end.

The days leading up to their date had been charged with even more tension each time they interacted at the hospital. Lane maintained a professional distance around their colleagues, but when it was just the two of them, she looked at Miranda as if she wanted to pin her against the wall and fuck her right then and there. The heated gazes and cheeky comments had left Miranda feeling as if she was constantly being seduced by a vixen. Now, with Lane holding her hand in her lap and tracing circles on her wrist just minutes away from her home, Miranda wondered if tonight would be the night Lane finally pinned her against a wall and fulfilled all the promises she had made at the gala. At that thought, nervous anticipation shot through of how their night would end.

"What are you thinking about, Miranda?" Lane

asked, her eyes still fixed on the window, interrupting Miranda's train of thought.

"I'm thinking about you, to be honest," Miranda answered, seeing no need to be evasive.

Lane turned toward her, the corners of her eyes crinkling with a smile. "What exactly are you thinking about me?"

"A lot of things. Some I'd rather not share," she replied coyly, her own teasing smile playing on her lips. "But I was thinking how different you are on a date than what I expected."

"Are you impressed by this side of me?" Lane purred seductively.

Miranda's eyes did a full three-sixty and back. "I wouldn't say 'impressed'. I'm not looking to inflate your ego any more than it already is… You're just softer… Less stern. More carefree. Although you have always been carefree with your flirtatious ways when it comes to me."

Lane lifted her hand and pushed Miranda's curls behind her ears. "Wonder what you'll think when you get the full Lane experience." She used her thumb to caress Miranda's neck as she stared into her eyes, the tension in the car escalating from one hundred to one thousand degrees in a matter of seconds.

Before Miranda could reply, the car came to a stop, breaking the charged moment. Just as she was about to ask Lane if she wanted to come inside, Lane opened her door and stepped out. The driver opened Miranda's door, and as she stepped out, she heard Lane telling him to wait for her. They walked in silence to Miranda's door, their fingers brushing causing a pleasant tingle to flow through her fingers.

Stopping in front of her door, Lane turned to her and said, "I had a wonderful time with you. What's your schedule like on Wednesday? I'd like to take you out again."

Miranda shook her head, still confused, wondering why Lane didn't want to come inside. "I'll be available after six."

"That's perfect. I'll pick you up at seven," Lane replied, still not making the move Miranda had expected. After a moment of silence, Lane asked, "Aren't you going to go inside, Miranda?" Her voice, low and sensual.

Miranda swallowed hard, her eyes dropping to Lane's lips before returning to meet her intense gaze. "Aren't you going to kiss me goodnight? Or are you always this chivalrous with your dates?"

Lane's top lip curved playfully on one side. "Depends on the context. Please, elaborate."

Miranda gestured vaguely to the small space between them. "I expected you to be more... um... dominant. Like you inviting me back to your place, ripping off my dress, and having your way with me."

Lane laughed—a loud, throaty sound that sent a pleasant shudder through Miranda's body. Lane took a step closer, closing the distance between them. "Oh, believe me, I am that kind of dominant, Miranda darling. But I want to do this at your pace. To allow you to work through your feelings without feeling pressured to have sex." Lane lifted her hand to Miranda's face and traced the outline of her bottom lip with her finger. "If you want me to take you inside and rip off your dress, then that can be arranged. But I need you to have no doubts about your feelings the first time that..." Lane dropped her voice an octave. "...I fuck you and make you... *moan my name.*" Moisture coated Miranda's underwear. "So, there's no need to rush. I've waited this long. I can wait a few more dates."

Miranda's breathing grew ragged as Lane's finger continued to tease her, the intensity in her eyes all-consuming, setting Miranda's core on fire. Before Miranda could find her words, Lane's lips were on hers —forceful and demanding. They moved over Miranda's, leaving her weak in the knees. The kiss was neither soft nor gentle—there was no hesitation as Lane parted Miranda's lips and slipped her tongue inside. It was rough and bruising, her teeth sinking into Miranda's bottom lip, blending pleasure and pain. Miranda whimpered, her body melting against Lane's, her hands lifting to Lane's hair, gripping the roots to pull her closer. This wasn't just a kiss, it was a claiming, an unleashing of passion—Lane taking what Miranda had denied her for months.

Miranda struggled to breathe as Lane's tongue explored deeper, then retreated, licking at the roof of her mouth before artfully sliding against hers. It felt as though Lane was mastering the art of kissing and Miranda was her canvas. Her head spun as sensations she had never experienced before assaulted her and every part of her craved Lane's touch. No one had ever kissed her with such ferocity. No one. Just as Miranda thought about reaching for her keys and dragging Lane inside, Lane pulled back, chest heaving, eyes blazing. Lane then pulled her in for a hug, holding her tight for a minute, and then kissed her cheek as she pulled away.

"Good night, Miranda. Sleep well," Lane said, her voice rough as if saying those words pained her.

Before Miranda could find her voice, Lane was

walking away from her, once more leaving her an aroused mess. Miranda wanted to chase after her, to demand she come back, but her legs wouldn't move as she thought about Lane wanting her to be sure. She leaned back against her door, still trying to come down from the high of Lane's kiss, trying to use the rational side of her brain to consider whether she was really ready for them to have sex. But she didn't have to think long, because based on how her body was crying for Lane's touch, she knew. She had been ready for weeks now. She ached for Lane.

Chapter 31

Lane once again found herself staring out her windows at Seattle's skyline, wondering why she kept punishing herself. She had never hesitated to bring a woman to her bed, but twice now she had denied herself what she wanted. The truth was, she had this overwhelming desire to make sure that Miranda was certain she wanted to be with her. She knew it was just sex and Miranda exploring her sexuality, but she didn't want Miranda to regret her first time with a woman because she rushed into having sex. She wanted the experience to be special, for reasons she wasn't even fully sure of herself. Over the years, she had been the first for quite a few women, and had never cared this much about whether or not they would regret it or realize it was mere curiosity, and they weren't actually bisexual. She admired Miranda for not wanting to rush into sleeping with anyone just to confirm her sexuality. A lot of heterosexual women often thought they were attracted to women and carelessly pursued a relationship with them as some sort of experiment, only to end up breaking that person's heart.

Before the date, Lane had been certain about bringing Miranda home, but by the end of it, she decided to take things slow. She wanted it to be about more than just sex. Maybe it was because the date had been so perfect. It had been a long time since she enjoyed spending time outside the bedroom with a woman—having meaningful conversations with someone who genuinely wanted to make the world a better place. From day one, Lane didn't understand her own behavior with Miranda. It was as if the usual rules that governed her life didn't apply where Miranda was involved. Miranda was the only woman who had ever rejected her and Lane still carried a torch for her months later. This was also the only time she would ever consider dating a woman she worked with. She thought she would be worried about what might happen if things ended between them, but strangely, she wasn't. Miranda was level-headed and would never create a scene. Come what may, they would deal with it like adults.

The elevator doors opened and Lane turned around to see Miranda stalking toward her, her fiery eyes fixed on Lane's face. Before she could form her next thought, she was being pushed against the windows, hot, demanding lips on hers, kissing her as if she were the air that Miranda needed to breathe. Lane allowed Miranda to lead the kiss as her tongue swept into her mouth, claiming her like no other woman had before. Miranda moaned deeply when their tongues met, dipping in and out, stirring the inferno inside of Lane.

Miranda suddenly pulled back, her breathing coming out in short puffs. "I don't need any more time to be sure. I want you to do everything to me that you promised at the gala," she demanded, her voice steady with conviction.

Miranda moved back in to kiss her, and when their lips met this time, Lane erupted. She didn't know if it was the certainty behind Miranda's words or months of pent-up frustration but she unleashed herself on Miranda's mouth. She couldn't help dragging her teeth across Miranda's bottom lip, earning soft whimpers from her. But she knew it wasn't the fact that she hadn't had sex in weeks. No, it was this damn infuriating woman melting against her body, who she had wanted to fuck since she laid eyes on her at Josephine's. She spun them around shoving Miranda roughly against the glass, pinning her with the full length of her body. There would be no more sweet kisses for them. She had wanted to do this for too long and well, Lane didn't do sweet. Her tongue swept into Miranda's mouth with sheer savagery as her hands dropped to Miranda's ass, gripping her hard. Miranda groaned at the act, and Lane felt a surge of satisfaction as the sound went straight to her clit, learning that Miranda didn't mind things being a little rough.

Her hands traveled from Miranda's ass up to find the zipper on her dress, tugging it down. She didn't break the kiss as she skillfully undressed Miranda, removing her bra and underwear as soon as the dress hit the ground. The feel of Miranda's naked skin beneath her palms forced Lane to stop the kiss, overpowered by the desire to see her fully. She took a step back and stared at the body she had fantasized about. Miranda stood there, looking back at her with lust-filled eyes, her chest rising and falling rapidly.

Lane reached out and cupped her cheek. "You're absolutely stunning. Not even my wildest imagination did you justice."

Miranda opened her mouth to respond, but before she could speak, Lane was on her, turning her around to face the glass. Lane swept Miranda's hair to one side and rested her chin on her shoulder, both of them gazing at their reflections. She wrapped her arms around Miranda, cupping and gently squeezing her breasts. Miranda melted into the touch, pressing her ass back into Lane's pelvis.

Miranda tried to close her eyes, but Lane pinched her nipples firmly and commanded, "Keep your eyes open, Miranda. I want you to watch yourself while I touch you. I want you to see yourself through my eyes as I touch you like this." Lane then softly bit Miranda's shoulder, soothing it afterward with her tongue. "Can you see how much I want you?" she murmured, her hand drifting lower across Miranda's stomach while the other continued its deliberate play on her nipple.

Miranda nodded, a sharp gasp escaping her as Lane's fingers grazed over her mons pubis and then retreated. Lane sucked on Miranda's earlobe, closely observing her reactions. Her gaze then dropped to Miranda's bare pussy, intensifying as she noticed the moisture there.

"How many sessions was your laser treatment?" Lane asked, her touch light as a feather over the smooth skin.

Miranda's eyes widened with incredulity as if to say, is that what you're asking now? But then she all but whined out, "Twenty-four."

"Mine was twenty," Lane responded casually, her fingers wandering lower, deliberately avoiding Miranda's clit to tease the wetness between her thighs. "You're so fucking wet for me." She used her middle and index fingers to separate Miranda's folds to see more of the reaction to her touch. "Do you always get this wet when you think about me fucking you, Miranda darling?"

"Lane... please," Miranda gasped out as Lane circled her entrance, withdrawing as quickly as she had entered.

"Hearing you beg is music to my ears, Miranda. As much as I'd love to draw this out and punish you for making me wait this long to fuck you, I don't believe in torturing myself any longer." Lane dragged her fingers coated in Miranda's moisture, up her stomach. "And while I have fantasized many times about fucking you against these windows, tonight won't be that night."

She turned Miranda around, intertwined their fingers, and silently led them to her bedroom. While the idea of taking Miranda against the glass was incredibly tempting, tonight wasn't just about her desires. She wanted Miranda's first orgasm with a woman to be more intimate, not standing up. Plus, Lane needed a moment to calm her racing heart. The adrenaline coursing through her veins from finally getting to touch Miranda like this would surely give her a heart attack if she didn't take a minute. Lane's entire body ached with need with each step, and for once, her self-control didn't fail her in Miranda's presence as she resisted the overwhelming urge to fuck Miranda hard and fast on the stairs.

As soon as they entered the bedroom, Lane's mouth was back on Miranda's, kissing her deeply as she guided them backward toward the bed. Miranda's hands roamed all over Lane's body, exploring and teasing her nipples through her blouse. Slipping her hand beneath the fabric, Miranda scratched her nails down Lane's back, eliciting a deep groan. At that moment, Lane felt as if just kissing Miranda would be enough. It was the most intoxicating kiss she had ever experienced, and she felt like she could spend hours just exploring

Miranda's mouth. As Miranda began to lift Lane's blouse over her head, Lane gripped her hands, stopping her.

She severed the kiss, causing Miranda to let out a whimpering protest. "Lay on the bed," Lane commanded.

"Does it turn you on to boss me around, Delaney?" Miranda asked as she took a step back, lowered herself to the bed, and slid up to settle among the pillows.

Not many people called her Delaney, but the way it rolled so sensually off Miranda's tongue made Lane want to insist she use that name exclusively. "Oh, you have no idea, Miranda darling," Lane replied, her voice thick with promise as she slowly removed her top and tossed it to the floor. She watched Miranda's eyes follow her movements, a thrill coursing through her as she saw them darken with desire. Next, she removed her bra, then ran her hands slowly down her stomach to the waistband of her pants. Holding Miranda's gaze, she removed her pants and underwear, intentionally baring herself completely to Miranda.

They stared at each other, each taking in the full view of the other's body. Lane had always appreciated beauty in many forms, but she appreciated the feminine curves of a woman more than even the finest, most expensive art in the world. To her, women were the finest art crafted by the universe—exquisitely beautiful and timeless. And Miranda Hayes, naked in her bed, her golden brown skin glowing against Lane's white sheets, was one of the most beautiful pieces of art Lane had ever beheld. Miranda was strikingly endowed with defined curves and ample breasts that could bring any deity to their knees.

"Are you just going to stand there all night and watch

me?" Miranda rasped, her voice sultry as her legs parted further in a welcoming invitation.

Lane smiled and placed one knee on the bed, then crawled toward her target, settling between Miranda's thighs. "I think I could watch you forever," she rasped softly, before claiming Miranda's lips with another intense, bruising kiss.

She lowered her pelvis to Miranda's, hissing as moisture coated her skin, the sensation like fire scorching her. Feeling Miranda grind against her, Lane felt her resolve to take her time with Miranda begin to crumble. She kissed Miranda wilder and deeper, snaking her hand between them to find and roll a nipple between her thumb and forefinger. Lane knew she should probably slow down, but how could she when she had yearned for so long to have Miranda writhing beneath her—to feel her pussy flutter around her fingers and to hear her scream her name? She had never wanted to fuck anyone as much as she wanted to fuck Miranda Hayes. Ever.

Still, this moment was more about Miranda than her own desire to fuck her. She wanted the experience to be unforgettable for Miranda, even if afterward she decided that being with a woman wasn't for her. Lane wanted to leave a permanent mark on her. But she had denied herself long enough and refused to hold back any longer. She would fuck Miranda in the exact way she wanted, by taking what she needed from her while giving Miranda everything she could have wanted from her first time with a woman.

With this in mind, Lane moved her lips from Miranda's mouth down to her neck, dragging her teeth over her pulse point while sucking roughly on the pulsing flesh. Miranda whimpered and dug her nails into Lane's back, undoubtedly leaving marks. The sharp pain only intensified Lane's desire, her mouth traveling lower to latch onto a nipple, sucking and gently nipping with her teeth. Lane's entire body felt ablaze as she indulged in one of her many fantasies about the woman squirming beneath her. She kissed a blazing trail across Miranda's chest, giving the other nipple the same fervent attention, moaning so deeply in her throat that she had to wonder if the sound was indeed coming from her.

"Oh, God," Miranda groaned out, her hand finding Lane's hair and pulling her even closer to her breast.

Miranda's touch acted as a catalyst, driving Lane to take as much of her breast as possible into her mouth. Her other hand found Miranda's opposite nipple, rolling and squeezing it as she contemplated whether she could bring Miranda to climax this way. Given how much wetter Miranda was becoming, it seemed like a possibility. But that wasn't the first type of orgasm Lane wanted to give her. She wanted Miranda to come pulsing on her tongue. Lane released Miranda's breast and kissed a path down her stomach, pausing to dip and swirl her tongue in her navel. She continued lower, biting and sucking on Miranda's hip bones, her own desire spiking as she neared the ultimate prize. Reaching Miranda's mons pubis, Lane sank her teeth into the tender flesh, causing Miranda's hips to arch off the bed. Lane gripped her hips to hold her steady as she continued to mark the sensitive area with small nips and bites.

"Lane... please... I need to feel you inside me," Miranda cried out, her voice pained.

The palpable need in Miranda's voice compelled Lane to lift her head and look at her. Miranda's head was thrown back into the pillow, her dark curls splayed out, her mouth open, and her eyes closed—she was a vision of ecstasy. Lane wished she could capture this moment on film. Sensing Lane staring, Miranda's eyes snapped open, and the raw desire within those hazel depths took Lane's breath away, igniting a fierce clench in her core. Miranda said nothing, her intense gaze fixed on Lane, silently pleading for her to continue. Lane, naturally dominant in bed, found the sight of Miranda so willingly submissive exhilarating, heightening the euphoria of the moment.

She rose to her knees between Miranda's legs, spreading them further apart. Forcing herself to break away from Miranda's mesmerizing gaze, Lane's eyes dropped to the glistening sex below her. Miranda's folds were drenched, moisture trailing down to her ass cheeks from how wet she was. Lane's mouth watered at the sight, electricity pulsing through every neuron in her body as she observed how much Miranda wanted her. Reaching out, she traced the length of Miranda's slit with her index finger, dragging the moisture up to Miranda's swollen clit, which caused her back to arch dramatically off the bed. Lane then lowered herself back onto the bed, sliding down and wrapping her hands around Miranda's thighs, placing them on her shoulders. She positioned her head at the entrance of Miranda's sex, inhaling deeply as the intoxicating scent overwhelmed her senses, nearly making her dizzy with desire.

"You smell so fucking good," Lane murmured, lowering her lips to Miranda's clit and sucking hard.

Lane's blood roared in her ears from her first taste of the woman she had wanted fuck for so long. Her mouth salivated as she savored Miranda's essence, relishing it like the finest wine she had ever tasted. God, she wanted this woman so desperately that she feared her need would never be fully satisfied, even as she took everything she craved from Miranda and more. Miranda's hips bucked off the bed, but Lane used her hands to hold her down as she continued to lavish attention on the hardened nub. Miranda's whimpering and the rhythmic motion of her hips only fueled Lane's need. She then dragged her lips down to Miranda's entrance, sliding her tongue inside, diving deep, curling, and flicking against her G-spot.

God almighty.

Finally getting to fulfill one of her many fantasies made Lane feel like she was having an out-of-body experience. She had always enjoyed sex and had plenty of amazing encounters, but what she felt as she devoured Miranda's flesh made Lane feel like it was her first time committing the act. Everything was just different. Maybe it was because she had waited so long, or maybe it was just Miranda and the strange effect she had always had on Lane.

"Oh fuck," Miranda screamed, her hips trying to rise off the bed, but Lane firmly kept her in place.

Moisture flooded Lane's mouth as she pulled back her tongue and lapped at Miranda's entrance. Though Lane had been with many women, she swore at that moment that Miranda's pussy was the sweetest she had ever tasted, and she doubted her own self-control to stop—each taste only intensified her craving. It was a maddening feeling as she dragged her tongue up

Miranda's length, alternating her focus between her center and clit. Lane felt insatiable as she continued her fervent exploration. She lowered Miranda's legs from her shoulders to slip a hand between them. Without pausing, Lane thrust two fingers inside her, pumping vigorously as she simultaneously tormented Miranda's clit with the tip of her tongue. Miranda's walls began to spasm faster around her fingers, signaling the approach of her orgasm.

"Please don't stop," Miranda cried out as Lane continued with long, deep strokes, relentless in her quest to deliver the most powerful orgasm of Miranda's life.

Vibrating walls clamped down on Lane's fingers, and although Lane wanted to heed her pleas to not stop, she wanted to feel Miranda come against her tongue, to feel her pulse and quiver. Skillfully, Lane replaced her fingers with her tongue, diving into the wet heat with a deep moan. She swirled her tongue inside, flicking the tip against Miranda's G-spot as she was drawn deeper by the contracting muscles. Lane closed her eyes, losing herself in the escalating sensations as Miranda's orgasm built intensely. No fantasy could have prepared her for the rush of fulfillment that flowed through her as Miranda unraveled on her tongue, making Lane feel like the happiest woman alive from just eating pussy. If she died at that moment, she would have died a very happy woman feeling Miranda's pussy fluttering on her tongue.

"I'm coming...I'm coming... Fuck..." Miranda screamed, her orgasm tearing through her with an earth-shattering force—the sounds echoing around the room as her body shook violently.

Lane continued to lavish attention on Miranda's tender flesh, not stopping until her body relaxed into the bed and the tremors subsided. Even then, Lane persisted, replacing her tongue once again with two fingers, each thrust deep and precise, curling against the rough spot. Miranda's back curved off the bed like a bow as her second climax crashed into her. Still feeling like a starved woman, Lane contemplated flipping Miranda over and taking her from behind. However, she decided to pause, allowing Miranda to catch her breath.

Lane peppered Miranda's stomach with soft kisses as she traveled up her body to meet her eyes. Resting on her forearms, she stared down at the woman beneath her, whose eyes were closed, skin flushed, and chest heaving—a breathtaking sight. *So very beautiful* she thought as she lowered her lips and placed soft kisses all over Miranda's face. Opening her eyes, Miranda wrapped her arms around Lane, her palms running soothingly up and down her back.

"Hi," Lane whispered softly, searching Miranda's face for any signs of regret.

"Hi," Miranda responded, her voice matching Lane's tone as a shy smile formed on her lips.

"Are you okay?" Lane asked, resisting the impulse to slip her hands between them and initiate another round.

Miranda squeezed her butt, and asked, "Do I look like someone who isn't okay?"

Lane grinned, pushing down her pelvis onto Miranda's and rotating her hips. "Call it me seeking confirmation that my expertise was well received."

Miranda laughed. "I'm surprised you didn't start with being this smug about being an excellent lover."

Lane's grin widened. "Dr. Hayes, did you just give me an A+ for my sexpertise?"

Miranda rolled her eyes. "I won't waste my time inflating your already gigantic ego."

Lane rotated her hips again, earning a moan from Miranda, who then wrapped her legs around Lane's waist, granting her even more access. Lane continued the slow, deliberate movements of her hips, driven more by the desire to make Miranda climax again than by her own need for release. Miranda whimpered beneath her, her eyes darkening as she stared up at Lane. Just as Lane was about to lower her head to capture Miranda's lips, Miranda tightened her grip with her legs, flipping them over. Landing on her back, Lane looked up at Miranda, who adjusted herself to straddle Lane's thighs. Her eyes roamed over Miranda's beautiful form, admiring her dark nipples and the marks she had left on her chest, curious to see what Miranda would do next.

"As much as I would love another orgasm from you, I think it's my turn to explore," Miranda said, her fingers tracing Lane's stomach, her eyes sparkling with curiosity.

"I'm here to serve at your pleasure, Miranda darling," Lane purred, her stomach quivering under Miranda's exploring touch.

******

Miranda stared down at Lane, her body still buzzing from the aftershocks of her orgasms, amazed at how skillfully Lane had mastered her body. The woman had touched her as if they had been intimate many times before, intuitively knowing exactly what Miranda liked and taking pleasure in giving her one of the best first experiences of her life. Her previous first encounters with men had often been unrewarding and usually required some coaching to find pleasure. She guessed there might be a lot of truth to the idea that women naturally understood how to touch each other properly. Or perhaps it was just Delaney Remington with her unabashed confidence. And indeed, the woman had plenty to be confident about. Because, God, when Lane fucked her, Miranda had felt like she was having sex for the first time and she couldn't quite find words to explain the myriad of sensations that had consumed her very essence. It was simply mind-blowing and her body was still quivering from the onslaught.

Miranda ran her fingertips along Lane's collarbone, the center of her chest, and across to tease a nipple. Miranda knew Lane could read everything she was feeling on her face. She knew this because of how strongly she felt it—the lust, the wanting, the ache. And she knew because even if she wanted to, she couldn't hide her desires from Lane. Not when the need to touch Lane pulsed through every fiber of being and she was ravenous for the woman beneath her. What she felt at that moment was unlike anything she had ever experienced—to want someone so much that she physically ached.

"Do you like what you see, Miranda?" Lane asked, her tone raspy with need.

"Very much. You're so very beautiful," Miranda replied with curiosity and wonder. She had always admired the beauty of women, but to experience a woman's body with lust and desire was a whole different version of beauty. To be so very aroused by the sight of pink nipples, that she was actually itching to feel on her tongue, was an intoxicating new form of exhilaration.

Miranda opened her hand, palming Lane's breast and massaging it, captivated by the instant reaction from the woman beneath her whose breathing grew more ragged as Miranda continued to tease her nipple. Lifting her gaze from Lane's breast to her eyes, Miranda found Lane watching her with a blend of mild amusement and patience. It was as if Lane was allowing Miranda to explore her body at her own pace, even if she was in need of urgent release. Such patience. Lane had been so very patient with her, and Miranda felt an overwhelming desire to reward her for that patience.

Leaning over, Miranda kissed Lane deeply and passionately, her tongue sliding into her mouth with ferocity. Lane's hands found her hair, pulling her even closer as she hungrily returned the kiss. Miranda sensed that although she was on top, Lane was still in charge, allowing Miranda to lead while guiding her. She suspected Lane would be dominant in bed and seeing her take control in this way made Miranda so very wet. She ground her hips against Lane's thighs, the kiss growing more urgent and sloppier as Lane palmed her ass and squeezed, urging Miranda to grind harder against her. Breaking the kiss, Miranda dragged her lips down Lane's neck, softly biting the hollow there—an act she intuited Lane would appreciate, given how Lane had touched her earlier. Lane moaned deeply, her hands tightening their grip on Miranda.

Miranda continued downward, gently wrapping her lips around the pebbled bud, moaning deeply as the sensation heightened her own arousal. She savored the moment, allowing herself to fully experience the pleasure as Lane's whimpers encouraged her further. *So, this is what all the fuss is about,* she thought, realizing this was something she could definitely get used to.

"Don't be afraid to suck it harder. I can take it," Lane rasped, her hands finding Miranda's hair again and pulling her closer.

Miranda followed Lane's orders, biting softly before swirling her tongue around the engorged nub. As she switched from one breast to the other, an overpowering need to taste Lane consumed her, persuading her to linger only briefly on the second one. She planted a blazing trail of wet kisses down Lane's stomach as she moved toward her ultimate target, guided by her own mounting desire. Positioning herself between Lane's thighs, Miranda adjusted to a kneeling stance and paused to admire the wetness coating Lane's swollen folds. Seeing Lane so very wet made Miranda feel an overwhelming amount of smugness, knowing she did that to this woman who always seemed so composed—as if untouchable by anyone or anything. Miranda licked her lips in anticipation, wondering what Lane tasted like. She had tasted herself on her previous lovers before but understood that women's essence varies, influenced by factors like diet and medication.

Miranda glanced up at Lane, who was looking at her with unmistakable hunger in her eyes—no trace of amusement, only intense desire, her chest heaving. The way Lane stared at her with such raw lust always sent shivers through Miranda's body. She had felt it from the very first time they met, although initially, she had misinterpreted the effect as annoyance. Now, that *look* only made her want to let Lane do whatever she wanted to her in bed. And God did that *look* make her want this woman with a fervor she didn't understand, or care to at this point. Because fucking Lane felt like being given her first taste of the of the forbidden fruit—an intoxicating blend of ecstasy and taboo that lingered long after the moment had passed, leaving an indelible mark on the soul.

"Do you plan to just stare at my pussy, Miranda? Or will you do what you've probably been fantasizing about, once you admitted to yourself that you wanted me?" Lane rasped out, low and seductive.

Struggling to find a sharp retort—because Lane's words hit close to home and she had indeed fantasized about being in this exact position with the woman—Miranda opted for a different form of response. She lowered her head and bit Lane sharply on the hipbone, a satisfied smile curving her lips when a loud hiss escaped Lane. Then, softening her approach, she kissed the inside of Lane's thighs, gliding her lips to Lane's glistening folds, moaning deeply from her first taste. Lane tasted like heaven, sunshine, and everything that could make Miranda feel as if she was floating among the clouds. As euphoria swept through her, Miranda's need to have Lane climax in her mouth overpowered her.

She ran her tongue along the length of Lane's slit, groaning deeply as she lost herself in her first exploration of the female anatomy. Lane's hips arched off the bed, and a loud cry escaped her, the sound encouraging Miranda to repeat the action. As Miranda continued a relentless back-and-forth rhythm with her tongue, she wondered why she wasn't nervous. She thought she would be, but nervousness was the last thing she was feeling. Lust, passion, and horny were the only emotions spiraling through her body as she feasted on Lane's flesh. Still, while this was her first time having sex with a woman, it wasn't her first sexual encounter. She knew what she enjoyed and was quickly learning how Lane liked to be touched. And given the way Lane was eagerly responding, riding her face with wild abandon, Miranda was confident she was on the right track.

"Add two fingers," Lane demanded, the rotation of her hips increasing. "While I want you to explore my body at your leisure, there is only so much I can take, and I need to feel you inside of me now," she added, widening her thighs to give Miranda more access

There was something about Lane's commands in bed that made Miranda's pussy clench. No one had ever bossed her around in bed quite like Lane, and to say she loved it was an understatement. Wrapping her lips around Lane's clit, Miranda sucked hard while sliding the two fingers Lane had requested inside her, reveling in the knowledge that her touch was making Lane increasingly wet. The sensation of Lane's walls quivering around her fingers sent a thrill through Miranda, making her eyes roll back with pleasure. It was one of the best feelings ever, and she could see herself doing it repeatedly. Miranda increased the pace of her fingers, driven by a growing desire to see Lane come undone beneath her. She set a steady rhythm, pulling out completely and then plunging back in deep. *Jesus, this feels amazing.*

"Oh...fuck.... argh... Just like that," Lane screamed, her hands once again finding Miranda's hair, holding her firmly in place as her hips continued to undulate at an erratic pace.

Miranda lost herself in the heat of the moment, letting her passion guide her movements as Lane's clit pulsed and her walls clenched tightly around her fingers. Following her instincts and recalling what Lane had done to her, Miranda curled her fingers, repeatedly hitting Lane's G-spot and propelling her over the edge with a loud scream. Opening her eyes, Miranda watched in awe as Lane threw her head back into the pillows, her back arching as she cried out Miranda's name. Hearing her name on Lane's lips as she fell apart was like a sacred prayer, lulling Miranda into giving Lane whatever she needed. As Lane's body relaxed into the mattress, Miranda slowed her strokes, tenderly flicking Lane's quivering flesh with the tip of her tongue, drawing out soft whimpers.

Lane reached down, grasped the back of Miranda's neck, and pulled her up to her lips. Her tongue slipped into Miranda's mouth with a force that left her breathless. Lane kissed her as if her sole purpose was to quench her thirst with her own wetness.

After what felt like an eternity, Lane softened the kiss and whispered against Miranda's lips, "Are you sure you've never eaten pussy before? Because that was incredible."

Miranda chuckled, a sense of relief washing over her, hearing that she had pleased Lane. It mattered more than she cared to admit. She eased back to look into Lane's eyes. "I'm happy to know that I lived up to your undoubtedly high expectations."

"Oh yes, you did," Lane replied, her voice thick with approval as she flipped them over and settled between

Miranda's thighs. "So much so that I intend to spend the rest of the night rewarding you by fucking you into oblivion."

Before Miranda could respond, Lane slipped two fingers inside her, and Miranda had no choice but to surrender to her fate—one she was very much looking forward to.

Chapter 32

Gentle breathing against her neck stirred Lane from the depths of a deep, restful sleep. Opening her eyes slowly, she became aware of a warm body draped over hers. Lane expected the unease she often felt when her lovers cuddled her to creep in, but surprisingly, it didn't. In fact, she felt like snuggling even closer and slipping her hand between the thigh carelessly thrown over hers. She wasn't against cuddling a woman after they slept together, but experience taught her that it could blur the lines between casual sex and deeper connections. However, this was Miranda, and after working together closely for months and their many interactions outside of work, she trusted that Miranda with her clear-headedness wouldn't misinterpret a morning cuddle as a sign of falling in love.

And she figured there was little she could do about it—Miranda took cuddling to an entirely different level. The woman didn't just cuddle, she took over Lane's body. After their many passionate rounds of sex, they had fallen asleep tightly intertwined. When Lane woke up and tried to create space between them, Miranda briefly stirred, only to wrap her arm around Lane from behind, pulling her close again. Whenever Miranda turned away from Lane, she would reach back, pulling Lane's arm around her. It was a novelty that Lane had never experienced before—she had never been with someone who instinctively sought her touch even in sleep. It was as if Miranda needed to feel Lane pressed against her to find comfort in her slumber. Even now, there was not an inch of space between them as Miranda slept on Lane's chest, one hand literally palming her breast.

She smiled as her mind pictured their night together. The whole experience had been intoxicating—a heady mixture of sleeping with a woman for the first time and finally getting what she had wanted for almost a year now. Everything about the night was intense—perfect. It had felt so much more than just sex, it was like sating a deep hunger that Lane hadn't been able to fill with anyone else. A hunger that still wasn't fully sated because lying there with Miranda's warm body on top of hers, she was still wetter than she had ever been since she started to have sex, her body thrumming with an insatiable need. She wanted Miranda as much now as she had before their night together. Lane saw it as a side effect of waiting so long to have her and now that she did, it was only normal to still crave her. It was also normal for her to accommodate Miranda more than she had ever accommodated any of her previous lovers, even more than Gabriella who had been her longest entanglement. Miranda's situation was unique, so Lane being patient with her and allowing her to cuddle her all night was fine. Nothing for her to overthink and freak out about. She was too rational for that.

Miranda shifting stopped her runaway thoughts and Lane glanced down to find sleepy eyes, slowly opening. *She's even more beautiful in the morning,* Lane mused, struck anew by Miranda's soft, unguarded expression.

Lane expected Miranda to release her, but instead, she simply adjusted her head to get a better view of Lane's face, her body remaining closely entwined with Lane's.

A shy, sleepy smile spread across Miranda's lips. "Good morning," she rasped out, her voice husky, likely from all the screaming she did the previous night. The throaty timbre sent a wave of desire straight to Lane's clit.

"Good morning," Lane replied, her fingers gently sweeping Miranda's curls away from her face.

Lane became even more aware of the hand on her breast, as Miranda's thumb started to move in a slow circle. "Have you been awake long?"

Lane pushed aside the rising need to push Miranda onto her back and sink two fingers inside her. "Not that long."

"Okay," Miranda responded, her voice coated with what Lane could only describe as self-consciousness.

Lane noted the soft, vulnerable inflection and it tugged at her as she scrutinized Miranda's face. Lane stayed quiet, allowing Miranda the space to voice whatever thoughts might be lingering in her mind. After a brief pause, sensing that Miranda was waiting for her to lead the conversation, Lane ventured playfully, "So, how did you find your first rendezvous on the dark side?"

Miranda chuckled, the sound light and content. "There is nothing dark about it. It was rather enlightening. Filled with plenty of fireworks and star-like explosions behind my eyes."

Lane couldn't help the laughter that bubbled from her throat. She also couldn't deny the flood of relief that washed over her that Miranda seemed to have no regrets. She knew it shouldn't matter to her, but it did. "I'm pleased to hear that," she said, trying to reel in her laughter. "Guess it's safe to assume that you want to continue your exploration and my services will continue to be needed."

"I think the bigger question is if you want to continue offering your services now that you've finally had me," Miranda replied, a little hesitant and apprehensively.

Lane stared at her intently. "Why would I want to stop having sex with you, when I enjoyed fucking you so very much," Lane paused, her lips drifting up into a cheeky smile. "Weren't the multiple orgasms proof enough?"

Miranda shrugged, her thumb now torturing Lane's nipple. Did she not realize the havoc she was wreaking on Lane's body? "You've wanted me for so long, and I know that sometimes, once someone finally gets what they've been chasing, the novelty can wear off instantly," she explained with uncertainty in her voice. "And since all you wanted from me was sex, maybe you want to move on to another conquest already."

Lane sighed heavily and gently adjusted their positions so that they lay on their sides, facing each other. She wasn't surprised when Miranda instinctively threw her leg over her hip. Lane carefully tucked Miranda's curls behind her ear to get a clear view of her face. "While I don't do relationships, Miranda, I'm very selective about who I sleep with. Yes, I've had my share of hookups, however, at this point in my life, I prefer to have steady sexual relationships with one person at a time, if possible. I enjoy sex a lot, and if I have someone I can have fulfilling sex with, I don't usually look elsewhere." As she spoke, Lane's hand gently caressed

Miranda's back, slowly drifting down to her ass. "And fucking you was very fulfilling and I'm looking forward to continue sexing you up."

Miranda playfully rolled her eyes. "You're so crude when it comes to talking about sex. So out of character compared to your poised demeanor outside of the act. Though, I shouldn't be surprised because you've always been rather crude when it comes to telling me how much you want to sex me up."

Lane laughed, marveling at Miranda's ability to easily draw laughter from her. "As if you're much better. You seem to have forgotten all the filthy things you were screaming last night." Lane pushed Miranda onto her back and positioned herself above her. "Maybe you need a reminder to confirm who talks the dirtiest during sex, Dr. Hayes," she added, settling between thighs that instantly widened to welcome her.

"I think you're just finding a reason to keep me in your bed," Miranda husked out as Lane's hand ventured between them.

Lane's reply was equally charged, her voice a rough whisper. "I think the evidence between your thighs says that I don't need to find a reason, Miranda darling," Lane purred, her voice full of deadly promise as she slipped a finger inside the molten heat waiting for her.

Miranda responded with a guttural moan, her hips rolling in response to Lane's teasing. "Well, I've always believed in science, so I can't really argue against your claim when there's such... compelling scientific evidence to back you up," she managed to say, breathlessly enjoying the sensations Lane was expertly invoking.

"I've always appreciated how rational you are,

Dr. Hayes," Lane murmured, her voice low and approving as she added a second finger, relishing the way Miranda's muscles tightened around her. "It saves us from wasting time on pointless arguments." She pressed deeper, feeling the responsive clutch of Miranda's walls. "So, it's settled then. We'll continue to have…" Her fingers pumped once. "A lot…." She pumped twice. "Of hot…" Her fingers pumped hard a third time, emphasizing the last word. "Sex." Leaning in, Lane captured Miranda's earlobe between her teeth and whispered, a hint of mischief in her tone, "And you're going to treat me to more of some of the hottest dirty talk I've ever heard." As Miranda's body responded with an even tighter grip, Lane lifted her head to stare into Miranda's mesmerizing eyes, the gold flecks glowing bright with desire.

"Have you ever thought that maybe you're the one who is rubbing off on me?" Miranda countered, arching her hips to match Lane's increasing thrust.

Lane's lips curved into a smug smile as she responded confidently. "Well, I always tend to leave a lasting impression on women or bring out a certain side they never knew existed before they had the Lane Experience."

Miranda laughed, looping her hands around Lane's neck. "That I can agree with since I'm here in your bed. And before your relentless insistence on banging me, I've never felt the urge to sleep with a woman."

"I feel so very special."

"That's because you are, even if you're the most insufferable person I've ever met."

Lane chose not to respond because Miranda telling her that she was special did weird things to her insides, as the ache in her lower stomach intensified. She could agree to an extent that she had thought that after sleeping with Miranda, her desire might wane, but that was the farthest thing from reality. While she didn't know how long Miranda would continue to explore her sexuality with her, Lane intended to make use of their time together to quell the relentless craving for this enchanting woman who had an inexplicable effect on her. But as she kissed Miranda, a nagging voice in the back of her mind whispered reminders of her dating history. And she wondered if, after a few weeks, her interest would diminish and she wouldn't be able to keep her promise of helping Miranda explore her sexuality. Only time would unveil the answers. Lane only hoped that no matter what the future brought, their ending wouldn't result in heartbreak for Miranda.

......to be continued......

Will Lane be able to keep her word and help Miranda explore sexuality, or will she move on after finally getting a taste of the woman she had lusted after for almost a year? Where will this new chapter of Miranda's life lead her? Will she continue exploring her newfound attraction to women, or will the novelty of being with a woman wear off, leading her back to dating men? What were the events in Lane's past that shaped her into the woman she is? In the end, what does *fate* have in store for them?

All this and more in **AN UNEXPECTED FATE**...... COMING SOON!!

ACKNOWLEDGMENTS

To you, my readers, I want to express my heartfelt gratitude to all of you who have read or will read my books. Your continuous support means the world to me. It's still so very surreal to see my books being loved by so many of you. Knowing that through my art, I can be a source of comfort for many of you who, like myself, use books as an escape from this harsh world, is incredibly fulfilling. Words will never be enough to say thank you, but I hope to continue writing amazing stories for you.

Noella, it has been an incredible journey having you as my editor. I've learned the hard way that an editor can make or break a book, and I'm so very grateful for an editor like you who takes immense pride in your work and goes above and beyond what is expected of you. Thanks for always treating my words as if they are your own and for making my stories even better.

Clara and Erin, thank you for your steadfast support and friendship. Thank you for understanding me without judgment, accepting me for who I am, and dedicating your time to being my beta readers.

Kim, Christine, Carolyn and Coral, thanks for allowing me to slide into your DMs and ask for your feedback, and for your kind words of encouragement. Kim, I dedicate Lane to you because you gave me the idea to turn her into a main character. I hope she is everything you thought she would be and more.

To my family and friends whose names I cannot list here, you know who you are and how much you mean to me.

AFTERWORD

Thank you so much for reading my work! If you enjoyed this book, please leave a review on Amazon or Goodreads. Even just a rating makes a huge impact for authors and means so very much to us. I look forward to reading your wonderful reviews, many of which were the light at the end of the tunnel during some of my darkest moments. So, please believe that your kind words make a difference.

If you're interested, you can sign up for my newsletter for updates on upcoming projects, sneak peeks and giveaways, or follow me on Twitter or Instagram.

ABOUT THE AUTHOR

Skye Von Triessen

Skye lives in North York, where she is maybe one of the few who loves the long winter season. Despite being born on a beautiful island where it is warm all year round, she absolutely despises the summer months in her current home country. Skye spends her days as a corporate analyst and spends her nights dreaming up stories, she desires to put on paper but oftentimes doesn't.

Her favorite thing to do is to lay in bed in the dark on Sundays doing absolutely nothing but watching TV shows or reading a good book. She absolutely loves food and despite her many attempts is unable to lower her monthly food bill to a reasonable amount which is hard to do seeing that she believes in eating the best quality food no matter the cost.

SKYEVON TRIESSEN

More than anything she believes that life is too short to be anything but happy.

Printed in Great Britain
by Amazon

48185588R00199